# REVENANT WINDS

## THE TAINTED CABAL: BOOK ONE

# MITCHELL HOGAN

REVENANT WINDS

Published by Mitchell Hogan

Copyright © 2017 by Mitchell Hogan

First Printing, 2017




Map by Maxime Plasse: maxsmaps.com

Cover by Damonza.com

# ALSO BY MITCHELL HOGAN

**The Sorcery Ascendant Sequence**
A Crucible of Souls
Blood of Innocents
A Shattered Empire

At the Sign of the Crow and Moon—novella

**The Tainted Cabal**
Revenant Winds

Tower of the Forgotten—novella

**Science Fiction**
Inquisitor

With love to Isabelle and Charlotte, who are too wonderful for words.

# ACKNOWLEDGMENTS

To the editors who have to endure my writing before it is polished, a mountain of gratitude: Derek Prior, Abigail Nathan, and Nicola O'Shea.

A great many thanks to those who volunteered to beta read this book and gave their valuable time and feedback: Ray Nicholson, Matthew Summers, Tim Chambers, Toby Lloyd, David Walters, Belle McQuattie, Mark Chamberlain, and Devin Madson.

I would also like to thank all those readers who took a chance on an unknown author and purchased *A Crucible of Souls* and then went on to finish my Sorcery Ascendant Sequence. Without you, this book would never have been possible. I am living the dream, and for that I will be forever thankful.

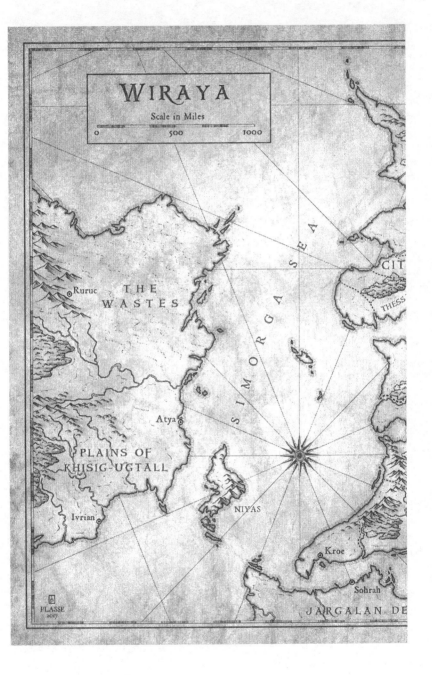

## PROLOGUE

# AN UNEXPECTED GIFT

S OMEONE HAMMERED ON THE door.

"Niklaus! I need to … Get your hands off me! I need to speak to Nik …" The strident voice of Volkmar trailed off as he was silenced by the heavies outside.

Niklaus du Plessis stared at the cards in his hand and stifled a curse. Another bad hand. He forced his face into as neutral an expression as he could muster in his inebriated state. Should he stay in on the hope his fortune would change? By the blood of his ancestors, that would be on his tombstone: *Here lies Niklaus. He hung in there, say that for him, until everything he was, or could have been, drained away to nothing.* Bloody fool.

A life renewed and perpetually extended by the goddess, but for what? An eternity of drinking and gambling? Had she granted him a gift all those centuries ago and then changed her mind? Or had it been a curse all along? He'd been in this forsaken city of Sansor for months and still hadn't discovered what she wanted of him. She'd used him for numerous missions in the past, but over recent months he'd had no instructions. *Abandoned …*

No, she valued him. He'd proven himself many times over. She wouldn't desert him.

He often found his thoughts lingering on the goddess whenever he had a spare moment, and sometimes when he didn't.

She was exquisite—in beauty as well as intellect—and he had become obsessed with joining her. Making her his, and ruling together.

He poked at his meager pile of royals and glanced at the other players in the smoke-filled room, eyes lingering on the cocksure noble who'd taken most of his coins. He'd forgotten the man's name—Al-something? As if the noble needed more money than he already had.

Volkmar might be an annoying ass and the city's craziest sorcerer, but he paid well. Damn well. For hardly any effort on Niklaus's part. There was no point wasting what little he had left continuing with the game; Volkmar's insane plans would fill his empty purse again.

"I'm out," he said, throwing his cards on the table and barely missing a puddle of spilled wine. He scooped up his remaining coins and stood, knocking his chair over as his sheathed sword tangled with its legs.

Niklaus intercepted the heavies at the entrance just as one of them was about to pitch Volkmar into the muddy street. "It's all right, Pirkko, he's with me." He stayed the bouncer with a hand and a brief smile. His reputation still meant something to some people.

Volkmar brushed down his patched robes and glared at Pirkko.

"He's just doing his job," Niklaus said. "Let's get out of here."

Volkmar nodded his bald head, jowls wobbling.

Dawn's half-light lit the sky to the east. Had it been that long? Niklaus felt a weary weight descend on him. Another night wasted. Still, there was tomorrow. Always tomorrow. Since the goddess had chosen him, time was all he had.

The sorcerer strode off, muttering to himself, then stopped abruptly. "Did you see that?" he said, peering into a dark alley.

"No. What was it?"

"Shadows moving. When they shouldn't. I know I'm close.

That's how I know. She's teasing me."

Crazy old man. No wonder the other sorcerers laughed at him.

Niklaus knew which "she" he referred to. The Lady Sylva Kalisia, one of the old gods, with dominion over the moons, pain, and suffering. A name whispered to children to scare them into obedience. Niklaus knew all too well what her presence felt like, and a fleeting shadow in an alley didn't come close. If the goddess wanted her presence known, you would feel it in your bones, in the animal musk and leather scent in the air, in the caress of her scorching breath on your skin, in the painful ache of your balls.

"I take it you need me to test your latest sword?" he said.

"What? Oh, yes. You're the best. She wouldn't want anything less. And I can't displease her."

"Thinking you're the best is a sure way to get killed," Niklaus replied. "But I could enter the annual Silver Blade competition at the Boneyards, see how I fare." Even as he said it, he knew he wouldn't. "But I've a lot on my plate at the moment. Very busy." His well-worn excuses sounded weak even to himself.

"You're the best," Volkmar repeated. "You train every day, no matter what. She wants the best. Deserves the best."

He was right, of course, about the goddess deserving the best. But Niklaus still thought the man was deluded. What use would the goddess have for a weapon?

"You're a fool," he said.

Volkmar nodded. "Maybe."

The sorcerer led the way to his laboratory, a decrepit house with a large yard. Niklaus waited outside while Volkmar retrieved the sword from its hiding place. Its wrapping of pristine purple velvet was incongruous against the sorcerer's stained robes. The gleam in Volkmar's eyes when he unwrapped the cloth to reveal his latest creation showed his devotion.

Niklaus drew in a sharp breath. The mottled blade shone like a ribbon of moonlight. It was forged from the metal of a fallen star, using techniques only powerful sorcerers were capable of. Etched into the first third of the blade and on the hilt were cryptic sorcerous runes.

He unbuckled and discarded his own sword and reverently took possession of the new blade, testing its heft and balance. Without thinking, he slipped into a basic form and completed it flawlessly, then started another, more complex. Soon he was sweating and breathing heavily—a good feeling, one he always missed. With a sword in his hand, he felt ... whole.

Niklaus stopped, form completed, the sorcerer's blade raised high in the upper guard. Reluctantly, he lowered it.

"It's ... perfect."

He couldn't think of another way to describe the blade. As it was, it was worth a small fortune. Imbued with sorcery, its value increased tenfold. And if Volkmar's crazy plan worked ...

Ever since the goddess had touched Niklaus, directing him, even gifting him with powers, he had wanted to be able to contact her of his own accord, not wait like some lapdog begging for scraps. And, dare he even think it, meet her as an equal.

It would be interesting to see what happened with Volkmar and the sword, but he'd grown fond of the sorcerer.

"I don't know if you should continue with this," he said. "Some things are better left alone."

"Old sorcery before the new," Volkmar replied, ignoring his advice. "Old when these hills were mountains."

"People have been messing with the old gods for ages, trying to leech their power. Not much remaining of them—the ones left alive anyway."

"Because they didn't ask. They just wanted to take. They didn't respect the old gods."

"You think if you ask nicely, they'll hand over their power for nothing? Fool!"

"No, not for nothing." Volkmar's head jerked to his right.

"There! She's here—or a messenger. It's a sign. Tonight, it is. Both the moons are full. I cannot wait any longer." He rubbed his hands together and chuckled.

"Enough," Niklaus said gruffly, tired and eager to be gone. "I can't see how you could make a better blade. Now, where are my coins?"

"Of course. Thank you." Volkmar spilled gold coins into Niklaus's palm, then gripped his arm with a liver-spotted hand. "You'll come tonight, won't you? At sunset. You must. I've invited all my colleagues to see the birth of my dream. A grand spectacle. They won't be laughing then, oh no."

Niklaus prized away the bony fingers. "Yes, I'll be there."

"Good! My triumph needs everyone's … participation. There is much to do to prepare for the rituals."

~ ~ ~

Niklaus stumbled from the tavern, guided by the hand of the establishment's bouncer. He tripped over his feet and landed heavily in the mud. He struggled upright and wiped his sticky clothes down as best he could. Another day gone. What was one more added to his eternal existence?

As he squinted at the orange sun disappearing behind the buildings, something tickled the back of his mind, and a soft, seductive woman's voice whispered in his ear, *Don't you have somewhere to be?*

He blinked blearily around. There was no one close. Passers-by were giving him a wide berth, like he had the plague or something. Didn't they know who he was?

Where had the time gone? Then he remembered: Volkmar. He was probably late and would miss the senile old coot's "triumph". At least he should turn up to console him. Drown both their sorrows in strong drink. A capital idea.

Volkmar's house was dark and silent. A cold wind swirled

leaves around the entrance. There was a faint sulfurous scent and the smell of hot metal, as if from a forge. Cloaks and coats hung in the entry hall, and many pairs of muddy footprints made their way toward and under the door to Volkmar's study.

The door was locked.

"Volkmar, you old bastard, open up!"

Silence.

"Blood and damnation!" Was this some sort of trick? He wouldn't be played for a fool.

He kicked the door—once, twice. A third time and the lock broke. He strode inside.

"I swear, if—"

The stench of iron and piss, fear and death. And underneath it all a woman's perfume laced with leather. *Her* scent.

Blood everywhere. A dozen corpses, eyes dripping scarlet. Clothes torn ragged. Faces rigid with terror. Mouths open, screaming silently. Volkmar's colleagues, come to witness his triumph or bask in his failure.

Well, he guessed the sorcerer had shown them.

Volkmar was sitting against a wall, a smile on his face. In his hands was the sword, but it had changed. Still perfect. Still a silver ribbon, but now it glowed faintly as the moonlight through the window struck the blade.

Niklaus licked his lips. He approached Volkmar and knelt. The old man was dead.

He touched the sword, barely a caress. A tingle of energy traveled up his arm, and his chest tightened.

Near the hilt was a new engraving of exquisite detail, worked into the metal between this morning and now: a naked woman, kneeling, wings extending outward from behind her shoulders. Her mouth was curled in a sardonic smile.

Sylva Kalisia. The Lady. Niklaus's goddess, who had touched him centuries ago.

Who better to wield such a blade than him?

Niklaus took the sword from Volkmar's grip and backed away. With trembling hands, he discarded his own blade and sheathed Volkmar's triumph.

He snorted. "Huh, I guess you did it, old man."

He looked around at the price Sylva Kalisia had exacted for the gift of her power. The sorcerer had to have known, and he'd wanted Niklaus to be here. One soul less, but the Lady had still accepted the sacrifice. It seemed she still had a use for him. Still required his unending servitude.

*The blade is yours,* Sylva whispered. *You will be rewarded above all others.*

Her words came from inside him, as if spoken directly into his soul. Niklaus swallowed, fear twisting his gut. But the sound of her, the scent of her, the thought she'd been in this very room caused his head to spin and his groin to ache.

*Burn this place,* she said. *There must be no trace of Volkmar's sorcery left behind.*

"I ..." Niklaus said, voice breaking. "As you wish."

*If you please me, your rewards will be great.*

Niklaus felt lips brush his ear, a hand pressing into his groin. He groaned, wits dribbling from his head like a lustful adolescent.

Before he left the house, he toppled candelabras into curtains and smashed lamps, spreading their flaming oil onto furniture and bedding. Once outside, he watched as flames ravaged the building, devouring all evidence of what had happened.

Pale light bathed the streets around him, and he looked up at the glowing moon. Realization hit that he'd taken—no, accepted—the goddess's sword, and maybe there was a debt to pay. Along with the niggling disquiet that sometime in the future, she felt he would need a blade enhanced with arcane powers.

Niklaus stood there for long moments and pictured his old life being consumed for the second time. As if the raging heat cleansed his soul, allowing him to be born anew.

# CHAPTER ONE

# HARD CHOICES

THE BROAD STONE DOOR of the ruins stood open. For the moment, all was quiet. Aldric Kermoran loosened his khopesh in its sheath. The crescent blade was sometimes difficult to draw and he didn't want it sticking at an inopportune time. Closing his eyes, he whispered a brief prayer to his god, Menselas. With a finger, he rubbed the catalyst implanted under his skin, close to his heart, without which sorcery was impossible.

Moving slowly, deliberately, he sidled through the entrance and peered down the steps leading into blackness. White, threadlike fungi grew around the door and trailed inside the tomb. Farther in, oyster-shaped mushrooms sprouted from the walls, their surface covered with fingernail-sized scales that glowed with a faint violet luminescence. Violet scaleskins were only found inside ancient ruins, and scholars thought the light they emitted was a product of sorcerous leakage.

Apart from the mushrooms, there was nothing chasing away the dark. Aldric breathed a sigh of relief. Whoever had broken the ancient wards to enter the tomb was far enough inside that there was no telltale glimmer from whatever light source they carried.

Simple treasure hunters were the likeliest culprits. Men and women who thought the enigmatic ruins contained valuable artifacts, metals and gems they could sell for easy coin. They were right, of course, but some of these forgotten places contained things much, much worse.

For thousands of years, these tombs and repositories had remained hidden, unplundered, the works of an ancient race about whom little was known, even by the most educated scholars. But what they did know was that whatever was sealed inside was better left undisturbed.

Whoever had entered the tomb would likely spend hours exploring. That meant Aldric had time to investigate their camp and decide on a course of action. He turned his back on the hole in the cliff face and made his way along the escarpment.

When he reached the camp, he saw it was ... disorganized. Hastily erected lean-tos, three of them, that would barely keep a drizzle off their occupants. The canvas was patched in many places, its edges frayed. A ripe stench came from behind nearby bushes where they'd dug a shallow hole to use as a latrine. Close by lay the half-butchered carcass of a deer, uncovered.

Aldric wrinkled his nose and frowned. Preparing meat this close to their waste, and leaving the carcass for any nearby scavenger to eat—either they were lazy or stupid, or didn't think they'd be here long. Judging by the state of their camp, he decided it was probably all three.

With a critical eye, he examined their gear. Mostly worn canvas packs, frequently repaired bedrolls, and battered pots and tin plates. An old mule tied to a tree stared at him as he walked a circle around the fire, which was still warm and trailed tendrils of smoke. Beside the fire sat a pot with the remnants of a stew. Flies buzzed around it, alighting on the rim and walking down the inside wall.

To all appearances, it looked like the treasure hunters were locals who'd stumbled across the ruins and decided to take a chance. But at least one of them had to have circumvented the wards woven into the door, and that meant sorcery. There was a chance, albeit a small one, that the locals were here only to help the sorcerer. Paid to do the manual work and to keep their mouths shut.

From the back of Aldric's mind rose another possibility, one that made him more than a little uneasy. The Church's ancient enemy still had followers, and they were as dedicated to their cause as Aldric was to his—if not more so.

Squatting by the tidiest lean-to, he picked through the gear. It was of better quality and looked well cared for. The backpack was double stitched, and the blanket newly purchased. Inside the pack were spare clothes, along with a sewing kit, a flask of rum, and writing materials. Nothing arcane, but that was no surprise. Talismans and other aids were no use unless you had them with you.

Aldric closed the backpack and stood. He hadn't expected to find evidence of demon worship, but it paid to be careful. He couldn't afford any slipups, not in his line of work. Cleaning up for the Church was dangerous business, and he took his vocation seriously. His god had given him gifts, so it was only right and fitting that he used them to benefit the Church. Or so the priests had drummed into him from a young age. For Aldric, sorcery was a necessary evil. A path he had never wanted, but he did what he was told. The Church had invested a great deal of coin in his training.

*Enough speculation.* There was no evidence so far that this was anything more than a simple raid to plunder the treasures of the ruin. But he loosened his khopesh in its sheath again, adjusted his long gray, time-worn coat, and made sure his sorcerous defenses were ready to erupt at a moment's notice. They weren't strong, but they'd gotten him out of a few bad situations. With any luck, he wouldn't need them.

Shrieks and cries reached his ears. Faint. If he hadn't been listening for them, they might have gone unnoticed. Back toward the ruin, startled birds scattered from trees. Aldric felt a pinch in his gut.

He made his way quickly back to the open ruin, this time not caring if he made noise. The gaping darkness seemed to welcome him. Ice-cold, dank air brushed his face as he stood just inside the stone door. In the glow of the violet scaleskins, he could see a dozen steps descending. Where they ended, a stone corridor sloped farther down, rime frost crusting its walls.

For a moment, he felt an absurd fear that he was wrong. That the sorcerer and his companions would survive. Then he felt sickened. What had he become, that he wanted people to die so he wouldn't have to do the terrible deed himself? It was his duty to ensure that none outside the Church knew of the ruins and how to breach them. The artifacts inside were better left undisturbed: sorcerous relics that would damn a weak soul and perhaps lead to the return of the demons.

As he squinted into the darkness, someone howled. A sound of pure terror torn from a throat.

With grim resolve Aldric descended the steps. He needed to see what happened, to bear witness.

Far along the tunnel, a brief flutter of light appeared and grew brighter. A man's voice shouted cants between gibberish outbursts. Aldric recognized some of the wards—against violence, and to create barriers. Incandescent flashes were followed by thunderous rumblings. Loud slaps reverberated off the frost-covered walls. The fungus glowed brighter as it absorbed arcane emanations.

Aldric saw that the tunnel descended only thirty paces before opening into an antechamber. On the far side of the chamber was another doorway. A man bolted through it, a talisman in his hand—a wooden rod festooned with feathers that spread a pale yellow light. His eyes were deranged, and his face a twisted mask of horror. Sweat dripped from his hair, spraying around him as he ran.

He cast a frantic glance behind him, breath steaming in the frigid air, and screamed to someone farther down the tunnel, "Run, you fool!"

Aldric swallowed, touched a hand to the catalyst in his chest, and prepared a cant himself. Whatever they'd disturbed was powerful, and his own sorcery couldn't hope to match it. But that wasn't his job, and he'd be stupid to try. No matter how much he wanted to.

Another light appeared behind the sorcerer, and the air filled with unintelligible murmurs that quickly rose to a drone as intense as the hum of a beehive. Aldric caught a glimpse of limbs flailing, and then the glow vanished and a spray of blood showered from the tunnel, splattering the sorcerer and the frost-rimed stone around him. Steam curled up from its contact with the cold, quickly dissipating in the air.

Aldric felt his gorge rise. He swallowed it back down, breathing heavily through his nose. Fear gripped him, but he knew it was a minuscule thing compared to the sorcerer's.

A violent gust howled through the chamber. When it tore at Aldric's hair, he smelled blood and sulfur and wood smoke—a combination he recognized.

A Reaper. *Holy Menselas.*

Reapers were sorcerous creatures, the knowledge of their making thankfully lost millennia ago. An amalgamation of human and animal parts, each one was unique. But they were all mongoose fast and bull strong and immune to all but the most puissant sorcery. Aldric knew he couldn't prevail against one. Neither his fighting skills nor his sorcery would suffice. Although if he could bring himself to access his dusk-tide repository ... No. The dark power was too unsettling and he disdained its use when he could. Its touch was ... unholy.

The sorcerer howled, feet slipping in the gore. His talisman jolted from his hand as he fell, clattering to the side and sending shadows flickering. His hands and feet scrabbled to find purchase as he attempted to regain his footing.

The urge to help rose within Aldric, and he took a stuttering step forward before retreating. The commands of his Church were very clear. And if the Reaper was so close, it was too late.

The sorcerer slipped again, then managed to get up and stumble forward, whimpering and cursing. He looked toward the exit, so close, and his eyes widened as he saw Aldric. Hope blossomed on his face.

"Help! Please …"

Curiously numb, Aldric shook his head. He didn't have a bow or crossbow to distract or delay the Reaper. And in any case, if he did, he'd use it to put the sorcerer out of his misery. For what was coming for him was far worse than a quick, clean death.

"I'm sorry," he said. "I cannot." And, hardening his heart, he took a step backward, then hastily ascended the steps.

As soon as he was outside, he uttered a cant, and his catalyst reacted. The ancient wards, so recently deactivated, flared anew. Stone ground against stone as the door began to shut.

"No!" screamed the sorcerer. "You can't—"

His words, along with the murmuring hum of the Reaper, were cut off as the door resealed the ruin.

Aldric took a deep breath, then another. He wiped his eyes.

*One final check.*

He awakened his divine sight bestowed upon him by his god along with his ability to heal others. The stone door glowed a pale rose, then brightened to a lurid purple as its sorcerous wards gradually re-established themselves. *Good.* The fell tomb was sealed, and it would take another foolhardy sorcerer to breach it again.

Aldric leaned against the door's rough surface. He felt drained, weak. And, ashamedly, relieved. He whispered a prayer under his breath for the dead.

Back at the camp, he built up the fire and dismantled the lean-tos. When the blaze was big enough, he burned all the men's belongings. Out here in the wilderness, there was no one to see the smoke.

When the fire died down, he extinguished the ashes with water from a nearby stream. The mule kept an eye on him.

"A hard day," he told it. "And I fear it won't get any easier. Come on."

Untying the beast, he led it back to where he'd secured his horse. It shouldn't be left out here for the wolves or the Dead-eyes.

~ ~ ~

It took three weeks of hard travel before the familiar haze of the seething metropolis of Nagorn City, Aldric's home for many years, came into sight. He'd left the mule at the first settlement he'd come across and hadn't taken any coin for it. It was hard enough in the wilderness, and the mule would go a small way to easing someone's life.

Nagorn City was ancient, older by far than the generations of farmers and settlers who'd toiled and died in the lands surrounding the great city. Historians believed it had survived the last three cataclysms, which made it older than Kharas in the hot southern reaches and Sansor in the heathen realm of Kaile far to the west, but not as old as Caronath in the north. Its enclosing wall had been built over centuries and showed the work of diverse hands and times: rough-hewn rock alongside sharper, regular stone carved by arcane means long ago, and cheap and hastily erected brick defenses on top.

Once inside the massive gates, Aldric had to breathe through his mouth until he became re-accustomed to the odor. He hadn't missed the overpopulated warren of tenements and businesses. The air was filled with a fine dust, and the paved streets were littered with dirt and rubbish and manure. It had clearly been a while since the last downpour had scoured them clean.

In his time away, nothing had changed. People still hurried about their tasks; dogs and cats and rats roamed the back alleys; and out-of-work citizens congregated around communal noticeboards. To Aldric's eye, there seemed to be more people down on their luck this year than any other before.

As he made his way through the streets, his gray skin elicited curious looks from farmers and traders and travelers. Surreptitiously, he tugged his sleeves down and his hood closer about his face. He forgave them their curiosity; after all, there were many races spread throughout the lands of Wiraya. And some were rarer in some cities than others. There weren't many of his race this far north. The San-Kharr were more plentiful in the south, where they originated, and those of full blood were much darker than Aldric with his diluted ancestry.

An hour later he squared away his gear and mount in the Church's stables, then made his way to the rooms allotted to him. Although small and furnished with dilapidated, mismatched pieces, they were enough for his needs. He washed off the dirt and grime he'd accumulated in the wilderness. There had been plenty of streams and lakes on his journey, but only a fool would splash around naked out there. It was a recipe for getting your throat cut or for being hacked apart by Dead-eyes—after they'd defiled you and made you wish you'd never been born.

Dressed again in shirt and trousers, he made a point of buckling on his khopesh and hanging his talisman from his belt. Every sorcerer used one—a concentration, logic, and mathematical calculation aid created at the start of their Covenant training. Arcane formulas were complex, requiring the sorcerer's awareness to split into many different parts, and a talisman made the difficult task slightly easier. Aldric's was a smooth, wooden, rounded-edged pentagon that snuggled into his palm when he used it, and hung from a chain on his belt when he didn't. It was etched with runes and had five sides: one for each of Menselas's aspects. Aldric had made it early in his tenure with the Covenant of the Evokers, which was where the Church had sent him when his arcane power became manifest—once they'd overcome their revulsion. The lessons and training had been hard, and made all the harder by Aldric's resistance. His colleagues never liked seeing the talisman, and showing it was a small act of defiance on his part. The god had given him his gifts, and he used them to further the Church's goals.

Casting his troubled thoughts aside, Aldric made his way to Archbishop Roald's office. As he passed novices and other priests, they lowered their eyes and sidestepped out of his path. Aldric ignored them in turn, but frowned at their attitude. Didn't they know he kept them all safe? Didn't they know that Menselas— god of the Five Aspects—had given him gifts only bestowed upon a few? Of course they did, but they also knew he was a sorcerer. As always, the knowledge of what he could do, as opposed to what he was directed to do, left him seething. All those months out in the wilderness, risking himself, and his own Church treated him like a pariah. It was unacceptable. Yet he'd accepted it for years. No, not accepted: tolerated. There was a difference.

When he found the archbishop absent from his office, Aldric decided to wait while he calmed down. He glanced around the reception room with its desk and comfortable lounges, shrugged, and entered the archbishop's study. It was tastefully decorated with polished furniture, tapestries hanging from the walls, and worn rugs covering the floor. Dust motes floated in the air, lit by windows on one side. Bookcases were filled to overflowing, and there was a faint scent of an alchemical cleaning solution. On one wall hung a circular brass astrolabe used to track the moons, planets, and stars. It was the size of a large dinner plate, of Kawib design, and powered, Aldric knew, by ensorcelled orichalcum, a rare metal prized for its ability to hold sorcery and its superior corrosion resistance. It would have cost far more than Roald could afford as an archbishop. Perhaps it came with the office.

Aldric poured himself a drink from one of the numerous bottles behind the large hardwood desk. It was after noon, wasn't it? Crystal chimed as the bottle's neck met the glass. *Expensive.* Both the glassware and the spirit showed the archbishop didn't skimp on luxuries.

Aldric gulped a mouthful of the liquor, which burned his throat and made his eyes water. He didn't normally drink, except at dinner, but for some reason he felt the need.

Deciding it would be best not to get caught trespassing, he returned to the reception room. In one corner, next to a leafy plant in a glazed ceramic pot, stood a padded armchair. He unbuckled his khopesh belt and leaned the blade against the wall, then sat down to wait.

He was debating a second drink when the door opened and a priestess walked in. She was wearing the usual drab gray wool dress, and her hair was covered with a dark blue scarf. Aldric recognized her bright blue eyes and dimpled cheeks. He'd seen her around the church and its grounds, but didn't know her name. There had been rumor of a dalliance between her and someone higher up—which itself was nothing unusual, as plenty of priests married; after all, one aspect of Menselas was the Mother—but unconsecrated sexual relationships between the clergy were frowned upon.

"Oh!" she said as he rose from his chair. "I didn't see you there. Archbishop Roald is booked for the day. You'll have to make an appointment."

Her eyes strayed to Aldric's khopesh and the symbol engraved into its hilt, and then to where the same symbol was embroidered on his shirt—a five-pointed star surrounded by a circle of runes, the meaning of which would be incomprehensible to her. She swallowed and edged around the desk until it was between them. Aldric knew she thought he was damned, that the mark of Menselas within him was an anomaly, a travesty of all that was holy.

"Roald will see me," he said. "When will he be back?"

"You have to make an appointment. He's very busy."

"When will he be back?"

Aldric's words came through clenched teeth. Each of these slights stung him like salt on an open wound.

Her eyes flicked to the door. "I don't know."

*Soon, then.* "I'll wait."

He sat back down and gazed out the window. The priestess stared at him for a few moments before sniffing and settling herself behind the desk. She shuffled papers, jotted notes, and generally made herself look busy. Aldric, pretending not to notice her fleeting glances at him, settled back into the chair and closed his eyes briefly. Any longer and he might fall asleep. His limbs were heavy, and his back ached. Not only was he tired, but his mind and soul were still troubled after what had happened at the ruin.

Shortly past the noon bell, the door opened again. This time it was Roald. His pale skin was dried and papery with age, but his black velvet robes were brushed and spotless, and five plain rings gleamed on his fingers, one unique metal for each aspect of Menselas. Apart from the pious bands, Roald wore no other jewelry. His archbishop's ring, presented upon ordination, was worn only at public functions. He radiated an air of sanctity and reasonableness.

His sharp eyes noticed Aldric immediately and he nodded in greeting. "Aldric, safe journey back, I take it?"

"Archbishop Roald, nothing untoward." Aldric couldn't say more in front of the priestess. He took up his khopesh and waited expectantly.

The archbishop turned to his secretary. "Dina, I need you to postpone today's lunch with Bishop Thormin. Make some excuse." Without waiting for a reply, he turned to Aldric. "Let's adjourn to my study."

They passed through the sturdy door, which Roald closed and bolted behind them, causing Aldric to feel a twinge of guilt at his earlier trespass.

"Did you find it?" Roald asked without preamble. He clasped both hands in front of him, fingers automatically tracing his rings.

Aldric nodded. "It was as you said. They'd found a ruin and opened it. How did you know?"

Roald waved a hand in dismissal. "What was this one like? Was it ... normal?"

It was the archbishop's job to manage the few specialists that operated for the Church, like Aldric, and he kept much of what he knew to himself. It was frustrating, but Aldric supposed it couldn't be helped. Unless he somehow proved himself worthy of a good deal more trust.

"As normal as any of them," he told the archbishop. "Standard square stone door with wards. The sorcerer who disabled them was middling. I don't know if he was experimenting and got lucky, or if he found an old book with instructions for opening the wards. I burned all their belongings to make sure. It was the best I could do short of spending weeks trying to find out where the sorcerer came from."

"Hmmm. No, you've done well. Did you go inside? Was there anything unusual?"

Roald's question was nonchalant, but Aldric sensed an eagerness behind it. The archbishop frequently sent Aldric and others like him into the ruins, supposedly to stop foolhardy treasure hunters from unleashing what they found there. But Aldric suspected the Church didn't just keep safe the artifacts they recovered. They used them. It was a suspicion he kept to himself.

"It looked to be a standard stage three ruin from the style and power of the wards. The walls were rimed with frost, but not thickly. The treasure hunters were all killed."

*I made sure of that.* Aldric rubbed his eyes. Their deaths weighed upon him heavily.

Roald raised his eyebrows, then moved to a narrow desk underneath a window, where piles of paper were held down with weights. He smoothed out a map and jotted a quick note next to a tiny red X, then tapped the pen on the page.

"Killed by you, or by what was inside?"

"Does it matter?"

Roald grunted. "I guess not. Unless it was something we haven't seen before."

"Nothing new. A Reaper."

"Huh." He made another annotation. "I'll send some people to clean up. The bodies might have something of note on them, especially the sorcerer's."

Aldric narrowed his eyes. "I should return with them. The Reaper needs to be confined again. It will require a sorcerer."

"Magister Zandra will hire appropriate assistance."

"I thought she was in Strindiya?" At least, she was supposed to be a thousand miles away on a mission in the burgeoning city.

Roald placed the pen on the table and began pacing back and forth. "I had to recall her, as I need you on something else that's come up. She's on a ship as we speak, and with good winds she'll arrive in a few weeks."

Aldric suppressed the urge to sigh. Something always came up, and it was never good. He wanted to rest, to visit the healers and work with them. But what he wanted never figured into the equation. He realized his hands were bunched into fists and forced himself to unclench them.

Roald hadn't noticed. "I need to make a few things clear before I give you the mission details," he said, ceasing his pacing to pick up one of the paperweights—a burnished metal sculpture of the Elder, one of the five aspects of Menselas. "First, know that we value you and the dangerous work you do. But there are forces rallying against the good of Menselas, and although we are all weary, we cannot rest."

Aldric nodded and said, "Thank you," when what he really wanted was to ask for some time off.

"You labor under a great burden," Roald said. "And Menselas has given you rare gifts. Your rise from priest to magister is but one sign of our appreciation. The missions I give you are another acknowledgment of your talents. You would be wise to see that."

A compliment wrapped in a warning. Aldric supposed it was the best he could hope for. The sideways promotion he'd received a few years ago had effectively removed him from the day-to-day workings of the Church. The Church of Menselas shunned sorcery, but they couldn't get rid of Aldric because Menselas had chosen him. As the god had chosen Zandra and Lyster, who Aldric hadn't seen in years. They were too useful. The Five had marked them, for good or for ill.

Aldric believed for good. He wanted to serve Menselas, to lead a virtuous life. But sorcery was a burden he had to bear.

"I only want to serve Menselas," he said, voicing his thoughts. "To do what is right."

The archbishop smiled. Roald was a good man of exceptional faith and strength. Perhaps that was why he'd been chosen to manage those novices tainted by the mark of sorcery. "That's excellent. As do we all aspire to do his will. You are also fortunate to be blessed with Menselas's gift of healing. Of his other aspects, no one has shown signs for centuries. We don't know why this has happened, but it leads us to believe those aspects are on the wane and our god's focus is on healing. And no wonder, with the state of the world we inhabit. I know you struggle with your place, but sorcery is a unique way of serving our god. Everyone has their own battles; they fight doubts you cannot know. I know things can be ... difficult for you, but the time has come for the Church to show how much it appreciates you."

Roald strode over to a metal safe and took a key ring from his pocket. Fumbling, he selected an ornate key and turned the lock. From the safe he removed a black wooden box that fit into his palm.

Approaching Aldric, he held it out. "Go on. Take it."

Aldric reached for the box, hesitating. "What is it?"

"Open it and see." A smile played across Roald's face.

Aldric stared at the box in his hand. It was crafted from blackwood, a rare timber known to dampen sorcerous abilities and emanations, and that fact gave him pause. He glanced at Roald before opening the lid. Inside, nestled in spongy felt, was a relic: a diamond the size of a quail's egg, caged in tarnished silver wire. At its core, a pale green light flickered.

Aldric's breath caught in his throat. He wondered if this was some sort of test, or if Roald was teasing him. Or could it be that after all these years, the Church was finally ready to accept him? He'd worked hard to gain their trust, but had never felt recognized. His hands trembled and his vision blurred.

He hid his emotion by moving the relic into the stronger light by the window. He'd handled such a relic only once before, for a single night during his training. Only given to the most trusted, the relics were used to relive the memories of dead priests.

Millennia ago, the Church of Menselas, along with many other faiths, had battled the demon lord Nysrog and the unholy sorcerers who were drawn to his power. Hundreds of thousands of people had died. The Church of Menselas had almost collapsed. It was a time of great upheaval and devastation, but eventually Nysrog was banished back to the hells. The demon might have been defeated, but his followers still worked to bring him back. That was the unspoken secret of the Church and why they kept their awareness honed. *Be forever vigilant*, their creed went, *lest the demon lord Nysrog is brought back to this world.*

"You will know this is a relic," Roald said. He cleared his throat uncomfortably. "And that it's past time for you to be offered a gift such as this. But"—he spread his hands—"you know why you have not yet been initiated."

"My sorcery," whispered Aldric. "My *taint.*"

"Yes. Because of the darkness within you. Many in the Church don't see things the way we do. Your talent is an anomaly, one that goes against all our teachings. Yet the Five must have a reason for giving you such a gift. Through long and hard negotiation, I've persuaded the archbishops this needs to be done. We couldn't have you unprepared."

Aldric nodded, not trusting himself to speak. A relic! He would have access to past priests' wisdom. Real memories, not prone to misunderstanding like the written histories were. And one day, his memories would join them. His knowledge and experiences available for any priest to learn from. Although he'd been promoted above the senior priests to become a magister, until now he hadn't been trusted. They'd withheld access to the relics. His heart swelled. He was on the brink of acceptance. If he didn't make any mistakes.

"This one is old and violent," Roald said. "It was decided you shouldn't bother with the mundane relics." He uttered a half laugh. "A violent relic for a violent man, one of the other archbishops remarked."

He watched Aldric for a reaction. But Aldric was past caring what was said about him behind his back. He knew his worth. And now, it seemed, the Church was taking him into its fold, deeper than he'd expected.

"My talent is for healing. It was the Church that molded me for violence." Why did he always need to remind them of that? "Nevertheless, I'll do my best to make use of the memories."

"Make sure you do. There are currents around the world that point to uncertain times. This relic is special. And, I needn't tell you, it's priceless. It's from the time of Nysrog." Roald's mouth twisted in distaste.

The diamond seemed to grow heavier in Aldric's palm: a direct link to a time of legend. Very few relics from that time remained, and they were never given to priests to learn from. What they contained was too harrowing. For the Church of Menselas, these were gentler times.

Aldric knew his worth; he'd contemplated it deeply. But of this gift, he was unworthy. "Archbishop Roald," he began, "I appreciate—"

"This is not an honor to be refused. Accept it with good grace, and learn from it. The time of Nysrog was an abomination. Hundreds of thousands of people died before we forced the formidable darkness back into the abyss whence it came."

Aldric knew the story well. It was drummed into all novices from an early age. Corpses stretching to the horizon. Sorcerers, fouled by Nysrog, perpetrating unspeakable acts. Men, women, and children could not weep, for they had no more tears to shed. Nysrog's defeat had been accomplished through an ancient artifact known as the Chain of Eyes, subsequently lost.

"I know the history. And I ... thank you."

Aldric closed the box and secured it in his pocket. He'd have to find a safer place for it. To lose such a priceless relic would be grounds for demotion back to acolyte, or even worse if they wanted to get rid of him once and for all. *Excommunication.* The thought sickened him. The Church was all he had. The sacrifices he'd made would be for nothing.

Roald stared at a faded tapestry on one wall, seemingly

engrossed in its details. "Take care not to lose yourself in the relic's dreams. You've not had the practice other priests have had."

*I'm a magister,* thought Aldric, but decided not to remind Roald. He was used to such slights, even from his direct superior. But a relic! He'd finally made it. Years of hard work and unquestioning obedience were paying off. Missions where he'd doubted his sanity seemed to pale into insignificance. But ...

"What has changed?" Aldric asked. "why now?"

"We have heard whispers. Possibly, the Tainted Cabal are planning something."

The Tainted Cabal ... the followers of Nysrog who had survived the great battle that had returned the demon lord to the hells. So far, in a decade of doing the bidding of his faith, Aldric had crossed paths with the followers of the demon Nysrog only a handful of times. Each encounter had left scars on his soul. And not a few on his flesh.

"What does this new mission for me involve?" Aldric said.

Roald gave him a serious look. He clasped his hands in front of him. "You need rest. But time is of the essence."

"I'm ready." He wasn't, but there was nothing else he could say.

"Well, you may recuperate on the way—you'll be spending some time at sea. Hierophant Karianne, in Caronath, has requested someone with your ... various skills. And Menselas knows, there aren't many of you. We can't really spare you, but the order came from their hierophant to ours, and the deal was done without my knowledge. We'll arrange passage for you up the coast, but you'll have to travel inland from the Port of Nantin. Unless you take a short cut through the wilderness."

Aldric brought up a map of the continent in his mind. Caronath was one of the northernmost cities, right on the border of the civilized lands. The country was harsh, with more than just

Dead-eyes to harass settlers and explorers. There were creatures of power that skirted the edges of mankind. Much of the wilderness was yet to be explored, and men fought a constant battle against nightmare creatures to maintain the foothold they had.

Roald was right. Nantin was south-east of Caronath. If Aldric was dropped off along the coast further north, he could cut weeks from his trip. It was dangerous, but it could be done.

"I'll pack my gear," he said.

Roald smiled ruefully. "I can always rely on you. But there's one more thing. Hierophant Karianne requested assistance for an unspecified period. It could be months. Years, even. I hope you see the necessity for this."

Aldric felt as if he'd had icy water dumped over him. The relic had led him to believe he'd finally made progress. Now, Roald was practically ordering him to remain in another city indefinitely. His fingers found the blackwood box in his pocket and caressed its smooth surface. They gave, and they took away. It was ever the case.

The Church was his life, but as usual his desires were pushed aside. Would he ever be able to settle down? To focus on healing again?

## CHAPTER TWO

# TESTS OF FAITH

AN HOUR'S RIDE FROM Nagorn City, Aldric reached the small village of Cranford, familiar to him from when he was a young boy. Half an hour beyond that, he arrived at his childhood home. There was no other place he would rather be—if it had remained as he remembered. But nothing stayed the same; change was inevitable. He knew this for truth, as solid and immutable as stone. Before he went away for so long, he needed to see his parents and provide what comforting words he could to his sister, who still lived with them. He couldn't stay for long, just as he also knew he could never return to his previous life.

The little brick house stood on a slight rise, surrounded by a dozen mature maple trees whose brilliant red leaves blanketed the ground. He could see a number of trails through them made by human footsteps: one from the rickety wooden gate to the front door, another from the porch to the sizable barn at the side, one to the well and its hand-pump, and the fourth to the outhouse. Aldric had spent many an hour working the pump for water until his arms burned, and emptying sewage from the outhouse into the fields.

His gaze took in the dilapidated fence and gate, the corrosion on the metal parts of the pump. The barn door was ajar even though evening was fast approaching. He sighed and shook his head. All tasks someone should have taken care of if they cared about their work and their family. Or if they had a son to help.

He strode to the side of the house and collected an armful of wood from a dwindling pile inside a lean-to—itself slanted dangerously to one side and missing a few shingles.

At the front door, Aldric paused, swallowed the lump in his throat, put on a smile, then knocked.

Movement sounded inside. A chair scraping on the floor. A man's gruff voice.

"Who is it?" asked his mother through the door.

His father hadn't even bothered to answer the door himself when a stranger knocked at sunset.

"It's me, Ma. I'm sorry to turn up unannounced—"

The door swung open, and Aldric found himself smothered in a hug despite his armful of wood. His mother's scent enveloped him—wood smoke and spices, a mix of perfumes from her flowers—and for an instant he was transported back to his youth. He squeezed her waist with his free arm, noting she had lost weight.

"Close the bloody door, Hesketh!" shouted his father. "You're letting the heat out."

"Oh, pipe down, Bastian." Aldric's mother wiped tears from her eyes and kissed him on both cheeks. Her gray hair was tied back in a braid, and her dark gray weather-worn face bore extra wrinkles since he'd last seen her. "Don't mind your father," she murmured. "He's—"

"I know," Aldric replied, more harshly than he'd intended.

Hesketh led him inside and closed the door. Nothing much had changed. The same oak table and chairs stood in the center of the room; the same faded burgundy armchairs in front of the fire, which had burned down to coals. The once plush rug from the far southern city of Gessa, where his father was born, was slightly more stained and faded.

Hesketh wore what Aldric could have sworn was the same dress he'd last seen her in, but he noticed it was less frayed. She was comfortable with the style, he guessed. Bastian's shirt and trousers were grubby and sweat-stained; and from the look of his dirty hands, arms, and face, he hadn't washed up before supper.

Aldric busied himself stacking the wood beside the fireplace. When he finished, Hesketh had prepared a plate of stew for him and placed it on the table in front of an empty chair. He'd been expecting to see his sister, but there was no sign of her.

"Where's Kittara?" he asked. "I was hoping—"

"She isn't here," said Bastian curtly. He used a crust of bread to sop up brown gravy on his plate, gnawed off a chunk and chewed.

Aldric gritted his teeth and took a breath. "Where—"

"Probably cavorting with some layabout."

Hesketh sat and placed a hand on Bastian's arm. "Kittara's helping the village healer harvest and dry herbs. She's taken a liking to it."

Bastian scoffed. "Waste of time. She should learn what you did, Aldric. Maybe then she'd be of some use."

Aldric caught the flash of irritation on his mother's face before she covered it with a strained smile.

"Well," she said, "sit, Aldric. Eat. Tell us what's happening in the world. How are you?"

"It's not something you can learn," Aldric told his father as he joined them at the table. "But you know that."

He picked up his spoon and pushed a few small chunks of meat and carrot around the plate. He wasn't hungry. The stew was thinner than he remembered, mostly gravy bulked out with barley. Empty whiskey jugs sat beside the door, and there were three stoppered jugs on a shelf. A cheap brand, but not the cheapest. So money wasn't too tight, then; and it shouldn't be, with the coin he sent home every month. If his father began making his own spirits, then Aldric would worry.

Bastian sniffed, then coughed. "It's sunset. Don't you have to be outside?" He raised both hands into the air, wiggling his fingers. "You know, the god's power."

Bastian knew full well that it was sorcery, not the god's power, that could be replenished during the change from night to day and day to night. He was baiting Aldric.

"I should," Aldric said, then shrugged. "But I have enough for now."

Sunset was a time of dark power—dusk-tide, as it was called—and Aldric held more than he wanted of such power.

"Sunrise is better, isn't it, Aldric? That's when there's more of the light sorcery," Hesketh said.

Dawn-tide, she meant. A time of clean and pure power, though still anathema to many in the Church.

"That's right," he said. "The two powers are different. The dawn-tide comes with the dawn, and dusk-tide with the dusk."

"That's obvious," said Bastian.

"Will you be staying the night?" Hope tinged Hesketh's voice.

Aldric reached over and squeezed her hand. It felt so thin and frail. "I'm sorry. I have to return tonight. I'm leaving on another mission."

Hesketh lowered her gaze and pretended to be interested in her food. "I understand."

"Just as well," Bastian said. "We can't afford to feed you. I have a hard time these days just feeding her and Kittara." He pointed his gravy-covered spoon at Hesketh before biting off another mouthful of bread and chewing noisily.

Under the table, Aldric slipped a hand into his trouser pocket and took out a calfskin coin purse. Moving slowly lest the coins make a noise, he slipped it into his mother's lap. She glanced up at him and gave a quick nod and a smile.

An hour passed, filled with strained conversation, suppressed acerbic replies, gritted teeth, and clenched fists. By then, Bastian had been drinking steadily from a jug for some time and trying, unsuccessfully, to repair a piece of leather tack. After the initial surprise of Aldric's burgeoning abilities had worn off, Bastian had realized he'd be left to look after Hesketh and Kittara on his own and had never forgiven Aldric. He'd expected to have his son's strong back to run the farm and do all the hard chores while he spent more time drinking with his friends and taking it easy.

When Aldric couldn't stand the tension any more, he made his goodbyes and spent a good deal of time trying to extricate himself from his mother's embrace. Finally, he closed the front door behind him. Only when his parents couldn't see him did he release some of his emotion. His face twisted as his chest tightened. Breathing became difficult.

He staggered away from the house, his booted feet shuffling through dry leaves. In the low light, their red looked black. His hand touched a tree for support and he clutched at its bark, as if its solidity could give him strength. He leaned his back against the trunk, head bowed, and drew in a shuddering breath. For long moments, he stood there deathly still, hands bunched into fists, knuckles white. Tears spilled down his cheeks.

"Oh, poor baby."

Aldric froze.

Kittara stepped around the tree and faced him. She looked older, though it was only months since he'd seen her last. Her homespun dress was too tight, and a few too many buttons were undone at the neck, revealing skin darkened by the sun. A woven basket filled with bunches of herbs hung from one arm.

Aldric wiped his face with his sleeve, embarrassed she'd caught him weeping. "I hoped you'd be home."

"Well, now you've seen me. Now you can go."

"Kittara—"

"Don't!" she spat. "Just don't. You can't imagine what it's

like."

Aldric stiffened. "Just as you can't imagine what I go through."

"Must be hard, being a sorcerer *and* favored of a god. If only I knew such hardship. Instead, I have to look after our beloved father and mother."

She kicked some leaves wet with evening dew, and the moisture left dark spots on her boots.

"She needs you." It was all Aldric could think of to say.

Kittara's lips twisted. "They need *you*. I do my best. I can't do more. But I won't be around forever."

"Kittara—"

"Enough. Just go. How long did you stay this time? An hour? Two?" She shook her head. "The prodigal son returns for an hour. How it must have pleased Mother. And Father will be in a mood for days. He drinks, you know. Far too much." She mimed surprise, her mouth open and both hands on her cheeks. "Shocking, isn't it? Still, Mother copes. I cope. We all cope. But not forever."

"Do what you must to make yourself happy. But make sure our mother is taken care of."

"Happy? I only want my own life. Is that too much to ask for?"

"I can send more coin."

"Ah, royals. Copper, silver, and gold—the universal cure. A salve for the soul."

"I can't do more at the moment," Aldric said, all too aware he echoed Kittara's words. "My work is important, and I'm hardly ever in Nagorn City. And now ..." He touched the hem of his sleeve, rolling the fabric between his fingers. "If I could visit more often—"

"It would be worse. You know it would." Her shoulders slumped. "Just go, Aldric. But know I'm getting older, and one day I'll be free of this prison. And who knows? Maybe I'll endure a quickening and become a sorcerer like you. Then I'll turn up on your doorstep. Wouldn't that be a thing?" She hugged her arms across her chest, eyes unfocused, a wistful expression on her face.

Aldric knew it wasn't likely to happen. At sixteen, she was already too old. Only rarely did a sorcerer come into their abilities later in life, and the quickening was more treacherous then. Almost all died; and those that survived were twisted, leaning toward the dark forces that arose at sunset.

He nodded, forcing a grin. "It would."

She smiled at him then, a shadow of her younger, more caring self showing through. It almost broke his heart.

"I think I can feel the sunrise sometimes," she said. "Like you told me you can. It makes my skin tingle." She hesitated. "What's it like ... all that power?"

"Frightening." Aldric cleared his throat. "If you discover you're a sorcerer, come find me. I'll make sure you receive the proper training. My Covenant is expensive, but the Church will pay for it, I'm sure. But it's ... not a path I'd choose, or recommend."

"But you can't *choose* it, can you, dear brother?"

"No," he agreed. "You can only submit."

"Submission isn't my strong suit."

"It wasn't mine either. Still isn't."

Kittara snorted. "Well, I can't stay out all night nattering. There's work to do. Stay safe, Aldric. I need you to be around when I become a sorcerer."

Without another word, she turned and ran to the house. Aldric watched her until she was safely inside. She didn't look back.

He shouldn't have come.

That was what he said every time. But still, he returned; and he knew he always would.

~ ~ ~

Aldric sat atop his horse a few hundred yards outside one of the many city gates that breached Nagorn City's massive fortified walls. He'd felt drained after his visit home and had rented a room for the night in a village tavern on the way back, unable to face the long trek with only his churning thoughts for company. He'd hardly slept and had headed out well before dawn, mind and body sluggish. Now, as darkness softened to gray, he knew he'd have to quicken his pace if he wanted to avail himself of the sorcerous dawn-tide and replenish his reserves. It wasn't just bad form to replenish a repository in the middle of a city street; it would probably lead to him being stoned or worse. And his Church wouldn't be pleased by the resulting scandal.

Aldric's dusk-tide power was relatively stable, but his dawn-tide repository leaked like a rusty sieve. Every sorcerer was different, though all power drained away eventually. One way to render a sorcerer powerless was to keep them underground, away from the dawn- and dusk-tides, until their power bled from them. With dawn fast approaching, he wouldn't make it back to his lodgings in time, but he had other options.

Passing through the gate, he urged his mount to a trot and muttered thanks to his god that the streets were still mostly deserted. He made his way along the Ithalt Highway and barely glanced at the dark, looming stone entrance to the Bartimus Catacombs. On the edge of the street, a few old women were setting up tables to sell candles, flowers, and assorted offerings for the dead to visitors to the catacombs.

He crossed a bridge over the fecund and oozing fester that the city's inhabitants called the Halle River, a brown stain that wound its way down to Raven Bay, where it emptied into the Trackless Ocean. A river barge lumbered through the sludge, partially obscured by "morning mist", which was mostly made up of smog from nearby manufactories. Aldric coughed at the river's stench and the pollution in the air, and not for the first time since he'd returned to Nagorn City wished he was elsewhere. Touted as one of the world's greatest cities, it reminded him of a rotting sore whenever he returned from the freshness of the wilderness.

Aldric came to an exclusive bathhouse known to its patrons as Little Fishes. Housed in a landscaped walled garden, it was divided into male and female bathing areas, as well as a building where, for a small fee, you could receive a massage or use one of the steam rooms. But he wasn't after a relaxing bath. On the roof of the bathhouse was a terraced garden separated into private areas. And before dawn, there was scarcely a soul around. He paid extra for a space on the edge of the building, as he'd done the other times he'd come here, and added his name to the record book.

The woman at reception chatted to him amiably. She had skin a darker gray than his and midnight black hair brushing her shoulders. She was always on duty at this hour; Aldric had never dealt with anyone different. If she guessed he was a sorcerer—which he thought likely—she gave no sign. But that was what the patrons of Little Fishes paid for: discretion. And Aldric hardly thought he was the only sorcerer to avail himself of such an establishment when dawn broke.

He hurried up flights of polished hardwood steps to the rooftop, where he closed and locked the door to the hallway and glanced to the east. Not long now.

He removed his khopesh belt and propped the sheathed blade against a low chair. His shirt came next, folded neatly. Then his boots and socks. He was more comfortable barefoot for this ritual, although not all sorcerers were. Replenishing was a different experience for everyone.

His hand strayed to where the Evokers had implanted the catalyst under his skin beside his heart. Such a valuable artifact couldn't be kept in a locket or somewhere else on the sorcerer's person. It had to be kept safe. Hidden. Impossible to steal, unless you knew exactly what you were looking for and the sorcerer was either unconscious or dead. And even then, their nascent wards would need to be dealt with.

When Aldric had completed his training and found out what the Evokers were about to do to him—cut him open and embed a hated sorcerous crystal inside him—he'd resisted, to put it mildly. Eventually, they'd held him down and used a cant of submission to render him pliant. When he came to, he'd vowed to one day cut out the catalyst.

He stood now in the center of the wooden deck, facing the soon-to-be rising sun. Manicured hedges surrounded him on three sides, shielding him from prying eyes, while the fourth side was open and looked over the city: timber and brick structures roofed with tiles or shingles, narrow cobbled streets, ground fog and dusty light.

As the first blush of dawn stained the sky and a sliver of sun appeared over the bay, turning the water silver, Aldric closed his eyes and opened his arms. His skin began to tingle, and his hair stood on end. Goosebumps covered his entire body and he trembled, no matter how hard he tried to stop it.

The power came almost imperceptibly at first. What felt like a soft breeze caressed him, then the sensation changed. He hissed in pain as the dawn-tide glided over his skin, feeling like stinging nettles. The red sunlight bathed him, followed by an unrelated warmth that slowly gained in intensity as more of the sun appeared. He breathed deeply and opened himself to the surge of power. Light. Clean. Pure. Scalding. It flooded over him, around him, threatening to wash him away with its strength. His consciousness clung on, buffeted and battered by the sorcerous energy as if he were standing in pounding surf. Tossed this way and that, his mind struggled to retain coherency amid the turbulent flow.

When he felt he had a semblance of stability, he opened himself to the dawn-tide. He drew in as much as he could hold— which, since his repository was small, wasn't a great deal—and closed himself off. He knew many other sorcerers would have opened themselves for much longer to the arcane emanations. The greatest sorcerers in history had frequently required multiple dawns to replenish their power.

He remained still, waiting for the roiling tide to diminish and eventually trickle away to nothing. Then he tested what he'd absorbed, feeling for his repositories. His mind skirted around the largest of the two, and the darkest. It was almost half full, despite Aldric not having used any of its power for months.

Every sorcerer's repositories leaked arcane energy and had to be topped up even if they hadn't cast any sorceries. But for Aldric, the power he derived from the dusk-tide forces was more viscous and leaked less than the purer dawn-tide forces. Even if he didn't consciously avail himself of the dusk-tide, his dark reserves remained high as he still absorbed some power every evening. A fraction of what he would if he'd exposed himself directly to it, but enough to offset the bleeding. His dawn-tide repository, on the other hand, had to be topped up at least every second day. He just wasn't able to hold enough—which suited him fine. The less sorcery he used, the better.

Guilt rose within him as he remembered the sorcerer in the ruin—helpless, about to be slaughtered by the Reaper. Aldric might have been able to save him, but his Church's orders and the cost of fouling himself with the dark forces of the dusk-tide had prevented him doing so. What did that make him?

He paused, staring at nothing for a few moments. Both of the powers ... it was like touching two parts of eternity. One was midnight dark and dense: a mammoth weight that bore down and threatened to crush him. The other was pure, light, and tempestuous: a storm tearing at his consciousness. Both hammered upon his mind, but only one could he bring himself to use.

Aldric shrugged and sighed.

His power replenished, he dressed and left the bathhouse. He nodded to the woman at reception on the way out and began the long trip through dirty streets toward the Kankin District. He had a final stop to make: a visit to his sorcerous Covenant, the Evokers.

~ ~ ~

Kankin District was set into an inside corner of the wall surrounding Nagorn City. It was the city's sparsest populated district, not least because it was where the sorcerous Covenants resided. Commoners were at best wary of sorcerers and at worst violently superstitious. Some associated sorcery with demons, which led to the occasional mob turning up brandishing kitchen implements and burning torches. The Covenants let the city guard deal with anyone unruly, knowing their own retaliation would create more trouble and possibly lead to bloodshed. It was, at the best of times, an uneasy truce.

Aldric had decided to tell the Evokers about the ruin and the Reaper. Anything arcane was of interest to the Covenant, even if it was Church business. Besides, they would know if he lied—they always did, a skill of accomplished sorcerers. Aldric had never been taught this ability, and as it involved dusk-tide sorcery, he didn't care to learn.

He passed the well-kept stone building with an abundance of windows that housed the Hidden Blade Covenant, then traversed a wooden bridge over a not too malodorous stream. Crossing a field of yellow grass—which could use a bit of rain, he noted—he halted in front of an unassuming red-brick structure with a roof of tiled gray.

Aldric remembered the first time he'd set eyes on the black varnished door with its brass knocker shaped like a whale. The priest who'd accompanied him had wanted to be there less than

Aldric did, and had thumped the knocker then almost tripped over himself in his haste to get away. It was Aldric's first experience of the taint that would follow him in the Church for the rest of his life.

This time, the door opened before Aldric could knock, revealing the cadaverous doorman who always seemed to be on duty. He stood a head taller than Aldric, which made his pallor and sunken face all the more striking. As usual he wore tailored black pants and a silver-buttoned coat.

Behind the doorman, a hunched figure swept the white-tiled floor with lethargic movements. The man's eyes were unfocused, and the veins under his skin were bulging and dark. One leg was withered, and the sole of the boot on that foot was thicker than the other. A burned-out sorcerer, someone who'd drawn too much of the dawn- or dusk-tide and let it slip from his control.

Aldric entered, grateful for the reminder of the dangers of sorcery, though his heart went out to the poor man.

A short while later he found himself in the presence of the Grandmaster of the Evokers, which was highly unusual. During his training, he had seen Shalmara only once, just before they sent him back to his Church. With her wrinkled skin, sharp cheekbones, and hair thinned to strands plastered to her scalp, she looked like one of the dried corpses Aldric sometimes found inside ruins—belonging to a sorcerer clever enough to pass the wards, but not clever enough to break back out. She sat on a wooden chair festooned with cushions, her waist and legs covered by a thin brown blanket, her torso swathed in a pale rose-colored silken robe, as if a tougher material would irritate her emaciated skin. Her eyes had sunk so far back in her skull they were lost in shadow. Encircling her neck was a scar, as if someone had cut her throat.

Shalmara was old; rumor put her age at a few centuries. But all the Masters of the Evokers were ancient, and no one truly knew if they could somehow prolong their lives.

A young boy in a rope-belted smock bustled around the room, stirring the coals in the fireplace, plumping the cushions, wiping a rag across dust-laden bookshelves. As Aldric stood in the doorway, waiting to be admitted, the boy stopped to stare, then dropped his dusting rag and hurried over to a table, where he began measuring dried tea leaves into a ceramic pot.

"Come closer, boy," Shalmara whispered. She spoke clearly and steadily, though her voice was as dry as autumn leaves.

It was a long time since anyone had called Aldric "boy". He was approaching his thirties, and his role and time in the wilderness had lent him a rugged appearance. He took a few steps toward the most powerful sorcerer in the known world and went down on one knee. His Church wouldn't like it, but she was a commanding force, and he would be a fool to insult her. But he hesitated before moving closer, and Shalmara noticed.

"According to reports, you were an unenthusiastic student," she said dryly.

Aldric always felt diminished when he returned to the Evokers, ashamed of being a disruptive and reluctant student. As a young man pulled from his divine calling and ordered to make the most of his burgeoning sorcerous talents, Aldric had been angry, and his teachers' concerned looks had only served to infuriate him further. In the end, they taught him what they could, considering his refusal to draw on the dusk-tide power. He sat through their lessons and did the bare minimum to be considered proficient. The Church had paid a great deal of money to train him, and he'd known the quickest way to escape was to pass whatever tests the Covenant set him and be returned to the Church. Still, he'd grown to understand his teachers in a way. They enjoyed sorcery and couldn't come to terms with why anyone wouldn't. It was a gift, they insisted. But the only gifts he'd wanted were his god's divine mark and the ability to heal.

"I was young," Aldric replied.

It would have to do. To tell the Grandmaster of the Evokers that he'd hated his time here would serve no purpose. And she probably already knew.

"You have your catalyst still?"

Aldric started, eyes narrowing. It wasn't the question he'd expected. Before he could stop himself, one hand moved to touch the lump on his chest. "Of course." Months of preparation and no small amount of sorcery went into manufacturing a catalyst; no cant could be transformed from words and calculations and thought into sorcery without one.

His eyes went involuntarily to her chest and saw beneath her robe the telltale lump. It stood out like a walnut and was larger than his. It had to be, to cope with higher-tier sorceries.

Someone tugged at his elbow—the boy, holding up a steaming cup of tea.

Aldric smiled his thanks and took the cup. He stood there awkwardly, not sure whether to sip or place it on a nearby table or just hold it.

"I've been told that you resist the dusk-tide," Shalmara said. "Foolishness. You cannot master sorcery if you use only one part of the whole."

She accepted a cup from the boy and slurped the tea loudly, heedless of its heat.

"I don't want to master sorcery," Aldric retorted. "I know enough to perform my role within the Church, and that's all I'll ever require."

"You must overcome your reticence. One day, you'll wish you had—when you are unable to draw enough power or fashion a complex cant to save someone you love."

"My work leaves me no time for love."

"Then what is its purpose?"

"I ..." Aldric hesitated. She was twisting his thoughts, trying to unnerve him. "You know what I do. Your agreement with the Church means you have all the details."

He took a sip of his tea to cover his nervousness.

"No," Shalmara said, "not all."

"Most. What I do makes the world a safer place."

"Partly. But as you and I know, there are far worse terrors out there than leftover ruins."

She was referring to the Church's millennia-old battle with the Tainted Cabal and their demons.

"You can barely fashion a ward to protect yourself," she continued, "a lowly second-tier sorcery. The higher cants are out of your reach. What will you do when you come face-to-face with a demon lord or one of their progeny?"

"That will probably never happen."

Aldric was comfortable with the cants he could perform. The higher sorceries, from third tier onwards, required more dedication than he was willing to give. A second-tier ward protected him from most physical forces. Third tier expanded to include heat and cold, and a fourth-tier ward excluded basic sorceries.

"But it *might*. The Tainted Cabal are out there, somewhere. Your Church knows this. We know this."

"They are scattered and lost. A shadow of their former power. No major demon has been seen for centuries. We've rooted them out, destroyed them. And those tainted with demon blood grow weaker with each generation. Their threat has diminished to almost nothing."

"Or perhaps they've grown smarter and are hiding."

Aldric shook his head. Impossible. He couldn't believe it. "The Church would know. Their informants would have seen something. You know enough of demons to realize their base cravings overrule their thoughts. They could no more hide from us than a hungry tiger could stay away from a herd of goats."

"We shall see. Well then, to business."

*Finally,* thought Aldric. "No, no, and no," he said, knowing her questions before she asked them. Every time he reported back to the Evokers it was the same: pointless questions he gave the same answers to. He didn't know what they sought, but answering to them was part of the agreement the Evokers had with the Church.

Shalmara held out her cup, and the serving boy rushed to take it.

"You try my patience, boy," she whispered, and Aldric saw a gleam in her darkened eye sockets. "First, have you found any sorcery you do not recognize?"

"No," he said.

"Have you found anything that absorbs the dawn-tide or dusk-tide?"

*Apart from sorcerers?* "No."

"Lastly, have you found the Chain of Eyes?"

"No. Your questions are cryptic," he added. "If I knew what you were after, I could answer them better. Or keep an eye out while I'm—"

"Just as your Church seeks signs of demons, so must the Evokers be forever vigilant in our task."

"And what task is that?"

"Join us, and you will find all the answers you seek."

"I am sworn to Menselas. You will not corrupt me."

Shalmara laughed, a dry, gasping chuckle. "Your Church already thinks you are corrupted."

Heat rose to Aldric's face. He clenched and unclenched his hands. Sorcery had been thrust upon him, unwanted. That the Church thought less of him was an open wound, one that Shalmara deliberately probed.

"I am touched by Menselas," he grated through clenched teeth. "Sworn to the priesthood. A healer."

"When was the last time you healed?" Shalmara said. She

waved a hand in dismissal. "Go now. I am weary."

The boy came and stood between her and Aldric, giving him a stern glare. Aldric looked for somewhere to place his teacup and eventually settled on handing it to the boy.

He left, still fuming. Luckily, it would be some time before he had to return. Facing the Evokers and their enigmatic questions was a duty he performed reluctantly. His primary duty was to Menselas and his Church.

## CHAPTER THREE

# DARK BUSINESS

THE BALL WAS A perfect opportunity for Kurio to infiltrate the heavily guarded Vandred Estate. She slipped in with the musicians and their carts loaded with instruments and trappings. It seemed they were an expensive troupe, for they set up their own props and alchemical lighting effects to add to their theater. She kept her head down and assisted by carrying a heavy box in through the servants' entrance. The musicians thought she was a household servant, and the servants that she was a musician.

She glanced around, made sure no one was looking, and stole away. Easy.

Finding a narrow back staircase, she ascended to the next floor. It didn't take long to locate the room where the valuables were secured—Willas, the noble who'd hired her, had given her a diagram of the residence, which she'd memorized before burning the paper to ash.

There were a few lamps around the room, but she lit only one and turned it down low, placing it in a corner where the flame couldn't be seen from under the door.

Against one wall was what she'd come for. A locked chest made of narrow strips of ironwood, its edges banded with ensorcelled orichalcum. She knew she couldn't break it open; and even though it measured only two feet square and one high, it weighed more than four men could comfortably carry. Set into the front of the chest was a locking mechanism: a circle of orange-tinted orichalcum with runed dials and a keyhole. Designed by the master craftsman Sandoval—his stylized initials were clearly visible in the lower right-hand section. Good. Her information had been correct.

The worst thing about taking on paid jobs was that the people you were stealing from inevitably expected someone to make the attempt, so they took extra precautions. Not that she couldn't handle it, but sometimes the bother almost wasn't worth it. Like in this case.

She sat back on her heels and examined the mechanically locked box. From somewhere below came the sound of music and people laughing over the hum of a hundred conversations. The noble house of Frederick hosted a ball every few months, and most of the nobles in Caronath attended. They brought along their children, dressed in the finest clothes the city's tailors and seamstresses had to offer, in order to parade them around and arrange matches. She breathed a sigh of relief that she'd escaped all that nonsense. Her family thought she'd run away and probably died somewhere, and Kurio was fine to leave it like that. No more being dressed up like a doll, no boring lessons on sewing and manners and whatever else a noblewoman was meant to know. And best of all, no more beatings and derision from her father and brothers. Even after all these years, her skin chilled at the memories, and her stomach twisted with revulsion.

She shook her head, bringing herself back to the present. *You have a job to do,* she chided herself. As her lazy, womanizing teacher of all things thieving had said to her countless times before being beaten to death in a tavern brawl: *Get it done and get out.*

Kurio sniffed and frowned. There was something familiar in the air she couldn't quite place. Perhaps it was the dust and the scent of polished wood and oiled locks, similar to her own apartment.

*No matter.* She flexed her fingers and rubbed her hands, then slipped her thin backpack from her shoulders. Taking out her toolkit, she unfolded the leather flaps to reveal her implements. She hesitated, then from her backpack withdrew her custom-made repeating crossbow. She made sure both mechanisms were loaded and cocked, then placed it on the floor beside her. The royals it had cost would have kept her living comfortably for years, but it had been worth it. The weapon had saved her life more than a few times. And if she wanted to live comfortably, she wouldn't have left her family.

*First things first.*

Kurio closed her eyes and calmed her breathing. She thought of clouds, then nothing, and as with every other time, she felt her senses extend from her around the room. Something wasn't right, although exactly what eluded her. There was ... danger ... but she couldn't sense any traps or poison, no alchemical devices or mechanisms that would scorch the flesh from her bones. She'd heard that was how Martiens had died on a job. What had remained of him fit into a child's coffin. She wasn't going to make the same mistake.

After several long moments, she let out her breath and opened her eyes. Nothing. The danger could be in her imagination, except her talent had never steered her wrong before. The problem was it was too sporadic and ambiguous. She'd been tested, and her talent wasn't sorcery. Which left ... nothing else. Maybe it was simply uncanny intuition.

She looked at the chest in disapproval, but it remained silent. There was nothing she could do but continue ... carefully. She hadn't lasted this long, or built her name up, by rushing and making mistakes, and she wasn't about to start now.

Kurio slipped a few picks and her L-shaped tension wrench

out of her toolkit. Humming to herself, she set to work. In a few minutes, the lock turned and clicked, and she gave a satisfied sigh.

She removed a slim leatherbound volume from her backpack and turned to the chapter on Sandoval mechanisms. It had been penned in Sandoval's native tongue, Durante. Kurio couldn't read it, but that didn't matter. Outlined over a few pages were schematics of most of Sandoval's locks, including this one.

She'd appropriated the book from the current leader of the Night Shadows' library. Less than intelligent Ritte probably didn't know what he'd inherited. And though it was unlikely he'd miss the book, he *might*. Which was why Kurio planned on returning it. They'd been after her to join their silly thieves' organization for years, and she didn't want them to have anything over her.

Examining the mechanism, she turned the dials until the swallow-shaped rune matched up with the squiggly triangle, the sun aligned with the moon, and the fish lined up with the tree.

*All right. That should do it.*

If she was wrong, a poisonous gas would be expelled into the room.

Kurio gripped her picks and wrench, which remained in the lock, then turned them clockwise. Multiple clicks sounded from inside the chest, and the lid popped ajar.

"Thank you, Kurio," came a voice from behind her.

She grabbed the crossbow, leaped to her feet, and whirled.

A shadow stepped from behind one of the curtains framing the window. The figure moved into the feeble light of the lamp, but she'd already realized who it was. The scent: cloves.

She cursed inwardly. *Damn it. I thought it was the wood.*

Gerret was a decent thief, but he had some strange notions. Probably because he lacked an education. And the pox-ridden whoreson was trying to steal her loot. Well, he wouldn't leave here with anything if she had any say in the matter. It was all hers. She'd worked for it.

"Gerret, you scumbag, what are you doing here?"

There could only be one reason, of course. The concerning thing was he'd been lying in wait for her. He'd known this was her job and when she was going to do it. Which meant her benefactor, Willas, had been compromised.

"I was just passing by," Gerret said. "Saw you duck in with the musicians, and thought there might be something here worth my while. Lower that crossbow of yours, and we'll divide the spoils."

He grinned at her, revealing crooked bottom teeth. Kurio kept her expression blank. His hands were empty, but she knew he was good with a knife. There was no way she was putting her weapon down.

"Divide the spoils?" she said incredulously. "You've done nothing. I opened the chest. How about you run along, and I won't tell the Night Shadows you tried to muscle in on my job? I'm not a member, but I pay their cut. If they find out, they'll whip you bloody."

And that, Kurio realized, was the problem. Gerret wouldn't risk punishment. Which meant there was a chance she wouldn't leave here alive.

*He wouldn't ... would he?*

"I know what you're thinking," he said. "Why would I risk it?"

"I wasn't—"

"You think I'm a fool, don't you? Uneducated and stupid."

"I don't—"

"Shut up! You think you'll go crying to the Night Shadows and they'll fix everything." He spat on the floor between them. "But you won't. Want to know why?"

*Because I'll be dead.*

Uneasiness whispered through her breast. Kurio gripped her crossbow harder and applied a little more pressure with her thumb on the trigger lever.

She spoke calmly, trying to sound reasonable. "Because there's plenty in the chest for both of us, and we'd be fools to let something like this blow up into something big. Neither of us should do anything we'll regret later."

She looked at him expectantly, hoping he'd follow her reasoning down the nonviolent path. The air suddenly felt hot and stifling, as if there were a roaring fire in the room.

Gerret stepped slowly along the wall, moving closer to the chest. Kurio mirrored him, stepping in the opposite direction to keep distance between them.

"I stopped regretting things years ago," he said, sounding amused. "That's what makes me better than everyone else."

Kurio had to stop herself from snorting. Instead, she let her gaze linger on the chest.

"Open it," she said. "We don't even know what's inside. I'm sure there's plenty for the both of us."

His blue eyes flicked toward the chest for an instant. "We won't be splitting it. I'm taking it all."

"That's not going to—"

"All of it!"

She clenched her teeth in frustration. "Will you stop interrupting me?"

"Why? Because what you have to say is far more intelligent than my words? You think you're better than all of us with your fancy education."

Unease rippled through Kurio. "I just read a lot, that's all."

"Stop lying. I know your secret. You went to the university here in Caronath. Where only the nobles' offspring go."

"I didn't."

But she had. How did Gerret know? She'd been so careful. Nothing linked her to her past, and good riddance to it. But if Gerret had found out something …

"There's an alchemist on Henwick Lane," he said. "Do you know it?"

"Of course. Everyone does."

"That's where you get your special tincture, isn't it?"

A fist squeezed Kurio's heart. She couldn't breathe.

Gerret smiled his crooked-toothed smile. "Nothing to say? Thought no one would find that out, didn't you?"

Kurio sucked in the barest of breaths through clenched teeth. Sweat made her grasp on the crossbow slippery, and she wished she'd spent extra on a sea-ray-skin grip.

"It's for womanly problems," she said.

Gerret shook his head. "No, it ain't. The alchemist gets her apprentice to prepare most concoctions, including yours. She's a lovely young girl and quite taken with a certain dashing thief."

Kurio wouldn't call him dashing, but then again, she wasn't a brainless girl. "She's making things up to impress you." A feeble lie, but she had to try.

"'For her eye,' she said. 'The tincture's got to be made just right, or the color won't match. As red as a rose,' she said. 'Red mixed with green makes brown, you see.' You use it to color your eye—the green one—to match your brown one."

As Gerret spoke, Kurio's stomach twisted and she felt ill. She'd been so careful, and now some stupid besotted girl had ruined everything.

"It's red for blood. I told you, it's for womanly problems."

But Kurio knew her words were weak. Gerret wouldn't swallow them. She lowered her crossbow, trying to set him more at ease until she could think of a way out of the situation. She switched it to her other hand and wiped her sweaty palm on her pants.

"You think you're so smart," he spat. "You think you're better than the rest of us. Always wearing expensive clothes, and keeping your blond hair brushed and shiny, and bathing every day, while we're born in the slums and likely to die in the slums. Well, I know your secret. And you know who's been looking for their runaway daughter for years—a girl with one green eye and one brown one and freckles on her cheeks like you have? You're playing at being a thief, like a mummer in a show. There's no risk for you. If things go bad, your family will bail you out, and you'll be fine."

"Who have you told?"

"No one … yet. And as long as you do as I say, I'll keep your secret. You work for me from now on. Put the crossbow down. You won't shoot me. You're too softhearted."

Kurio shook her head. "You're so very, very wrong, Gerret. You think I'm a stranger to violence? I'm not. I grew up with it. It's an old friend. I don't enjoy it, but I got comfortable around it after a while."

"What are you—"

Kurio raised the crossbow and thumbed the lever. Her barbed bolt thudded into Gerret's chest with a crunch. He stumbled backward.

"Wha—" His hands clutched at the bolt as crimson spread across his shirt. He groaned and fell to his knees.

Kurio loosed the second bolt, which struck home close to the first.

Gerret's eyes rolled into his head, and he pitched forward, hitting the floor with a thump.

What he'd been too stupid to realize was she wasn't playing. And she certainly wasn't softhearted.

Kurio cranked the crossbow and loaded two fresh bolts. Lightly sprung clips held them in place so they didn't fall out. It paid to be prepared, and she never liked to leave the weapon uncocked, even though it meant replacing the strings frequently, as the strain stretched them.

She prodded Gerret with her boot to make sure he was dead. Falling onto his face would have driven her bolts in further, but she had to make sure. He didn't move. Good.

Blood seeped from under his body, and she hopped back before any got on her custom-made boots. Her vision blurred, and she wiped angrily at her eyes.

*Bloody fool. Why couldn't you leave me alone?*

Breathing deeply, she kneeled in front of the chest, hoping the gods would favor her. She opened the lid and took in the contents. A few smaller lockboxes, a lumpy velvet pouch—probably gemstones—and a shiny metal cube covered with indecipherable script. She sighed with relief. She'd been hired to steal the cube, though she had no idea why it was so valuable. In her business you didn't ask those sorts of questions.

She stuffed the velvet pouch into her backpack, her nimble fingers confirming it did indeed contain gemstones. She debated opening the lockboxes to see what was inside, but Gerret's rapidly cooling corpse beside her was slightly unnerving.

She reminded herself that whoever had hired Gerret would have disposed of him once he'd delivered the goods. So he would have been killed tonight anyway.

*Keep telling yourself that.*

She grabbed the metal cube and secured it in her backpack, along with her cracking tools. The cube rested on a round wooden holder, but she wouldn't need that. Then she noticed a folded piece of paper resting on the holder. She hesitated. Her job was for the artifact only, but she'd already taken the gemstones as well. She shrugged and picked up the paper. It was covered with lines of an ancient script she recognized from her studies: Skanuric.

Kurio stuffed the paper into her pants pocket and turned her attention to getting out of there. If someone was working behind Willas's back, her planned escape route was most likely compromised.

Gerret had thought he was killing two birds with one stone: taking a job out from under Kurio, and blackmailing her into working for him. But he'd proven many times that he lacked intelligence or common sense. She thought it likely that whoever had sold her out would have men waiting to kill her if she left the same way she'd entered. But like any good thief, she had a backup plan.

Gerret had probably had the same idea, so his gear … Ah, there was his backpack, hidden behind the curtain he'd appeared from. She dug out a coil of thin, blackened rope. No point wasting hers if there was a spare. After all, Gerret wouldn't be needing it.

She tied one end of the rope to the leg of a sturdy side table, which she pushed up against the wall below the window. Crouching atop the table, she tugged out the window's locking pin and opened it. A cold blast of air ruffled her hair and clothes.

She pulled on calfskin gloves, tossed the rope out, then turned to give Gerret's corpse one final look. Then she pulled the rope tight against her back and leaped into the darkness.

~ ~ ~

Kurio wound her way along dank alleyways until she was a few dozen streets from the Vandred Estate. Her face felt hot, and she had to stop herself from grinning. She'd done it! Another successful job—albeit with complications. But she'd come out on top, and that was what mattered.

Now all she had to do was convince the Night Shadows that she hadn't killed Gerret. Except, with two bolts in his chest and the loot stolen, it wouldn't take a genius to figure out it had been her. Punishment for killing one of your own ranged from a whipping to being drowned in the murky waters of the Brown Canals, commonly referred to as "the stew". The city governors had passed strict laws to keep the river clean, but the manmade canals that joined it were another matter.

She doubted she'd be able to convince the Night Shadows she'd acted in self-defense; and even if she did, she'd still be looking at a flogging or death. It was too risky. Kurio cursed as many gods as she could remember, which was quite a few. When she'd finished, she felt a little better, but not much.

She kept moving, surreptitiously glancing behind her, peering in the reflections of windows and sprinting around the occasional corner to make sure she wasn't followed. A short time later, she entered her apartment and clicked each of the four locks shut. She paused, then barred the door for good measure. Someone wanted the loot she'd stolen tonight and her dead. This was no time to be lazy. Lazy got you killed.

She realized she was breathing heavily, and not from the five flights of stairs she'd just climbed. She rolled her shoulders and took a few deep breaths to calm herself. There was too much left to do to start panicking. She needed to deliver the cube to collect her payment, then give a message to the alchemist's apprentice that wouldn't be forgotten. After that, she needed to disappear. The Night Shadows knew where she lived, and they'd come for her.

*Bloody Gerret!* He should have left well enough alone.

Kurio looked around her sparsely furnished room. It was totally enclosed with no window. There was a wide cot with an extremely comfortable mattress, a writing desk she hardly ever used, and a closet filled with everyday clothes. In one corner stood a brazier. She wouldn't miss anything, and that was the point. She could easily leave and not look back. Her thieving gear and valuables were in her other apartment, which she was sure no one else knew existed.

She sighed. She would miss that mattress. It had cost a great deal and had taken two big men to lug it up the stairs. Oh well.

Using the iron poker, she stirred the embers in the brazier to life and added more charcoal. Once it was hot enough, she ripped off her blond wig and threw it on. The shiny hair burst into flames, and she coughed at the smoke that enveloped the room.

She ducked down low and coughed again. *Hells, that was stupid.*

She opened the closet and pushed a back panel open, ducked through it, and emerged into a constricted room. Replacing the panel so the entrance was once again hidden, she moved to the narrow window and ran a hand through her short sweaty hair. She grinned at the thought of the Night Shadows busting down her door and finding the room empty, with no way out, not even a window. She'd give a few gold royals to see their faces.

She'd built the false wall on her own. Easy as pie. Not a bad job too, if she did say so herself.

The window swung open soundlessly on oiled hinges, and Kurio dangled from the ledge by her fingertips, then dropped six feet to the tiled roof below. Landing lightly, she dashed across the tiles and was soon lost in the shadows.

~ ~ ~

The alchemist's apprentice's room looked more like it belonged to a little girl than someone learning a trade. Pink curtains embroidered with red flowers moved slightly in the breeze from the open window. A colorful patchwork quilt kept the girl warm, and there was a stuffed rag doll at the end of her bed.

The girl slept peacefully, her lovestruck head no doubt filled with thoughts of her dashing, handsome thief. Kurio sniffed disapprovingly. The apprentice was young. Too young to be taking up with the likes of Gerret, the disgusting animal. Well, she wouldn't be seeing him again. Maybe she'd grow wiser from her experience.

She slipped through the window and crossed the floor to the bed. Kneeling beside the apprentice, she tugged her hood tighter to make sure her dark hair was concealed. Then she blew lightly in the girl's face.

The apprentice stirred and opened bleary eyes. "Gerret?" she whispered.

Kurio clamped a hand over the girl's mouth. Her eyes opened wide, and she uttered a muffled scream.

"Keep your mouth shut, or I'll shut it permanently," growled Kurio.

The girl looked wildly around. Ragged sobs escaped her lips.

Kurio pushed her hand down harder, forcing the girl's head into the pillow. "Do you understand?"

A frightened nod.

"Good. Don't worry, I'm not going to kill you. I'm here to deliver a warning on behalf of the Night Shadows."

She'd be whipped or worse for using their name, but that was just one more infraction to add to her list. They'd probably kill her if they found her, but she aimed to disappear as best she could.

She leaned close to the girl and waved a shiny knife in front of her terrified eyes. "You've been telling secrets. Your loose lips make you untrustworthy."

*Loose lips in more ways than one, stupid girl.*

"You've put your life and your mistress's business in peril. The Night Shadows are not pleased. Tonight, we will spare you."

Relieved sobbing came from underneath Kurio's hand, now warm and wet from the girl's tears and saliva.

"But if we hear you've been spilling secrets again, we'll be back. And you won't like it. Nod if you understand."

The girl nodded vigorously.

"Good." Kurio removed her hand and wiped it on the quilt. She backed away to the window, then paused, one leg over the sill. "You'll never see Gerret again. The Night Shadows have determined this will be his punishment."

She left the girl lying there, tears streaming down her face. At least this way, she wouldn't know Gerret was dead.

~ ~ ~

Kurio's benefactor stood staring into a dwindling fire that sputtered feebly beneath a massive mantel of carved sandstone. The huge thing looked out of place in such a small room, but rich people like Willas could do whatever they wanted, she supposed. Although she didn't believe for a moment the gaunt man's name really was Willas.

Dawn's pale light peeked through gaps in the thick curtains. Around the room were signs of a collector with expensive tastes. Wooden display boxes of different sizes were stacked against two of the walls, completely covering them. Almost all contained an object of some sort. A few Kurio recognized from her first visit: mechanical contrivances mapping the movement of the stars, bleached skulls of creatures most people thought only inhabited tales, a rough hunk of metal, vials and jars filled with liquids and powders. Others she thought were talismans for sorcery, along with an egg the size of her head that might be from a flightless bird in the far south. Her fingers itched to open some of the locked boxes, but she kept her hands to herself.

Willas turned as she stepped into the room. "Ah, Kurio, I half expected never to see you again."

He laughed briefly before convulsing into a coughing fit. She stood silently until it ended, and he drew out a kerchief and wiped his lips. It came away with a dark stain.

Kurio looked aside and only then noticed another man sitting in an armchair in the shadows. At least, judging from his size, it was a man. She'd never seen someone so big. It was a wonder she'd missed him when she'd walked in.

He sat upright, as if afraid to slouch. Like her, he was hooded and cloaked, so she couldn't see his features. But there was something about him … a presence that made her skin tingle. He was dangerous.

She resisted the urge to point her small crossbow at him, which hung from her belt under her cloak. Nevertheless, she kept one hand on it just in case. Someone had told Gerret where to find her, likely someone close to Willas. If Willas wanted her dead, he would have attempted it in their first meeting, but the sooner she was done here and had her fee, the better.

Willas stumbled to a desk, where an alembic bubbled away on an open flame. Crimson droplets slid down the discharge tube to gather in a flask. He poured a measure of the thick liquid into a glass, where it sparkled with phosphorescence, and drained it in one gulp. He stood motionless for a moment, then shuddered before leaning on the table to steady himself.

Was it a bloody pox he had, or the result of years of smoking strong herbs? Either way, it didn't look good, Kurio thought.

"So," Willas said, clearing his throat and turning to regard her, "I've been wondering—are you also curious by nature? Curious for curios? Is that why—"

"No, I'm not curious," she replied flatly. "Are we going to do business?"

She'd heard the same jokes a hundred times over the last few years. Mostly from nervous benefactors and stupid thieves.

A chuckle came from the man in the armchair. He stood quickly for all his size. His head almost brushed the ceiling, and Kurio heard the telltale clink of mail underneath his expensive clothes. He took a step forward into the light, and Kurio gave him a once-over. His pants and coat were impeccably tailored and clung close to his lean form. Splashes of crimson across his silk vest added a colorful accent. A sheathed sword hung from his belt, which was why he had sat like a lamp pole.

One of the rings on his hand caught her eye. Three were plain silver bands, while this one was gold, with a square face divided into four smaller squares. Each segment contained a Skanuric rune. Out of habit, Kurio committed them to memory.

Her gaze traveled up to his face, and her breath caught in her throat. Chiseled cheeks set in sun-touched skin. Full lips that ended in a cute smirk. His eyes were a startling blue, somehow shy and daring at the same time. He wasn't just handsome, he was exquisite.

When she remembered to breathe, Kurio caught a hint of his scent and felt herself stir. It conjured visions of sweaty midnight sex.

She knew straight away there had to be something wrong with him. Wasn't there always a flaw, especially with beauty? But part of her was drawn to him, intrigued.

"This one's impatient," he said, amused. His voice sounded like honey: sweet and thick.

"The best business is done quickly," Kurio retorted, flustered. "The less I know about you, the better."

"How forthright of you. It must serve you well in your chosen career. But wise words nonetheless. Well, Willas, conclude your business with Kurio here. I'm sure she wants to be gone as soon as possible. Back to"—he raised his eyebrows—"whatever nocturnal activities she desires."

Kurio's face warmed as she flushed.

Willas chuckled nervously. "Of course, your … ahem. Were you successful, Kurio? Do you have it?"

There was eagerness in his voice. He looked almost like a dog begging for a bone.

Kurio took out the cube, which she'd wrapped in a cloth, and held it out. "Here. Now, my payment?"

Willas stepped forward excitedly and took the artifact from her hand. Kurio's fingers tightened on her crossbow, but his eyes never left the package. He took it over to a lamp and unwrapped it. Metal glinted in the light as he turned it round and round, drinking in the sight.

"Yes …" he said.

"You can examine your trifle later," the handsome man said. "Give Kurio her payment, and she can leave. I'm sure she wants to be gone as soon as possible, no?"

Kurio nodded. She didn't know why this man was here, but his attempt to hold himself at a distance from her and Willas's transaction didn't fool her. He had some part in it, though what it might be eluded her.

He stepped closer, maintaining eye contact, as if examining her. She couldn't look away. Her breaths grew shallow and hurried.

"My name is Gannon Chikaire," he said softly, leaning forward. "An old name, but my parents were ever fond of making things awkward for me. These days it makes me stand out. Tell me, Kurio, are you fond of standing out?"

Despite her caution, Kurio found a smile playing across her lips. "Sometimes. Though often I find myself standing out more than is healthy."

Gannon chuckled, and his breath caressed her neck, stirring tendrils of her hair. It felt like steam from a hot bath.

"You thought this final transaction with Willas would be quick and easy," he said. "Although now you're not so sure. Is this one of those times when you stand out?"

"I hope not," she replied. "I have enough trouble at the moment."

"Don't we all," he said, and broke his eyes from hers and stepped back. "Willas, conclude your business. We have much to discuss."

"Yes, yes," mumbled Willas. "Of course."

He absently thrust a purse at Kurio, still staring at the cube. She weighed it in her hand and the coins inside clinked. It felt about right, and she wasn't going to count the royals in front of these two odd birds.

She turned to leave. "Right, then. Farewell."

"One moment," said Gannon.

Kurio swallowed her unease and turned to look at him again, drawn to the lustrous blue of his eyes.

"You were never here," Gannon warned. "You've never met Willas. Never stolen anything for him. Your thievery will go unnoticed for some time, and you'll forget it ever happened."

Kurio thought of Gerret's corpse still in the room with the chest. If no one discovered it sooner, in a day or two the smell of decomposition would be noticeable. She debated telling them that someone else had been after the strange metal cube, then decided she didn't need more complications.

"Yes. Is that all?"

Gannon nodded, then frowned. "No. I'd like to call upon you. If I may?"

*Call upon me?*

"You want to see me again? I don't think—"

"A brief meeting. You intrigue me, Kurio. And I find life is … pleasurable when I indulge my curiosity."

She was interested too. There were depths to this man she'd like to explore. He was beautiful. Seductive. Whatever he was mixed up in with Willas, it would be dangerous—but when had that ever stopped her? As long as she was lying low, she might as well have some fun. Though she should still be wary.

She nodded, smiling. "All right. Where can I find you?"

Gannon answered her smile with one of his own and reached out to clasp her hand. His skin was hot, and she felt the heat penetrate deep into her flesh. Her mouth parted, and she suppressed a gasp.

"Excellent," he said. "I'm sure someone of your talents could find me if she were to look. Or perhaps I'll find you."

He released her hand, and for an instant the room swam around her. She breathed deeply to steady herself.

"Go," Willas said. "Our business is done."

Kurio didn't have to be told twice.

## CHAPTER FOUR

# A RELUCTANT BARGAIN

EVER SINCE THE GODDESS had chosen him centuries ago, time had been a nebulous and indistinct concept for Niklaus. In the years since she'd gifted him her sword, he'd traveled a great distance to Caronath, that he knew. And he'd killed. For her, always for her. Well, mostly.

The goddess's sword clung to his back wherever he went. A weight he couldn't forget. And when he drew it … Ah! Such bliss. He was transformed. The blade was perfection. His skill unmatched. Blood flowed, and dangerous men and women fell before him. They had to be dangerous to her or about to thwart her plans, as otherwise she wouldn't have directed him to them. He'd killed lords and ladies, members of the Tainted Cabal, and once—so he'd read in his journal—a king.

He couldn't remember many of the deaths detailed in his handwriting. It seemed there was only so much a memory could hold before it began spilling its contents like an overfilled glass.

And sometimes, as a reward, she came to him in his dreams, whispering sweet words of approval, her lips touching his ear and burning with a fire he couldn't get out of his mind.

Leaving his rooms in a tenement next door to the Crossed Keys, a seedy dive of a tavern he played cards in most nights, Niklaus stopped by a nearby fountain to quench his thirst. Men and women of all ages were filling jugs and buckets from the pool of water under spouting mermaids. His stomach rumbled, eliciting a giggle from a girl beside him. He winked at her and set off.

He wouldn't break his fast until he'd visited Sylva Kalisia's church. He wasn't much for prayer and figured he didn't need to be, as the goddess was keeping an eye on him anyway, but he felt better when he'd paid his respects. And he liked it when his appearance agitated the priestesses and set them scampering around like bugs whose rock had been overturned.

By the time he reached her church, the sun had risen a few fingers. Not many of the goddess's worshipers came out at this time, which suited Niklaus fine. As he ascended the wide granite steps, a gust of cool wind sent leaves skittering across his path. He paused, wondering if they signified something. Then shook his head and muttered to himself about seeing signs in everyday events. He hadn't before and had laughed at Volkmar when the sorcerer thought the goddess was directing him. Over the centuries she'd instructed Niklaus to kill many sorcerers, so he'd decided that she must hate them. Because of Volkmar he'd learned better.

That was the problem. His encounters with the goddess were fleeting and ephemeral, and each one left him wanting more. Wanting *her*. The more she visited him, the stronger was his desire to see her in the flesh. To join with her as a man with a woman. Goddess and … god?

Deep down, a tiny part of him realized perhaps that was what she wanted.

Niklaus was a warrior. He believed in strength of arm and strength of will. Now, somehow, he was in a fight to resist losing his soul to Sylva Kalisia. And for all his training, all his skill with a blade, he had no idea what to do.

Victory would mean survival, continued life. Failure would mean … he knew not what, but it wouldn't be pleasant. Gods and goddesses didn't care for mortals, except for how they could be used. They only cared about other gods.

So if Niklaus wanted the goddess to care about him, did that mean he should try to become a god?

He shook his head as he approached the church's open doors. Two mercenary guards stationed on either side watched him without emotion. He didn't mind. It was better they didn't know who he was. The priestesses did though: they called him Sylva Kalisia's Chosen Sword. He didn't think much of the title, or the ownership it suggested.

Inside, the vast open space was cool and dim. Light entered from the open doors, marking a bright rectangle on the stone floor. Human-sized statues lined the walls to the left and right. Carved from stone or cast in bronze, they depicted naked men and women in a variety of poses. One woman ate a bunch of grapes; a man raised a sword high; a girl held a small branch in her outstretched hand. Some of them were touching themselves sexually, while others ran nails down their bare chests, marking themselves and drawing blood. After so long, he knew this was the kind of worship the goddess wanted.

The priestesses knew too; some even spoke regularly to the goddess. If he was honest, Niklaus would admit to jealousy of them. He hardly ever spoke with Sylva except when she came to him in his dreams. And then all he could think about was wanting her.

He knew that some of the priestesses prosecuted their own agendas in the goddess's name. Rage bubbled up inside him at the thought. For a priestess to hold the sanctity of speaking with the goddess in such contempt—the very thought was sickening. Perhaps that was why she had drawn him here to Caronath: to kill such faithless priestesses. To clean out the chaff so her Church remained strong.

In the center of the room was a multitiered rose-quartz

structure, much like a stepped pyramid from the southern kingdoms. It rose from the floor to twice his height, and each level was crammed with offerings: bowls filled with liquids; bottles and vials; dried fruits and meats; coins of all denominations and from different countries; flowers in varying stages of freshness and decay; necklaces and earrings, amulets and rings. Around the base of the structure were scattered donations that had been displaced when worshipers made their sacrifice, or had overbalanced when piles became unstable. A couple of young novices in rough-spun woolen robes collected them in wicker baskets.

Worshipers kneeled and sat around the offering steps, mumbling prayers and chanting hymns, filling the air with a constant hum.

A priestess he'd never seen before emerged from an alcove in one corner of the large space and walked slowly toward him. Someone must have taken her word that he'd arrived. He resisted scratching a sudden itch between his shoulder blades.

She approached, smiling and scrutinizing him. When she was within a few paces, she dropped to her knees. Her black robe hugged her body, and she wore a silver belt that cinched the material tight to her narrow waist. Her dark hair, long enough to touch the small of her back, shone even in the dimness of the church. As the priestess bent and touched her forehead to the stone, her robe drew tight around her buttocks.

So this was how they were going to play it. Another priestess who supposedly looked like the goddess. *Fools.* They should know, as he did, that for some things there was no substitute. The goddess knew he'd tried.

"Chosen Sword of the Goddess," the priestess said huskily, rising again to a kneeling position, "to what honor do we owe this visit? There are refreshments in our quarters if you are hungry or thirsty. Or perhaps you require our knowledge or guidance? We are here to serve you."

Niklaus had to hand it to them: they'd taught the young woman well. She wasn't obvious, apart from her beauty. He wished they wouldn't keep trying to control him. No one pushed him around or made a tool of him. No one human anyway.

She wriggled forward and tried to grab his hand.

Niklaus jerked it away. "Don't call me the Chosen Sword," he said sternly.

"But you are. The goddess has gifted you with her blade—"

"It wasn't hers, and it's a gift with many strings attached."

The priestess gasped, a hand covering her mouth in shock.

He liked to upset them, but this morning he wasn't gaining his usual pleasure.

"Go and fetch the Matriarch," he ordered. "I'll wait here."

The priestess glanced fearfully over her shoulder to the alcove she'd emerged from. No doubt she'd be punished for not succeeding in whatever it was they wanted her to do. But that was none of his concern. The girl needed to learn her looks wouldn't gain her whatever she wanted.

A calmness settled over him, familiar and welcoming. He felt it whenever he drew a blade. He was a rock in a river of turgid water, while others floundered. His thoughts were deliberate and composed.

"Go!" he shouted.

The girl fled, bare feet slapping on stone.

Niklaus waited. A short time later, another priestess emerged. An old woman with hair turned gray, but eyes and mind as keen as a freshly whetted blade. The Matriarch. They met occasionally to trade gossip and small talk, and play subtle games with each other. He knew that with her he had to be careful. If he put them off side, they could make things difficult for him. They wanted him to follow the goddess's path, but could be touchy if he didn't give them due respect.

"You scared the poor girl," Matriarch Adeline said. She had to look up at him, for although she was tall, he stood a head higher.

"You shouldn't have sent her out to me," he said, meeting the meddling bitch's hard eyes.

"You flatter yourself. Not everything revolves around you. She was on duty; she saw you come in and was a trifle overenthusiastic. Can you blame her?"

Niklaus let it slide. The priestesses couldn't help but interfere where they weren't wanted. It was in their nature. They hated that they didn't control him, yet were in awe of him being chosen by the goddess.

"I have some questions I'd like answers to," he said instead.

Matriarch Adeline motioned for him to follow her away from the worshipers. "I'll answer as best I can. But there are things about our order that are secret unless you're an ordained priestess. But first, tell me why you scared the girl away?"

Niklaus shot her a cautious glance. The fact that she referred to one of her own ordained priestesses as "a girl" said a lot about her. Then again, at her age, almost all the priestesses under her must seem like girls. But she had to know why he'd acted as he had, so her question was designed to create a bond between them. A closeness. *Be wary*, he told himself. The Matriarch was used to manipulating others and extremely good at it. It took more than faith and devotion to rise to the top in the dog-eat-dog Church of the goddess. Only the fit survived, unlike in other Churches, such as the Church of the Five.

"She annoyed me," he said.

It was the truth, though the Matriarch would not take the correct meaning from his words. The priestess had annoyed him because her attempt to entice him was so see-through, so blatant. And for the fact she did indeed resemble the goddess, as much as any normal woman could without the magnificence of the divine.

"She worships the goddess, as do we all. She was doing what

she thought right."

Blood suffused Niklaus's face. He tried to dampen his anger. "She doesn't know me. You don't know me."

"The goddess knows you," the Matriarch said quietly.

"And *she* guides me. Best you remember that. I go where she directs."

"And where is that these days? She brought you here for a reason, but you haven't done much these past few weeks."

*Don't tell her,* Niklaus thought.

But maybe the goddess's priestesses deserved to know something ... What if she wanted them to know?

*Then she would tell me,* he decided.

"I've felt vague urgings only," he said. "But the goddess has never before had me wait when she wants something done. So patience, priestess. I'll tell you when I know."

The Matriarch's eyes flashed in anger at his lower form of address. But she looked away, swallowing her fury. He shouldn't have pushed her, but hadn't been able to help himself.

"Please make sure you do," she said through tight lips. "We can help. We are here to further her glory."

"As are we all," he said, echoing her earlier words. "Now, tell me what you know about the gods. Did they spring from nothing? Or are they gifted people who have ascended far above us?"

He knew what he'd been taught by his tutor when he was young: the gods were coalesced from powers unknown. But the man had been a fool, more interested in chasing the maids than searching for truths.

The memory of his childhood sent a pang of longing and regret through him. He clamped down on it, pushing it aside. Memories were nebulous things, bringing a myriad of emotions from joy to anger. There were gaps in his memories, he knew, and he figured it was because of new ones pushing out the old to make room. Some details of his early life he could remember clearly, while others were hazy and indistinct, or simply not there at all. Sometimes he wondered how much he had forgotten and whether not remembering changed who he was.

"That is a question many scholars have pondered," the Matriarch said.

"And you? I'd trust your thoughts over those of a hundred dried-up old bookworms. What is the nature of the gods? Where did they come from?"

It was best to start with generalities and let the Matriarch believe her answers led him along a certain line of thought.

She smiled wryly. "We are *taught* the goddess has always been. But there are old histories, tomes thought lost long ago, that I have seen ..." She eyed him sideways. "Some speculate that the gods and goddesses were human once—sorcerers and wielders of some other power the texts are vague about. The more powerful they grew, the less they cared about mundane matters, and the more obsessed they became with guiding the world. Of course, with so many of them 'guiding', the world couldn't help but be twisted this way and that."

He wasn't sure he could trust her words, but they were a start. He wondered what Sylva Kalisia would do to him if he found out the Matriarch had lied to him, and he lost his temper and killed her.

"Yes, the gods have made a bit of a mess of things," he said.

She frowned and glanced around, as if expecting one to pop out and chastise him. "It's best not to speak ill of the divine. Although I suppose you have nothing to fear, being under the goddess's protection."

Niklaus grunted. "It's not that simple. And I've scars to prove it."

Time to dangle a carrot for the shriveled prune. The priestesses had been at him to examine the sword ever since he'd arrived. They considered it one of the goddess's artifacts, a holy relic or some such.

"I want to know if it's possible for a human to become a god," he said. "Consult your dusty tomes; buy any you think might have answers, no matter the cost; and speak to whoever you need to. If I'm satisfied, I'll hand over *her* sword for you to examine. For a short time."

Adeline's breath caught in her throat. "Can I see it now?" Her eyes went to the hilt of the sword poking over his shoulder, then narrowed. "Why now, after we've asked so many times, and you've refused? Is this information you're after part of the goddess's mission?"

"Yes," lied Niklaus. "And you'll get your hands on the sword when I'm ready and you've proven your worth."

Her lips tightened. "I'm a Matriarch. I've already proven myself many times."

"Not to me you haven't."

She sighed. "Very well. I'll do as you ask. But only because *she* wills it."

"We all follow her path," Niklaus said slowly, to give the words weight. "Search for the information I need quickly and thoroughly. The goddess will make sure you're rewarded for your efforts."

Adeline hissed through clenched teeth. "You go too far. Don't you dare speak for her. And serving her is its own reward."

Niklaus inclined his head in false apology. "Of course it is. Please, forgive me. Sometimes my eagerness to serve her makes my words clumsy. I'm not an educated priestess like yourself. I'll come and see you when I'm back."

"Where are you going? Perhaps we can help."

Niklaus shook his head. "I work alone, except for her presence."

*Let the conniving bitch chew on that.*

It was possible the Matriarch could help with his quest to join the goddess, but he wanted to know what he was getting into before asking her for help. She might think he owed her a favor then, and that was something he didn't want. Besides, he was getting ahead of himself. He hadn't met with the necromancer he'd tracked down yet, and wasn't sure if this was the right avenue to follow. But if he was to reach his goal, no stone could be left unturned. Crossing the veil between life and death was a puzzle he'd long sought to solve.

"Well," Adeline said flatly, "let us know if you need anything."

Without another word, Niklaus left the Matriarch standing in the church's gloom.

## CHAPTER FIVE

# NORTH OF THE WORLD

A S THE SHIP SAILED north along the coast, Aldric prepared himself for his new role as magister in the benefice of the Church in Caronath. More than likely it would be the same work as before, though he could not help hoping for something different. After all, he had been touched by Menselas, which was rare, and his healing skills were not insignificant.

Every few days they stopped at a port or town to take on fresh provisions, exchange passengers, and deliver goods and letters. Thankfully, Aldric didn't succumb to seasickness, seemingly to the disappointment of the crew. Although many times while pondering his new position, he found himself anxiously picking at his fingernails. Every day he washed in cold seawater and came to enjoy the salty scratchiness as his skin dried. His horse, on the other hand, wasn't too happy with the voyage and the lack of sunlight below deck.

While in port they ate whatever they wanted, and at sea consumed mostly salted and spiced fish with rice and noodles. When the sailors sparred to keep their weapons skills keen, they invited Aldric to join in, but he begged off. Along with sorcery, combat wasn't something he was comfortable with. There were a few injuries to heal, mostly minor bruises and grazes from the sailors' weapons practice. Luckily there were no major injuries, since the weather wasn't rough, and there were only brief rain showers. Manning a ship in a storm often led to mishaps among the sailors, when decks and spars were slick with water and the ship rocked something terrible.

The crew considered it a blessing to have a priest of Menselas and a healer aboard. One sailor, a grizzled man named Dillan, so devoid of body fat you could see the sinews of his muscles, often asked if Aldric would stay with them and become the ship's healer. It was a nice idea, but Aldric declined each time. "I go where Menselas tells me," he always said. Meaning, where the Church sent him.

They were halfway into the relatively straightforward journey when Aldric was woken by the clanging of an alarm bell. He pulled on a shirt and hastily tugged on his boots.

"Pirate!" someone shouted, the rest of his words muffled by the cabin walls.

Grabbing his khopesh and his talisman, Aldric joined the crew as they rushed along narrow corridors and stamped upstairs to the deck.

A gray glow lit the eastern horizon—dawn wasn't far off. He situated himself at the prow, which dipped and rose, spraying sea around him. The crew were all staring to the east, where the black outline of another ship was visible.

Aldric glanced at the captain, who was engaged in vigorous debate and hand-waving with the first mate. They didn't look pleased. No doubt they imagined they offered easy pickings for a pirate crew hardened to violence. At least this was something Aldric could avert, even though it would change his relationship with the sailors forever.

Each use of sorcery felt like another step down a path he'd never wanted to tread. Even if he only tapped into his dawn-tide power, he couldn't help feeling it brought him closer to the darkness of the dusk-tide. His teachers in the Evokers had forced dusk-tide lessons upon him, coercing his reactions so he'd become more intimate with the darkness than he'd wanted. Aldric knew that if the pirates attacked, he'd be forced to use that hated dusk-tide power now.

Reluctantly, he voiced a cant, and a perfect sphere of sorcerous energy surrounded him.

Exclamations of wonderment and fear erupted from the crew. A few made superstitious signs to ward off evil.

Aldric siphoned power from his dawn-tide repository and uttered a few words in Skanuric, an ancient language none of the sailors would understand. His shield glowed, its pale yellow light brightening. He held it for a minute, grimacing at the discomfort it exerted on his mind. Sweat beaded on his forehead, dripping into his eyes.

*The pirates should have seen my sorcery by now.*

Aldric chanted a dismissal, and his shield winked out of existence.

The crew's mutterings grew until he was afraid their fear of sorcery would overcome their fear of the pirates. He kept his eyes on the pirate ship, and gradually it turned. It was going to leave them alone.

It disappeared in their wake, and a few of the crew clapped him on the back or clasped his hand, relieved they hadn't had to fight. But many more did not meet his eyes; and from that point on, although he had probably saved them, all were polite to him to a fault. Even Dillan avoided him.

It was after the encounter with the pirates that Aldric drummed up courage to use the relic Roald had given him for the first time. Shalmara had told him to learn more powerful sorcery, and he wondered what he would have done if the pirates had boarded the ship. Perhaps the relic would provide answers.

He disabled the wards protecting the box and took it from where he'd hidden it at the bottom of his saddlebags. Aldric lifted the caged diamond from the felt. Its pale light unnerved him, the gem warm in his hands. He settled onto his bunk and closed his eyes. His pounding heart and swirling thoughts made it difficult to relax, but eventually the rocking of the ship lulled him. He drifted off … and his dreams were not his own.

He looked down from a hill over a great encampment. Fires twinkled on the plain below; and to the north, a citadel reared from the ground. Its smooth stone walls were without joins— raised by the darkest sorcery and the blood of innocents. It stretched between the walls of a wide gorge, a dam that held back a dark tide. Nysrog was inside, along with the remains of his sorcerous cabal.

"It will all be over soon, Marthaze," said Sian.

Marthaze turned to face her, and Aldric stared through his eyes. He was Marthaze. Platinum hair hung to Sian's waist, and a talisman carved from driftwood was suspended around her neck.

He suppressed the urge to spit. *Unholy.* All sorcerers were, even those who aided them against the demon.

"And then what?" Marthaze said. "Nysrog's cabal will still live on. They'll try to bring him back even if we succeed."

"We'll hunt them down."

Sorcerers fighting each other in a never-ending war. It had to be stopped. But Marthaze didn't know how. His Church was growing in power, in influence, but they were healers, not fighters. The power the Five had gifted him could only be used to heal, never to wound. It couldn't halt Nysrog or his corrupted sorcerers, which was why the Church had made an alliance with the Covenants of sorcery.

Sian looked into his eyes. "You've done well. We've come so far. Almost to the end. Trust in us."

*Never.*

~ ~ ~

Every night after that first experience, Aldric clutched the relic tight before falling asleep. Some of Marthaze's memories were bland—everyday life and situations—while others were terrible: the horrors of war, of demons, of suffering, and loss. Some of the priest's thoughts and actions were reprehensible, not at all what Aldric would expect from a follower of Menselas. Then again, Marthaze had lived in a harsh time and had fought an extraordinary evil.

Each morning Aldric woke sweating and nauseous; and for the rest of the day, his thoughts were skittish, and he found it hard to concentrate. But he forced himself to repeat the experience. He felt he owed it to the priest to learn from his life. Aldric had been given the relic for a reason, and not using it because it made him uncomfortable would be foolish.

~ ~ ~

The ship docked at Nantin for a full day, and the crew and dockhands hurriedly unloaded and refilled the holds with new goods. Then they sailed farther north until Aldric was satisfied he'd be able to cut a great chunk of time from his inland journey.

The captain anchored in a cove, and a small group of sailors rowed Aldric to shore in a boat large enough to transport his horse. Getting the animal into it was troublesome, but that was what the loading rigs were for.

"Good luck," one of the sailors said as they pushed the rowboat back into the sea. His tone indicated he thought Aldric was mad.

Perhaps he was. Not many braved the wilderness, only a few trappers and treasure hunters, many of them forced to it by circumstance. Those who did it out of choice were a hard-bitten lot, prone to violence. But that was what was needed to survive in the wilds. It took a certain type of person to venture out voluntarily, either capable or desperate.

For ten days, Aldric prodded his horse through the forest, passing mighty red cedars that thrust into the sky, so wide and tall they seemed gigantic pillars holding up the roof of the world. Moss and lichen covered their bark, and vines twisted about their bases. He kept his eyes on the trees and thickets to either side, stopping occasionally to peer through an extendable spyglass. A layer of decomposing leaves spotted with ragged patches of sunshine muffled the thud of his horse's hooves.

This part of the world, he knew, had once been the eastern marches of Swaidal. One of the Confederate of Skoiden nations, it had ceased to exist during the Fifth Cataclysm, wiped from existence, from most of the history books, and from memory. Once quilted with fields, the land was now covered by the trees that had crept slowly across it for millennia. There was a serenity to the forest, stemming from the absence of humankind, that both comforted and unsettled him.

The air was cold and bitter, and somewhere in the near distance a stream gurgled. He tugged his coat about him, his other hand curled around the leather reins, red and chapped from exposure.

A scattering of birdsong disturbed the quiet, and he relaxed slightly, though his unease remained. He let the reins drop from one hand and touched the hilt of his khopesh where it stuck out from a saddlebag. He tried to order his thoughts using the ancient techniques taught to him by priests, but, as always, they didn't suffice. Sighing with disappointment, he turned to the other, less accepted mind exercises of sorcery, which imposed the order he sought.

He was becoming convinced this short cut had not been a good idea. True, it had cut weeks from his trip, and he'd likely arrive at Caronath before he was expected. That would give him time for a well-deserved rest before he had to report for duty, and also to investigate the fortified city he'd only ever read or heard tales about. But such untouched wilderness had its own dangers: there were frightening creatures out here. Less dangerous for a sorcerer, to be sure, but still harrowing. The wilderness was these creatures' home and had been for thousands of years.

The roads he should have traveled were busy enough, with inns and way stations to make the journey safer and more hospitable. And there were wards set into milestones and markers to reduce the chance of a violent encounter with such creatures. Any that came too close would be dealt with by patrolling soldiers. But Aldric had been unable to resist the lure of the unknown, the chance to tread where no man had for hundreds, if not thousands, of years. In the forest, the air was alive, scented with pine and rich dark soil; and the water he drank from sparkling streams was sweet and icy. But he had to remain constantly alert, as he would if he wandered down the worst streets of a city where you could be knifed for looking at someone the wrong way, and your corpse stripped of valuables and left to rot. Except here, in the wilderness, you'd likely be eaten instead.

To his delight, the next day he came across an ancient ruin in the forest. Parts of some walls still stood, though they were covered with roots and moss. Elsewhere, blocks of granite taller than a man and twice as wide lay scattered across the forest floor, and slides of earth partially obscured what had once been stone steps. Everywhere, the forest reclaimed the broken works of ancient races. A destroyed work of man, the stain of a broken civilization. Whoever had built this place, and what had happened to them, was something that would never be known.

If Aldric hadn't been on a mission, he would have liked to investigate the ruins. Perhaps there were artifacts and lost knowledge here that could prove useful. A distinctive angular script was carved into some of the stones. He debated making a charcoal rubbing of it, then discarded the idea. The stylized script and alien thought patterns of the old races would be indecipherable to even the most experienced scholars.

He found a clearing where the great trees had failed to take root. Far above, open blue sky beckoned, though it was darkening rapidly. He gazed at it for a few moments, watching the birds zipping through the light and butterflies floating in the breeze. He enjoyed the wilderness and felt far more comfortable out here than among the lifeless stone and timber of the cities.

He made camp and sparked a small fire to cook food rather than for its warmth and light. He was comfortable with the darkness: he knew it, and it knew him. The rituals and tests he'd passed under the Evokers had made sure of that.

In the side of one wall he spotted a stone doorway. Around it were mounds of earth, as if someone had dug it out of a landslide. Bones cluttered the ground in front of the door, broken and chalky with age. After poking through the piles with a stick, he found at least three human skulls and many slightly smaller ones with pointed teeth. He cursed. Treasure hunters who had been set upon by Dead-eyes, and it hadn't gone well for them.

After a quick examination, he determined no one had been able to get past the wards guarding the entrance. Good. What was inside was better left alone.

He ate dried wafers and cooked the last of a rabbit he'd snared the other day. Taking off his riding boots, he uttered a relieved sigh, then set them and his socks by the fire to dry. He warmed his feet and thought about the forest for some time until his fire died and only coals remained. Then he set up his canvas bed, placing his sheathed khopesh beside it.

From a secure pocket sewn into his saddlebags, he removed the relic his Church had given to him for this journey: the green-glowing caged diamond.

A priest's memories, or "past magisters' wisdom", as the teachers had told him. "Not frail or prone to misunderstanding, like writing is. Real memories. And one day, yours will join them."

He wondered what it might be like to be interred in a relic like this. It was a form of immortality, he supposed. Of a sort.

He settled down and wrapped his blanket around him. A vast scatter of stars carpeted the night sky. A cricket chirped close by, and in a nearby stream, frogs croaked.

Aldric held the relic tight in his fist. Its silver wire bit into his flesh. He closed his eyes.

The chaos of battle raged all around him. Weapons clanging. Horses screaming. Shouts of pain and triumph. Dust from the dry plain clouded the air, stirred up by thousands of mounts and studded boots.

Marthaze hunched over a woman whose arm was almost severed, his crimson-painted hands working furiously to sew the ragged ends of the artery back together with an iron needle and hemp thread. His god's power infused him, flowing from his mark into the woman's flesh and bone. He finished with the slippery tubes and used crude, hasty stitches to reattach her limb. Giving the god a helping hand, they called it. Usually, his work was more considered and precise. But here, with the fight against Nysrog raging around him, he did the best he could.

He wrapped a bandage around the wound and hollered for helpers to take the woman away. He didn't know her name; she was just one of many he'd worked on. With the god's healing working on her arm, perhaps she'd be able to use it again. Perhaps.

Marthaze turned to see more wounded being dragged into the makeshift tent. Other priests worked feverishly on soldiers and sorcerers alike. One man's face was seared to the bone, one eye as white as a boiled egg. Another's leg had been crushed under his falling horse. They all screamed, begging to be healed, pleading for the pain to be taken away.

He blinked, eyes burning with exhaustion, and stumbled outside. Using the god's power came at a cost, and he was so very tired. But the battle had been raging for hours and didn't look like ending any time soon. There could be no end, not until Nysrog was defeated and sent back to the hell he had escaped from. The hell he had been summoned from—curse the Tainted Cabal sorcerers and their lust for power.

He poured water into a bowl and washed his hands, then discarded the red liquid and walked a few steps away from the hospital tent. A buzz filled the air, and something punched him in the chest. He staggered backward and fell to the ground.

An arrow protruded from his chest.

He gasped, reaching for the Five's power. Was denied. Power could only be used to help others. His hands pressed down around the shaft, attempting to stem the flow of blood.

"Help," he croaked.

Aldric woke suddenly, thoughts foggy, dripping sweat. Something had disturbed him.

Somewhere in front of him, a horse snorted.

He came instantly alert and leaped to his feet, brandishing his blade.

The horse was large—a destrier—though riderless. It hung back at the edge of the feeble light cast by the glowing coals of his fire.

Aldric tapped his dawn-tide repository and voiced a cant. A glowing orb appeared high above him, painting the ruins and trees with a pale yellow light. The horse's reins hung loose, dragging across the forest floor.

In the shadow of one of the granite blocks, something moved and stepped into Aldric's vision: the horse's owner. He was tall and garbed in a dark cloak. Finely wrought mail glinted underneath. He wore the cloak's hood pulled over his head, obscuring his face.

His deep voice broke the quiet, speaking Skanuric, the ancient language of scholars. "I smelled the stench of your sorcery. What do you do here?"

Shadows flittered at the edge of the light, quick and darting. White stick limbs crept forward. Glazed-over blind eyes peered from jerkily moving heads. Noseless faces snuffled the air, then retreated into the darkness. Dead-eyes, each one the size of a grown man, but half the weight.

Aldric shifted into a fighting stance, crescent blade lowered but ready. In his mind's eye, he traced the sphere of influence around him, the boundary that delineated his killing zone. Outside it, an opponent was safe; inside, his warded steel could cut flesh in an eye-blink. The man was too far away; Aldric would have to get closer.

"I am merely passing through," he replied.

Underneath the mail, the stranger was strong, built like an ox.

Aldric's globe hissed and sputtered as a drop of water fell onto it from the trees. The man glanced up at it, then back to him.

"You bear the mark of one of the new gods," he said. "But I see you are also marked as a manipulator. You are a student. And you have been taught things that were best left alone. You meddle at the risk of releasing great destruction."

Aldric realized what he faced. His stomach twisted, and his mouth went dry with fear. *A wraithe.* The first he'd ever seen. One of the elder races, a myth come to life. Older than old and possessed of power he couldn't hope to match. Aldric was as good as dead. The creature would crack his bones and abuse his corpse, and then the Dead-eyes would have their perverted fun with it.

Aldric licked his lips and lowered his khopesh, all the while preparing a cant of protection.

"We survive," he said. "We use what tools we can to aid us."

"Everything fails, in time." The wraithe gestured at the ruin around them. "This fallen place is but an example. Your race will also fail. But we will remain."

Several moments passed, and the silence grew deeper. The wraithe was as still as a statue. Of the Dead-eyes there was no sign, but they had to be lurking in the darkness. Whatever control the wraithe had over them, it was strong. Normally they would have attacked Aldric without hesitation.

"I will leave if my presence disturbs you," Aldric said.

The wraithe laughed, a deep sound that rumbled from its chest. "Does a fly disturb a deer? Does a mouse disturb a wolf? Sometimes. I remember when your race first appeared. But I am too old to feel much any more. It is the way. Time … *flattens*. Do you understand?"

Aldric nodded. The wraithe was implying that its kind, its culture, had been diminished by the passage of time. And perhaps it was right. But its sorcery hadn't diminished and was far stronger than Aldric's. A touchy subject, one's lessening. Perhaps it tormented him?

"As it does mountains and the works of man," Aldric said, hedging around the wraithe's meaning.

There was a long silence before the wraithe hissed a reply. "Do not mock me, human. I am beyond your ken. I have worked sorcery that would leave you weeping. My ensorcelled blade has taken a thousand lives. Without your weapons, your clothes, your stolen sorcery, could you survive this forest? Could you cross the trackless plains of Khisig-Ugtall? Could you endure the battering heat of the Jargalan Desert for days without water? Your race is weak and ignorant. Mine was mature when mankind was clawing its way out of the swamps."

Aldric backed away a step, licking his lips. He didn't dare speak.

Suddenly, the wraithe voiced a word. Dusk-tide sorcery.

Aldric's dormant wards triggered an instant before a blow hammered into his chest. He was flung backward like a rag doll, tumbling across the dirt and loam. He rolled and lurched to his feet, a perfect sphere of sorcerous energy surrounding him. His blade was nowhere to be seen. A cant formed on his lips, though he knew it would be useless. Sorcery far greater than his would tear the flesh from his bones.

But the wraithe had disappeared.

Its horse regarded Aldric blankly, then trotted away into the darkness of the forest.

Chest aching, Aldric spoke a cant, and his globe brightened to a furious white that banished the shadows and scoured the ground. He peered into the darkness between the trees, searching for the telltale glint of his curved blade, wincing as the very act of breathing hurt. He found the khopesh ten feet away.

Shadows flickered around him, and cold air bit his lungs.

"Man!" the wraithe called from somewhere, everywhere. "Do not venture here again."

Aldric packed his things as quickly as he could and found another game trail heading north.

## CHAPTER SIX

# A DIVINE GOAL

ROWNING, NIKLAUS STOPPED IN the middle of the alleyway and went over the directions he'd been given. He'd thought he'd followed them exactly, but he wasn't where he wanted to be—at the residence of the necromancer Eckart the Lost.

*The name should have warned me*, Niklaus thought. *Perhaps that's why I can't find him.*

Dark gray clouds had gathered during the afternoon, and rumbles of thunder grew louder. If he didn't get this over with, he'd be caught in the storm. His search for a way to join his goddess had already led him to some strange places, many of them a waste of time. And he couldn't trust information from the priestesses of Sylva Kalisia. They were like scavenging dogs baying for scraps while fighting among themselves.

Ah, there was the entry—more of a narrow gap between two buildings. As passages went, he'd seen better: it was dark and damp and reeked of mold and refuse.

Niklaus edged along it sideways, boots squelching in the mud. He made sure he led with his cane in his right hand, his thumb on the button that would cause a foot-long blade to spring out. In the open, he could deal with anything, but cramped spaces were a nuisance.

He didn't like to count on the goddess warning him of danger, like she had on his way to Caronath when his traveling companions had tried to make off with his belongings and leave him a corpse rotting in the sun. They'd quickly learned that a rough upbringing and thick limbs counted for nothing when steel was drawn.

If you relied on others, you were bound to be disappointed eventually. And that applied to gods and goddesses as well. They had their own plans, and you had yours, and you wouldn't realize you'd been abandoned until the blade slit your throat. Niklaus's stomach twisted, and he took a few deep breaths. No, she wouldn't abandon him. Not yet.

His legs wobbled. The thought of never seeing her again left him trembling and weak.

*Damned fool, get a grip.*

He scraped his knuckles across the rough brickwork, and the pain cleared his head.

Lightning flashed above, illuminating the alley. Ahead, in the mud, lay a dead rat teeming with maggots. Well, he'd seen worse and would in the future. It had probably been placed there by Eckart to deter visitors. Although those who truly wanted his services wouldn't blink an eye at a dead rat.

A dozen paces later, Niklaus was in a courtyard just as squalid as the passageway. There was a little more light here, and he could see a trickle of brownish-gray ooze flowing across the courtyard into a drain. Withered vines in pots scaled the walls and climbed a stairway that ended at a door painted blood-red and covered with indecipherable symbols.

Niklaus liked a good show, but perhaps Eckart had overdone it.

A sudden wind twisted dust into the air and blew dead leaves in swirls. A faint sound ... Was it the flapping of vast wings? Fear gripped Niklaus's heart. He froze, sweating. The goddess was here. Had he gone too far by wanting to become a god? Was she displeased and ready to vent her anger?

He waited, aching for the sound to return, and at the same time hoping it didn't. He could barely hear anything over the blood pounding in his ears.

When the fear left him, it was replaced with anger. He resented being treated as a slave, manipulated by her sexuality, powerless against her attractions. He became more determined to meet Sylva on her own terms, to become a god worthy of her. She wasn't omniscient, he'd figured that out a long time ago.

When strength returned to his limbs, Niklaus tapped his cane on the door and waited.

It creaked open to reveal a hooded and robed figure lit from behind by a brazier spilling a lurid green light.

"Who dares—" the figure began.

"You can cut the theater," snapped Niklaus, irritated by his weakness outside. He stepped forward and pushed past Eckart.

"You can't—"

"Spare me your protests, sorcerer. And get some more light in here. I'm not some greedy noble out for revenge against imagined slights, so you can dispense with the mummery."

Thick shutters covered the windows, and the room was stifling. In the dimness, Niklaus made out numerous tables cluttered with what looked to be sorcerous paraphernalia and talismans. At least to the uninitiated. Niklaus had learned a lot over the years and knew most of the objects were there for effect: skulls of various creatures, polished and painted; bones and feathers; glass jars filled with body parts and embryonic blobs; labeled vials; semiprecious stones holding down papers covered with symbols and squiggly diagrams. If it wasn't for the real sorcerous items interspersed among the junk, Niklaus would have cursed the necromancer for wasting his time.

"Now listen here," growled Eckart. "I don't know who you are, but—"

"And you never will. That's the second time I've had to stop your whining. There won't be a third."

Niklaus threw a calfskin pouch onto the closest table, where it landed with a solid clunk. Coins spilled out, flashing gold in the dim light. Eckart's tongue flicked out from between thin lips, and his eyes narrowed. He turned to Niklaus, and now his face was lit by the green coals in the brazier. Shoulder-length lanky brown hair framed pale features, and a slim leather band holding a star sapphire pendant hung around his neck. His eyes shifted from Niklaus's cane to the goddess's sword across his back and then to the shorter blade at his hip.

"You look like you can take care of most problems on your own," he said. "You're a swordsman by your build, and your blades aren't just for show. So it must be something big for you to want my services. Or subtle. Do you want someone killed so no one suspects? Perhaps a love rival?"

Niklaus snorted. "I could do that myself. But no, nothing so mundane. Does my gold buy your services and your silence?"

Eckart pursed his lips and pretended to ignore the gold royals spilled across his table, but Niklaus knew what he was thinking. Of course it would. These sorcerers were all alike: toying with powers they barely understood, thinking they were better than everyone else. But they still had to live somewhere and eat. And the materials for their experiments weren't cheap.

The necromancer nodded. "All right. But we've a way to go before I determine a price. My methods are ... unusual, not for the faint-hearted."

"As long as you're effective, I'll do whatever it takes. I'm told you're discreet, a trait I value in those I employ."

Niklaus watched as Eckart absorbed the message behind his words. *Yes, you're a tool I'm buying.*

Eckart moved to one of the tables and picked up a metal pen—one of the new ones with an internal ink reservoir. He opened a leather folder crammed with paper and inserted a blank page.

"Tell me what you want done, and I'll make a list of the materials I'll need. Some may not be cheap," he warned. "And others may be ... difficult to obtain."

Niklaus was silent for a time, and Eckart let him think. The necromancer must be used to people hesitating before spilling their darkest secrets to him.

Niklaus wandered over to a bookcase set against one wall, examining titles as he ordered his thoughts. One was *The Way of Sorcery*, a lesser treatise by Szander Satchid, who had gone on to pen many more complete guides. Another was *The Sorcery of Souls* by an unnamed author. Niklaus had read both and hadn't been impressed by either. What he needed was a specialist. He couldn't tell Eckart everything. But he could hedge around what he really wanted.

"It is said," Niklaus began, "that the gods and goddesses inhabit a place between life and death, a netherworld. I serve the goddess Sylva Kalisia; her hand guides me. I want"—*need*, he thought—"to know more about her. And, if possible, to contact her. If I could see her ..."

He would show her he was worthy, and then they would be together. She'd *chosen* him. She wanted him by her side. He was certain of it. His heart raced, and blood surged to his groin.

To hide his emotions, he took a dusty book off the shelf and flicked through the pages, not seeing the text inside. Eckart might think he was deluded, but he'd do his job. And Niklaus knew enough to determine if he was fudging. Not something the necromancer should risk if he valued his life.

Eckart set the pen down and rubbed his hands together. "You've come to the right sorcerer! I've made a study of the veil between life and death. An intriguing subject, but not one appreciated by the usual timid sorcerers. They leave that sort of thing to the priests and priestesses. Which makes me wonder why you haven't gone to them ... or have you?"

Niklaus narrowed his eyes, and his hand twitched toward the hilt of his short blade. "What I have or have not done," he grated, "is not for you to wonder."

Eckart laughed nervously. "Of course, of course. I'm sometimes too curious. I'll be forthright with you though. What you're asking is one of my interests, but ..." He spread his hands. "The materials required to investigate further are, shall we say, hard to obtain. I need dead bodies. Recently deceased."

He fixed Niklaus with a stare that was probably meant to intimidate.

*He wants freshly killed bodies.* It wouldn't be that hard to arrange. After all, people turned up dead all the time. A visit to a mortuary or a church, a few gold royals to grease palms, a way of transporting the bodies, and it was as good as done.

"Is that all?"

"By no means. I need other materials, but fresh corpses are the key. Well, someone in the process of dying would be better, but I don't think you'll get any volunteers." Eckart chuckled. "I can obtain the other constituents myself. As for a price ... work of this magnitude doesn't come cheap. A hundred gold royals each week, for a minimum of ten weeks. We can evaluate progress then."

Niklaus nodded. "All right."

Money was no object to him. And if Eckart needed someone dying to do his best research, that was what he'd get. Niklaus didn't want any half measures. Not when the reward could be so great. To become a god! He turned the thought over in his mind. There were tales of men and women ascending to godhood, but they were old fables, the truth behind them lost in the mists of time. But gods came from somewhere. Was there really a way to find out? Possibly. But it would be dangerous. It had to be, else everyone would attempt it, and there would be gods and goddesses coming out of the woodwork.

And Niklaus wasn't just anyone. Immortality he had already, bestowed by his goddess. But now he wanted to take his destiny in his own hands, to no longer be beholden to another. He'd grown weary of this world and hoped life in the netherworld of the gods would be an improvement on this dreary existence.

Knowledge, training, planning, and preparation were needed. And, above all, timing. There were uncertainties, and he had to make sure it was truly possible before attempting anything. Gods were jealous beings, and perhaps they sought to prevent competition.

When she'd given him the sword, Sylva had virtually promised to lie with him, to consummate their relationship. Why should it only happen once? Was it impossible that he could remain with her as her consort? Ascend to godhood, and take his rightful place at her side?

~ ~ ~

In the end, finding a dying person was easier than Niklaus had imagined. Discreet inquiries led him to a hospice on the western edge of Caronath. Run by the Church of the Five, the building was run-down but good enough for the job. Niklaus handed over some gold coins, asked a few questions, and found he had more than a couple of people to choose from. In the end, he decided on a frail old woman who looked like she hadn't eaten anything for months and was in constant pain from a wasting disease.

She sat in a frayed lounge chair, her legs covered by a striped blanket. Her white hair was unbrushed and patchy. On an empty wooden crate next to her sat a jug and three glasses, one with a reed poking out the top.

He had to wait until the woman had a lucid period between doses of a painkilling concoction the priests made her drink. He could have left the deed to the carers he'd bribed, but he felt this was something he had to do himself. When the woman's eyes cleared, and she began to look around her, Niklaus wandered over.

"Good evening, my lady," he said, then swallowed and looked away. What was he becoming? But this was important. He had to take his place at the goddess's side.

The woman smiled and looked at him expectantly. "Hello there, young man. Where am I? This isn't my home. Where's Jensin? He always comes to have supper with me. Such a good son."

Niklaus's thoughts swirled and settled on an indistinct vision of himself kneeling beside the bed of a different crone. Before he could hold it in his mind, it dissipated. He almost cursed out loud at his erratic memory. He remembered … something … a woman … a lover … In one of his journals there were entries about a wife he had no recollection of. Perhaps that was her. He resolved to read the section again when he had the chance.

He looked around, expecting to see one of the priests of the Five rush up to ask him what he was doing, but none did. Perhaps they were all busy with more important work, like collecting tithes.

"Jensin sent me," he told the woman. "You had a bad turn, and he had to bring you here so the priests could heal you."

The woman gasped. "Oh no! What happened?" She frowned. "I've been here a while, haven't I?"

*Not that far gone, then.*

"Yes, my lady, you have. But the priests say you're much improved. In fact, they'd like me to take you to meet Jensin now."

"I'm thirsty," declared the woman. "Would you be a dear and get me some water?"

Niklaus nodded and poured water from the jug into the glass with the reed. He held it under her chin and pressed the reed to her lips. She sucked greedily, then sat back panting, as if drinking had exhausted her.

Niklaus placed the glass back on the crate. He thought about making more small talk, but what would be the point? He was set on his course, and it was best to get any unpleasantness over with quickly. That way he could forget about it as soon as possible.

He beckoned the two carers he'd bribed. The skinny one pushed a wheelchair over, and the muscular one lifted the woman into it.

Niklaus arranged the blanket on her legs and patted her wrinkled hand. "We'll get you some more medicine before you go so you'll feel better. Then we'll be off."

"Good. Just make sure to pack my things. They must be in my room, wherever that is. I can't remember. Why can't I remember?"

The skinny carer took a flask from his pocket and poured a thick yellow liquid into the glass. Oil of poppy mixed with a few other alchemical ingredients, Niklaus had been told. It was supposed to knock her out for a few hours. The skinny man urged the woman to take a few swallows, then nodded to Niklaus. Already, her head lolled, and her eyes had a glazed look, as if she stared into another realm. A trail of drool leaked from one side of her mouth and down her chin.

The carers wheeled the woman to a side entrance where the litter Niklaus had hired was waiting. They bundled her inside and propped her up in the seat. Four thickset men with muscular legs stood ready for the order to depart.

"One moment," Niklaus told them, then jerked a thumb toward the side door. "Inside," he said to the carers. "You'll get your payment away from prying eyes."

The fools grinned greedily. They hadn't considered anything

could go wrong, even in this disused section of the building. The moment the door closed behind the three of them, Niklaus drew his short sword. One thrust, two, and it was done. They didn't even have time to shout. He wiped the blade on the skinny one's shirt, sheathed it, and went back to the litter.

The goddess's sword wouldn't do in situations like this. He would use it only for her work. To do otherwise defiled the blade and his complex relationship with her. Though it had been ages since he had felt her pull, seen her signs. He was still trying to work out what his purpose was in coming to Caronath. He felt like he was wandering, directed only by shadows, whispers, and the goddess in his dreams.

And he was sure most of his dreams were of his own making. When she came to him, when she really *showed* herself, she was exquisite—both in body and mind. Niklaus's hand tightened on the stingray-skin grip of his short blade. Clamped down on it hard until his knuckles ached. He ached for her, even when he wasn't dreaming.

~ ~ ~

The litter bearers stopped in a dingy alley at the rear of Eckart's residence. A nondescript wooden door at the top of a rickety staircase denoted a second entrance.

Niklaus knocked, waited, knocked again.

Eckart opened the door and took in the litter and Niklaus with one look. His face broke into a smile. "Excellent. This is perfect."

Niklaus rubbed his eyes. "Just get the job done, sorcerer."

He felt dirty. He needed a bath and a few drinks.

## CHAPTER SEVEN

# DEEP WATERS

TWO SILVERS," SAID THE librarian, a pinch-faced young woman. She licked her lips, glancing to either side to make sure she wasn't overheard.

"It was one silver yesterday," protested Kurio. "And the day before." She held out a silver royal. "Here, take it and don't be greedy."

"Two," the woman said firmly. "I've had some unforeseen expenses."

Kurio's gaze took in the librarian's frilly new dress and the silver hair clip in the shape of a swallow that held her mousey-brown hair away from her face. *Maybe I'll find it today,* she thought, sighing with resignation.

"Two, then," she agreed. "And remember not to tell anyone."

She toyed with a lock of her shoulder-length red hair to draw attention to it. If anyone asked about her, the greedy librarian should remember the color. The wig didn't suit her, and she'd been meaning to get rid of it, but thought she might as well get one more use out of the thing. She was dressed as a wealthy student, in a smart dark gray skirt and cream knitted shirt, and dark gray boots with silver buckles. She'd chosen the disguise to be allowed access to the library, but the librarian obviously thought it meant Kurio could afford to pay more.

The librarian wrinkled her nose. "I'm not looking to get thrown out. Though perhaps I should get you to pay me three just in case."

*And I should throw you off a tall building.*

"If you ask for three, I'll not come back." Kurio dug out another coin. "Take two, or I walk away."

The woman sniffed, then snatched the coins from Kurio's outstretched hand. They quickly disappeared into the folds of her dress. Kurio strode past her before she could utter another word.

The library was dark and musty, and there was a rank stench in the air the librarians didn't seem to notice. *Rotting paper and glue,* Kurio surmised. *And probably mice and rats.*

She did an entire circuit of the large room, making sure the windows she'd unlatched previously remained so. It wouldn't do to be blocked by a locked window if she had to leave in a hurry. There was no way she'd have been able to smuggle her crossbow inside, so she'd left it back at her new apartment. A dagger strapped to her thigh and another tucked into the back of her skirt made up for it.

Satisfied, she made her way into a side annex. Here, she again checked the windows, wishing she could open a few of them to let in some fresh air. But the librarians would throw her out, as the parchments and tomes in this room were ancient and had to be protected. Not that the librarians were doing a good job of that: most were covered with a layer of dust, and some were in advanced states of decay. One scroll had practically fallen apart in her hands when she picked it up, and she'd hastily gathered the scraps together and left them in a pile on one of the shelves. She'd even seen a book in one dark corner covered with a white mold that looked a bit like coral.

Alchemical lamps burned in chandeliers hanging a few feet above the shelving. Their pale yellow light wasn't the best to read by, but it was enough if she squinted. Three days of research, and she was no closer to deciphering the Skanuric script written on the paper she'd found underneath the cube. Someone had considered it important enough to hide it under the cube in an impenetrable ironwood chest banded with ensorcelled orichalcum, and secured with an obscure Sandoval lock. If that didn't signify value, she didn't know what did. Kurio smelled opportunity, and she was never one to let it slip through her fingers. With the Night Shadows probably hunting her, this paper could lead her to a stack of gold royals—enough to flee the city and start anew elsewhere.

Kurio had invested most of her ill-gotten gains and didn't have much coin on hand. And if she divested herself of some of those investments now, she'd come out with less than a tenth of what she'd put in. She just couldn't bring herself to do it.

Besides, the Skanuric script intrigued her. Whatever it said, it had to be linked to the metal cube. And Willas and his bearlike companion had paid a goodly sum for her to snatch the cube. Unfortunately, most of that money was gone, as she'd had to pay for new lodgings and make them secure.

Kurio wandered to a bookshelf at the back of the room, reached up to the top shelf, and took down two books she'd secreted before leaving yesterday. Both looked promising: a text listing Skanuric words translated into their modern Dakuni equivalents, and the other on Skanuric symbols and their multitude of meanings. Now all she needed was a translation manuscript from Dakuni to some other language she could speak, plus texts on idioms and subtleties for each.

A lot could get missed through that many translations. She could spend days or weeks on it and come up with a final version that made no sense. Or she could just find someone who could read Skanuric … A scholar perhaps.

As she stood there thinking, a cockroach crawled out of one of the books and over her hand. She yelped and jerked away, causing the books to tumble to the floor in a puff of dust and the cockroach to disappear into the shadows. She sneezed and wondered what the hells she'd been thinking. She wasn't spending any more time here. Four silvers wasted, and she was no wiser. There had to be a better way.

Leaving the books on the floor, she went around the room and relatched the windows. She didn't want anyone noticing and taking steps to ensure they remained locked.

As she passed the librarian on her way out, the young woman frowned at her. "Found what you're looking for?" she said in a disappointed tone.

"Not yet," lied Kurio. "So there'll be plenty more royals for you."

The woman smiled.

*Maybe the greedy girl will spend more than she can afford,* Kurio thought as she walked away. *It'd serve her right.*

~ ~ ~

The letter was waiting for her when she arrived home—if home was what you could call her current bolthole. It had been slipped under the door. A crisp, expensive, cream-colored envelope with *Kurio* written on it in an elegant hand.

The problem was, no one was meant to know about this place.

After bolting the door, Kurio stared at the envelope as if it were a poisonous snake. It couldn't be from the Night Shadows, she was certain of that. If they knew her location, she'd be dead or trussed up like a feast-day pig and just as likely destined for hot coals.

Well, there was no point delaying.

The envelope was sealed with a dark crimson wax imprinted with a square divided into four smaller squares. *Gannon Chikaire.* Though the symbol was missing the Skanuric runes his ring bore, it was easily identifiable.

That reminded her: she should look up the runes and translate them. Kurio shook her head. Time enough for that later, after she'd read the letter.

That Gannon had located her set her nerves on edge. Strangely, it also set her heart pounding with excitement. It had been a long time since she'd experienced such stirrings for any man. He intrigued her, of that there was no doubt. And, dare she hope, it seemed she also intrigued him.

Moreover, he was mixed up in something with Willas, which could prove useful if she knew more about it. Thievery filled her pockets and taught her many skills, but it wasn't enough for Kurio to live from one job to the next. If she was to set herself up for life, to be entirely independent, she'd need far more capital than she'd gathered over the years. And connections. She knew how the dark underside of business worked, and unless you knew the right powerful, wealthy, ruthless people, you might as well be pissing into the wind. She sensed an opportunity here that might provide some advantage.

Kurio broke the seal. The same hand had penned the letter inside, which was on even better-quality paper than the envelope. She wasn't even sure where to buy such stationery.

*Miss Kurio,*

*I hope this correspondence finds you well. Please forgive both my familiarity and the method of delivery of this correspondence. The direct approach may unsettle people of uncertain temperament, but I believe you are not so easily disconcerted.*

*My thoughts keep returning to you and our conversation the other day. I will be lunching alone in two days' time at midday at The White Rabbit, and it would be my pleasure to entertain your company, if you should so desire. It is my fervent belief that you will find the assignation stimulating. I do hope you accept.*

*Leaving our engagement entirely in your hands.*

*Faithfully yours,*
*Gannon Chikaire*

Kurio refolded the letter and slipped it inside the envelope. She strode to her desk and deposited it in a drawer, then poured herself a shot of alchemically enhanced wine and downed it in one swallow. It slid down her throat cold, then exploded with warmth in her stomach.

She noticed her hands were trembling and poured herself another drink, intending to sip this one slowly.

*Well, well, well.* How did Gannon find out where she lived? He must have extremely competent retainers, but even so … She couldn't think of any way they'd have found her.

She shouldn't go to the meeting. But Gannon was intriguing, and she found his lure hard to resist. She had to see him again. She wiped her damp palms on her skirt, her eyes moving involuntarily to the drawer that held the letter.

The White Rabbit was an exclusive club for the obscenely rich, built on the bank of a manmade lake in Lichfields, a district almost wholly populated by the wealthy and their mansions. Membership at the club was on her to-do list, though so far down it was among the least likely, below *Own ten merchant ships.* Money wasn't enough to buy your way into The White Rabbit; you had to have connections. And here was one, fallen into her lap.

She had to know more first.

It was late, though, and she was tired. The sun had set hours ago. Kurio rummaged through her nightstand drawer for her bedside clock. Although it had been expensive, it ticked too loudly for her liking. It would be midnight soon. She debated with herself, then shrugged.

A few minutes later, she'd changed into her dark, nondescript work clothes, loaded her gear into her backpack, primed her crossbow, and was on her way.

~ ~ ~

Gannon Chikaire's residence was easy to find and surprisingly unremarkable. It was situated at the termination of a dead-end street, with similar dwellings to the left and right.

Kurio tugged her hood closer about her face as a man wheeled past a barrow of what looked like bloodied heads wrapped in hessian cloth. A thin trail of liquid leaked from the barrow, and the man pushing it had to walk with a wide stance to avoid getting his boots wet. Kurio wouldn't be surprised if the barrow did actually contain severed heads. She'd heard human heads sold for quite a bit of coin to the right people. As did other body parts of the freshly deceased. She'd put that business in the "too risky" basket, but the Night Shadows had their hands in such trade up to their elbows, as they did with everything.

The front of Gannon's building was flat and uninviting. It was three stories high and constructed from brown bricks, with sandstone around the doorway and windows. Two iron-encased alchemical lamps on either side of the black-painted door kept the darkness at bay, but judging from the lack of light in the windows, the servants were all asleep. Their master had to be out or residing somewhere else tonight.

Still, Kurio waited. Rushing a job was the surest way to make mistakes and get caught. And she was close to the main entrance to the Northern Catacombs, so there would be all sorts of people about at night.

A short time later, one of the windows on the second floor opened, and a man dressed in a nightshirt leaned out. In one hand he held a pipe, and in the other a burning taper. When he proceeded to light and puff on the pipe, Kurio knew Gannon had to be absent. No servant would display such a blatant breach of etiquette if their master was home.

Satisfied, she made her way down dimly lit streets to the rear of the house, where a wall topped with iron spikes loomed up from a narrow back lane. A servants' door and a wider delivery gate were set into the wall. Her footfalls made barely a sound across the cobbles, though she had to skip over the sludge-filled gutter running down the center of the lane, and around piles of refuse.

After a quick glance around to check she was unobserved, she bent over the lock in the servants' door. It was old but obviously frequently used. Her nimble fingers had it open in a few moments, and she slipped inside. Keeping to the shadows, she made her way across the paved inner courtyard to another narrow door. Peeking through the window beside it, she saw it led into a kitchen. The door wasn't locked.

*Lazy,* she thought as she crept inside.

A faint orange glow came from coals in the fireplace. Kurio took a few moments to note where everything was. If she came through here in a hurry later, she didn't want to run into anything. Large jars of flour sat on a sturdy table along one wall, surrounded by smaller containers of salt, sugar, and various spices. Recipe books were stacked neatly in one corner.

An entire wall was covered with shelves containing baskets of vegetables and fruits. It seemed Gannon ate healthily, which didn't surprise her. Sausages and hams dangled from hooks set into the ceiling; and a covered plate contained baked biscuits, each with a nut delicately placed on the top. Kurio took one and nibbled on it as she crept to the doorway on the far side. It was good. If she had time on her way out, she might acquire a few recipe books.

Popping the last of the biscuit into her mouth, she found the servants' stairway and ascended to the second floor in pitch darkness. At the top, light filtered in from a hallway window. Not much, but enough that she didn't fear bumping into any furniture or tripping over a cat.

With the servants all asleep in their quarters at the back of the house, all she had to do was avoid the man who was smoking—

and probably his master's tobacco too. From the placement of the window, he was in the second room on the left.

Kurio peeked in the first room, which seemed to be a snug of some sort. Good for relaxing with a cozy fire and not much else.

She tiptoed past the second door, fervently hoping it wasn't Gannon's study, as that was her goal. Luckily, the third door opened into a room dominated by a large mahogany desk finished with a marble top laden with ledgers and stacks of papers held down with polished stone weights. Bookcases stuffed to overflowing covered the walls, and there was a medicinal scent in the air. Whatever cleaning solution the servants used, they were overzealous with its application.

To her surprise, the hairs on the back of her neck stood on end. It was an uncomfortable feeling, creepy and frightening at the same time. Her talent was telling her to beware, but of what?

Taking a length of cloth from her pack, she stuffed it into the gap at the foot of the door to block any light, then vigorously shook her alchemical globe. Within seconds it began to glow with a soft, pale blue radiance—just enough to read by.

After ten minutes of riffling through Gannon's ledgers and papers, she hadn't found anything of interest. Household expenses, bills, details of income received from various investments—a good deal of money, but nothing suspicious. Reluctantly, she gave up. If Gannon had any secrets, she'd need a more thorough investigation to reveal them.

Tapping a finger on her cheek, Kurio took a slow turn around the room. She should trust her talent, which had proven uncannily reliable in the past. Something to do with Gannon was amiss, but what?

With a resigned shrug, she secured her globe inside her pack, along with the cloth from under the door, and slipped into the hallway. There were a number of other doors she hadn't investigated, but she was already pressing her luck. As she stood there hesitating, chewing her bottom lip, a soft breath of air brushed her cheek. A draft, from where?

She held out her hands and slowly crossed the hallway. As she reached the middle, the draft caressed her fingers. It seemed to be coming from a massive gilt-framed painting that covered much of the wall.

Kurio took a step back and frowned. The paint was cracked with age, though she could see it had been restored in places. A stern-looking family gazed down upon her: a man wearing a high-buttoned suit centuries out of date; a wife dressed in a voluminous skirt, with a waist so small it had to be cinched; and two children, a boy and a girl, both clothed as miniature versions of their parents. They all wore grim expressions, as if the beloved family dog had just died.

Kurio felt around the frame, smiling as she easily found a locking mechanism. The painting swung out into the hallway, supported by well-oiled hinges. Behind it, an opening. A staircase led down.

Kurio ducked inside and pulled the painting shut behind her. Blackness. In a few moments she had her alchemical globe in her hand again. She'd expected dust and cobwebs, but the stairway was as clean as if it had been scrubbed yesterday.

Carefully, she descended. The steps kept going until the wooden walls were replaced with stone, and Kurio was sure she was a few stories below ground level. Maybe this was a secret entrance to the catacombs. Or to ruins from the cataclysms, which were even deeper.

At the bottom, she found a strange door. It was made of an orange metal—orichalcum—as was the frame it was set in, and plain and polished, as if it had been installed recently. She could see her reflection in it, slightly distorted.

Her breath caught in her throat. It had a Sandoval lock above a handle. His stylized initials were etched into one corner. Which meant the door was a thousand years old.

There was no keyhole, just a series of four coded dials. Each one had ten different Skanuric runes, which meant there was roughly one chance in ten thousand of guessing correctly. It looked like she was out of luck.

Unless ...

Kurio recalled the four Skanuric runes on Gannon's ring. She didn't know their meaning, but that didn't matter. That the dials contained the same runes as the ring gave her confidence.

*Could it be this easy?*

Turning each dial, she selected the four runes in order. Inside the lock, mechanisms clanked and whirred. She gripped the handle, prayed to a few different gods, and pulled.

The door swung open, and a foul reek invaded her nostrils—the stench of old meat and rancid fat. Kurio heaved, clamped her nose shut with her fingers, and breathed through her mouth. Her stomach churned as she imagined the air invading her mouth, on her tongue. She gagged, then swallowed thick spit.

*Bloody hells, what's this about?*

Beyond the door, a corridor led into darkness. She rushed along it, wanting to get this over with and get out of there as quickly as possible.

The walls were rough-cut stone, ancient. This must have been part of the catacombs. Someone had delved deep into the earth until they'd broken through into the ancient ruins. It seemed to Kurio like a great deal of effort, for what reason? A builder could easily include a decent-sized secret room in a house as large as Gannon's, and no one would suspect a thing.

Dust stirred underfoot, coating her boots and the cuffs of her pants. She must have gone a hundred yards before the corridor ended, opening into a circular room.

Hanging from the ceiling, like the sausages and hams in the kitchen, were two human bodies.

Iron hooks stuck through their feet held them upside down, limp arms dangling above the floor. The bodies were hairless with red splotchy skin, just like butchered pigs that had been scalded and scraped. Both were men, and not small either. Their throats had been cut. An incision ran from chest to groin, and their innards were missing. In the pale light of her globe, their skin sparkled in places, and Kurio decided it had been rubbed with rock salt for preservation.

A long bench caught her eye as she tried not to look at the corpses. As in the kitchen on the ground floor, the bench held large jars of flour, several smaller containers, and an enormous bowl of rock salt. And books. Recipe books.

*Oh, gods. They're eating them.*

A half-barrel against one wall seethed with maggots—the source of the stench and presumably the resting place of the missing organs. Kurio felt her gorge rise and looked away, swallowing bile.

A faint noise from the other side of the room made her jump. There was another door, this one wooden and bound with iron.

*Don't, Kurio.*

But she had to.

She skirted around the edge of the room, keeping as close to the wall as possible to avoid the butchered men. Her skin crawled, and she wanted to run away as fast as she could. But there was that door …

Gripping the handle as hard as she could, she tried to calm her mind and steady herself. A noise meant something moving. There could be a prisoner locked in here, chained up until they were ready to be butchered like an animal.

*Calm down. Deep breaths. No, not deep breaths. Just open the door, take a look, and leave.*

She inched the door open and thrust her alchemical globe in front of her through the gap. The vile stench was even worse now.

A dozen pairs of orange eyes punctuated the darkness. She caught a glimpse of wrinkled, yellow-skinned limbs with blood-covered hands, fanged mouths, and finger-length horns jutting from heads and backs. Clumps of rotting meat were scattered across the floor.

*Dead-eyes! Here, in the city!*

She stopped breathing and whispered a prayer. Her alchemical globe trembled in her grasp. She pulled it back and slowly closed the door. Its hinges creaked, and the orange eyes turned toward the sound. Screeches and snarls erupted as claws scrabbled across stone. Almost as one, the monsters burst toward the door.

Kurio slammed it shut and ran. She ducked under the hanging corpses, cringing as their fingers brushed her head. Panting like a dog and sweating rivers, she raced along the corridor, flung herself through the orichalcum door, and shouldered it shut. Hands shaking uncontrollably, she spun the dials, not caring if the runes didn't match the pattern she'd found them in.

Even in her panicked state, she realized those creatures couldn't be Dead-eyes, as she'd first thought. Dead-eyes were said to have white pupil-less eyes and thin white limbs. Those hideous creatures had to be … demons.

*Gods help me!*

Before she knew it, she was flinging open the painting and dashing down the corridor.

"Hey! You there! Stop!"

Kurio ignored the man's voice. She didn't think she'd stop for quite some time.

She threw herself down the servants' stairs, hearing thumping footsteps behind her. In the kitchen, she grabbed a jar of flour and dashed it against the wall, groaning under the weight. It broke with a satisfying crash and enveloped the kitchen in white powder.

The footsteps trailing her faltered, then stopped. "Thief!" the man shouted, obviously trying to wake the other servants.

But Kurio knew he was too late. She was almost free.

A dozen quick steps, and she was outside. Moments later, she slammed the door to the lane behind her, jammed a pick into the lock, and snapped it off.

Sweat cold on her face, limbs trembling, she raced down the lane and was soon lost in the surrounding streets.

## CHAPTER EIGHT

# A FORTUITOUS ENCOUNTER

MARTHAZE'S SHADOWY VISIONS CUT Aldric to his soul, as if they were made from razor-sharp blades. He watched through the long-dead priest's eyes as a wave of Mutinate cavalry—warriors from an empire long since turned to dust—charged a seething horde of demons. Lances pierced flesh and bone and shattered against toughened hides and armor. Horses screeched, joining the wailing of the demons that threatened to drive men crazy. Sabers were drawn. Dark purple demon blood whipped from their flashing blades, but scarlet blood was torn from humans too. One pocket of cavalry fought the hardest, and Aldric realized the demons were targeting Lord Beremas, the last ruler of the Mutinate. New demons rose from where they'd lain hidden amid others; larger, darker, carrying serrated blades as long as a man was tall. The massive demons made short work of the cavalry surrounding Beremas, and the lord was hammered down, black steel blades chopping until there was no hope of survival. Aldric cried out, although he knew this battle against Nysrog had been fought in ages past, and Beremas was long dead and turned to dust.

Then the sorcerers arrived, their glittering lights blowing demons and Dead-eyes into bloody mist. Too late, as usual. Even in the dream, Aldric could smell the charred meat, the blood, sweat, and piss of battle.

Demons and Dead-eyes matted the land. The dusty haze that surrounded the demons stank of decay and bitter feces. A river to the west was jammed with bloated bodies, the land around it covered with sheets of flesh that festered and decomposed in the heat of the arid south. Valleys were clogged, and hills seethed. Dust choked the air, turning snot and tears to mud.

Marthaze turned to the woman by his side, the sorcerer he hated. "Lord Beremas has been slain."

Sian only nodded, eyes narrowed in concentration.

"I should be out there," he muttered. "Healing the injured."

"It's too dangerous," she replied. "You know this. The gift of your god is too valuable to risk. Content yourself with healing those who survive and are brought back."

*Bloody sorcerers,* he cursed. But he knew she was right, and that galled him all the more.

"There!" she shouted, her tone gleeful. "Can you see it, Marthaze? The Chain!"

Another atrocity, but that thought he kept to himself.

Sian's Grandmaster strode through the battlefield, surrounded by her wards. Around her neck she wore the Evokers' prized possession, the Chain of Eyes, said to have been crafted by three different gods and gifted to mankind to help them defeat Nysrog and his abyssal minions. Though the Grandmaster was the youngest ever to have risen to the rank, her power was immense. She waded into the mass of demons, trailing lesser sorcerers behind her. Around her, a burnished conflagration erupted. Sparks whirled like butterflies caught in a circling wind.

Where they touched the demons, the foul creatures shrieked and died, their bodies blasted to ash and dust. Nysrog's fell minions, Dead-eyes, and corrupted humans alike were unable to withstand the strength of the Chain of Eyes. Even the demon-worshiping sorcerers—what they'd taken to calling "the Tainted Cabal"—fled its wrath.

Sian clapped her hands in delight, and Marthaze reluctantly admitted that corrupt sorcery sometimes had its place.

She turned to him. "Once the demons are defeated and Nysrog is sent back to the abyss, the sorcerers will guarantee the demon lords will not return."

"Guarantee?" Marthaze spat. "How can you say such a thing? You know his cabal will work toward his return."

"I don't know the details. Only that the Evokers are working on something that will prevent Nysrog from ever rising again. It is rumored they will release such power that the world need never live in fear. It will seek out and destroy any sorcerer who grows skilled enough to breach the veil between our world and the hells." She moved closer to Marthaze, a conspiratorial gleam in her eyes. "They are calling this creation 'the Revenants'. It will save the world."

Any rogue sorcerer's death could only be a good thing in Marthaze's book. But to kill *anyone* who had such skills? What if they had no intention of summoning demons? To preemptively slaughter someone for growing their knowledge—the idea sat ill with him.

"Your work begins," Sian said, gesturing down the dirt track toward a train of wagons bearing wounded soldiers.

Marthaze's heart sank, though he drew himself up, steeling himself for the long days ahead.

The first injured soldier brought to him was a woman. Both her arms had been severed at the elbow. Blood-soaked bandages covered the charred flesh of a hastily implemented cauterization. Despite all he'd seen in the years of war against Nysrog, Marthaze wept.

The woman's eyes were glazed, and her movements sluggish, no doubt the effects of a heavy dose of poppy oil. But some glimmer of awareness broke through, and she gazed at Marthaze. He wiped his eyes, not wanting her to see his despair.

"My hands," she said dully. "I can't feel my hands. Will I be able to hold my children again?"

Marthaze almost fell to his knees as hopelessness and anguish swamped him. "I'll do my best."

That was all he could do. All that Menselas required of him.

Aldric woke, slick with sweat under his blanket. His fire had burned to ash, and the silence of the forest around him seemed as loud as the clamor of war it replaced.

He sat up, hugged his knees tight against him, and wept as Marthaze had.

~ ~ ~

"Caronath," Aldric whispered, enjoying the sound of the city's name. It was a place he'd only heard about in stories or read about in books.

He had finally arrived after more than a month in the wilderness, joining a paved road a few days ago. Slowly, the forest had thinned, replaced with tilled fields and villages—signs of civilization carved from an unforgiving land. His heart had lifted at the sight of wood smoke pluming from chimneys, farmers in the fields, cattle grazing. But he couldn't help wanting to turn back to the forest. There were mysteries there. Lost knowledge and treasures that could benefit everyone—if a person could survive to bring them back.

His encounter with the wraithe had been a week ago, but his bruised ribs were still sore. He'd thought about the chance meeting often as he'd traveled. A being so old, it defied logic; and one of many, if the legends were to be believed. The whole world had been theirs once, their sorcery propelling them to greatness. But they were much reduced, both in number and culture. Time had a way of wearing anything down, making dirt out of mountains.

His mind turned to the Revenants in the priest's memories. He hadn't learned any more of this power through his use of the relic, and had to assume the sorcerers of old had either failed or abandoned whatever mad plan they'd created.

Crops in the fields were slowly replaced by herds of animals as the city neared. Cows and pigs; barns filled with clucking chickens and quacking ducks. Food for the city's inhabitants, raised as close to the city as possible so the animals weren't killed or defiled during the night. Timber buildings began appearing, then brick houses, as the city walls loomed closer.

Aldric joined the throng at the gates and breathed in the dirt-laden air. He passed under the gatehouse's shade and into the dusty sunlight of the streets of Caronath, where the road's massive pavers gave way to cobbles. He guided his horse along the main street, eager to take in the sights, but also wanting to ease his way into what would be his new home for the foreseeable future. Until he was inevitably ordered elsewhere.

This close to the gates, the city was as crowded as a marketplace. As he'd expected, there were more of the fair-haired, pale-skinned people of the cold northern climes here, but he could see many other races mingling with the northerners. A few Illapa, with their greenish skin and dark hair; the occasional dusky-skinned Inkan-Andil from the far west; and some San-Kharr, like himself, with dark gray skin.

One young San-Kharr woman carrying a basket of fruit reminded him of his sister. Hopefully his family was well, and Kittara … he'd have to talk with her in more depth when he returned home. It wasn't good for her to dwell on things that just weren't possible. The chance that she might quicken and become a sorcerer was minuscule.

Suddenly, the crowds and noise and closeness of other people was too much for Aldric. The stillness of the forest had faded from him too quickly. He found himself chafing at humanity and steered his horse down a side street to separate himself from the masses.

Deep parallel ruts marred the stone streets: worn by countless carts and wagons—a testament to the age of the city. He saw a few wards nailed above doors and windows. Weak talismans, but good enough to deter anything that made it through the city's defenses, sending them after easier prey.

A flaxen-haired woman walked toward him, her mark of sorcery plain to his eyes. This was a slice of luck. Sorcerers were rare, and even rarer to meet one in the street.

"Excuse me," Aldric said, leaning from his horse slightly. "Could you tell me where the nearest sorcery merchant is, please?"

He needed to replenish his supplies before he reported to the Church. Especially since what he did, what he *was*, wasn't well tolerated by his brethren.

The woman looked him up and down and sniffed disparagingly. "Cheapest ones are on the main streets. Plenty there to choose from."

"I'm after a high-quality shop, not a cheap one that sells worthless charms," Aldric said. "I used up many of my materials on my way here."

The woman frowned and squinted up at him. Her gaze traveled over his dusty clothes and horse, to the emblem stamped into his leather saddle. Her eyes widened as she recognized the holy seal.

"Oh!" she said. "Excuse me, ah …?"

"Magister will do."

She nodded, swallowing. "Magister. Why do you need a sorcerer's … Oh. Yes, well … Pearello's shop is on North Sorrel Avenue." She pointed up the street. "Maybe ten streets farther. Turn right and look for the sign."

Aldric nodded and gave her a smile. "Thank you." There was

no need to ask what sign. Anyone with arcane power would recognize it.

The woman scurried off, casting frequent glances at him over her shoulder. She'd have an interesting story to tell her friends.

He followed her directions and was soon drawing up outside a building with a red door. Above the entrance was a metal talisman that flickered with light, even though the sun was behind the building, leaving this side in shadow. The runes inscribed into the sign were complex and powerful, the work of a master.

Grunting with satisfaction, Aldric dismounted and tied his horse to a rail, then dusted his clothes off as best he could. He slung his saddlebags over his shoulder. They contained his valuables and personal items; he wouldn't leave them unguarded in any city. He buckled his khopesh across his back.

Inside, the warmth of sorcerous lamps chased away the chill, their light bathing the interior in orange. They spoke of a knowledge of sorcery that far surpassed his own—an innate talent and hard-worked-for skill.

Shelves and display cases were filled to overflowing with raw materials, with sorcerous items in glass-doored cabinets under lock and key. Of the materials, most were familiar to him: ingots of different metals, blocks of rare woods, vials containing liquids that themselves could only be created through sorcery. Feathers of all kinds, dried herbs, and fragments of stone. Talismans and trinkets: some complete and some half-made, ready for their owner to stamp his or her mark upon them.

Some cases held weapons: daggers and swords of various lengths, worked with runes and symbols. One wall was entirely covered with sheets of tacked-on paper, each one showing intricate geometric designs and calculations. Notes were scrawled alongside patterned runes following the lines. Aldric knew some of the cants, but many were beyond him. The logic and mathematical calculations of the sorcery on display eclipsed his talents, not to mention many used a mixture of dawn-tide and dusk-tide power.

A petite woman wandered among the shelves and cases, her long dark hair sprinkled with braids that she occasionally toyed with. She wore a pair of black woven pants and a scarlet shirt with silver buttons. As she peered into a glass display case, she tutted, then withdrew a bunch of keys attached to a chain from her pocket, unlocked the case, and took out a palm-sized bronze statue. Yellowed birdlike bones with shattered ends had been grafted onto it somehow, sticking out like quills on a porcupine.

"I knew it was around somewhere," she said, turning to Aldric. She flashed him a smile, and he found himself answering it with one of his own.

Her brown eyes were slanted, and her skin was pale, so much so, it made her seem as if she were wearing red lipstick. Her beauty made Aldric catch his breath. Having grown up among people with dark gray skin, paleness was still an exotic oddity to him, even after all these years. She had some Soreshi blood in her, he realized. How much was impossible to tell. The nomadic clans that inhabited the vast grasslands to the west were secretive and usually hostile to outsiders. How she came to be here would likely be an interesting tale.

He examined her again as she left him and made her way to a polished wooden counter. She wrapped the talisman in a rough cloth, then placed it inside a box. Her figure was strong, muscles firm, and Aldric found himself wanting to know more about her.

"Is there anything I can do for you?" she said, pushing the box to the side and meeting his eyes. "Feel free to look around. And if there's anything you like … You seem fresh off the road. Are you looking for lodging?"

Aldric shook his head, then stopped. "Actually, yes, I am. Do you know of anywhere close by?"

Although accommodation would be provided to him by the

Church, one of the perks of arriving early was he had time to relax and take a break from his duties.

The woman walked around the counter and approached him, her head tilted, wide eyes staring into his. She pointed to his saddlebags. "I know that seal."

Aldric felt her sorcerous mark surge as she worked something. Her mark was deep and fierce, a profound fissure. For an instant, jealousy flared in him, to be pushed aside by sorrow. He quashed both feelings and turned his face away as it grew hot with shame.

"I'm just after some simple talismans," he said stiffly, the first thing that came to mind.

He faced her again and saw she was regarding him with concern and a little sympathy.

"No need for falsehood," she said softly. "We're both sorcerers, after all."

"I'm …" He swallowed. "I'm a dabbler, nothing more."

"Your mark is small, but it is there. How did you find yourself following Menselas, or the Five as he's commonly known? Though the Church makes use of us occasionally—for which they pay dearly—they don't like us much."

*An understatement,* he thought. And then, *She knows.* She had realized he was cursed in the eyes of the Church.

The thought clenched his hands into fists, and he struggled against the anguish that threatened to overwhelm him. Being alone in the forest for so long had given him too much time to think. It was a few moments before he mastered his sorrow enough to speak.

"I'm sorry," he said weakly. "I'll come back."

He strode from the shop, the woman's concerned voice following him out, though for some reason he couldn't understand what she was saying. He unhitched his horse and led it away, aware of the woman standing in the doorway, staring after him.

~ ~ ~

A platter of roasted bird and vegetables was plonked down in front of Aldric, followed by a tankard of beer. He picked up knife and fork and set to with gusto. He couldn't tell what sort of bird it was, but there was plenty of dark and tender meat on its bones. Speckles of charred herbs spotted the crispy skin. He swallowed a few mouthfuls of pale beer and puckered his mouth. Too fruity for his taste, but he'd heard they liked it that way this far north.

The Cask and Squirrel was but a few blocks from the sorcerer's shop, and the first reasonable place he'd stumbled across. A few silver royals later, he'd booked a room for the week, along with morning meals and a stall for his horse.

As the hour was getting late, he'd dropped off his gear and come downstairs to take the edge off his hunger. He'd found a booth to the side of the room before the inn became too packed with the evening crowd. There was a brick wall at his back, and the roaring fireplace was to his right. He could see the front door and also the entrance to the kitchen at the side of the bar.

He was halfway through the bird when a steaming berry tart was deposited next to his platter. Aldric paused, considering abandoning his meat to eat the tart while it was still hot.

"That looks nice," someone said, sliding into the seat opposite him.

Aldric swallowed his mouthful and wiped grease from his lips. The woman from the shop. She must have worked a divining to find him. Sorcery beyond his ken.

"Magister Aldric Kermoran," she said, confirming his suspicions.

She wore a dark jacket over her shirt to keep out the night's chill, and this close he could see colored strings woven into her braids: red and black and yellow. Her Soreshi clan colors, he realized.

"You seem to know more about me than I know of you," he said, not unkindly. "I don't even know your name."

She held out her hand, and he clasped it in his. Her grip was firm, though her hand was small and her fingers delicate.

"Lady Pearello," she said. "Though my friends call me Soki. It's short for Sokhelle."

Aldric smiled. "Lady Pearello it is, then. We are not yet friends."

"No. But that could change. You intrigue me, Aldric, if you'll forgive my familiarity. There is much to study with sorcery, but so few men are as … memorable as you."

Aldric stared into the froth of his beer. The conflicting emotions he'd felt when she'd mentioned his god had mostly subsided. But the implication still hurt.

"I don't care to be examined like some strange animal," he said.

"No, I don't suppose you would. But I wasn't planning on doing that. Ah … do you mind?"

He looked up to see her greedily eyeing his berry tart. He laughed. "Go ahead."

"Oh, thank you!" She bit into it, heedless of the heat. "It's good," she mumbled around a mouthful.

Aldric picked up the remaining bird's leg and finished it off in short order while watching the sorcerer devour his dessert.

"Lady Pearello," he began.

"Please. Just Soki. I have a feeling we'll become good friends." Her eyes sparkled in the firelight.

"Soki, then. I'm new here …"

An impish smile crept across her face. "Would you like a guide?"

"I do need someone to show me the neighborhood and the rest of the city. Perhaps we could start there?"

She nodded slowly, still smiling. "The day after tomorrow?

Tomorrow, I'm ... working on something. It can't be put off."

Aldric wondered what kind of sorcery Soki was involved with. Presumably something significant and difficult. She was driven, he decided. And attractive.

~ ~ ~

There were many sights in Caronath that Aldric wished to see. His youthful ears had been filled with tales of the fabled city, and his eyes had devoured many historical tomes about it during his novitiate training with the Church. With Soki on his arm, all seemed greater and more vibrant than he had imagined. She proved to be a goldmine of information about Caronath and the areas around the city, as well as the ruins and wilderness that spread from the city to the north.

By a bend in the river loomed the Temarine, an impossibly tall tower with a slight lean. Abandoned centuries ago due to poor foundations, it now housed a population of swallows in its upper tiers and bats in the lower.

An unremarkable tomb in a cemetery held a shaft dug deep into the earth, and at the bottom were ancient ruins from a cataclysm.

They visited a huge warehouse where the river's fishermen brought their daily catch and sold over a hundred types of fish amid shouts and smoke and flies.

They traversed the Living Bridge, made from the roots of a tree woven together and able to support the weight of thirty people.

And all the while, they spoke of themselves, their pasts, their hopes for the future, and occasionally of sorcery. Despite that, all the time he was with Soki, Aldric kept the relic hidden away. He didn't want anyone other than his direct superior to know he possessed it. Besides, while he was having a well-earned break, he also wanted a rest from the relic. Using it wearied him, physically and mentally, and a few days away from the nightmares and unsettling truths it showed him would be welcome.

Just as the sun was setting, Soki led him to a brick-walled garden deep inside the district of Bitter End, an area with many mansions and wealthy residents. At this time of day, the streets were busy with carriages and passers-by. She took a key from her pocket and unlocked the garden's wrought-iron gate. Inside, a trimmed hedge blocked the main part of the garden from outside observers. They skirted around it, and Aldric saw a lake surrounded by shrubs and carefully placed rocks. On the far side, swans glided silently away.

"Come," Soki said, and took his hand. "No one will disturb us. This is a privately owned garden."

She led him along the lake's bank until they reached a wooden pier, at the end of which was a platform extending twenty paces over the water. Their boots clunked on the polished timbers, and Soki briefly shook three globes that sat in metal cages fixed atop square posts. A pale light shone from them; and as the sun began to set, painting the sky hues of orange and red and violet, they were enough to see by.

A wry smile formed on Aldric's lips, and an uneasiness in his belly. He knew what Soki was doing. The dusk-tide was coming, and he'd mentioned his reticence to use its power.

She gave him a questioning, impudent smile and backed away until she stood in the center of the platform. She closed her eyes, breathing deeply, and Aldric's skin began to tingle. Like a tidal wave, the dusk-tide was coming.

Soki shrugged off her shirt and slipped her trousers down her hips to pile at her feet. Underneath, she wore scanty underclothes of pale red. She kneeled and folded her clothes with quick efficient movements, then stood again, stretched her arms toward the night sky, and waited.

Although he knew she was simply doing what was most effective for harnessing the dusk-tide, the sight of her near-naked form aroused Aldric. He couldn't help it. Her pale skin and lithe body scattered his thoughts until the only ones that remained were lustful and indecent. His face grew hot, his breath short.

"Join me," Soki said. "You need to put your inhibitions aside. Dark counters dark, remember? How can you defend yourself if you refuse to learn? To embrace your power?"

Aldric removed his shirt, but that was all. Something about the dark power of the dusk-tide unsettled him, and to weather it naked, or almost so, filled him with dread.

It seemed Soki had no such reservations.

Staring at Soki's striking figure, Aldric forgot to prepare himself as he opened to the arcane energy. Perhaps that was what she had planned. Unlike the dawn-tide, which approached stealthily and softly, the dusk-tide hit them like a wall of water. Aldric's skin burned as if thousands of needles penetrated his flesh. The energy roared around them, buffeting him as if it held a physical weight.

Soki cried out in ecstasy.

Aldric staggered, cursing. Darkness entered him, cloying and choking. He closed himself off, not needing the dusk-tide power and not wanting it. Its blackness diminished immediately, leaving him gasping for breath.

He looked up. Soki was awash with the darkness. Midnight waves chased with silver painted her skin, touching and caressing. Her fists were clenched, and there was a rapturous smile on her face, which was tilted to the heavens. For long moments she drew in the dusk-tide, imbibing its energy, standing as if turned to stone. Her capacity both awed and frightened him. His own repository was supposed to be large, but if it had been empty, he'd have been replenished by now. Soki's must be immense. And he could tell she had used dusk-tide sorcery recently, and often.

By the Five, she was exquisite. Blood-red lips and feline eyes, midnight-black hair and pale skin. Aldric had never met anyone like her. Arcane power shone from her, rippling and swirling across her skin, and his blood stirred at the sight. His eyes drank her in.

The dusk-tide vanished as quickly as it had appeared. Soki remained still, chest heaving, exposed skin glowing with sweat. She opened her eyes and pursed her lips, gazing at his chest.

"How can you not enjoy it?" she gasped, breathless.

"It is dark power, and many who use it are twisted."

"Not all," Soki said.

"No," Aldric admitted. "Not all. Some are ... exquisite."

Soki seemed to belie his belief that the dark power would lead to his corruption. She clearly reveled in both dawn-tide and dusk-tide power, and she showed no sign of wickedness. On the contrary, her immense power hadn't changed the person she was. It had merely given her self-confidence and the certainty that sorcery itself was neither good nor evil.

Or perhaps she was a temptress. A temptation he should avoid. No, he couldn't believe it. Though a niggling thought did come to him: perhaps he should re-examine his firmly held beliefs.

They dressed themselves in silence before leaving the garden for the busy streets.

~ ~ ~

Aldric was enjoying himself immensely. The restaurant Soki had brought him to was, from the look of the place, far more expensive than he'd usually spend on a meal. But as a sorcerer of considerable power, Soki probably wasn't short of gold royals. Located at the top of a tall building, the restaurant's walls were mostly clear glass and overlooked the sparkling lights of the city. To the east, just above the horizon, the red moon, Jagonath, peeked out. Soon it would rise and provide a decent glow through the night, chasing its cousin, cold white Chandra, across the sky. The tables were set at a distance from each other to afford some privacy. Soki had wanted to sit close to one of the many fireplaces, but he had steered her to a table against a wall. He liked having something solid at his back and a view of the entire room.

When a neatly dressed waitress came over, Soki ordered for them both. The names of some dishes were foreign to Aldric, but that wasn't unusual. And he'd learned long ago that his stomach could handle almost anything.

A chair scraped across the floor to the right of them, and he half turned, hand reaching for his khopesh before he remembered he'd left it in the establishment's cloakroom. He shrugged and turned back to face Soki.

"Have there been many sightings of Dead-eyes lately?" he asked. His encounter with the wraithe and its minions still concerned him.

She snorted and leaned her elbows on the table. "Dead-eyes? Plenty. Mostly on outlying farms. They come out of the forest or down from the mountains and try to steal chickens or calves. The farmers chase them off, kill one now and again. That's just the way out here: you live wary, or you die careless."

Their meals arrived, deposited on their table by a surly-looking waiter. He flashed Aldric a stern look, then hurried away.

"I don't know what's gotten into him," Soki said. "I usually eat here alone, and he's always smiling and chatty."

Aldric had his suspicions. "Perhaps he's had a bad day?" he suggested dryly.

One large bowl was filled with spicy noodles, and Aldric licked his lips. After his weeks on the road and in the wilderness, he still craved food that wasn't flatbread or cheese or dried meat, even after the decent meals he'd enjoyed since arriving in Caronath. Another dish was heaped with crustaceans the length of his palm, their shells orange and shiny from being tossed in herb butter, while yet another held roast lamb along with some sort of purple peas.

He served both of them, with Soki asking for an extra helping of a green vegetable side dish.

"Try the bugs first," she said, pointing to the crustaceans. "They're very good. Delicate. They're found in freshwater streams, but they've started farming them in pools too."

Aldric set to with a will, and it was a while before they spoke. The bugs, as Soki called them, were good. He glanced at her as she licked herb butter from her fingers, then dipped them into a wash bowl, and wiped them dry on a cloth.

"So your family are back in Nagorn City," she said. "In the city or somewhere close by?"

He nodded. When he'd finished chewing and swallowed, he added, "A village outside the city. My parents run a farm. Well, my father ... he thought I'd be there to help out and eventually take over. My mother does the best she can, and my sister too, but she has big dreams."

Soki chuckled approvingly. "It's fine to dream, but it's better to plan. Is she training to become a sorcerer? Where one child has the talent, it usually manifests in others."

"She hasn't shown any signs, and it galls her. She thinks what I do is heroic or some such nonsense. Maybe she just wants to see the world."

"I understand. That's what I wanted. Still, there's a chance she'll manifest a talent. It's a shame we've lost the knowledge to push someone over the edge."

He knew she was referring to a practice from many centuries ago that, so the histories told, had released latent sorcerous talent. What she couldn't know was that it was a talent only found in demons, and they'd used it to coerce the weak-willed to join them. His Church possessed ancient knowledge lost to most scholars and institutions; and to the majority of people, demons existed only as vague legends.

"Yes," was all he said, "it's a shame."

Soki began to tell him about her childhood and parts of her training, the bits she was allowed to reveal. In exchange, he told her about his travels and the work he performed, the parts he was allowed to. Secrets lay between them. Some they might reveal later perhaps, but many they couldn't.

By the time dessert came, Jagonath had risen out of sight of the windows, though its glow still painted the buildings outside. Aldric's breath caught as the waiter deposited a bowl in front of him. It held a mound of dark brown mousse sitting atop a crunchy base, with bright red berries sprinkled haphazardly around, along with tiny purple flowers.

He looked at Soki. "Is that ...?"

She grinned at him. "Chocolate? Yes. Some of the traders bring it up here from the southern kingdoms. It has a long way to come, so it's expensive. I hope you enjoy it."

Aldric took a spoonful of his and closed his eyes. "Gods," he murmured.

Soki chuckled pleasantly. "So, now that I've bribed you, can I ask some more personal questions?"

"You didn't need to bribe me to get me to reveal more," he said without thinking.

She raised an eyebrow. "My, my, forward, aren't we?"

Aldric felt heat rise to his face and averted his eyes. "I didn't mean—"

He broke off when Soki chuckled.

"I know you didn't. But I do have more questions."

He busied himself with another spoonful of the slightly salty mousse, crumb, and berries. He'd spent several days in her company now, but how well did he really know Soki? Enough to know she was a decent person. Although sometimes wild, if his experience with her during the dusk-tide was anything to go on.

"Ask away," he said around another mouthful of the extraordinary dessert.

"I was trained by the Sanguine Legion," she said, not asking a question, but revealing a secret.

Aldric searched his memory. The Sanguine Legion was one of the smaller Covenants today, but had been the premier power on the west coast hundreds of years ago. Like many of the larger Covenants, factional infighting had split them asunder as sorcerers desired to follow different directions. Within the Sanguine Legion, the fight had been particularly bloody. Some sorcerers had begun research into summoning creatures from outside this world. Not demons exactly, but their likeness to demons had caused the other Covenants to unite against them. Many of their sorcerers had perished, and now only outposts of the Covenant remained. The Sanguine Legion's sorcery was among the most powerful though, and some would say the most elegant.

"Not so legion any more," Soki continued. "One of their sorcerers lived close to … where I was born. So, what Covenant do you belong to? I can sense your mark, but that doesn't tell me much. And I've always been interested in the workings of sorcery, how others do things."

Of course she would ask about his Covenant, Aldric thought. She was an accomplished sorcerer herself, after all.

"They … the priests of the Five sent me to the Evokers."

Soki let out a low whistle. "A powerful Covenant, and expensive. Not just in terms of royals either. Why did they … Oh."

"Yes. The priests saw a use for me. A way for me to … matter in some way. Though they also believe I am cursed."

"Fools," Soki said, then shook her head. "I'm sorry. You were trained and looked after by the priests of the Five, so they must mean a great deal to you. When did they, or you, realize?"

"That I had the mark? It manifested during puberty. I'm one of the rare cases where the mark didn't appear at birth. That's why I was trained by the Five."

"Because you also bore the mark of their god? Which I can't see."

"Only others with the god's mark can see it. Unlike sorcery, where any sorcerer can see another's mark. My training with the Evokers was quite thorough and the best the Church could afford. When I was young, I wanted to be a healer. I enjoyed learning about the human body and how to cure illnesses." Aldric sighed and shrugged. "But now ... let's just say I don't get much opportunity to practice healing. When my sorcerous mark became apparent, the priests decided the Five had other uses for me. So my training turned to sorcery and more martial skills."

"I can sense your repositories, Aldric. You must be more proficient in the dusk-tide, seeing as it's the largest of—"

"No. I'm not."

His curt words caused an awkward silence between them. Soki stared into the distance, as if unsure whether to meet his eyes after he'd interrupted her.

Eventually she said, "I understand. You see the dusk-tide as a dark power, as many do. It's not, but such prejudices run deep."

Aldric wasn't about to let a virtual stranger lecture him on dark sorcery. He knew what he'd felt during his training. The cloying, sticky dusk-tide felt wrong to him. And the malicious cants it could be used for only reinforced his opinion. But he had to admit it could be useful, and it hadn't seemed to corrupt Soki.

"Anyway," she continued, "what rank have you reached in your Covenant? What cants have you been taught?"

This was a subject he was more comfortable with. "Only second tier, I'm afraid. Scarcely more than an apprentice." His unwillingness to use his dusk-tide power had limited his advancement. "I can construct a decent personal shield and only require my talisman for more complex cants. But to tell the truth, most of the sorcery I use is defensive. The offensive cants are … not something I or my Church find acceptable."

"Because they use mostly dusk-tide power?"

"Yes."

According to scripture, dusk-tide sorcery came from the hells and the abyss. The Evokers scoffed at this, stating that both tides were natural forces. Aldric didn't know himself what the truth was, but the fact his god had made him a sorcerer seemed to fly in the face of his Church's teachings. He immediately clamped down on the thought. It would do him no good, and possibly a great deal of harm, to question scripture.

"A healer and a warrior, a priest and a sorcerer. You're a rarity, Aldric, one I mean to investigate further." Soki's hand reached across the table and enfolded his. "If we have time. You haven't reported to the priests yet. They must know you've arrived."

Aldric nodded. "I know. I'll go to them soon. I … needed some time to myself."

Soki let go of his hand and stood. "It's late, but I'm not very tired. Do you need to spend time alone tonight? Or would you like some company?"

"I … not tonight," Aldric said, and coughed to cover his embarrassment. "I'm still tired from my journey." A poor excuse, but he'd never been good at lying.

Her offer enticed him, although was too soon for his liking. And part of him still recoiled a little from what Soki represented: a sorcerer with no inhibitions, fully in control of the dusk-tide portion of her power.

CHAPTER NINE

# RED FINCHES AND ASSASSINS

ALDRIC FILLED HIMSELF WITH dawn-tide power surreptitiously, taking in what he could through the open window of his room at the inn. He hadn't used any sorcery recently, but leakage meant he still had to replenish the energy. As soon as he'd recovered, he dressed and left for the hill where the Rafic-ur-Djasir monument was located. Scholars had named it in Skanuric, which translated as Ladder to Darkness, or the Night Steps, as the locals called it. Aldric could have asked Soki to act as his guide, but he was avoiding temptation, and he'd always imagined being alone to see the prehistoric structure.

Fires were lit on the hill at the end of summer to burn off weeds attempting to gain a stranglehold. Rain and wind cleaned the area after, so all that remained was a grassy zone around the edifice at its center: a stepped pyramid made from blocks of rough-hewn obsidian, with five tiers reaching sixty yards into the sky.

Early explorers had found the site the obsidian was sourced from: a volcano a hundred miles to the north. Why the monument had been constructed, and by whom, remained a mystery hotly debated by scholars. Many of the tomes that mentioned it were old and prone to translation errors. But all novice priests became fascinated with the structure, and Aldric was no exception.

The pyramid had been originally located outside the city, but Caronath had spread as its population swelled, and now the Night Steps were inside the city walls. The dwellings close by, Aldric noted, were mostly dilapidated and vacant. It seemed to be one of the poorest districts in Caronath, which was hardly surprising given no one wanted to look out their window and gaze upon the disturbing structure. Plus, people's pets tended to go missing and wind up mummified at the pyramid's base, or so he'd read. And occasionally a human body would be found there too. Unmarked, but dead all the same, mouth stretched into a horrified grimace.

He climbed the rough path that ran up the side of the hill. A brightly colored finch flew past his head, close enough to almost brush his ear. He jerked his head back, startled. The bird circled and landed twenty paces in front of him, appeared to look back, then hopped along the path before taking flight toward the top of the structure. When Aldric reached the summit of the hill, he found a flock of finches congregated on the upper tiers of the pyramid, chirping noisily. Red-bodied with black wings, they seemed to burn in the bright morning light.

He admired the glassy stone of the structure; it too was bathed in sunshine. It was a greenish color on the illuminated side, and black on the shadowy reverse. Aldric thought it a miracle that no one had dismantled some of the blocks for their own building purposes, but perhaps the rumors surrounding the pyramid had scared away would-be scavengers. Locals generally left the area alone, save for a cult that had reportedly sprung up around a century ago.

As Aldric neared the pyramid, he could see offerings laid at its base: mummified animals—cats and dogs and a lamb—along with dried fruits and nuts, cheeses and jerked meats. Curiously, no rats or mice had disturbed the offerings, which he supposed gave credence to the myth there was a powerful entity interred inside.

If myth it was …

In the historic tomes his Church hoarded, one tale told of a stand made here by adherents of the Tainted Cabal as they attempted fell sorcery to tear a breach in the veil between worlds that Nysrog could emerge through. That was why Aldric had wanted to see the place for himself.

When he was young and in training, he and the other novices had spent many a night enthusing about the wonders of the world and where they'd travel and what they'd see. The Night Steps were impressive, of that there was no doubt. But somehow Aldric had expected more. An energy in the atmosphere, perhaps a chill, even though the sun was warm. He admitted a little disappointment to himself, then laughed at his foolishness.

It was then he noticed a small girl standing next to the first tier, watching him. Her face was grubby, and her dress torn, but she was well fed, and her golden hair was intricately braided and tied with a pink ribbon. She noticed him noticing her, and nodded and walked toward him, picking her way around the dead animals and bowls of offerings. She stopped ten paces from Aldric and looked him up and down with her brown eyes. Her nose wrinkled, and she tilted her head to the side.

"Do you have a sweet?" she asked.

Aldric didn't move for fear of frightening her. "No. I'm sorry."

She stamped a bare foot in annoyance. "She said I'd get one. Maybe she has it."

"There might be some with the offerings, but I don't think taking one would be a good idea. Where do you live?"

"Why not? She doesn't want them. She doesn't even have teeth!"

"Your mother? Do you live around here?"

"No, silly. The old lady. No one lives around here except her."

It didn't surprise Aldric that few chose to live close to the pyramid. The old lady was probably a hedge-witch, wanting to make a name for herself by setting up business in an area the locals considered cursed.

"Would you like me to walk you home?" he said.

He didn't think it was dangerous out here, but the girl was too young to be wandering around Caronath by herself. She should be playing with friends, or with dolls, or … What did girls her age do? He had no idea. He'd been busy working on the farm when Kittara was this girl's age.

"She wants me to take you to her," the girl said. "Come on."

She skipped away, nimbly avoiding the dogs and cats staring sightlessly at them.

Aldric glanced at the Night Steps, sighed, and followed.

The girl disappeared around the side of the pyramid, and when Aldric turned the corner, he found her staring at a spot in the wall. To him, it looked no different from any other.

She looked around furtively, as if suspecting someone might be watching, then said, "Open up!"

Aldric cleared his throat. "I don't think—"

One moment the wall was solid, the next there was a hole in it. Aldric's dormant wards hadn't triggered it, so it wasn't sorcery. Then what was it?

"Hey!" he yelled as the girl ran inside. "Bloody hells!"

He checked his khopesh and plunged in after her, ducking his head to avoid the ceiling. He was in a corridor, and pale purple light radiated from violet scaleskins growing on the walls and floor. Surprisingly, the air wasn't stale. Rather it smelled faintly of charcoal and roses.

The shadow that was the little girl grew smaller, her bare feet slapping on stone. Aldric glanced at the bright square of light behind him: outside, and presumably safety. But he couldn't turn back. Here was a mystery, and one his Church would need to know about.

He crept along the corridor, his heart pounding, and his hands slick with sweat.

"Where's my sweet?" he heard the girl ask.

Then he stepped into a chamber concealed in the heart of the pyramid. The floor was comprised of rectangles of obsidian pavers laid in a basket-weave pattern. An old woman sat on a stool by a fire of flickering red flames that gave off no smoke. Beside her was a large flat bowl filled with rose petals. The girl stood next to her, hand held out. The woman reached into the pocket of her frayed robe and handed the girl something. She squealed with delight and popped it into her mouth.

"Go now, *nothfoljer*," said the old woman. "Your parents will become worried." Her voice wavered slightly, but was loud in the silence of the chamber.

Aldric tensed. *Nothfoljer* was Skanuric for "successor" or "replacement". What nefarious purpose did this crone have planned for the girl?

"Leave her alone!" he shouted, drawing his crescent blade.

The girl gasped and ran away screaming.

The crone stood abruptly. "Halt!" she commanded.

Aldric felt himself gripped tight by an invisible force. Again his dormant wards were quiet, not triggered by any arcane emanation. He couldn't move his head, but out of the corner of his eye he saw the girl was also frozen.

The old woman tutted at him and ambled over to the girl. "There, there," she said softly, and hugged the girl, who unfroze and collapsed into her arms. The old woman laid her on the floor gently, and stroked her hair.

Turning, the crone stepped close to Aldric and met his gaze. Her eyes were two red-glowing crystals of fire. Within them stirred the primordial hotness of the sun, an intensity of torment, and whirling storms. They pierced Aldric to his very core, rifling through his innermost thoughts, searing his soul.

"Mmpf," he managed.

Fire eyes. Obsidian. Sorcery that wasn't. Holy Menselas, this wasn't just a monument; it was a temple to an old god that predated the founding of Caronath! If he hadn't been held motionless, Aldric would have fled in blind terror.

"When I release you," the woman said, stepping back, "you'll put your sword away, and we'll have a discussion." She smiled, revealing a mouth devoid of teeth, as the girl had claimed. "Don't try anything, or I'll have to get nasty. You wouldn't like that."

The force holding Aldric vanished, and he staggered. He drew in shuddering breaths and tried to control his trembling limbs without success. He felt wrung out, sapped of strength.

"It'll pass," the woman said, "in time for you to do what I need you to do. But I forget. Too long with only myself for company, I expect. That's been the hardest. I don't expect you'd know, but one day you might. If you're worthy." She cackled without mirth. "Remember me, if that happens."

*At least she thinks I'll still be alive one day,* thought Aldric. That was slightly reassuring.

"You can call me Etia," she continued. "Though even my *nothfoljer* over there doesn't call me that. She calls me Wrinkly. Can you believe it?" A shake of her head. "I think I'm holding up quite nicely. Respect, that's what young people are missing. That, and brains."

"I'm ... I'm Aldric. You're a ... goddess?"

Etia cackled again, this time sounding genuinely amused. "Oh, dear me, no. I'm like you. One of the chosen. I can use the power of my god, though he's almost forgotten out there. I get by. I send my helpers out and do what I can. The birds do well enough."

*The finches,* realized Aldric. "Who is your god?"

She waved a hand with knobbed knuckles and parchment-thin skin. "Does it matter? What's in a name anyway?"

"Some names have power, hold knowledge."

"Bah! Foolishness. A name is only an identifier. But I didn't open my door to you to argue about trivialities. Someone's come knocking. They've been attempting to breach my wards and break inside for weeks. My power has weakened and doesn't reach far these days. You're the first competent person to visit lately, so you're what I have to work with."

Cursing silently, Aldric shook his head. "You'll not use me like some game piece," he said firmly. "I'm no servant."

"Of course you are! The same as I am. You think your god's power comes without chains?"

He knew it did, but some burdens were born willingly. "You've survived for this long. No one knows you're here. And you have your god's power. It's been enough to keep you safe so far."

Etia's eyes flashed. "Someone does know. And I'm not worried about the temple. I'm worried about my soul. There are those who want to, shall we say, bottle my essence. They've tried before. They need both types of sorcery and the *puske*. At least they think they do. They're very determined and not very nice. I'd rather stay alive and myself, thank you very much."

"The *puske*? What's—"

A bony finger jabbed into Aldric's chest. Hard. "Don't they teach you anything? It's what the gods' power is made of. The gods can gift it, as they have with you, but they cannot rescind it. So if you can control someone who has been gifted, then you can control their power."

Aldric had never heard the term before. Then again, he'd never been taught Menselas's power was made of anything; it just *was*.

"Who is it that needs sorcery and the *puske*?" he asked.

Etia rolled her eyes. "You really are ignorant, aren't you? No, don't answer that. I can see for myself. You're like a baby left out in the wilderness."

Bridling at her tone, Aldric felt his face flush with heat. "Educate me, then. You brought me here for a reason."

"The Tainted Cabal," said Etia, giving him a penetrating look.

"I take it you have at least heard of them?"

The heat left Aldric's face as a chill swept through him. The pieces fell into place: the legend of the Tainted Cabal's defeat outside the pyramid. Etia was under siege from the Cabal. They wanted her power—her *puske*—for themselves. A step along their plan to return Nysrog to the world. They'd tried, and failed, before. But this time, Etia was worried. *Holy Menselas.*

"I can get help," Aldric said quickly, thinking of his Church, the few warriors he could gather. But what good would Menselas's sacred healing power be? It wasn't a weapon. "I know a little sorcery, though I'm far from powerful. As for Menselas's gift, I can heal, but that won't be of any use unless there's bloodshed."

The old woman tilted her head, much like the girl had earlier, and frowned. "You don't know, do you? Ha! How foolish your priests have become over the centuries. Did they deliberately withhold the information from you, I wonder? Or have they forgotten themselves?"

His mind raced, trying to decipher her words. "What are you talking about?"

She scratched an armpit. "Never mind. There's no time anyway. My suitor approaches." She looked toward the entrance. "They've found a way in. And if you're all I have to work with, may the gods help us."

A faint light illuminated the tunnel, and Aldric realized she hadn't closed the door behind him. She'd invited them inside, whoever they were. The light dimmed as someone blocked the opening. Hard leather scuffed on obsidian paving stones. Footsteps echoed, drawing closer. Shadows moved.

"With any luck," Etia said, "we'll both get out of this alive."

Aldric glanced at her, but her attention was focused on the approaching threat. He gripped his khopesh hilt tighter, knowing he was out of his depth, forced into an alliance with an unknown priestess against a nameless enemy, with only his limited sword skills and sorcery to defend himself.

The footsteps stopped. Silence reigned for long moments, the only sound Aldric's heavy breathing in his ears. Unexpectedly, there was a surge of sorcery. Fueled by the dusk-tide. It subsided as quickly as it had appeared, but there was a strangeness to it, as if it was somehow stale.

Aldric's free hand reached for the talisman inside his belt pouch, and he tried to clear his mind and concentrate on the forms and calculations of sorcery. His dormant wards would erupt when needed, but once they did, he had to maintain them. If he was required to use his khopesh at the same time, it wouldn't go well for him. He couldn't concentrate on sorcery and wield a blade with any skill.

A short, slender woman emerged from the gloom. She withdrew a hand from a pocket, as if she'd hastily stashed something inside. Her clothes were … odd. A man's trousers and a shirt of expensive material, too big for her frame. A plain sword hung from her belt, and Aldric wondered if she could even wield such a large weapon. She flashed Aldric a smile, hitched the pants up, tightened her belt, then brushed a strand of long black hair from her tanned face. Her eyes were a startling blue, slightly slanted, and somehow daring and intelligent. She could have been Soki's sister, a darker version.

"'Ware the *idmoni*, Aldric. It knows your desires," Etia said. She stepped forward, and Aldric saw she clutched a handful of rose petals in one hand. "Be gone from this hallowed place!" she shouted. "Your kind is not welcome here."

A tinkling laugh came from the intruder. "The door was open … I took it as a sign you'd reconsidered. But where are my manners?" She looked straight at Aldric. "What an unexpected pleasure. My name is … Darya, and I'm pleased to make your acquaintance."

"I'm Aldric," he said before he could stop himself. There was a sensual energy to her, a look that promised pleasure and excitement. She was a smoldering version of Soki, unnerving in her beauty.

"Bloody men," he heard Etia say.

"You look like a reasonable man," Darya said. "Perhaps we can come to an agreement. I promise you a substantial reward should you stand aside, and let the crone and me settle our differences amicably."

Etia scoffed. "That's not going to happen. I'd rather die."

"If need be."

Aldric heard fluttering wings that grew to a crescendo as loud as an angry swarm of hornets. A red stream poured out of the opening behind the woman: a flock of finches, chirping and swooping around the chamber. Almost as one, they landed to form a circle around Aldric and Etia, and alighted on the sleeping girl until she was a feathery mound. Hundreds of tiny heads turned to regard Darya, whose only reaction to the display was to raise her eyebrows.

Etia brought the rose petals to her cheek. Blood dripped from her hand and trailed down her arm.

"You look like someone I know," Aldric said to Darya.

His mind felt sluggish, his thoughts slow to form. This woman was Tainted Cabal, and all he could think about was her beauty. It struck a chord within him, vibrating through his senses and his soul.

"Do I?" she said.

"Yes. A woman named Soki. Are you related?"

Another tinkling laugh. "No. But I can be Soki if you desire. I sense a difference in you, Aldric. A divine gift." She placed a finger on one dimpled cheek and pursed her lips. "We should get to know each other better. If you'd like?" Her tone suggested she'd be extremely disappointed if he declined.

"You're wasting your time," Etia spat before Aldric could

respond. "His god is strong and won't take kindly to your meddling."

"Unlike yours," Darya retorted.

The motionless finches unsettled Aldric. They just sat there staring at Darya, covering the floor like a red carpet. Or a pool of blood, with Etia and Aldric at its center.

He grasped for his sorcerous power, and instantly his mind cleared, like a strong wind blowing away dense fog. He knew his khopesh would probably be useless and prepared a cant on his lips.

Dark, dusk-tide sorcery erupted from Darya. A small circle of finches dropped to their sides. Dead. Etia hissed in anger, and Darya raised a mocking eyebrow again. Another surge of dusk-tide sorcery, and another circle of birds fell senseless to the floor.

Darya laughed. "I've come for you, Etia, servant of a dying god."

"I do not fear death, demon."

*Demon?* wondered Aldric. She was human. Wasn't she? A fist of terror squeezed Aldric's heart. Light countered light; darkness countered darkness—this he knew. It had been drummed into him during his sorcerous training. Along with the fact that dark sorcery was malevolent and should not be used.

Darya smiled knowingly. "Your desires are as plain as the sun to us. You grow old. Weak. You fear withering away to nothing like the others of your kind. The world has forgotten you. You no longer matter."

"I matter!" screamed Etia. "I am still able to influence the world!" She fell silent, as if fearing she'd revealed too much.

"Those little birds tweeting in people's ears? Come now. Even here, in what was once the seat of your power, you are insignificant. Look at your servants. You cannot even save them."

Without warning, the warmth and serenity of his god's power flowed through Aldric. He felt a directive to go to the birds. He stepped toward them, and they opened a path for him, hopping to the side. He kneeled beside the tiny dead bodies, a puddle of red feathers. Menselas's gift surged out of him stronger than he'd ever felt before, encasing the birds, curving over their inert forms. Their tiny bodies, once lifeless, stirred. One by one, they chirped and hopped to their feet.

Before Aldric could do more than wonder at the birds' divine resurrection, his skin prickled, and an immense pressure descended upon him, pushing from all sides until he felt encased in honey. Etia and Darya must have been affected too, as they both moved sluggishly. The sensation brought the warmth of a summer's day to Aldric's skin. But Darya's mouth opened slowly in a scream of pain, her words inaudible through the syrupy presence.

*Menselas,* Aldric realized with wonder. *It has to be.*

The force disappeared as quickly as it came.

Etia stamped her foot in triumph. "Menselas has made his wishes known. The Tainted Cabal has been rebuffed. Begone, *idmoni.*"

That word again. Aldric didn't know what it meant.

Darya sighed with annoyance. "Such a tawdry name to hang upon us. Pettiness has ever been a flaw of those without the vision or ability to rise above their station."

She turned her piercing eyes on Aldric. "My offer still stands. Come to me. I sense you are troubled, perhaps … unhappy. Or … unappreciated. Yes, unappreciated. I can show you beautiful things. With us, you will become what you've always desired."

Without waiting for an answer, she spun on her heel and strode back down the tunnel. The finches followed her, but formed a mass in front of the doorway, not venturing out of the chamber. The little girl remained asleep on the floor, unaware of what had just occurred.

"You can relax now," Etia said. "And thank you. Though you

almost lost yourself there. I guess the old saying is true: *Use fire to test gold, gold to test woman, and woman to test man.*"

"What just happened?"

Aldric felt the need to have Etia confirm that one of the Tainted Cabal, an exquisite woman, had wanted to kill Etia and steal her power. Her *puske*, but had been stopped by Etia's god, whoever that was, and Menselas. That about summed it up.

"At first blush, you'd think some gods put aside their differences to stop something evil from enacting their wicked plan. That's partially correct, but it goes deeper than that."

"My god protected you, which proves you're trustworthy," he said.

"It doesn't! And he'll ask for something in return."

The very idea offended Aldric. "Menselas doesn't trade favors."

Etia barked a laugh. "Of course he does. They all do. You're young still; you'll learn eventually. Anyway, I've been doing what I can to thwart the Tainted Cabal's plans, so they sent Darya to silence me. My *puske* would be a bonus to the *idmoni*. The demons. They've been after it for many years."

Centuries, if Aldric's guess was correct. Perhaps her ancientness was a gift from her god?

Etia stumbled over to her stool and fuel-less fire and sat down. One of the finches alighted on her shoulder and chirped. She passed a weary hand over her face. "I have to sleep. I'm not as young as I once was."

"But—"

"Go," she commanded. "Darya, if that was truly her name, won't bother me for some time, if ever again. With two gods opposing her, she'll pursue easier targets. In the meantime, perhaps you should seek to learn more about the Tainted Cabal."

"Yes," Aldric said slowly. After all, he would be here in Caronath for some time. "I'll see what I can dig up. This Darya cannot be allowed to roam free. Wherever she is in Caronath, I'll find her."

To his amazement, Etia laughed. "No, you won't. She'll be hidden too well, if indeed it's a she. And besides, you're leaving the city soon."

"What? How do you know? Will Menselas give me a mission?"

The priestess gave another dried-out laugh. "His Church will. And you'd best be wary. There are old evils, and new ones, stirring. Beware the wolf in sheep's clothing."

Aldric frowned. "Aren't we allies now? Shouldn't we work together?"

"I'm indebted to your god. You could say my god is as well. That doesn't make us allies. But I'll give you some advice: Heavy currents are moving in and around Caronath. Whatever your mission, it's not going to be as simple as you think. You hold a darkness within you, Aldric."

He knew she was referring to his repository of dark-tide sorcery. "I also hold a light, and I have been touched by Menselas's gift."

"The difference between good and evil is how they use power. Now, get out of here and leave these old bones to rest."

## CHAPTER TEN

# HUNGERS

NIKLAUS FOLLOWED THE MADAM across the opulent room and into a private area to one side. His nose wrinkled at the stench in the air. Burning incense tried to cover stale sweat and mustiness, and failed. Large mirrors adorned the walls, and men of all types and ages sat on red velvet lounge chairs, each with two women draped over them. The women all wore sheer dresses that left little to the imagination, and their faces were made up, lips and cheeks red. It was an expensive establishment, and the patrons were men of means: successful merchants, bankers, and business owners. They drank and laughed and joked, while the women pretended to be amused by their jests.

The madam was provocatively garbed in a dress so tight her voluptuous figure threatened to spill out, and her long golden hair was artfully curled. Niklaus watched her ample buttocks as she walked in front of him, which was probably the point. He strode across the polished marble floor, brushed through heavy curtains into the private area, and waited patiently as the woman recited her patter, which she probably used on every customer. Lewd paintings covered the walls, which themselves were a dark red, probably designed to incite passion. Except to Niklaus, they looked drenched with blood.

He unbuckled the goddess's sword from his back and sat on a lounge. It was red, of course, and velvet. He laid the sheathed blade across his lap next to his cane, his fingers trailing the leather covering. In his mind, he could see, and imagined he felt, the design she'd scored into the blade. The goddess, *his* goddess, naked and kneeling, wings extending behind her.

A single lamp burned atop a holder, hardly enough to see by. Shadows lurked in every corner, making him uneasy. To his right was a round table, its veneered top crowded with bottles. He reached over and poured himself a glass of a golden liquor. He gulped it down, not tasting it, and not caring. Potent fumes invaded his nose, and he coughed and wiped the back of his hand across his nostrils.

The madam was staring at him. Niklaus realized he hadn't heard a word she'd said. He wiped his nose again and sniffed. "Get on with it."

"So, long, dark hair, with tanned skin?" she asked.

"That's what I said. I'll pay extra for violet eyes. A fair bit extra."

"Violet eyes? I don't think I've ever seen a girl with that color before."

Niklaus rubbed his face with both hands. "I have. She wasn't a girl though. Never mind."

The madam gave him a practiced smile and backed away through the curtain. Niklaus sighed and poured himself another drink. This one he nursed carefully, only sipping occasionally.

A few minutes later, the madam returned with three girls. She lined them up, and he saw that each one was dressed much as the other girls he'd seen, with too much skin showing and too little emotion on their faces. But what did he expect, coming to a place like this? Goddess, why was he even here? The goddess, of course. She was a part of him. Everywhere he went, everything he did, it was for her. To become closer to her. He obsessed over her, his every thought tinged with her presence. He couldn't get her out of his mind and in truth didn't want her gone. This was a poor substitute, but the next best thing.

He gulped down another mouthful of liquor while examining the girls. The madam had done her best, he supposed, but had he really expected to find the goddess here? He almost laughed at the thought. Perhaps one day she would surprise him, then probably kill him. After all these years, it would be a relief. After centuries of wandering, at least he'd get to see her.

He waved his glass towards one of the girls. "Her hair is too short."

The madam jerked her head toward the curtain, and the girl hurried out. The two that were left both smiled at him, and one drew her shoulders back so the material of her dress tightened over her nipples.

Niklaus dropped his empty glass on the table, where it wobbled, then tipped over. He stood, clutching the goddess's sword and his cane in one hand. The girl on the left was taller, but her skin wasn't as smooth or blemish-free as the other. Still, she'd do. In the dim light, with her height and her long dark hair, she came close to what he'd seen of the goddess.

He gestured to her. "That one."

Fumbling with his purse, he handed the madam some coins, and she and the other girl left.

"Thank you for choosing me," the girl said. "I won't disappoint you."

"No talking," Niklaus said.

She nodded, mouth twisting into a wry smile. Her hands moved up to undo the clasps of her dress.

"Not yet," he said. "Come here and ... love me." He closed his eyes at the desperation he heard in his own voice.

Fabric rustled as she approached. Her fingers stroked his

cheek, his chin, his neck. The scent of her wafted across him: orange blossom and amber. His pants tightened as his groin swelled. He groaned. The girl wasn't his goddess, but she was the closest he'd come to touching her, tasting her. Maybe, if he kept his eyes closed, he wouldn't know the difference. But deep inside, he knew he would. He always did. All the girls he'd used were but pale imitations of her glory. And after, the guilt and shame and longing would come crashing down on him.

He felt the pressure in his groin ease and whimpered. No! He wouldn't lose her. Not this time.

He brought his head down and touched his mouth to the girl's. The goddess's. She responded, her tongue slipping between his lips, over his teeth. Her hand crept down and pressed against him. He tangled his fingers in her silky hair and felt himself return.

Yes. The goddess was with him.

~ ~ ~

Remembering the goddess, and what he hoped to achieve, was key to not succumbing to the pit of insanity he always seemed to be circling. Nights like the last, with the goddess substitute, kept him grounded. In the beginning, when he'd realized he wasn't aging, his mind had flirted with madness, and it had taken him years to recover. Many men and women had died while anguish and desperation gripped him; and many more had died to make him whole again. But they were of no significance. *She* was all that mattered. Although at times like this, he wondered if part of him still plumbed the depths of despair.

"How can I be sure I'm getting what I'm paying for?" Niklaus asked the alchemist.

The portly man, bespectacled, with long gray hair tied back in a greasy tail, smiled as if he completed transactions like this daily. "A moment," he said, and pulled on a pair of calfskin gloves, followed by a thicker pair of leather gloves.

Using tongs, he withdrew the dull green crystal from inside its metal flask. He held the thumbnail-sized gem at arm's length and approached a table, on which sat a wire cage that held a white rat. The alchemist pressed the crystal to the cage, and the rat came sniffing. Its nose touched the gem, and the alchemist pulled it away and hastily deposited it back into the metal flask. He placed the tongs into a water bath, then screwed the flask lid on tight, sealing the gem inside.

It paid to be careful, Niklaus thought. The almost-extinct worm of Ak-Settur produced a venom that killed with the slightest touch. The crystal was supposedly imbued with the venom through some unknown sorcerous and alchemical process. It was rumored the poison was strong enough even to kill demons, who were supposed to possess an uncanny resistance.

Unaware of its fate, the rat scurried across the cage, then froze. It fell down, paralyzed except for its breathing. Its fur rippled, as if maggots moved underneath its skin. Its eyes were still, though Niklaus knew it must be in excruciating agony. Suddenly, its limbs contorted, and its neck twisted as its muscles spasmed. Slowly, its body ballooned, like a bladder filling with air. Its skin tore along one side, and a gush of thick red liquid spurted out. The rat deflated as if it had been crushed. Even its bones had dissolved.

"As you can see," said the alchemist, "the efficacy of the venom is assured."

The venom was certainly potent, Niklaus thought. On a larger animal the effects would be diminished, but a painful death was certain.

He handed over a purse bulging with gold royals and another filled with gems. Coin meant nothing to him; he could always ask the goddess's Church for more. Though the priestesses were uncertain of him and feared him, they also knew he'd been chosen by *her*.

It was the withered old Matriarch who had sent him here, claiming the goddess had given her a vision, and he was inclined to believe her. The goddess punished those who used her name without her permission, often severely, no matter how small the transgression. Once, a priestess had claimed the goddess spoke through her, and the next day she was found lifeless in her bed, pillow covered with congealed blood, her own fingers buried deep in her eye sockets.

Niklaus grasped the metal flask and left the alchemist's premises. "Be extremely careful," the man called after him. Likely, he was relieved to have survived the transaction without being killed.

After all, there was only one use for the crystal. And given the sum Niklaus had paid for it, the venom was probably intended for someone powerful. If the alchemist was wise, he'd take his coin and gems and disappear, lest the murder be traced back to him. But men were rarely wise.

~ ~ ~

"Knock on the back door, and ask for Missa. She's a scullery maid there. She's one of us."

"One of us?" echoed Niklaus.

Matriarch Adeline scowled at him. "You know what I mean. Just because you don't have breasts and a slit doesn't set you apart."

"Language, Matriarch. What would the goddess think?"

"A name is but a name, and one is as good as another. Missa will let you inside and point the way to the hidden room. Make sure you kill all the—"

"I know what to do," said Niklaus.

In order to get answers about the gods from her, he'd agreed to a few tasks as long as they were reasonable. But he didn't have to like them.

Adeline glared, but refrained from barking at him. "This is important. The goddess wills—"

"You don't know what *she* wills, old woman."

"Still your tongue! You may be her Chosen Sword, but I have served her almost my entire life. More years than you have."

*She doesn't know I'm immortal, and thinks of me only as a killer*, he thought. *She has no idea of my potential, or what I'll become. When I ascend and sit at the goddess's right hand, only then will Adeline understand. At this moment, I'm but a male she has no control over, and she hates that.*

"She appears to me," he said. "She shows me signs."

"Any fool can see omens in everyday occurrences." But her tone held uncertainty.

Niklaus let the silence grow.

"I am also visited by the goddess," Adeline continued eventually, "sometimes. This is what she commands."

"Then I'll do my best to obey. Now, if there's nothing else?"

The Matriarch shook her head. "Return when it's done. We'll be able to scry the dwelling to perceive the results."

A short time later, Niklaus was knocking on the back door of the expansive house. A timid, mousy woman let him in. Her eyes were slightly too wide apart, no doubt from some Charral blood in her ancestry. It was rare these days, as the Charral were a much-diminished species.

*Probably a good thing*, he thought. *She looks like she couldn't count to twenty with her shoes off.*

"Thank you, Missa," he said.

She bobbed her head. "May the goddess protect you," and her voice held more fervor than many of her priestesses'.

"I find it advisable never to expect anything," replied Niklaus. "That way you're never disappointed. I presume no other servants are awake? Good. Then lead the way."

She crossed the kitchen, her skirts rustling. "Please be quiet," she said softly. "There was a disturbance last night, a thief. The master was informed, but he wasn't concerned, so I guess nothing of value was taken. Still, the servants are wary and suspicious of strange noises."

"Then let's be quick. Show me the door, and get yourself back to bed. If there's a ruckus, it's best you're not found walking the corridors."

Missa nodded solemnly, as if both proud and humbled she had found a way to serve the goddess. He wondered if she'd be so proud once the bloodshed started.

She led Niklaus out of the kitchen, and they ascended a narrow servants' staircase at the back of the dwelling, keeping to one side so the boards didn't creak. They paused midway along a hallway where a massive painting adorned the wall. A family probably: a man, woman, and their two brats. Missa groped behind the gilded frame, presumably triggering a locking mechanism as the painting swung open on well-oiled hinges. She stepped back, her skirt clenched in her hands. Her task was complete.

"Go now," Niklaus said gently. "You will be above suspicion. The goddess thanks you."

A timid smile broke out on her face, and she hurried back down the hallway and then the stairs. Niklaus waited until her footsteps had faded. Then he waited some more. The house was quiet, as it should be at this time of night. But wouldn't remain so for long.

He drew *her* sword from its sheath. As always, his breath caught at the sight of the magnificently crafted blade. His eyes were drawn to the exquisitely detailed figure of Sylva Kalisia, her mouth stretched in a sardonic smile. Goddess, she was beautiful. His fingers traced her outline in the metal, tingling as they caressed her. She'd touched the blade herself, here in the material world.

Niklaus swallowed and shook his head. With any luck he

wouldn't need to use *her* sword, but the unprepared usually got what they deserved. Death.

Behind the secret door, the space was devoid of light. He paused, allowing his eyes to adjust. The wooden walls and floor took on a gray cast, and he could see as if it were dusk. One of the gifts *she'd* bestowed upon him.

He swiftly reached the bottom of a set of stairs, where a metal door blocked his path. Orichalcum. With a Sandoval locking mechanism.

Sandoval had been a grumpy old prig of a man who'd somehow managed to leverage slightly above average talent into a huge success. That memory, at least, was clear to Niklaus. Sandoval had died from choking on his own vomit after a three-day drinking spree when the woman he was courting, thirty years younger than him, had spurned his advances. Good riddance, Niklaus thought. He'd never liked the man.

Squatting, he placed his ear against the door beside the lock. With his free hand, he turned the first dial until he heard a tiny click of metal, too faint for any normal person to discern. Another of *her* gifts. He had all four dials aligned correctly in a few moments. The handle turned smoothly, and he entered a corridor reeking of decayed flesh.

He lifted *her* sword, prepared for anything, but nothing stirred.

Breathing through his nose, Niklaus found he could stand the stench. It was bad, but he'd smelled worse. The field strewn with days-old corpses in the aftermath of the Battle of Yellow Plain had been ghastlier than this, with maggots and flies, rats and vultures feeding on the dead. He'd had to burn his clothes to be rid of the smell.

The floor was dusty and marked with trails denoting numerous comings and goings. The corridor opened into a round room with a wooden door opposite. Hanging from the high ceiling were two butchered men. The stench seemed to be coming from a half-barrel against one wall. He glanced inside to see their discarded innards.

Scratching noises came from behind the door. At least he knew he was in the right place. It seemed the Matriarch's sources were good, though why she was concerned about demons was another matter. Usually, the goddess left such creatures to their own devices, not caring what they got up to in the world of men. Their domain was not hers to meddle in. Which begged the question: what had changed?

He observed the corpses hanging from the ceiling. Demons didn't eat their meat the way these men had been prepared. They preferred live prey, its blood hot and spurting. Which meant something, or someone, else was at play here. And to be active in Caronath, indeed, to have servants, they had to remain unnoticed. What creature that ate human flesh was also able to pass as human in a city this size? Niklaus could count the options on one hand, and some would require considerable sorcery to disguise their true nature. In Caronath, with its powerful sorcerous practitioners and high priests and priestesses of numerous gods and goddesses, such a sorcerer would likely be found out in short order.

Which left only one possibility: a follower of Nysrog. And not a weak one either. Powerful enough to operate in Caronath undetected. And a flesh-eater, a human corrupted by demonic sorcery or possessed of demon blood themselves.

*Blood and damnation.*

And the goddess was making a move against them.

Niklaus smiled. Perhaps this was an opportunity. The Tainted Cabal, as the followers of Nysrog were known, had to know more about the veil between life and death, and godhood, than anyone else alive. If alive they truly were. Perhaps the goddess was showing him the way, providing him with an opportunity to further his knowledge, to aid his quest. The thought warmed him, making his chest swell. She was guiding him. She did want him by her side.

Carefully, he removed a wooden rod from his pocket. There was a metal knob on one end, fastened with a cunning latch. He removed the covering to reveal the green crystal imbued with venom from the worm of Ak-Settur. To his goddess-aided sight, it seemed to glow from within.

*The bodies first,* he thought. If he contaminated the innards first, the smell would transfer to the curing meat, and the demons might become suspicious. That wouldn't do.

He rubbed the crystal over the butchered men, then over the intestines and livers, hearts and kidneys, lungs and stomachs in the half-barrel. The poison immediately killed the maggots writhing on the offal, but that didn't concern him. The demons wouldn't recognize the danger. It was whatever had summoned them that he had to watch out for.

Niklaus dragged the half-barrel toward the wooden door. It was unlocked, and the scratching noises ceased when he turned the handle. He jerked the door open and shoved the barrel inside. Snarls erupted from fanged mouths beneath orange eyes. He yanked the door shut and listened as the demons devoured the tainted innards. Tearing sounds were punctuated by growls and wet slaps as offal hit the floor.

It didn't take long. One by one, the demons grew still. Some mewled pitifully before succumbing to the venom, but most made no sound.

When there had been silence for a few minutes, Niklaus opened the door. He prodded the closest limp body with his boot. They looked like minor demons: yellow leathery skin with a scalelike pattern, and mottled brown horns jutting from their heads and backs. Their offal-covered mouths were open, their eyes unseeing. He was glad he hadn't had to use her sword on them. It would have felt like he was polluting the goddess-touched steel.

The demons might have been weak, but there were many of them. A dozen or so. Whoever controlled them was powerful, probably protected by sorcery and perhaps even a major demon.

Niklaus sighed. He should have known the goddess wouldn't make his task easy. After all, he had to prove himself worthy of her.

Well, this task was done. Time to leave. He chuckled at the thought of the Cabal member's face when they found their demons slaughtered. With any luck, they wouldn't think their own meat was contaminated. Niklaus didn't think they'd be that stupid, but it was worth the attempt.

As he turned to go, a small book on a side table caught his eye. The diagram on the cover was unmistakable. Stitched with silver thread, it showed a clawed and winged being ascending from flames. A demon. And its image on a book such as this could only mean one thing. The book was a grimoire. Evidence and mysteries of the unholy cabal, there for the taking. Secrets upon secrets.

He peered closer and saw that a clasp locked the book, its metal gleaming in the dim light. Demon sorcery, no doubt, a deadly trap to claim whoever tampered with it.

He hesitated, then, overcome by temptation, tucked the fell tome into his pocket. The Tainted Cabal must know more about piercing the veil between worlds than anyone else, and it was likely the grimoire contained information he would find useful, if not outright revelatory.

But he'd need to find a sorcerer to unlock its secrets. Either one who didn't fear the Cabal—and, as such, a fool. Or one to whom such valuable knowledge was worth any risk.

Eckart was too weak, but perhaps he would know of such a sorcerer.

## CHAPTER ELEVEN

# AN INITIAL TASK

ALDRIC STOOD IN THE middle of the paved square in front of the Church of Menselas. In truth, the word church didn't do the building justice. It was—he searched for the right word—imposing. Steeples rose into the cloudless sky; archways and buttresses punctuated the stone walls, every inch of which were decorated with carvings. There were many stained-glass windows, ranging from smaller simple depictions to the great scarlet rose above the entrance: a complex symbol made from intricate patterns.

He shaded his eyes against the sun to peer at the wooden scaffolding that enclosed one section, where workers scrubbed away grime and bird droppings. The edifice was magnificent, but there were many nooks and crannies where birds could nest. Even the god wasn't immune to nature.

A number of lesser churches lined the square. Closest to the Church of Menselas were the houses of worship dedicated to Antiam, the supposed mother of all creation, and the Lady Sylva Kalisia, a goddess for degenerates. Worshipers of all faiths mingled among the numerous market stalls set up in the square. Many sold hot food to the hungry people finished with their worship: meat on wooden skewers cooked over charcoal; pies and pastries warmed in portable ovens on the beds of wagons. Children dressed in their best clothes chased each other, dodging around people and between stalls, their shouts rising over the general hubbub.

Aldric had put off this day long enough, and it was already close to the predicted time of his arrival. He'd enjoyed his time with Soki as she showed him her city; she'd been a source of much knowledge for him, and they'd gotten to know each other quite well. But after what had happened with Etia at the Night Steps, he'd decided his break from responsibility had to end. He was here on secondment to assist the Church in any way he could, and it was time he informed them of his arrival. Besides, they needed to know about Etia and the Tainted Cabal's attempts to steal her power. That the demon worshipers were active in Caronath wasn't to be ignored. Or perhaps that was why the Church here had requested help.

Bells began to toll, marking the end of the afternoon's service. Birds scattered from the bell tower and flew around in a circle until the clanging stopped. Worshipers filed down the steps, hundreds of them: men and women who bowed their heads to Menselas and sent their prayers to one of his five aspects. Couples held each other's hands, and their children's, while youngsters helped the elderly negotiate their descent to the square. Nobles chatted with businessmen and women, and commoners were treated almost as equals.

Such a situation, Aldric knew, only lasted until the warmth of the service left them, and they lost sight of the church. He sighed. It was a start, but human nature was human nature. And here in the north, on the edge of civilization, where existence was so much harder than in most other places, it was the best that could be hoped for.

He adjusted his khopesh, which hung from his hip, and straightened his collar. Running a hand through his hair, he ascended the steps. Inside, the pews and paintings and altars were illuminated by sorcerous lamps. Five marble statues stood at the center of the cavernous space, one on each side of a tessellated pentagon, each lit from all angles by lanterns of a specific color.

Aldric made his way up the nave, in between rows of pews, noting a number of worshipers still praying: an old woman, a young girl barely out of her teens, a weeping man with a bushy gray beard. Acolytes were busily sweeping, mopping, and dusting. One would approach him eventually, but he was grateful for the time to adjust. He paused to examine the statues. Each was a masterwork, likely having taken months to produce. Aldric faced the Elder first and bowed his head, then did the same to the other four: the Mother, the Healer, the Warrior, and lastly the Hooded One—or Death, as he was originally known.

A blue-robed priest approached, seeming hesitant if Aldric should be disturbed or not. "May I help you?" he said eventually. His eyes widened as he noticed the crescent blade hanging from Aldric's hip, and he grimaced in distaste. "The Warrior's service is—"

"I'm here to see Hierophant Karianne. I've traveled a long way at her behest."

"I can take your name and add it to the list of petitioners waiting to see Her Holiness." His tone indicated it would be a long time, if ever, before Aldric was seen.

There were murmurs from one side of the church. Aldric turned to see a white-haired man in a frayed scarlet robe rushing toward him past open-mouthed priests. He wore battered sandals and was sweating by the time he was close enough to talk to. The worn symbols on his robes signified he was an archbishop, but clearly he didn't care for material wealth. The sign of a dedicated holy man, Aldric thought.

"Tell the settler to wait for us outside," the archbishop told the priest, who nodded and hurried away.

The archbishop guided Aldric through a doorway and into a side room. Aldric concealed his irritation at the fact the man seemed to want him out of the way.

"Please, sit," the archbishop said, and turned his penetrating pale blue eyes on Aldric. "We were wondering when you'd show up."

His white hair stuck out from his head, above prominent features: a hooked nose, jutting eyebrows and cheeks. His face was tense, eyes hard and unflinching, and his bloodless lips were drawn into a line, as if he struggled to contain his disapproval. It was exactly the unfriendly welcome Aldric had expected, and one of the reasons he'd delayed reporting for his new position. A cold reception, from the people who'd asked for him and held his reins. He would simply do his best, as he always did, and hope his actions and manner went some way to persuading the priests of Caronath of the depth of his faith and his desire to serve Menselas.

Aldric unbuckled his khopesh and hung the belt from a hook next to the door. There were a few padded armchairs, and he sat in one, while the archbishop sat across from him. The man adjusted his robes as if stalling for time, or trying to think of what to say.

"My name is Archbishop Hannus," he said finally, with a thin smile. "And I take it you're Magister Aldric Kermoran. There wouldn't be anyone else of your bearing and demeanor coming here. I saw the god's mark on you from the other side of the church. It is a deep one."

As was Hannus's. To Aldric's divine sight, it shone a brilliant green. He quickly closed those senses, and the room dimmed to normal.

"I hope to use it as Menselas sees fit," he replied. "To help people."

Hannus glanced at Aldric and frowned, then lowered his eyes

and pretended to examine the archbishop's ring that adorned his finger. It was set with a cut emerald—green, like the mark of the god. Against his pious appearance, it stood out like a sore thumb.

"You also have other talents," Hannus said. "And it is those we are in need of. Your course may not be in the direction you would like, but it is the one the god has set you on."

Aldric stiffened at the words, then forced himself to relax. Here was a man he could respect. To lash out at him because of his own circumstance wouldn't do anyone any good.

"I know I was sent here at the request of the Hierophant. I'd rather talk to Her Holiness about what I'm to do in Caronath."

Hannus let out a weary sigh. "Her Holiness doesn't want to meet with you," he said bluntly. "Which is why you're talking to me. Your other talents don't sit well with her."

*She doesn't want to be polluted by me,* Aldric thought. He hadn't expected that here, of all places, where they needed his help.

He kept himself under control and said, "I will do Menselas's will."

Hannus nodded and rubbed his hands together. "Good. And just as well—something has come up."

"Before you begin, I must tell you of my experiences since I arrived in Caronath."

"That can wait—"

"No. It cannot."

Hannus stared at Aldric with barely concealed annoyance. He probably didn't get interrupted often.

As quickly as he could, Aldric gave a summary of his encounter with Etia, and with Darya of the Tainted Cabal. He paced as he spoke, unable to keep still in his chair. When he'd finished, he listened as Archbishop Hannus listed half a dozen reasons why his encounter with Etia wasn't significant. He was beginning to think reporting to the man was a mistake. It seemed it wasn't just Her Holiness who wasn't comfortable with Aldric's sorcerous abilities.

"Etia is a high priestess," Aldric added. "If I had to guess which god she serves, I'd say some sort of old volcano god, based on the red finches and fire and the obsidian."

"She is not unknown to us," Hannus said.

"Someone tried to kill her," repeated Aldric. "The Tainted Cabal. Menselas intervened."

The archbishop laughed. "So you say, but what evidence do you have? She's the servant of an old god, one with no relevance any more. She was probably deceiving you. And what does it matter if she disappears? Good riddance, I say. We have enough problems of our own to worry about without adding to them."

"But, Archbishop—"

"Enough!" barked Hannus. "Although we requested assistance, you're here on sufferance. We will not replace you and send you back in disgrace, but we will send dispatches to Archbishop Roald, detailing any wayward conduct. And I won't lose any sleep over it."

"I understand." Aldric kept his voice devoid of emotion. He'd run out of things he dared say. Hannus's cold and bloodless logic sat uneasily with him. The archbishop's office seemed oppressive, and Aldric now regretted coming to him and sharing what he knew. But what was done was done.

Etia's words came back to him: *Heavy currents are moving in and around Caronath*, and *There are old evils, and new ones, stirring. Beware the wolf in sheep's clothing.*

Was he being guided by Menselas? Or was he only a pawn in whatever Hannus had in motion? Aldric had been used enough by the Church to know his true value to them. He had to believe his god steered him, or he might abandon his faith entirely. Already, he clung to it by a thread.

"There is more going on here than you're allowed to know," Hannus said. "Trust the Church. Trust me. Focus on the tasks we give you. There are mysteries here, but we have them under control."

Aldric remained silent. Was this another test? When would the Church stop testing him? Never, probably. He scratched the stubble on his cheek, then glanced at his khopesh. He knew what the archbishop would want. The Church had decided how his talents might benefit them best, and they would make full use of him.

"May I spend some time with the healers?" he asked eventually. "My skills are getting rusty, and I'd like to brush up on them. It helps me to reconnect to the Healer aspect of Menselas." Seeing Hannus begin to shake his head, Aldric quickly continued. "The god gave me this talent also, to be used, revered, and given freely. On my journey, I took a short cut through the wilderness, where I gathered rare herbs and plants when I came across them. The healers will be glad of them."

Hannus clasped his hands together and shifted in his armchair. "All right. I suppose they could use your assistance, briefly. A few hours tomorrow morning. This far north, away from most of civilization, there are a lot more run-ins with Dead-eyes and the like. Evil creatures."

Aldric felt his chest loosen a little and looked away from the pity in Hannus's eyes. A few hours were better than nothing. He could insist on longer, and Hannus couldn't use his rank to stop him—the gift of the god's mark was venerated and useful, there was no denying it. But making enemies on his first day would be a bad start. Especially with Her Holiness already shunning him.

"What is the situation you need help with?" he asked. "I've traveled a long way to get here and was taken off another job for the Church."

"Well, it's nothing mundane, I can tell you. And there's already a complication. First, some settlers found a nice valley, and by all accounts have been living there for years. But now they've had a run-in with Dead-eyes."

"A run-in?"

"Dozens of the creatures. Came down from the cliffs surrounding the valley, apparently, and they weren't just after chickens or smaller livestock. According to what I've been told, they attacked the settlers over a period of days—well, nights, really. At the time of full-dark, when the Dead-eyes are usually most active. Eventually, they were driven off, but these people aren't warriors. They're hurt and scared and need help. Since then, there have been a number of attacks, though not of the same ferocity as the first. They are worried the Dead-eyes might come again in force, which could spell the end for the settlement."

Full-dark was when both moons stayed below the horizon, and in the inky darkness the Dead-eyes were most active.

Aldric's hand drifted toward his belt where his khopesh usually hung. He stopped it. "You have brought me here to help defend a settlement against Dead-eyes? Why can't soldiers do it?"

"This happened after we'd requested someone of your ... abilities. But there's more. The settlers searched for where the Dead-eyes had scaled down the cliffs, to see if they could do anything to block their return. It was thought they came through one of the nearby caves, which could lead to an opening outside the valley. They discovered a ruin inside one of the caves: a great door surrounded by carvings, and some orichalcum sheets covered with ancient writing. You know the type."

Aldric shifted restlessly. There was something the archbishop wasn't telling him, he could feel it. "You want me to attempt to translate the writing? Or to explore the ruins?"

"The writing isn't important," Hannus said, looking away. "But from our historical records and the shared memories of the Church's relics, we think this ruin is unique."

*The writing is important,* realized Aldric. Why was Hannus lying to him? "Were soldiers sent to deal with the Dead-eyes?"

"They were, except the fractious creatures never appeared

again. Probably because the nights of full-dark have passed, and the moons light the night sky again."

Fractious. A callous way to describe the terrible frenzy of the Dead-eyes when they raided, and the deaths and chaos they caused.

"The soldiers waited," Hannus continued, "but when the Dead-eyes didn't return, they left. The settlers have sent a representative to petition us for help—an old man they could easily spare from the look of him. A few idealistic priests took up his cause and have petitioned the bishops to take action. My peers were reluctant to do so. Only I saw it as our chance to show solidarity in the face of evil. We are not a callous, uncaring faith." He shook his head. "In the name of charity and our service to Menselas, we must take a stand against the Dead-eyes. The creatures have plagued us for far too long."

Hannus's enthusiasm was palpable, but Aldric saw the task for what it was. *A babysitting mission.*

"You want me to travel to the settlement, train the people there, and deal with the Dead-eyes," he confirmed.

"Correct. This will be your first task. And ... the settlers might have taken more from the ruins than they admitted. Find out if they have, and what it is. Bring everything back to me."

And there it was: what Hannus really wanted.

"Do they have a firm idea of the number of Dead-eyes we're talking about?"

"A few dozen. The settlers have had a bad time of it. That's why they sent to us for assistance. In truth, I welcome the opportunity. The Dead-eyes are evil, and the fewer of them in the world, the better."

Aldric had never heard a priest of the Five refer to the other races that shared this world as evil. They just ... were. And he was concerned that if there was a tribe of Dead-eyes preying on the settlement, instead of groups of nomads or scavengers, he wouldn't be able to cope on his own. Then again, perhaps Hannus didn't care if the settlement was destroyed. No, that was uncharitable. As an archbishop of the Five, Hannus had to be good-hearted, didn't he?

"I can't take on an entire tribe on my own," Aldric said. "If—"

"We've already assembled a team. And someone from another Church will be joining you, a mercenary of some sort. This will be a joint effort to show harmony among the gods."

"I'd rather choose my own men. I need people I can trust—"

Hannus cut him off with a sharp gesture. "I'm not giving you an option. We've gone to the effort of putting together a team for you, so the least you could do is be grateful."

Suppressing a sigh, Aldric nodded. "As long as they're experienced fighters. If it is a tribe of Dead-eyes, we might have to track them to their clan and destroy them all."

Hannus waved a hand, and his emerald ring glittered in the light. "Two faiths are cooperating here. I needn't stress to you how important it is we put our best foot forward in everything we do. You'll be given gold and whatever equipment you need. The … talismans"—Hannus spat the word—"you use … well, you can use some of the funds we give you for them."

Aldric gave Hannus a flat stare. "I only require one. And I try to use sorcery as little as possible."

"Yes, well, be that as it may, you must use whatever talents you have to complete this task. And remember, find whatever artifacts the settlers have taken from the ruins, and bring them to me." Hannus pursed his lips and narrowed his eyes as if a thought had just occurred to him. "Although perhaps it would be better if you investigated the ruins yourself. Eventually the settlers will become curious, their fear overcome by greed. If they were to commission a rogue sorcerer and explore the place themselves, that could be dangerous. Those not bound by our agreement with the Covenants are selfish and despicable."

Aldric was getting mixed messages, and he didn't like it. It was obvious that Hannus trusted him far less than Roald did, which was hardly at all, and consequently was giving him as little information as possible.

Having had enough of the charade, Aldric stood. "Very well. When do I meet this mercenary? And where is the team you've already assembled?"

He didn't like having unknown warriors thrust upon him, but it seemed he didn't have a choice. And if he fought with Hannus the first time they met, it wouldn't bode well for his appointment in Caronath.

Hannus rose to his feet and smoothed his faded robes with both hands. His fingers found and picked at a stray thread. Once again Aldric was impressed by the man's apparent poverty and sanctity. But Hannus's coldness toward him reminded him of Etia's comment about wolves in sheep's clothing. Maybe she was warning him against the archbishop. Immediately he felt ashamed for thinking badly of one of his god's servants, a man no doubt far holier than Aldric was himself.

"You'll meet him tomorrow," said Hannus, "and the team shortly after. In the morning, spend a few hours with our healers; then you'll need to take charge of the mission. We don't know when the Dead-eyes will strike again, though we strongly suspect at the next full-dark, in around eleven days. Now, come and meet the old settler."

On the way out of the room, Hannus paused and frowned, as if only just remembering something. He touched Aldric's arm, and they halted, Aldric just outside the room, Hannus a step inside.

"I was told you were given a relic to bring with you," Hannus said cautiously.

"I was," Aldric said, equally as cautious. "Though it wasn't given to me to bring here. It was given to me for my personal use."

He knew the relics were a favorite gossip subject among the priests. Through centuries of guesswork, the Church had surmised the relics were ranked in some indefinable way, and priests had to prove themselves to gain access to different experiences. While the dreams the relics brought weren't secret, talking about what you'd experienced was discouraged and could lead to harsh punishment.

"The missive said the relic was one of the rarer ones, from the time when Nysrog walked the earth and gathered his filthy cabal of sorcerers. I would like to borrow it. For a few nights, at least."

What Hannus was suggesting was against the strictest rules of the Church. Aldric steeled himself to reply.

"The relics granted to priests are for their own use and not to be given to anyone else. Such an act is a serious crime against the Church."

"Traditionalists!" exclaimed Hannus. "I suppose you got that from Roald, Menselas bless him. Such a stickler for the rules. Those of us with a more progressive leaning prefer collegiality and sharing. I would have thought someone of your reputation within the Church would want to get off on the right foot here."

Aldric fumed inside. What the archbishop wanted was unconscionable, and he knew it.

"I'll consider your request," he replied tersely.

"Good," Hannus said with a thin smile. "But not for too long. Now, let's go and see this settler."

~ ~ ~

The settler was the old man Aldric had seen weeping in the church. He was standing by the great doors, a scruffy hat crumpled in his hands. His rough-spun clothes were patched and stained, as though the dirt was ingrained into the fabric. They were wrinkled too, as if he'd been sleeping in them. Up close, Aldric could see the man was fit for his age, his bearing solid and strong. A man used to physical labor, face and hands weathered by the sun.

He shook the old man's hand, then gripped his shoulder. "I'm here to help," he said, meaning it. "Hopefully, it will only take a day to get the men ready, and then we can get you back to your settlement."

"Another day?" the man said. "I've been here too long already."

"My good man," Hannus said, "you can't rush these things. Sending a few mercenaries instead of a full team of warriors won't do much to help."

"What's your name?" Aldric asked.

"Neb."

"Well, Neb, I promise you I'll do everything I can to keep your settlement and your people safe. The Dead-eyes came on a moonless night, correct? If they're going to come back, they'll wait for another one. They don't attack in numbers unless it's full-dark."

"Well, I still need to get back. We can't spare any hands at the settlement. You look like you can handle yourself. We'll need more of your type."

"And you'll get them," Hannus interjected. "Just remember the deal we struck. We need everything of interest you found outside the ruin, and no exploring inside either. Leave that to the experts. Though I'm sure you wouldn't be able to pass the door." He looked outside at the darkening sky. "It's getting late, and Magister Aldric here has an early start, don't you, Aldric?"

"Yes. Meet me in front of this church at midday," he said to Neb. He should be finished with the healers by then.

"Excellent," said Hannus. "I'll bring your companion from the other Church at the same time, and you can all get acquainted. Now, if you don't mind, it's time for my prayers, and then I have some urgent business to attend to."

Neb watched the archbishop's retreating back with an expression Aldric couldn't identify.

"Where are you staying?" Aldric asked.

Neb's eyes shifted to his. "About. We couldn't spare much coin."

Aldric took a few silver royals from his purse. "Here."

"I don't need no charity."

Aldric pressed them into his hand. "Take them, from the Church of Menselas. Get a good night's rest and some hot food into you. We'll be leaving as soon as possible, and I want to travel hard. Do you have a horse?"

"No. Walked here."

"I'll get you one."

"I don't need no—"

"It's not a gift; it's a loan from the Church. I'll take it back with me. As I said, get some rest. And meet me here at midday tomorrow."

He left the settler standing alone on the steps, his hat scrunched in his grip.

## CHAPTER TWELVE

# ONE STEP FORWARD

NIKLAUS STRODE THROUGH THE darkness and drumming rain. Only a few others were walking the streets, the downpour keeping most at home or at work, waiting for a lull. He wore an oilskin coat and a wide-brimmed hat, both of which had served him well over the many years since he'd taken them from a dead man. His boots were soaked, but the workmanship was of good quality, and his feet remained dry.

The tavern Eckart the Lost had told him about was up ahead. Niklaus ducked under the awning above the door. This had better be the right place, or Eckart would become as lost as a corpse floating in a canal.

*No,* Niklaus admonished himself. *I need him.*

At least the necromancer had been of some use so far. His work was progressing well, or so he said. And he'd been able to tell Niklaus of a scholar who had delved deep beneath the city and recently found an artifact that might assist with Niklaus's task. With the expedition Matriarch Adeline wanted him on leaving soon, Niklaus had to follow this lead up now and make sure the business was concluded before he left Caronath. He'd likely be gone weeks, which was annoying, but what did he have if not time?

From inside the establishment came the sounds of merriment—the hum of conversation and laughter. After the chill of the rain, the warmth of the place hit him like a wave. Against one wall was a large brick fireplace, though now only smoldering coals remained. A scruffy man with a bristly beard bent over them to ignite a splinter of wood, which he used to light a cheap corncob pipe. The atmosphere was humid and stale, and Niklaus's nose wrinkled at the stench of unwashed bodies, smoke, damp wool, and stale beer. Dirt had been swept into corners, and the stained tables shone with grease and spilled drink. Most of the crowd was in a cheerful mood, drinking, carousing, gambling, and pawing the whores. There were rowdy thugs from the dark back streets of Caronath; travelers with accents from distant lands who'd come to the city for unguessable purposes; mercenaries sporting too many weapons and scars; and seductively clad prostitutes whose laughter rang false to Niklaus's ears and never reached their hard eyes. A few card games were in progress, coins neatly stacked in front of the participants. He suppressed the urge to join one.

In the corners of the room, small groups of men hunched over their drinks and spoke in low whispers, ignored by the rest of the patrons. A person's business was their own, and in this tavern the city guard rarely appeared, except to collect bribes. A man sitting alone at a side table caught Niklaus's notice, and he let his gaze slide casually over him, as if he didn't observe anything out of the ordinary. The man was huge, and the hands clasped about his mug were deeply tanned and calloused. All brawn and not much brain, if Niklaus had to guess. A slight twitch of his head when he'd noticed Niklaus had given him away. *Someone with an interest in me.* Well, he'd find out what soon enough. Then perhaps there'd be another corpse added to Caronath's many other deaths tonight. Murders happened all too frequently in cities, especially in the poorer districts.

Niklaus's gaze turned to the tavern keeper, a scarecrow of a man with a thin smile plastered on his gaunt face. Pale skin attested to the fact he spent most of his time indoors, no doubt busy with the tasks required to run such a dive.

Taking off his hat, Niklaus made his way to the bar and signaled to catch the tavern keeper's attention.

"What'll it be?"

"I'm here to see Ikel."

A man known for his nefarious connections and access to almost anything you wanted to get your hands on—even extremely rare artifacts of power looted from ruins that most of these scum would kill for, though most of the men in this bar would be too terrified to go near a ruin.

"What drink?" The tavern keeper spoke as if he hadn't heard Niklaus's request.

"A beer. Something pale. With no bugs in it."

Taking a tin mug, the man filled it from one of the barrels behind the bar and placed it in front of Niklaus. "That'll be a gold royal."

Niklaus paused. Obviously, he was paying for more than the drink. A gold royal would buy the entire barrel. He clicked a gold coin onto the counter and slid it toward the tavern keeper. A stranger standing next to Niklaus glanced at the coin, then away.

The tavern keeper's pallid fingers picked the coin up and tapped it on the counter while his shrewd eyes considered Niklaus. After a few moments, he sniffed and jerked his head toward a heavy curtain covering a doorway next to the bar. "Back rooms. Third door on the left. Knock three times."

Niklaus nodded and drained his mug. To his surprise, the beer was actually quite tasty. He licked foam from his lips and pushed his way past a few of the tavern's patrons. A stocky mercenary wearing a scuffed leather harness festooned with blades glared at him, but looked away when Niklaus returned the stare. Most dogs knew their betters when they came across them. You didn't live long in the business if you misjudged people.

The hallway was quieter, the thick material of the hanging deadening sound and filtering out most of the stink.

Niklaus knocked on the third door three times, waited a moment, then entered.

An old man clad in homespun trousers and coat sat on a low chair behind a desk. Next to him was a brazier filled with glowing coals. He glanced up as Niklaus entered, then went back to making notes in a thick ledger. His liver-spotted skin was a greenish-brown, but despite his age his black hair was still thick, though trimmed short. Perhaps he dyed it.

"I take it you're Ikel?" said Niklaus.

The description matched: the man's Illapa blood showed in the color of his skin. The Illapa were a usually passive race of people who lived in the forests and worshiped nature and weather or some such nonsense. From what Niklaus recalled, they were fond of smoking hallucinogenic herbs and fungi.

"Indeed I am." Ikel pointed the end of his pen at an empty chair against one wall. "Please, sit."

Niklaus placed Ikel's accent as from the Pristart Combine in the far south-west, a very long way away. But that wasn't surprising. Caronath was a lure for many opportunists. His manners were a contrast to his rough clothes, but Niklaus well knew you couldn't judge someone based on their appearance. One of the deadliest killers he'd known was a man only a hair over five feet tall, with a thin frame and a boyish face that made mothers offer him cookies and milk.

Niklaus perched on a corner of the chair. *Her* sword on his back was awkward sometimes, like now. But he would never leave it behind or remove it.

"My name is Niklaus du Plessis."

"I've heard your name before. The priestesses of Sylva Kalisia don't seem to know what to make of you."

That Ikel knew this gave Niklaus pause. Not many in Caronath knew of him or his involvement with the goddess. Ikel must have little birds everywhere, telling him all manner of secrets. A dangerous man.

"The priestesses are flustered by what they can't control," he replied. "They like to keep everything in a box they hold the key to, or on a leash."

"Indeed. And you look like a man who would chafe at a leash. And perhaps bite the person holding the other end." Ikel cleared his throat, then took a sip of water from a crystal goblet. "Forgive my abruptness, but my time is limited. Can I help you with something?"

"I'm looking for the scholar Valter. I've heard rumor he's been unearthing some … intriguing items. But I can't find him. I'm conducting my own research and hope to gain his insight, as well as view any special items he might have in his possession."

Ikel gave him a considering look. "Pardon me if this seems discourteous, but you don't exactly have a scholarly look."

Usually Niklaus would remain silent in such a situation, encouraging Ikel to underestimate him, but he had nothing to fear from this man. And this was his best chance to find Valter.

"I have a particular interest in the cataclysms," he began. "And have qualifications from the Arcanum in Riem and the Thaumaturgy School in Kroe. I've studied *The Epistemologies of Eilwyn* extensively and *The Annals of Terrant.*"

Dissecting or critiquing either of these thick multi-volumed works was usually a lifetime's endeavor for a scholar.

"Eilwyn, eh? A thoughtful woman. A scholar's scholar."

Niklaus inclined his head. He knew from personal experience that her version of some crucial moments in history were incorrect, but there was no point arguing.

"So, tell me," continued Ikel, switching to ancient Rho-uric, a later variant of Skanuric, "what do you believe happens after death?" His accent was atrocious, and he faltered slightly as he searched for the next word.

He looked at Niklaus expectantly, waiting for him to plead ignorance. No one who hadn't studied for years at one of the prominent universities would be able to speak, or read, Rho-uric. It was spoken only by scholars, as many of the surviving histories were written in the later variant. In his clumsy testing of Niklaus, Ikel had revealed a detail about himself.

"Really, Sur-Ikel," Niklaus replied in flawless Rho-uric, using the common form of address, "was it too hard to imagine I am telling the truth? Enough of these games. Either you can lead me to Valter or you cannot. Which is it?"

Ikel switched back to the common tongue. "My apologies, Niklaus. Please forgive me. Despite my precautions, a few fraudsters find their way to me. I was merely trying to ascertain your legitimacy. I see now that you are genuine." He cleared his throat noisily. "Valter is known to me, but I must tell you he values his privacy."

"I can pay well."

"Good. That's good. But coin isn't the only consideration. However, I think Valter wouldn't mind meeting with a knowledgeable researcher such as yourself."

"Then let us make arrangements. And by the way, when most people die, they are consumed by maggots and worms and become dust. It is impossible to construe a mind that continues in an afterlife. But for a very slender few, there is godhood."

Ikel smiled thinly. "That's two theories. Neither of which I ascribe to."

~ ~ ~

It was almost midnight by the time Niklaus reached the hills behind Caronath. They were thinly treed and scarred by swathes of deforested areas and canyons. The Crystal River, fed by snowmelt from the high Ymaltian Mountains far to the north—the home of Margebian, the so-called Witch of Winter—cut a twisted path through north Caronath and then flowed east to spill into the Trackless Ocean. Named for its clear waters, which swelled in the spring and summer months, the river was the lifeblood of the city, providing a plentiful supply of water, along with fat salmon in the winter months. Niklaus had only lived a short time in the city and already he was heartily sick of the fish.

Niklaus looked around, making sure to keep his guide in sight—a half-wild mountaineer supplied by Ikel who talked to himself and constantly chewed cravv leaves that stained his lips and teeth black. The guide, Grogan, wasn't long for this world at the rate he consumed the addictive narcotic. It was a wonder he could still walk and talk coherently. But he knew his business, Niklaus had to admit. They'd traveled along barely discernible trails into the hills, which were honeycombed with tombs, some of which descended to the cities buried by the cataclysms underneath Caronath—or so the rumors went.

Only the hills closest to Caronath were still used for burials, a few miles north of the city, and the paths and tombs farther out around here were abandoned. The people of Caronath rarely interred riches with their dead, only burial clothes and occasionally jewelry hardly worth a few copper royals. So there was nothing to tempt grave robbers. Besides, the ghouls and Dead-eyes, and worse, kept away anyone intent on making mischief. Not many citizens of Caronath would brave the inhuman custodians that had made the abandoned tombs their homes.

The late hour didn't bother Niklaus, who seldom slept these days. But at Matriarch Adeline's request he had to meet an archbishop of Menselas early in the morning, so hoped his business with Valter would be relatively quick and easy.

"This way," Grogan said gruffly.

He led Niklaus along more tortuous trails and over rock slides. Fortunately there was enough light shed by the waning red moon, Jagonath, to prevent them tripping over stones and branches. Soon they were traversing a narrow path up a cliff face, with a dark drop of unknowable depth to their right. Niklaus's boot skidded on a loose rock, and he gripped the cliff with one hand for security. Then the path widened, and they emerged onto a wide ledge. Shadowed openings arose from the cliff face, hand-hewn and rough, carved through the rock by long-dead slaves to house their masters' corpses. Iron gates had kept the tombs free from invasion by wild animals and creatures of the night, though many of these were missing now or hung on rusted hinges, having been forced open at some point.

Grogan looked around, as if expecting to see whatever monster that had the strength to rip asunder the iron gates. Niklaus's guess was a pack of ghouls, or a wraithe on arcane and unknowable business.

Each opening was pitch black, darker than the night around them, and the air stank of moldering decay. Scurrying sounds came from inside one of the tombs, along with a soft shuffling. Niklaus moved away from the doorway, and his boots crunched on fragments of bone scored by tooth marks.

Grogan chuckled mirthlessly. "Something ate them." His jaw worked ceaselessly on the wad of leaves.

"I believe you're right," Niklaus said.

If Grogan hoped to disconcert him, he was going to be disappointed. A few old bones were nothing to be worried about. The sounds were most likely rats. Old corpses weren't of interest to most creatures in the wild. Some, but not many.

"Hurry up," Grogan said. "I want to be done here and back with my wife and kids."

Niklaus glanced back along the ledge to see if the big man from the tavern was still following them. He was. Without Niklaus's goddess-gifted vision, he would have remained undetected. Whoever the man was, his luck had run out. Although, Niklaus was curious about how he was tracking them. A puzzle.

Grogan had already entered one of the musty tombs, brandishing an alchemical globe for light. Finished stone framed its entrance, carved with hieroglyphics and old script, denoting it had been built for a person or family of importance and wealth. Niklaus followed the guide inside the tomb and along a tunnel that turned right, then left. Stone coffins lay in niches in the walls, lids cracked and broken on the floor, their inhabitants long since taken or eaten.

They came to a door made from saplings covered with tough hide. Grogan lifted it slightly and pushed it open, beckoning for Niklaus to follow him through. Inside, light shone from a number of alchemical globes set around a chamber. Columns supported the ceiling, and dark stone slabs lined the walls, carved with more hieroglyphs and arcane symbols. Niklaus peered at one wall and determined the symbols were a series of ten repeated again and again.

On the ceiling were carved stars, some with fragments of yellow paint still attached. Toothless and superstitious spells to protect the dead from being plundered in this life and to protect their spirits in the afterlife. They hadn't done much good, Niklaus thought.

Three massive granite sarcophagi dominated the room, their lids lying haphazardly on the floor. Shadows lurked everywhere, but Niklaus could see the space had been furnished for human habitation. There was a chair, which Grogan deposited himself in, sighing with relief. He fingered through a pouch and took out another black-coated leaf, which he popped into his mouth.

"Where is Valter?" asked Niklaus.

"He'll be here in his own time. Doesn't keep much to a

schedule. He doesn't know we're coming, so that's why he hasn't laid out his best silverware." Grogan convulsed into a fit of laughter at his own wit.

Niklaus ignored him and cast about the chamber. Three doorways led off it, though only one looked like it was regularly used: bones and broken pottery had been shoveled aside to create a path to it. To one side was a pile of straw covered with large pelts and a thick woolen blanket. An old table of grayed timber held one of the alchemical globes, along with an unlit lamp, several bottles of wine—one open, two unopened—and a number of books and writing implements.

Niklaus held his hand over a pile of ash. Still warm. Beside it were the splintered remains of several wooden coffins. *At least they're serving some purpose for the living,* he thought.

Scattered about the floor were several wooden crates, recently built, containing an assortment of ancient daggers and axes, and parts of armor and helms, all rusted to brittleness. In one corner was a haphazard pile of bones—presumably belonging to the coffins' occupants. Some still held rings and necklaces; clearly Valter hadn't bothered to take them to sell, not that they'd be worth much. Some of the bones also showed tooth marks from something substantially larger than a rat. *Bloody ghouls and Dead-eyes.*

A shadow emerged from one of the openings off the chamber—not the well-used one, Niklaus noted—and a thin, pale man clad in well-made but dirty clothes stepped toward them. He carried a basket filled with oddments in one hand, and in the other a shuttered lantern, which he placed on the table. He glanced at Niklaus and Grogan, who was nonchalantly picking dirt from underneath his fingernails with a knife.

Straightening his metal-rimmed spectacles, Valter, presumably, scraped the top layer off the still-warm ashes and placed a few handfuls of crumbling wood on them. The tinder began to smoke almost immediately, then, when Valter blew on it, burst into flame. He threw some larger chunks of wood onto the fire. In the darkness of the tunnel Valter had emerged from lurked another man pointing a rather large crossbow at Niklaus.

Of course. Valter wouldn't survive out here without a bodyguard.

"Who's this?" Valter asked Grogan. "He has a sword. Two, in fact. I hate swords."

Not waiting for Grogan to answer, Niklaus stepped forward. "My name's Niklaus. And I don't like having a loaded crossbow pointed at me. Tell your man to stand down, and we can talk. Otherwise I'm leaving."

Valter shrugged. "What's it to me if you leave? You came seeking me. Go, then. At least I can get back to my work without interruption."

"You've found a way down to deep ruins that few people have seen," Niklaus said. "You've walked ancient cities, seeking their secrets. I've been told you've found something ... special. And I want it."

Eckart wouldn't tell Niklaus what it was, curse him, no matter how much he'd threatened the sorcerer. *See for yourself,* was all he'd said.

Valter froze. "No one knows about that. No one could know. Who told you?"

He wasn't much good at subterfuge, Niklaus observed. A quick denial would have served him best. "Tell your man to disappear. This is best discussed in private."

"And Grogan?"

"No one would believe him. Cravv addicts will say anything to get their next fix."

Grogan stared daggers at Niklaus, but said nothing.

Valter bent his head to examine his toes. He mumbled to himself for a few moments, then looked up. "Very well." He turned to the other man. "Jakub, go back, and bring the haul from today, there's a good lad."

The man who thought himself hidden in darkness lowered his crossbow and disappeared down the tunnel.

"I have a necromancer in my employ," Niklaus said. "He sensed it when you took the item you found from its resting place. I've brought you a gift in exchange for it."

He took the grimoire he'd found from his pocket and held it out. Even from this distance, he saw Valter's eyes widen. The demon stitched in silver thread on the book's front cover was unmistakable.

"A grimoire," Valter breathed. "Where did you get this?" His tongue moistened his lips while his eyes remained greedily on the fell book. "They'll kill you, you know. The ... Tainted Cabal."

"I'm still alive. And no one knows I have it. Nor that it has passed to you."

Valter laughed nervously. "Grogan does."

Niklaus drew his short sword and plunged it into Grogan's chest. The man groaned and clutched at the blade; it sliced deep into his hands. He glared at Niklaus, then fell slack. Black leaf juice and saliva trickled from his mouth and down his chin. As Niklaus withdrew his sword, the body slumped off the chair onto the dirty floor. He wiped his steel clean on Grogan's shirt.

"As I said, no one knows I have it, nor that it passed to you."

Cursing, Valter went to the table and poured himself a cup of wine. He gulped it down, then wiped his mouth with the back of his sleeve.

"Ikel will want to know what happened to Grogan."

Niklaus shrugged. "He fell. Slipped from the path. It was a dark night."

"Truly, this place has its dangers," said Valter, nodding. He held out a trembling hand. "The grimoire first, please. Then tell me what you think I've found. I can assure you, if you kill me, you'll never find it."

Niklaus studied the insipid fool. The scholar's quest for knowledge had made him weak. He heard sounds from the tunnel: the bodyguard returning.

"This tomb," he said, "was built to protect its inhabitants, though they were already dead. Already doomed. There was no afterlife for them with their useless spells and carvings. They knew not the difference between mysticism and myths and reality."

Valter frowned. "They were ignorant. I am not."

"As any ignorant person would say." Niklaus handed over the grimoire, which Valter snatched greedily, as if he feared it would disappear if he waited too long to claim the malevolent tome.

"Study it well," Niklaus said. "I will return to discuss what you've learned."

He knew that Valter would plumb the knowledge contained in the grimoire in the same way he had plumbed the depths of the ancient cities, searching for knowledge and artifacts. The Tainted Cabal had a unique perspective on immortality, and Niklaus meant to unravel their secrets. By obtaining the artifact from the scholar and using him to unravel the mysteries of the Cabal's grimoire, Niklaus could kill two birds with one stone.

Valter hastily stuffed the grimoire into his shirt as his bodyguard stepped into the chamber. Jakub carried a sack slung over one shoulder and his crossbow in his other hand. He was only a young man, barely ready to shave, but he had wise eyes. He'd seen much violence, surmised Niklaus, for one so young.

"The … ah … what I've found," began Valter, "it is unique. I wonder how you know of it?" He looked at Niklaus expectantly.

"It suffices that I know. No more questions."

Eckart's progress was slow, but he had found a way to track perturbations in the veil, if only across a short distance. The necromancer had sensed the artifact being unearthed and had felt its power. And had known the artifact was a flawed, but still valuable resource he required to experiment with crossing the veil.

Furthermore, he'd discerned the faint trace of another object to the north. Curiously, this aligned with the fresh task Matriarch Adeline had proposed to Niklaus: protecting some squalid village in the north from Dead-eyes.

"I don't know what it does," Valter said nervously. "I don't know its true value."

"Are you trying to bargain after accepting the grimoire? That wouldn't be wise."

As Niklaus expected, Valter backed down. The scholar chuckled nervously, then gestured to Jakub. "Retrieve the object," he said shortly.

Jakub frowned, but did as ordered. He thrust his arm deep into the pile of discarded and gnawed bones and drew out a cloth-wrapped bundle. He handed it to Valter. Bone dust lifted from the cloth as Valter unwrapped the parcel, and he waved it away.

Niklaus saw a glint of metal that quickly dulled, as if drawing the light into itself. The object was a mask, with two empty sockets for eyes and a wide-open mouth, but there its resemblance to humanity ceased. Tiny scales were worked into the face, with small horns dotting the cheeks and chin, while finger-length horns sprouted from the top. It was almost demon-like, though perhaps its creator had seen only drawings, not a live demon. Despite its age, not a spot of rust marred the hideous visage. Valter turned the mask over, and Niklaus saw that its inside surface was covered with sharp spikes the length of a fingernail.

"As you can see," Valter said, "I haven't tried to wear it."

When Niklaus took hold of the mask, a chill wave swept through him. He heard something: a weird droning of insects, with unintelligible words weaving in and out of the rustling. A force tugged at him, not physically, but latched onto his soul, as if contorting his very being …

He flapped the cloth to rid it of more bone dust and rewrapped the mask. For a heartbeat, the world stopped, and the shadow fell from his soul.

"Where did you find it?" he asked.

"A long way down. The third city underneath us. There's ..." Valter hesitated.

"More artifacts? I care not for anything else."

"It's part of a set. At least, that's what the writings speak of."

Niklaus blinked. Possibilities exploded in his mind. "Writings?"

"The chamber where we found the mask was protected by sorcerous wards, and the floor covered with script. It spoke of an ancient champion, a being who stood against a mighty enemy." Valter wrung his hands. "Possibly a wraithe, though it could have been one of the Tainted Cabal or a summoned demon. There really is no way to tell."

"Were there any other details?"

Valter nodded eagerly. "There was a name, or at least I think it's a name. *Mert-no-Carysut.* It's Skanuric and roughly translates as 'divine metal'. The mask must have been crafted from a fallen star."

Slowly, Niklaus nodded. *A competent translation, but incorrect.* Valter's mistake was one of time. As the centuries passed, texts were damaged or lost, or mistranslated. Current scholars translated "mert" as metal, though at its root, in earlier dialects of Skanuric, it meant "armor". Armor of Divinity.

Niklaus breathed deeply to calm his racing heart. He'd seen a reference to divine metal once before, in a fable that told of a hero who'd donned a suit of ensorcelled armor to battle the gods in their own territory. And lost.

"Metal of divinity, to be exact," he said, going with Valter's mistranslation. The scholar didn't need to know what he'd stumbled onto.

"Yes, indeed. You are well educated."

"I've picked up a few things over the years. Thank you," he added abruptly. "I'll leave you to your work."

"Er, Grogan …"

*Really, do I have to think of all the details?*

"Have Jakub throw him over a cliff."

Niklaus turned his back on Valter and Jakub and stumbled across the chamber, clutching the mask. He drew a deep breath of the tomb's musty air into his lungs. The mask. The Armor of Divinity. He needed time to think. He had to get out of here.

He turned his back on Valter and Jakub and stumbled across the chamber.

"Wait!" Valter cried. "When will you return?"

Niklaus ignored him. Outside, he stopped and leaned against the cliff face. For some reason, he felt dread and longing, an ache in his chest and groin. After searching for centuries, he'd stumbled across a path to his goal. A smile stole across his face.

The man who'd been trailing him emerged from behind a tree. He was bigger than he'd seemed in the tavern: over seven feet tall, and muscled like he wrestled lions for a living. His arms and neck were ribbed with ritual scarring, and his eyes were sinister glinting spots of blue in the darkness. A massive sword dangled from one overlarge hand; it glowed with an unearthly green hue and had serrated edges.

Niklaus saw leprous bodies heaped about the base of the tree. It seemed his follower had run into a pack of ghouls, enough to take out half a dozen men. Yet he still stood.

"The Tainted Cabal have decreed you are to die." The words were roughly spoken, as if pulled from the man.

"Oh, come now," Niklaus said. "I hardly inconvenienced them, and that was years ago. Don't tell me they're still looking to even the score? After all this time? Or perhaps this is about what happened the other night?"

"The Cabal know you killed their demons, and they remember your previous slights. They have long memories."

They had to have scryed it was him who'd killed all those

demons. Or perhaps Missa had talked? If so, she was probably dead. "And are short on brains, it seems."

The big man remained silent.

Niklaus had expected as much. The warriors the Cabal sent to do their dirty work were usually devoid of humor or conversation. Whatever demonic sorcery was used to control them corroded their minds, but they were deadly all the same.

He placed the mask on the ground out of the way, then released his chest-harness clasp. The goddess's sheathed sword swung down to his side. There was always an obstacle in his way. He dealt with one, and ten more appeared.

"You know what my father said?" he asked the Cabal's warrior. "No? He said a good big man will always beat a good little man. But he was a fool in so many ways."

The green-hued sword lifted, then came toward him with blinding speed as the assassin leaped across the space between them. Niklaus ducked and rolled, coming to his feet in time to draw *her* sword and deflect another slash of the massive blade. Sparks flew.

Niklaus moved, too quick for the man to counter. He stepped inside his long reach, drove *her* sword deep into the Cabal's servant's guts, ripped upward to disembowel him, and danced backward before the assassin had time to register what had happened.

A few faltering steps, and realization dawned. Long-fingered hands clutched at his bloody intestines as they slid free. The assassin's sword clattered to the ground, and a mewl escaped his lips as he stumbled to his knees.

He looked at Niklaus in horror. "I ... I was promised ..."

Niklaus flicked his blade and cut through the assassin's neck. Crimson spurted, splashing the dirt. The huge man's eyes rolled into his head, and he fell face forward with a thump, like so much dead meat.

As always, Niklaus's eyes were drawn to *her* sword as the blood coating the blade seemed to evaporate or was absorbed, leaving the metal immaculate. A thrill coursed through his body at the confirmation she still watched over him. He remained hers, chosen.

And one day, she would be his.

So the Tainted Cabal wanted him dead. But by sending this oaf, they obviously had no idea who they were dealing with. And it would be months before they realized their assassin had met an untimely end. Niklaus was confident there wouldn't be any more attempts on his life, at least from the Cabal, in the short term. They might know he'd stolen the grimoire, but the death of one of their twisted minions was no mean feat. That should give them pause.

He bent and picked up the mask. One piece of the Armor of Divinity. Even just this fragment had secrets to reveal to a sorcerer competent enough. Eckart? Or someone else?

And if the other pieces were lost, could they be forged anew?

## CHAPTER THIRTEEN

# A GATHERING OF STRANGERS

I T WAS A STRANGE sensation, the warmth and serenity Aldric felt when he used the gifts his god had given him. With every healing, the memories of his childhood came back. Sorrow intermingled with the joy of the god's power flowing through him.

He found himself transported back to when he was ten, and his father had been injured by a Dead-eye while looking for a lost goat. He'd suffered a gashed arm, almost to the bone. Aldric had been drawn to it, heedless of the blood, and the god's power had coursed through him. Muscle and skin had knitted in front of his eyes before a heavy weariness overcame him, and he'd fallen unconscious. But not before he'd seen the look of wonder and pride on his parents' faces. He was one of the chosen.

When he'd recovered, his mother and father had taken him to the closest church of Menselas, or the Five as they knew it. The priests had taken him in, and he didn't see his family again for three years.

Aldric opened his eyes and looked down at the young girl lying on the cot. The red pustules that had erupted on her arm—the result of a brush with a poisonous caterpillar—were already fading. Weariness came over Aldric, and he sat back in his chair, dropping the girl's hand.

"Thank you, thank you," whispered the girl's mother between sobs.

Aldric smiled at her. "Thank Menselas, or one of his five holy aspects."

The girl wouldn't have died if she hadn't been healed, though her arm would have atrophied and become mostly useless. And there were other priests that bore the god's mark and could have healed her if he hadn't been there. But ... he'd *needed* to do it. Healing was the thing that kept him sane. Aldric was one of only a few sorcerers among the Church's priests, and the only one gifted with his holy power. Menselas had a purpose for him, he was sure. He just hadn't revealed it yet.

Aldric tugged the blanket up to the girl's chin, rubbed his eyes, and stood. "She should wake in a few hours. Make sure she drinks some bowls of broth. The priests will provide it."

The girl's mother wrapped her arms around him and hugged him tight. "May the Five bless you, good priest." She fumbled with her belt pouch and took out a gold royal. "Here, we don't have—"

Aldric held up his hands and backed away. "I don't need payment," he said, a little too harshly. Then, softer, "If you feel the need to donate, see one of the other priests."

He left without another word. He'd already spent too long here ministering to the injured and sick who came seeking help, and he was tired. His meeting with Neb and the mercenary was soon, and he needed a quick rest and some nourishment.

A short time later, he was wolfing down a bowl of thick beef stew along with dark bread in the church's kitchen. He widened his eyes periodically, trying to wake himself up. A cold front had swept down from the north overnight, chilling the air to almost freezing, and the hot food was welcome, especially as his reception in the kitchen was as cold as the wind. Despite the five-pointed star embroidered on his shirt that identified him as a priest of the Five, none of the other priests sat near him. As it had been everywhere else he had worked, so it was here. Perhaps he would gain acceptance once he settled down and focused on healing, though every year that goal seemed farther and farther away.

~ ~ ~

Neb was standing at the top of the steps when Aldric arrived, the Church of Menselas stretching into the sky behind him. And so were Archbishop Hannus and a man with shoulder-length black hair—presumably the mercenary. The stranger was tall with wide shoulders and carried himself with an easy grace. His arms were long and corded with muscle, and his skin was dusky, which put him as probably of Inkan-Andil descent. If so, he was a long way from his home on the far western shores. He wore leather armor, but it was of exceptional quality—supple and worked with flat metal rings inscribed with flowing script. A sword was strapped to his back, and in one hand he held a thick metal cane etched with swirling lines. A shorter-bladed sword swung from his hip.

As Aldric approached, the mercenary's green eyes bored into his, confirming his Inkan-Andil blood. Under their penetrating gaze, Aldric had the feeling he was being assessed. The man had an unyielding manner, as if nothing mattered beyond what he desired.

"Ah, Aldric," Hannus said, "this is the man who'll be joining you. Niklaus, this is Magister Aldric Kermoran."

Niklaus's grip was limp, as if he couldn't be bothered expending the energy to shake hands. "A warrior-priest?" he said. "Excellent! The settlers might need your skills, if what they've said is true."

"It is!" cut in Neb. "Else I wouldn't be here. We trailed some of the Dead-eyes back to their camp, a few days from our settlement. It looked like a few tribes gathered together. And we guessed it'd only be a matter of time afore they came in numbers. We can't face them alone. We aren't fighters."

Aldric thought the settler looked less haggard than the day before. A good night's rest and a hearty meal had done him some good. He saw Niklaus smirk at Neb's words, and decided he didn't like him.

"I can heal," he said, "if it's required. But I can also wield a blade fairly well."

He mentally chastised himself for exaggerating. The mercenary had already gotten under his skin.

Niklaus glanced at Aldric's khopesh. "Can you now? I guess we'll find out."

Aldric's dislike intensified, but he decided it wasn't worth making his feelings known. After all, they'd be in each other's company for weeks.

"You're a long way from home," he said instead.

Niklaus frowned. "What do you mean?"

"Your skin. You have Inkan-Andil blood."

Niklaus gave him a blank look, and Aldric had a strange feeling the mercenary was confused.

"From the western shores," he added. "Over a thousand miles from here. Isn't that where your family is from?"

"I don't remember," Niklaus said. "It's not important."

"Well," said Hannus, "now the introductions are out of the way, Aldric can help himself to the Church's equipment and—"

"And we'll kill some Dead-eyes," finished Niklaus. "So these good people can live in peace."

Aldric wondered why Hannus thought he needed the dubious assistance of a mercenary he didn't know. Or why this had to be a joint mission between two faiths. Come to think of it, by allowing Hannus to get under his skin yesterday, he'd neglected to ask which other faith they were cooperating with.

"What god do you serve?" he asked Niklaus.

"He's in the service of the Lady Sylva Kalisia," answered Hannus. "If people see the servants of different gods working together, they'll understand how much we value peace and harmony. There's been too much trouble lately between worshipers."

Sylva Kalisia ... one of the degenerate goddesses.

"Trouble?" Aldric prompted, not voicing a dozen other questions, and complaints, that sprang to mind.

"Fights," Niklaus said. "Beatings and murders. This close to the wild, people get on edge, and tensions boil over. Usually over stupid things. Idiots."

Hannus bridled at Niklaus's words. "Defending one's faith isn't stupid."

"It can be."

"We'd better get going," Aldric said, attempting to head off an argument. And he did want to get started. There was a lot to do. "Archbishop Hannus, when can we meet the warriors you've put together?"

Hannus was still glaring at Niklaus, who held his gaze, then stifled a yawn. The archbishop's mouth twisted in distaste as he looked away.

"They're close by," he told Aldric. "In a building owned by the Church on Locust Street. The door is marked with Menselas's holy symbol. The place is distinctive enough. In fact, it used to be a haggle yard in years gone by."

Most of the haggle yards—trading places for horses and livestock—had been relocated when the city's population grew and residents began complaining about the stench of the beasts.

"I'd have preferred to put my own team together," Niklaus said. "I don't like strangers watching my back."

The mercenary's words echoed Aldric's thoughts, and he

couldn't help but nod, which drew a disapproving glare from Hannus.

"We went through an intermediary," the archbishop said. "Someone both our Churches trust. They vetted the warriors, and we're satisfied they'll get the job done. They've already been paid to wait for you as well as for the mission."

Niklaus sniffed. "So long as they're proficient at killing Dead-eyes. I'm not babysitting anyone."

"I'm sure they'll be sufficient," Aldric said. He felt the need to be gone from Caronath, not to mention Hannus's influence and barely concealed condemnation. Despite that, he added, "It's getting too late to leave today, plus we have to organize gear and mounts. That will take the rest of today and tomorrow. Perhaps we should join the men for the night. It will help if we know each other a little better before we set off."

Niklaus nodded and turned to Neb. "Come, farmer, we'll find a room for you too. And with any luck, we'll be on the trail as soon as we can."

"Have to get my stuff," Neb said.

"As do I," Aldric said. "I'm staying at the Cask and Squirrel."

Niklaus raised an eyebrow. "Not at the church?"

Aldric glanced at Hannus, then shook his head. "I've become accustomed to fending for myself."

"I'll join you there," said Niklaus. "I know where it is. It's best if both our Churches' representatives greet these mercenaries at the same time. Neb, meet us at the inn as soon as you can."

As Neb descended the steps to the square below, Hannus took Aldric's elbow and drew him aside.

"About your relic," Hannus began, but left the question hanging.

Aldric had no intention of handing his relic over to the archbishop. "I'll consider your request," he said. "There's no time now in any case."

"When you return, then."

Aldric made his way down the steps to the square, with Niklaus trailing him. All the way, his back itched between his shoulder blades.

~ ~ ~

Locust Street turned out to be a main thoroughfare close to a seething market square. The three men slowed their pace as they weaved through the throng; it didn't help that they were leading horses. A few people stared at Aldric because of his dark gray skin, but quickly looked away and returned to their business. Caronath was used to oddities.

"There," Niklaus said. The mercenary smelled of spirits, and his eyes were red. He looked like he'd been up all night drinking.

Close by, a squad of Caronath's city guard stood at an intersection, surveilling the crowd. Their surcoats were emblazoned with the city's emblem of a black swan on a green background, and underneath they wore armor of metal scales over leather.

Aldric looked away from a stall selling strange fruits he'd never seen before, and followed Niklaus's gesture to a dilapidated building to their left. The five-pointed star of Menselas stood out like a sore thumb with its gold lines and symbols, as shiny as if it had been painted yesterday.

On one side of the building was an open space separated from the street by railings. The original haggle yard, Aldric presumed. From the look of things, the disused yard had become a place for those looking for work. There was a board built from scrap timber with numerous papers tacked to it, no doubt notices of employment opportunities. The yard's corrals were covered with canvas awnings that offered protection from the sun and rain. The men and women waiting there looked unskilled and mostly destitute, presumably willing to take any work that would pay enough to stave off hunger for a day. Aldric hoped the warriors who'd be accompanying them hadn't been chosen from the sorry lot hanging around the yard.

The haggard men and women stared at Aldric, Niklaus and Neb as they approached, until their attention was drawn away to a group of traders who were putting together a caravan and looking for muscle. "Nagaraf," one of the traders shouted. It was a city a few weeks to the west of Caronath, along a road that was troublesome and dangerous. A merchant caravan would likely make a good return, though, if they made it through without too many assaults from Dead-eyes and the like.

A few big men, scared and wary-eyed, pushed to the front of the crowd gathering around the traders. Words were exchanged, and several of them shouldered packs and stood in a group to the side. The chosen ones. They'd be kept busy and fed for a few weeks. The traders turned away from those still clamoring to be picked, ignoring their pleas and imploring hands.

Aldric leaned against the wooden fence rail and scanned the groups of men and women who hadn't bothered to approach the traders, knowing they wouldn't be chosen. Some talked softly among themselves, but most remained silent. He figured they knew each other from their time waiting here, and their conversation was sparse, as anything they had to say had likely been said many times before.

Neb nudged him in the side. "Maybe we should get some extra men? Can't be too careful, can you? Though these lot look—"

"Useless?" cut in Niklaus. He sniffed and tapped his metal cane against the rail.

Aldric saw the swirling lines were a depiction of vines with thorns and intricate flowers blooming from the occasional bud. From his healer training, he recognized the plant as a kronnir vine, rare and valuable. The stamens from its flowers were used as an aphrodisiac and a stimulant, although it was highly addictive.

"Thieves, thugs and cutthroats, that's all we'll find here," continued Niklaus. "The honest ones will be looking elsewhere. And I doubt any of them has much skill with weapons. Bunch of pants-pissers. Maybe they'll manage to do in a few Dead-eyes, but we need more than that from what Neb said."

Aldric grunted. Much as he disliked the idea, he had to admit Niklaus had a point. "Let's see what we have to work with first."

Neb's eyes were still on the yard. "Some of these men look handy. Wouldn't trust them as far as I could throw them though."

"Trying to find decent fighters in a haggle yard is like trying to find a weevil in your porridge," Niklaus said, and chuckled at his own wit.

Neb ignored him and stepped up onto the lowest fence rail, stretching his neck and gawking at the men and women.

Niklaus poked him in the side with the tip of his cane. "You look like you haven't been here before, old man. Why not? Surely places like this were your first stop to find men to help defend your village, or whatever it is?"

Neb stepped down and scratched an armpit. "We're poor settlers. We barely have enough to get by. Even sending me here was a stretch." He met Aldric's eyes briefly and nodded, a thanks for the coins Aldric had given him.

"How are you paying our Churches, then?" asked Niklaus.

"They agreed to help for free. They care for everyone, even those not of the same faith."

"For free, eh? That'd be a first."

Aldric didn't care for Niklaus's tone. "Maybe for your Church, but not for mine. I've often helped people because they needed it, not because I'd be paid."

The mercenary chuckled. "Good people do good things, that's a fact. But the Churches and the merchants and the nobles are all as bad as each other."

Aldric didn't want to get into a debate with Niklaus, at least not when they had other more pressing concerns. He guessed there would be ample opportunity for discussion on the way to Neb's settlement and while they were there. With the next full-dark more than a week away, the Dead-eyes shouldn't be back in numbers before then, which meant there would be plenty of time to sound each other out. *What a waste of my abilities,* he thought. Maybe Hierophant Karianne wanted him out of the way. If so, he couldn't blame her.

Neb looked between Aldric and Niklaus. "Where are the swords? The archbishop said we'd get weapons. We don't have much at the settlement."

"Probably not your only problem," Niklaus said dryly. "But you won't be getting any swords. Short spears, maybe clubs and daggers."

Aldric nodded. They had no idea how much time they'd have to train the settlers, so simple was best.

"How about we take some extra men, like him?" Neb pointed to a huge man who'd just arrived in the yard. Like everyone else, his clothes were dusty and dirty and frayed, but he was well muscled and stood a head taller than most of the others. "He'll kill plenty of Dead-eyes, for sure."

"No, he won't," Niklaus said. "He'll steal what he can and maybe kill some of you if he's caught in the act. Look at his yellowed eyes, the trembling in his hands, the sheen of sweat on his skin. He's an addict, probably to cravv, the bad kind."

Cravv was a mixture of several pain-relieving herbs combined with the hallucinogenic sap of a cactus. Aldric knew of at least eleven different types, all as bad as each other as far as he was concerned. He reached for his god's power, and the big man transformed before him. A sickly red aura surrounded him, and his veins pulsed brown, as if filled with river sludge.

Aldric's attention was caught by a shadow that flickered around

Niklaus. He turned to see what it was, but it vanished. Strange.

"He's right," Aldric told Neb as his vision returned to normal. "The man's an addict. Best we see what our Churches have put together first."

Neb cursed, and Niklaus smirked, as if amused by the settler's consternation. Aldric could feel a headache coming on and wished Archbishop Hannus had found a different mission for him.

"Why didn't the Church of the Five send some of their own soldiers?" Niklaus asked.

"We don't have a standing army," Aldric replied. "A few guards, that's all. We don't need more than that. Everyone knows we're here to help people, to heal them, and there's rarely any trouble. Archbishop Hannus told me that soldiers were sent initially, but they couldn't find any Dead-eyes and so returned. Which is why the settlers had to approach our Churches for help."

Niklaus spread his hands. "But one of Menselas's five aspects is the Warrior. And your curved blade's not for show, apparently, so I guess that's where you come in."

Aldric replied through clenched teeth. "Yes. Sometimes."

He wondered why Hannus had paired him with this man from the Church of Sylva Kalisia rather than one of the more mainstream Churches. There was something disturbing about the people who followed this goddess, and this mercenary definitely rubbed his skin the wrong way.

Niklaus raised his eyebrows, then swung gracefully over the fence. He landed in the dry dirt, barely raising a puff of dust. Aldric had to hand it to him: he moved well.

"Let's go in the side door," Niklaus said. "We'll see how ready these warriors are. I don't trust the Churches to be the best judge of a fighter."

Aldric followed Niklaus over the fence, albeit less gracefully, and across the yard. Neb decided to slide between the top and middle rails and lost a button doing so.

Niklaus hammered a fist on the side door, and they walked straight in. Aldric squinted as his eyes adjusted to the dim light and the heat of the room after the cold outside. There were scuffling sounds, and he smelled wood smoke and roasted meat, sweat and leather. The room was large and had three doors leading off it, one of which was the larger front entrance.

"Hey!" a man shouted. "You can't come in here. This is Church property."

He was sitting at one of three broad tables around the room, and his chair creaked as he rose to his feet. He was tidier than the down-on-their-luck people outside, though a little on the short side. His pants and shirt sported numerous patches, but they were neatly sewn, and it looked like he'd shaved this morning. His hair was gray, and dark eyes looked out from a weathered face. He watched them warily, one hand on the pommel of a dagger sheathed at his belt.

"What company?" asked Niklaus.

The man frowned as he examined them, then visibly relaxed as he saw the symbol of Menselas embroidered on Aldric's shirt.

"The Eighth Wall," he said. "Pikemen. You're from the Church? They said someone would come today."

A soldier, Aldric realized, a few breaths behind Niklaus. Judging from the man's appearance, he still maintained some of the habits. A good sign.

"The Eighth Wall," Aldric said, racking his memory. "Out of Thessalika?"

The man gave a nod.

Thessalika was one of the city-states to the south-west, on the edge of the inland sea. One of a dozen or so that always seemed to be at war with one another, as if there wasn't enough trouble without that.

"Pikemen we don't need," Niklaus said. "The Dead-eyes are too quick. But I'd wager you can handle other weapons."

"Not the sword, but mace and shield. Some dagger work." The ex-soldier chewed his lips and shuffled his weight from foot to foot. There was something he wasn't telling them, but he didn't have the feel of a deserter.

"What's your name?" Aldric asked. "And why did you leave the Eighth Wall?"

"Razmus, sir. It was—"

"That's Magister to you," Niklaus said.

Aldric held up a hand. "Just Aldric is fine. I have a feeling we'll all know each other well before this is over." He nodded encouragingly to Razmus. "Go on."

"My wife died. Of the brain pox. There was nothing …" Razmus looked at the floor of packed earth. "We have a daughter who needed looking after. I had to be there for her. Started taking on odd jobs, but times aren't what they used to be."

"They never are," said Niklaus. "So you found yourself taking on thug work? Cracking skulls and breaking bones?"

Razmus kept his eyes on the floor. "A few times. Now I'm here. Thought we could have a new start. We took a caravan and worked for our passage. I've killed a Dead-eye or two."

He looked and sounded the part, Aldric decided. They should have no trouble with him, and he'd be up to killing Dead-eyes and protecting Neb's settlement. Before Aldric could say anything, Niklaus tossed a purse to Razmus. It hit the ground with a solid clink of coin. Aldric frowned. Hannus had said the men had already been paid.

"Wait a moment," he began.

"Train some men," Niklaus said, ignoring Aldric. "Kill some Dead-eyes. Do whatever else we want, and the purse is yours, plus more to come. Deal?"

He held out a hand to Razmus. The soldier hesitated.

"Your daughter," Aldric said. "She's still with you?"

Razmus nodded. "She can help. She's worth ten of those scum

outside." His eyes dropped to the purse on the ground, and he licked his lips.

"Hardly scum," Niklaus said. "Down on their luck maybe. In need of some guidance. And a good bath."

Razmus nodded again. "As you say." He bent and picked up the purse.

"I do say." Niklaus clapped Razmus on the back. "You'll do."

Aldric sighed, not sure about the complication of the daughter. "This is no mission for a girl. Maybe the Church of the Five could look after her."

"No," Razmus said sharply. "I'm sorry. They won't want her there. She's ... marked."

The implication was plain, especially to Aldric, who'd often borne the brunt of his Church's scorn. Razmus's daughter was a sorcerer. Or at least had the mark, if not any training. Luck was on their side, it seemed. Sorcerers were rare and required years of expensive training. And Aldric's own skill wasn't the most powerful or complex, so it could be a good thing if there was another sorcerer accompanying them. To stumble upon one who would likely join them was ... fortuitous. Or perhaps divine providence. He breathed a prayer to Menselas.

"She's welcome," he said. "As long as she has some control over her abilities."

Razmus smiled briefly. "That she does."

Neb sidled around from behind Niklaus, staring at Razmus as if to size him up. Aldric couldn't blame him. After all, the survival of his settlement rested upon the team the Churches had put together.

Niklaus moved to the table Razmus had been sitting at. It held bottles of wine, a plate with a whole roast chicken, and a loaf of sliced dark bread. On one edge was a small wooden cask with tin tankards beside it. The wine bottles were still corked, and there were three plates, cutlery, and some ceramic wine bowls.

Counting Razmus and his daughter, that left one other. Hannus had put together a team of only two people. *They'd better be good*, Aldric thought.

"Looks like the Churches have supplied you well," said Niklaus, uncorking a bottle and splashing wine carelessly into a bowl. He slurped it like it was water. With his other hand he ripped off a chicken leg and took a bite out of it.

"Help yourself," said Razmus.

Niklaus grinned, lips shiny with grease, and kept chewing.

Razmus moved to the table and poured dark beer from the cask into the tankards. He handed one to Aldric and one to Neb, who gulped the beer as if he'd been trudging through a desert all morning.

"It will be good to have another sorcerer along," Aldric told Razmus, "not to mention someone with your experience. You will be able to train the settlers."

Niklaus snorted. He wiped fat from his lips and took a bite from a slice of dark bread. "We'd be better off going alone. No offense, Razmus."

"None taken."

"You and me against the Dead-eyes, Aldric," Niklaus continued. "What do you say? Back to back, we could hold off a horde of them. Well, I could. I'm not sure about your skill."

The thought of trusting Niklaus at his back sent a cold shudder through Aldric. There was no chance he was leaving here without the admittedly small team the Churches had put together. The fact Niklaus didn't want more people around led Aldric to think back to what Hannus had said, and why Niklaus was even here. *Bring whatever artifacts you find back to me*, the archbishop had said.

Aldric swallowed a mouthful of the nutty-tasting beer and looked up to find Niklaus staring at him, as if the man knew his thoughts exactly.

"It will take more than the two of us to defend the settlers' village against the Dead-eyes," Aldric said. "I'm not leaving without the team."

The mercenary shrugged and dropped the mostly eaten chicken leg onto a plate. "Time's a-wasting. Let's hope the settlement is still there when we finally arrive."

Neb cried out in dismay.

"It will be," Aldric assured him. "It's not full-dark for a while yet. We'll leave as soon as we get the horses and gear together. Likely the day after tomorrow."

"Didn't Hannus arrange them as well?" asked Niklaus.

"*Archbishop* Hannus didn't know when we'd be leaving, so no," replied Aldric.

A hulking man emerged through one of the back doors, carrying an armload of firewood. His long brown unbound hair made him seem wild, though there was a deliberateness to his movements. Scars covered his sun-dark arms, showing he used to be a warrior. He lumbered over to the fireplace and dumped his load to one side, then disappeared outside again.

Niklaus glanced at the newcomer, shrugged, and sipped his wine. Aldric swallowed a mouthful of beer, content to let their conversation die.

After a short while, the big man reappeared, carrying another stack of wood. The pieces clacked together as he unloaded his burden by the fireplace. He crossed the room to the table, hacked off some chicken, sandwiched it between two slices of bread, and grabbed a tankard of beer, then disappeared outside again.

"That's the other mercenary," said Razmus. "He doesn't say much. His name's Stray Dog."

"Only two warriors?" said Niklaus. "It seems both our Churches are holding tightly to their purse strings. I don't fancy the idea of playing wet nurse to these settlers. I think we need at least one more blade."

Aldric agreed, but he had questions first and wasn't sure he'd like the answers the mercenary gave. "A thug for hire? A cutthroat? No, thank you."

Niklaus took another bite of bread and chewed slowly. "No. A real fighter. It'll cost a bit, but as our Churches are covering expenses, it won't be a problem."

"What kind of fighter are you talking about?" Aldric said. "A caravan guard, a bodyguard? We don't have a great deal of time before we have to get moving."

Niklaus shook his head. "Guards have easy jobs with regular pay—they wouldn't want to give that up. Plus, it's blind chance if they ever encounter Dead-eyes. With us, it's a certainty. We'd be better off with a treasure hunter, the type that searches ruins for whatever artifacts the Dead-eyes have managed to squirrel away. That's not a job for the unwary. The wilderness and the ruins are dangerous places, and the unskilled amateurs get culled early, leaving only the best alive."

*Or the worst*, Aldric thought. "If you can find someone decent, I'll consider them."

"If I find someone suitable, I'll hire them on the spot. I'm not waiting for your approval."

Aldric took a deep breath and let it out slowly. "Just don't pick someone who'll cut our throats in our sleep."

He expected a comeback, but instead Niklaus coughed and spluttered, spraying wine across the table. He'd gone as pale as a Dead-eye, and his gaze was fixed on the front door, where a woman had entered.

Aldric realized they hadn't asked Razmus how old his daughter was. She was of average height, but held her head high, as if a run-down building wasn't the type of establishment she'd usually frequent. Hair as dark as the abyss hung down her back, and her travel clothes were supple leather and did nothing to hide her figure.

As she approached, Aldric could see she carried a number of

talismans tucked into her belt: carved wooden sticks festooned with feathers and knotted cord. They would do their job—aiding a sorcerer with calculations and concentration—but their simplicity and the materials they were made from showed she was short of coin. An oddity for a sorcerer, as their skills were in demand.

Niklaus held out his hand. Aldric noticed that it trembled slightly. "A pleasure to meet you," he said. "Please, sit with us. Have you eaten?"

The mercenary barely glanced at Razmus, only having eyes for his daughter. But it wasn't lust coming from Niklaus; it was something else. Aldric couldn't work out what.

Razmus moved so he was between Niklaus and his daughter. He ignored Niklaus's extended hand, pulled out two chairs from the table, and they sat down. "This is Priska," he said gruffly.

"Pleased to meet you," Aldric said, inclining his head.

Priska's wide brown eyes flicked between Aldric and Niklaus, as if undecided who to rest on. She chose Aldric.

"I thought priests of your faith didn't like my kind," she said bluntly.

Niklaus chuckled. He peered at Razmus, then at his daughter, then back at the soldier. "Are you sure she's your daughter?"

Razmus bridled at the question, but although he looked like he wanted to say something, he remained quiet.

"We're sure," Priska said. "My mother was ... like me. And I have my father's ... disposition."

Aldric reluctantly reached for his sorcerous power and quested his senses toward her. Priska's mark was fierce and brilliant, a torch to his candle. Nowhere near the bonfire that was Soki's power, but Soki was almost unique in her talents and knowledge. If Priska had been trained, she would be a welcome addition to their party.

"What Covenant do you belong to?" Aldric asked. Someone would have sensed her. Someone would have taken her on. With her power, it was likely one of the bigger Covenants.

Priska's mouth twisted, and she looked down at the table. "Gray Hand," she said softly.

Her answer surprised Aldric. It wasn't a well-known Covenant, and he doubted many sorcerers today would even recognize the name. His Church had spent a lot on his education though, and the Evokers had drilled him mercilessly. The Gray Hand was a weak Covenant, its existence almost lost in the mists of time. Hundreds of years ago, its adherents had decided to take short cuts, using rote learning rather than teaching understanding, and consequently their sorcery had suffered. They had an incomplete mastery of their talents and had become increasingly distanced from the other Covenants. Eventually, they'd turned to the sorcery of summoning, attempting to bring forth and control creatures from the abyss. Most had been killed by their own creations; the few survivors had broken from the Covenant and scattered. Clearly, some of them remained somewhere, if Priska had been trained by them.

And the cause of her discomfort was plain: she had vast potential, but had been hobbled by inferior training. Aldric wagered no other Covenant would take her on now. Which was probably why she and her father were scratching out a living. His heart went out to her.

"I know of it," he said.

A connection came to him, niggling at his thoughts. Soki's Covenant, the Sanguine Legion, had also delved into summoning sorcery. Both Covenants had fallen because of their desire for power and the dark paths it had led them down. Was it a coincidence he'd met two sorcerers in a matter of weeks from Covenants with similar pasts? The sorcerous Covenants chafed at their low societal standing, and some were always scheming to get one over on the other Covenants. Surely none would be so foolish as to repeat the mistakes of the past?

"So do I," said Niklaus.

Aldric jerked his gaze back to the mercenary. How could Niklaus know of such an obscure Covenant?

Razmus's hand clasped his daughter's. "Hardly anyone does, so it's surprising you both do."

"That it is," Aldric said.

Niklaus merely shrugged. "You pick up a few things over the years."

Priska cleared her throat. "I ... I don't do any of that summoning sorcery. I don't know any. My master taught me as well as she could, and I do the best I can with what I have."

*Maybe she doesn't know her potential,* thought Aldric. *Or perhaps ...*

"Have you approached other Covenants?" he asked. "One of them might take you on."

Priska shook her head, face downcast. "None of them wanted me. They said I don't have enough talent."

More likely the real reason was her Covenant's reputation, and the fact that much of her training would have to be unlearned. She was also older than the usual fledgling sorcerers the Covenants took in, less impressionable. That opinion was confirmed when Priska finally looked up, and her eyes flashed with suppressed fury, her jaw clenched tight.

Niklaus stood abruptly. "I have to go." He glanced at Priska, then back to Aldric. "There's a lot to do before we leave."

He stumbled away, pushing past Neb, whose muttered curses followed him out the door. They all watched him go.

"Too much wine?" asked Razmus, turning back to Aldric.

"It must be," Aldric replied. But he realized Niklaus hadn't drunk anything since Priska had joined them.

The young woman was still a puzzle to him, and he was glad the mercenary wasn't around to hear what he was about to say.

He smiled encouragingly at her. "You said before you didn't think priests of my faith liked sorcerers."

"They don't."

"I know," he said, folding his hands on the table. "But I'm going to tell you something not many people know. You see, I'm a sorcerer as well."

Razmus gasped. "But ... you're a priest of the Five."

"And a liar, it seems," Priska said.

Aldric cleared his throat and took a sip of his beer. "See for yourself."

That she hadn't immediately recognized him as a sorcerer said volumes about the quality of her training. It was a shame she'd been stunted, but perhaps he could guide her a little, or at least try to strip away some of the ingrained teachings that hindered her.

Priska closed her eyes and placed a hand on one of her talismans. Her fingers moved over the knots, which were tied in patterned groups—calculation aids. He wasn't sure why she needed them to open her senses to him, but that would be the first thing he'd work on with her. He didn't carry his own talismans out in the open because they marked him as a sorcerer. That choice hindered his ability to concentrate when using sorcery, but it was a price he paid willingly.

And at least her actions proved one thing: she had a catalyst on her.

Her jaw dropped as she saw his mark of sorcery. *My stain,* he thought.

She opened her eyes. "You ... He is."

"What's going on here? I thought this job was about killing Dead-eyes." Razmus half rose from his seat, but stopped when Aldric held up a hand.

"Calm down. It's not a trick. I'm a magister of Menselas, of the Five, and a sorcerer. Sorcery can do things that priests marked by the gods can't, and sometimes it's needed."

"You don't look like any sorcerer I've ever seen," said Razmus. "Your armor, that curved sword—a khopesh, isn't it?"

"That's part of what I do," admitted Aldric. "Though truth be told, I'm not that proficient a fighter."

He wasn't going to reveal his Church's secret: that thousands of years ago the khopesh had been forged from the metal of a fallen star, which was anathema to demons.

Priska laughed, a warm throaty sound. "An enforcer. You do the Church's dirty work."

"No," said Aldric, a little too quickly. "My faith is peaceful. Some of us are healers. I'd rather heal people than fight Dead-eyes, but ... I do as the Church asks of me. I believe in its work, in Menselas."

All of a sudden, he didn't feel like talking about sorcery any more, or his faith. He drained the rest of his beer and exited through the same door the big man had used. It led onto a paved path, with outhouses constructed of rough-sawn timbers to the left and a shoulder-high stack of logs straight ahead. He heard the thwack of an axe splitting wood.

Aldric skirted the logs and came across the hulking man, Stray Dog. He was stripped to the waist, dark skin exposed to the frigid air. He stood in front of an old, hardened stump. An axe was in one hand, but due to his bulk it looked almost like a hatchet. Split logs lay to either side.

The man glanced at Aldric, then buried the axe in the stump and tied back his dark mane of hair with a leather thong. His sweating torso was decorated with scars as well, though not nearly as many as on his arms. Some, Aldric noted, were puckered spots—puncture wounds—in places that should have proved fatal, which meant a priest must have healed him. Whoever this Stray Dog was, he'd fought and survived many battles, if only by the grace of one of the gods.

He pulled the axe out and circled the stump, making sure Aldric was in front of him. He'd moved closer to his weapons: two war axes resting against another pile of logs—single-bladed with a short spike on the back. They weren't anything fancy and looked well-worn and cared for.

The man positioned a log on the stump, and the axe came down, splitting it neatly in two. He didn't look at Aldric, just continued with his task. Aldric found a log to sit on.

"Can I help you with something?" Stray Dog said eventually. His voice was smooth and cultured, belying his appearance. He placed another log on the stump and chopped it in half. His movements were economical, and the log had split effortlessly.

"Not really," Aldric said. "I'm just curious."

"Curiosity can be dangerous," the man said, his voice flat.

He gathered the log halves and split them into quarters. Aldric shrugged, watching as he easily lifted another log to the stump.

"Have you done much fighting?" he asked.

Stray Dog glanced at him sidelong, knowing Aldric could see his scars. "I try to avoid it. There are so many enemies out there, and, well, you can't kill them all."

Aldric nodded thoughtfully. "It would be foolish to try. Something a young man would do."

Wood cracked, and more split logs joined the piles.

"We all do foolish things when we're young," Stray Dog said. "Sometimes they work out for the good, and sometimes not."

That struck close to what Aldric himself believed. "We do the best we can."

"That's true."

"Razmus said you're called Stray Dog. That's hardly a name."

"It's as good as any."

Aldric shrugged. "I suppose so. Do you have another?"

"Nope."

Stray Dog kept chopping logs, splitting the halves into smaller sections. Aldric felt comfortable with the man for some reason, far more than he did in Niklaus's company. He scratched his chin. The man would be a good fit for the team. He was a warrior, that was certain. The Church seemed to know what it was doing.

Aldric stood, and Stray Dog paused, axe held high.

"How do you feel about our mission? About killing Dead-eyes?" Aldric asked.

The axe descended, splitting another log. "There's no end to those creatures," Stray Dog said, shaking his head. "They breed like rats. They're quick too. If you're not ready, they'll be on you before you know it. But they die like any other animal." He paused and scratched his arm. "Your star shows you're from the Church."

Aldric nodded. "Yes. I'm a magister of Menselas. Also joining us, from the Church of Sylva Kalisia, is another warrior named Niklaus. You would have seen him earlier when you carried firewood inside. We plan on leaving the day after tomorrow, once we've organized horses and gear."

"Good. I've had about enough of this place."

Aldric didn't hide his satisfaction at the big man's words. At least with him, he knew there wouldn't be another agenda. "Is there anything you need?"

Stray Dog's eyes narrowed in thought. "Food—the usual. I have my own camping gear. But … I have a request."

Aldric rubbed the back of his neck. He didn't need any more complications. "What's that?"

Stray Dog smiled. His teeth were small and white. "I do most of the cooking. These northerners are useless. Their food lacks taste."

Aldric snorted in amusement. "You'll get no argument from me." His own culinary skills left a great deal to be desired.

Stray Dog returned to chopping firewood.

Aldric waited a few moments, then went back inside. To his surprise, another woman stood near the front door.

"Excuse me," she said imperiously.

She wore a cloak, as if the warm room was too cold for her

liking. Her brown hair was pulled back and tightly braided, the ends secured with a silver chain. Her pale skin and high cheekbones made her face look severe. As far as Aldric could tell, she wasn't carrying a weapon.

"Yes?" he replied. He moved to take her arm and guide her outside, but she stepped away from him like an unbroken colt. He dropped his hand, not wanting to frighten her further.

"I heard you're heading up north to one of the settlements," she said.

As far as he was aware, the Churches hadn't spread word about the mission. He didn't know how this woman had heard about it, but it didn't feel right to him. If she wanted to join their group, she wouldn't get his agreement.

"We have all the people we need," he said.

The woman raised her eyebrows. A faint line of irritation appeared between them. "Really?" she said. "I'm sure having one more along couldn't hurt."

"We don't need anyone else. Now, if you'll excuse us, this is a private residence."

The woman's hand shot out to snag his sleeve. He looked down at it and frowned. Her nails were impeccably manicured and painted a purple so dark it was almost black.

"I'm afraid I have to insist," she said firmly. "You have a partner, do you not? He'll agree to me accompanying you."

Aldric removed her hand from his arm. "Will he now? Who are you? And why are you so keen on joining us?"

"I serve the Lady Sylva Kalisia. I want to see these poor settlers saved."

Aldric cursed inwardly. The degenerate goddess again. Niklaus would get a few choice words for setting him up like this. But ... the priestess had approached Aldric, not the mercenary. Could it be he didn't know about her? He thought about Niklaus's blunt manner. If he'd wanted this woman to join them, he would have just said so.

"Whatever's going on, it's between you and Niklaus," Aldric said.

The woman showed no recognition of the name, but she didn't look puzzled either.

"If he says you're coming," Aldric continued, "so be it. I can't do much about it. But don't drag me into your games."

The heat of the room suddenly felt stifling. He had a strong urge to take a walk in the cold air outside. He knew it wouldn't look good, but he needed some time alone. And maybe to visit Soki.

He turned to Razmus and Priska. "I'll be back later. We leave the day after tomorrow."

The woman's soft laughter followed him out the door.

# CHAPTER FOURTEEN

# UNPLEASANT ANSWERS

THEY WERE STRANGE, THE feelings inside Kurio. Dread, terror, yet … she also felt drawn to Gannon. He was beautiful and seductive. And quite possibly evil.

He had to know it was she who'd broken into his house and discovered his secret. But even so, here he was, lounging at his ease at The White Rabbit, waiting for her to join him.

Kurio looked down from the mezzanine level, where she'd secreted herself. It hadn't been much trouble to flit over the rooftops and find a way inside the building through a window in the attic. It seemed this level was closed to luncheon patrons; a red velvet rope barred people from ascending the stairs. So she was undisturbed, and the unlit booths were ideal places to conceal herself.

Gannon Chikaire occupied one of the tables in the center of the ground-floor dining room, a low-set, polished walnut affair surrounded on three sides by lounge chairs. He was dressed impeccably in charcoal gray pants and jacket, and a purple silk shirt fastened with pearl buttons. Apart from the ring on his finger, he wore no other jewelry. His boots were polished black, but weren't dress boots; they looked comfortable and serviceable, out of place with the rest of his outfit. He picked up a glass filled with pale green liquid, leaned back, and sipped. From what she could see, his eyes remained on the entrance to the dining room.

Kurio's heart hammered in her chest. She didn't want to go down there. Yet … she had to. He knew where she lived, and she had no idea how. She'd thought about moving again, but knew it would be no use. She couldn't hide from him. A shiver ran through her.

She checked her weapons and smoothed her clothes. Her crossbow she'd had to leave behind; it wasn't something she could conceal under the dressy clothes she'd had to wear to the club. A few daggers would have to do.

At least if she was to confront him, it would be in a room full of patrons. Usually she preferred to do business discreetly, but in this case it was probably wise to meet in a public place. Every fiber of her wanted to run, but that was a quick way to end up dead for certain. There had to be a way out of this situation.

She descended the stairs and made her way toward Gannon. One of the servers noticed her and glided in her direction, a frown on his face.

"Ah, Kurio," said Gannon when she was a few paces from him. His back was still to her, but somehow he'd been alerted to her presence. "I wasn't sure you'd accept my invitation."

The server hurried over and bowed obsequiously. "My apologies, sir, I don't know who this woman is, but—"

"She will be joining me," said Gannon, waving a hand at the server. "Please bring us a bottle of the Locyl-Sertral, something more than twenty years old."

The alchemical wines from the Locyl-Sertral region were famous and among the most expensive. Kurio had a bottle she'd stolen stored in a dark place, to be opened in celebration of her earning enough to finally give up thieving.

She perched on the edge of the chair opposite Gannon. "There's no need. I won't be staying long."

Gannon shook his head in disappointment. "Please reconsider, Kurio. We have much to talk about." He turned to the server. "Bring the bottle."

She kept her gaze on the tabletop, hands clenched in her lap to stop them trembling. She had visions of orange eyes and horned yellow skin. *Bloody hells, I should never have taken the job for Willas. Well, too late now.*

She cleared her throat. "I won't tell anyone." The words came out thinly, and she cursed herself for her weakness.

"Kurio, you wrong me." Sorrow tinged his words. "But that's not so surprising. People fear what they don't understand. But I hope to persuade you that my intentions are good."

*Good?* thought Kurio incredulously. *Harboring demons and eating human flesh?*

"You see," continued Gannon, "I'm employed by the ruling council of Caronath to investigate certain anomalies. And the creatures you saw are part of this commission. Their ... food source is supplied by the council from ... unfortunate accidental deaths."

"Really?" drawled Kurio.

Gannon flashed her a smile, and in spite of her misgivings, her heart skipped a beat.

"Truly. Everything is aboveboard. And although it may seem distasteful—"

*That's one word for it.*

"—it is essential. I implore you to look beyond the superficial and trust that what we're doing is for the benefit of all people. The creatures are part of a threat we're investigating."

He stopped as the server appeared bearing a blue-tinged glass bottle. The man turned the label for Gannon to examine, but he merely nodded and waved at him to be about his business. Soon there was a glass in front of each of them, half full of a sparkling blue wine. Kurio knew the bottle would have cost a small fortune.

And people who cared little for coin were the most dangerous sort.

She concentrated on keeping her hand still as she reached for her glass. The liquid danced on her tongue, the flavor gorgeous and hard to describe. It brought forth one of the few happy memories from her childhood. She immediately quashed it. That part of her life was dead to her.

She considered what Gannon had told her. Either he was lying, or he was telling the truth. Either way, she was in trouble. She doubted the council would like a thief not under their control knowing what they were doing.

"However, what you saw is of no relevance now," he continued. "The fell creatures were killed last night."

Kurio gasped. Did Gannon think ... "It wasn't me," she blurted.

"I know, Kurio. It was a coincidence, nothing more. Someone has brought forces to bear against me. Destroying my research is one part of their strategy." He sighed, as if disappointed that anyone would oppose him. "They will regret their actions."

"What is it you want from me?" Kurio said.

His blue eyes pierced hers. "Nothing onerous, I assure you. Indeed, it is my hope you will learn to enjoy it perhaps? You are ... different. As am I. And to be different is a power of a sort, is it not?"

"I guess so."

"It is," Gannon said firmly. "And even among all the wonders of this world, I find people to be the most intriguing. You do not belong among the masses. In short, I would enjoy your company, if you were able to forgive the rocky start to our relationship. I can promise ... adventure."

Bloody hells, he was tempting her. And her nature meant she couldn't just walk away, however much she wanted to. He was practically asking to woo her, and she found the prospect enticing.

It had been a long time since she'd had any feelings for a man. Her last fling had lasted only a few weeks before she got cold feet and fled. But Gannon was something else entirely. She had a sense she'd never be bored with him.

She stood abruptly and drained her glass in a few gulps, as if it were cheap ale. She placed the empty glass back on the table. "Consider me intrigued, Gannon Chikaire. But I usually avoid polite society. A bad experience when I was young."

"And it's easy for you to avoid notice, isn't it? It's one of your talents."

"It's part of my job, if that's what you're getting at." She'd had enough of this banter.

"Are you leaving so soon? Without eating? I understand. I rarely eat outside my home. You never know how the meat has been prepared. Do I have your permission to call upon you?"

Well, if he wanted her dead, she'd be a corpse floating in a canal by now. And her best option for finding out more of what was going on was from the inside. Besides, he'd aroused her curiosity—and something else.

"I warn you, I'm dangerous," she said.

"As are all beautiful things," he replied.

*Like yourself.* "Very well. You have my permission to call upon me."

"Excellent! I'm arranging something in a few days that you might find amusing. I'll send word to your apartment. I'm unable to see you sooner, unfortunately. There's something I have to deal with—a commotion around an ancient ruin that's been found. A couple of the Churches have sent representatives to investigate."

Nothing to do with her. "I'll bid you good day, Gannon. I have business to attend to."

He smiled knowingly, as if aware of her false excuse. "Until we meet again. Farewell."

Kurio nodded and left, this time through the front entrance. It would take her an hour to walk back to her bolthole, and she could use the time to think. Was Gannon playing with her, as a cat did with a mouse?

One thing was for certain: she needed more information, whether to align herself with him, or to extricate herself from this mess.

~ ~ ~

Kurio returned to her bolthole to change clothes and clip her crossbow to her belt under her coat. She felt better having the weapon on her. A short time later, she scaled the wall surrounding the university and made her way through bushes before strolling nonchalantly along a worn track as if she belonged there.

The university was much as Kurio remembered it. Self-important students hurried along paved paths crossing a grassy courtyard surrounded by sandstone buildings. They clutched leather satchels filled with books and notepaper, and all of them spent more on clothes in one week than the average person spent in a few years. Education and knowledge, it seemed, were only for the rich.

In one corner of the courtyard, a tree dropped purple blossoms, so many the area underneath was completely covered. Kurio remembered slipping on them once and almost falling on her face.

One of the masters strolled by at a distinctly slower pace than the students. Her name was Roselin, if Kurio remembered correctly. Puffy-faced and always late to the classes she taught. Her specialty was alchemy, which, while interesting, and something Kurio had a few questions about, wasn't the discipline of the master she was looking for.

A group of students walked past the column Kurio leaned against, and she turned her head away. Though her hood concealed her face, she couldn't take any chances. She'd swapped her red wig for one close to her natural hair color and style back when she was a student; otherwise the master she wanted to see might not recognize her. It was a risk, what with her family still looking for her; but on balance, the paper she'd found underneath the metal cube was more important. If someone reported her presence here to her family, she'd be long gone by the time they came looking for her.

A short, squat man dressed in the black robes of a master came out of a side door. *There.* Master Okas still looked the same: his lank dark hair needed a wash, and his fingers were stained with ink. She'd fallen asleep in his classes, but apparently he spoke and read Skanuric like a native.

Kurio followed a discreet distance behind Okas as he wandered along lost in thought, head bowed to gaze at the path just in front of him. She glanced at the clock above the main entrance to the great hall. Almost midday. Classes would be over soon, and the students would crowd the place as they made their way to lunch. Okas had left to avoid the crush.

The master wandered through a tunnel and passed the ivy-covered history and philosophy buildings before entering the masters' residence. Kurio cursed. Of course he was coming here. She should have realized.

She slipped inside and trailed him up a flight of broad wooden stairs. When he turned down a side corridor, she quickened her pace. He'd withdrawn a key and was about to unlock a door—presumably to his rooms—when Kurio cleared her throat.

Okas looked up, eyes wide with surprise. "You shouldn't be here, young miss. This is the masters' private residence. Now, please—"

Kurio waved the paper in front of his face. "Skanuric writing. I need it translated. I heard you're the man for the job. I'll pay well."

Okas's eyes narrowed as he looked at her. They flicked to the paper, then back to meet her own. "Don't I know you? You were a student here once."

"A long time ago." Kurio jingled a heavy purse in front of his face. Due to her disturbing lack of funds, she'd had to fill it with mostly copper royals, but the top layer was silver. "Here," she said, opening it. "Silver, and a lot of it. For your trouble and discretion."

"Bah!" Okas waved the purse away. "If I need coin, I've plenty of options. And none of them mean my lunch will go cold."

*Bloody hells.* She hadn't counted on him refusing. *Everyone wants royals, don't they?*

"Listen," she began.

"Piss off," growled Okas. He inserted the key into the lock and opened the door a crack. "I don't know who you think you are, but my time is—"

Kurio kicked the door wide open and shoved Okas inside the room. He stumbled to his knees, and she slammed the door shut behind them.

"What the hells do you think you're doing?" he shouted, red-faced. He lurched to his feet.

Kurio spread her hands, one still clutching the purse. Her movement had stirred a copper to the surface. "Calm down," she said softly, squeezing the purse shut. "You'll want to work on this. Trust me."

"Trust you?" he said incredulously. "You kicked my door in and shoved me to the floor!"

"It was already open."

"Get out before I call for the guards!"

"What guards?"

Okas hesitated. "The other masters will come. We'll throw you out, and you'll be banned from the university for life."

*That'll make twice.*

"Listen to me," Kurio said, enunciating every word slowly. "I found the paper in an ironwood chest banded with ensorcelled orichalcum and secured with a Sandoval lock."

*No need to mention the metal cube also covered in Skanuric script.* Gannon had to be linked to the cube in some way. Despite his lack of interest in it at the time, she couldn't see him staying away from something like this. His hands would be all over it.

Okas frowned and crossed his arms over his chest, resting them atop his belly. "Found it? How?" The skepticism in his tone was unmistakable, but at least he'd calmed down and wasn't shouting.

Kurio kept one ear trained on the door to make sure no one was coming to investigate the disturbance. With any luck, the masters would all be feeding their faces and guzzling expensive wine, and no one would notice.

"That's none of your concern," she said. "But I know it's valuable. It could reveal the answer to a mystery that's been lost for thousands of years." She was warming to her task now and injected more excitement into her words. "Just think of it! You'll be famous. I mean, more famous. What ancient secrets will this paper unlock? It could be a ... map! Directing us to untold treasures. To ancient sorcerous artifacts of immense power." She lowered her voice and stared Okas in the eye. "Someone died to get this into my hands."

*That was true enough.*

He snorted. "The paper looks new to me."

"Well, yes, but it's obviously valuable."

Okas sighed loudly, like she was an unruly student he was going to fail unless she passed this one final exam. "Hand it over, then. And once I'm done, you'll get out of my room and leave the university grounds. I don't want to see you again. Is that clear?"

He reached for the paper. Kurio jerked it out of his reach, and his fingers closed on empty air.

"What—"

"I need reassurances," she said firmly. "This stays between us. You don't tell anyone else. And you forget you ever saw me."

Okas squinted at her. "Wait. I do know you. You're the student that—"

She shoved the paper at him. "Just read it."

"The mess took days to clean up. There are still stains in the stone floor."

Kurio gritted her teeth. "Just read it."

Okas took the paper from her. He frowned, tutted, then went to the closest window. Holding it to the light, he studied the writing, lips moving slightly. Blood drained from his face.

"Nysrog," he whispered. His eyes followed more lines of script; then he threw the paper at her. "Get out! You get out of here!"

"Calm down. What is it? What or who is Nysrog?"

Okas's face went even paler. He pointed at the door, hand trembling like he was an alcoholic who hadn't had a drink in days. Or like Kurio's had when she'd encountered the demons, and when she'd met Gannon for dinner …

"Get out! You've put me in danger. You're likely dead yourself. Go." His voice cracked. "Please. Just go."

Kurio bent to pick up the paper. "Not until you tell me what's going on."

"By all the gods." Okas staggered to a chair and collapsed into it. His hands clutched at his chest.

"Are you all right? I'll get you some water."

"Forget water!" he shrieked. "If you have any sense, you'll return the paper to where you found it and disappear. Go far away. Maybe you'll live. Who knows? I'm too old to run."

"Come on, old man, I haven't killed you."

"You bloody well have." He buried his face in his hands. "You stupid girl."

"Tell me, then—what does the paper say? Why should I run?"

Okas's reaction gave her pause, but he was a fat old man who'd lived most of his life closeted at the university. He wasn't like her. No one was. As Gannon said, she was different.

Maybe she should try another tack. "If I'm going to die, I want to know why."

Okas spoke as if she wasn't in the room with him. "Much of history has been lost, destroyed because of the cataclysms," he whispered. "By people who didn't want the truth to be known. I found hints and followed them. It took years … but all the tales are true, and terrifying. The demon … its darkness blotted out the sun. The world almost ended."

"What are you babbling about? The gods keep the demons imprisoned. That's one of their burdens."

Okas laughed weakly. He lifted his head, and she saw shiny tear trails down his face. "Such truths hidden in simple tales. The Tainted Cabal were reckless sorcerers lusting after power, and they brought forth a demon lord, Nysrog. Eventually, they were defeated, and Nysrog was returned to whatever foul pit it came from. Its progeny scattered and were eventually hunted down and killed."

*Interesting.*

"There's no mention of this in the histories," Kurio said. Which meant it had been deliberately left out or removed. And to do that would take many years and many men with a single purpose.

"History belongs to the victor," said Okas. "And this victor wanted such knowledge scoured from our minds and records. The books where you'll find mention of it are rare and coveted." He wiped his eyes with the palms of his hands. A sigh escaped him, and his body deflated, like he'd given up all hope. "Just go."

Kurio shook her head. "Not before you tell me more."

"Foolish girl. You stole that paper from the Tainted Cabal. Or from someone who wanted to hide it from them. Whoever it was, they'll come for you. And you'll wish for death long before they're done with you."

So filled with conviction was Okas's tone, a chill ran through Kurio. He honestly believed they were both dead.

"What is the Tainted Cabal?" she asked.

"Worshipers of Nysrog. Sorcerers who banded together and summoned a demon they thought they could control. They were wrong. The demon ... warped their minds. Dominated them, so in the end they became its tools." Okas leaned back in the chair and rubbed his eyes. "It was thousands of years ago. And afterward, the Churches made sure they destroyed any records. Eventually, the demon, and the Cabal, became a legend. Now, the Cabal has almost disappeared. Some remember, though, and wait."

"Wait? For what?"

"To bring Nysrog back. The paper you showed me mentions a cube that supposedly contains immense sorcerous power. An artifact that could either return the demon lord to our realm or imprison him."

Kurio looked at her hands. It all sounded so ... crazy. But Okas certainly believed it, and he wasn't insane or stupid. Was Gannon part of this Cabal, or was he involved in something else? Was he telling her the truth earlier, that he was just a researcher? Perhaps Willas was the mastermind and was using Gannon?

"So, this Cabal, they work to bring back Nysrog, but after thousands of years they've been unsuccessful. Why? And after so many years of failure, why haven't they given up?"

"The sorcerers of the Tainted Cabal cannot die. Nysrog corrupted them, and they can do nothing but seek his return. The desire burns hot within their souls."

"They wait." Kurio repeated Okas's earlier words.

"Exactly. And now you've stolen something from them. They

will come for you. And for me."

It didn't make sense. There hadn't been any sorcery protecting the chest. Was this Cabal so incompetent they couldn't repeat what they'd done thousands of years ago? No … there was more to this story. Something, or someone, had to be opposing them.

"For an evil sorcerous organization that worships demons, they haven't done much in a few thousand years. You've not told me everything. Tell me what you know."

Okas chuckled humorlessly, like someone had told a joke at a funeral. "After they were defeated, the sorcerers were much reduced. They fled, went into hiding. Though they'd gained much knowledge from the demon, they weren't powerful enough to implement it. And the Churches and their sorcerers decided on two actions: they would create an order to forever oppose the followers of Nysrog, and they'd construct traps for them."

"You mean sorcerous traps of some kind?"

Okas nodded. "The Tainted Cabal are always seeking to expand their expertise and power, and for that they need sorcerous artifacts."

"From the ancient ruins around the place?"

"Yes. Most of the ruins are harmless, at least to competent sorcerers. But the ones concealing true power, they've been … taken over, I guess you could say. If someone with enough power meddles with certain artifacts hidden in ruins, a virulent sorcery is unleashed. Disaster follows. Destruction. Just after Nysrog, it was thought the best course of action was to prevent the return of the demon lord at any cost. People were desperate; they'd been through such horrors as you wouldn't believe. The cataclysms weren't natural occurrences. They were caused by the Revenants, which were created by the Churches and sorcerers to limit sorcerous power in the world and hopefully to prevent the return of Nysrog."

Kurio squirmed under the intensity of Okas's gaze. She

decided to come clean.

"I don't think," she said slowly as her thoughts coalesced, "I stole ..: I mean, I don't think this paper was in the Tainted Cabal's possession. There wasn't any sorcery protecting it. And the house where it was held was just a noble's residence. Nothing malevolent about it."

Okas perked up. By the time she'd finished speaking, he was on his feet, chewing a thumbnail. "This noble—don't tell me his name—is he powerful? Is there anything unusual about him?"

Kurio thought for a moment. "I guess he's powerful. He has a lot of coin, anyway, and commands a lot of soldiers. Even has an elite squad, from what I'm told."

Okas began pacing. "Maybe ..." he said softly. "Could it be?" He turned to Kurio, exhaling hard through his nose. "We might be saved. You have to take the paper back to him."

"What? I'll do no such thing. He'll lock me up!" *Or kill me.*

Okas gripped her shoulders with surprising strength. "Listen to me," he said urgently. "Just as the Tainted Cabal works in secret, so does the organization opposing them. If this noble is involved with them—"

"Then he'll string me up! And if he's with the Cabal, he'll definitely kill me."

Kurio thought back to Gannon giving Willas orders, and the chills she'd felt when she entered the room. *Bloody hells. Have I just aided the Cabal? Is Okas right—am I dead already? But if so, why didn't they kill me then? And who sent Gerret to the house?*

"You must give it back!" Okas repeated, shaking her violently.

She grabbed the hilt of a dagger and almost punctured his lung before pushing his hands off her and backing away. Maybe she could send a messenger to return the paper, a street urchin perhaps? But she knew she couldn't trust anyone else with it now.

"I'll do it," she said softly.

*Why did I say that? I should run far, far away.*

"Then go," Okas said. "Never mention my name. Come back here if …" He trailed off, dropping his eyes to the floor.

"If I'm alive?" she finished with a wry smile.

Kurio left the old master to torture himself with fear. If he was right, maybe she could flee the city and hope they never find her—not a palatable option. Or she could return the paper and hope they didn't kill her. And if Okas was wrong, and there was no weird Tainted Cabal, the owner of the paper would likely pay her some royals to regain it. She'd have to be careful though, as they might suspect she knew something about the theft of the cube. But that was why fences were in business.

Exiting the masters' residence, Kurio glanced around. A few students strolled by, talking quietly. No one had followed her here, and no one knew she'd stolen the paper. The old fool's tales had made her nervous.

She strode down the path, heading for a narrow alley that would save her some time. She turned the corner and stopped. In front of her were two men, both staring at her with flat eyes. She could see scars on their fingers and hands: cuts from many a sword fight.

"Excuse me," she said, backing away, her hand reaching for her crossbow. "I think I've—"

Something covered her head from behind. A scratchy hessian sack.

"Fire! Fire!" she shouted, knowing that calling for help was useless.

She scratched at the hands holding the sack. Something struck her head hard enough to rock it sideways. Stars erupted before her eyes, and she felt the world spin around her.

## Chapter Fifteen

# Sorcerous Attachments

SOKI RUMMAGED THROUGH A pile of papers she'd pulled from a leather folder. Each page was covered with calculations and geometries: formulas and methodologies for controlling and shaping sorcery.

They were in her private study located at the back of her shop. Aldric had been surprised to find she lived on the second floor rather than in a lavish mansion somewhere. With her power and skill, she could charge an exorbitant sum for her services. But it had pleased Aldric to find that she cared more about her work than about coin.

The room was cozy, with a fire burning in one corner. Tables and shelves lined the walls, all filled with curiosities and knick-knacks: colored rocks, polished woods; bleached skulls of different creatures; jars containing a yellow-tinged pickling solution, and animals he didn't look too closely at. From one, an eye the size of his fist stared out at him.

Aldric watched Soki as she examined each piece of paper, the tip of her tongue poking from between her lips as she concentrated. He relaxed in his armchair and sipped his tea, letting the warmth of the cup seep into his hands, comfortable for the first time in quite a while.

"I noticed a small flaw in your dormant wards," Soki said, glancing at him, then going back to her schematics. "If you'll forgive me, I think I can fix it. Do you use a talisman when you construct them?"

"Yes," Aldric said. "But ... I try to use sorcery as little as possible."

Her dark eyes locked onto his, and he looked away.

"Because of ...?"

"My god, yes. And the Church's attitude toward us."

Her hand reached over to clasp his. It felt hot on his skin. "Aldric, sorcery isn't a sin or a curse. You were born—"

"I wasn't born a sorcerer. My mark appeared later."

"It doesn't matter when it appeared. You were born a sorcerer. You should embrace what you can do. I can teach you, guide you, if you're here for a while. I assumed ... you are staying, aren't you?"

He nodded. *Until they've had enough of me and shuffle me off somewhere else.* "Yes. I've been assigned here, and my guess is it'll be for a few years. It takes time for the priests to get used to me, so they don't move me around much. No matter, there's always someone who can't reconcile their faith with what I am."

Soki flashed him a smile, then went back to looking through her designs. "Good. I think there's much we could learn from each other. And I enjoy your company."

"And I yours. I have a mission already though. I'll be gone for at least a few weeks, probably longer."

Once the settlers were trained to his satisfaction, he couldn't see them waiting for the Dead-eyes to come to the settlement. They'd probably have to hunt them down in the mountains, but at least that would shorten the trip.

"Oh." Soki stopped riffling through the pages and reached for her tea. "Damn, it's gone cold." She whispered a cant, and steam rose from the cup.

Aldric was impressed. She showed such a fine control of her abilities, something that was far beyond him, even if he studied and practiced for decades.

"Where are you going?" she asked.

"There's a settlement that's come under attack from some Dead-eyes. The Church of Menselas has joined with another Church to help the people there. A show of unity, or so I'm told."

"Filthy creatures. The Dead-eyes, I mean. They're always a nuisance up here. I don't know why they keep harassing us. There's enough grubs, worms, bugs, and mushrooms for them to live off in the forests and mountains." Soki cleared her throat and sipped her tea. "I thought we'd have a bit more time together before you became too busy with your new duties."

"I'll buy you an expensive dinner when I get back. Or three."

Soki laughed. "Pleasant company is what I need, not expensive food. Street-vendor fare is good enough for me, if I'm with the right person."

*Am I that right person?*

"That sounds … enticing. There's still much of the city I haven't seen. I'd like it if you showed me more."

Soki frowned and blew the surface of her tea. "This settlement … Is there a ruin close by? That would …" She trailed off.

"So the archbishop says. I gather he's keen for me to recover some artifacts from it, though I don't see the point."

"Aldric, I …" She hesitated. "I have to tell you something. I agreed to do some work for your Church a few days ago. A priest came to see me. Standard contract conditions: artifact examination and analysis, with recommendations. He paid well—not that I need the royals, but something this big piqued my interest. And making the connection with your Church didn't hurt. They avoid sorcery, as you know, and I thought it a golden opportunity."

It was one thing for Hannus to order Aldric to bring back what he could find in a ruin, but another entirely to engage a sorcerer to examine such artifacts. A sorcerer not of the Church, no less.

"What's the artifact?" he asked.

"That's the strange thing. He didn't have it yet. Said it might be a few weeks until it was in their hands."

Aldric grunted. His Church was playing some sort of game, and they'd dragged both him and Soki into it. "Bloody hells!" he said under his breath. "I don't know if Hannus or Hierophant Karianne is behind this, but I mean to find out. Have you ever been asked to examine something found in a ruin that turned out to be ... beneficial?"

"To have power? An artifact that could be used?"

"Yes."

"A few times. Just small things. Once there was a dagger—a knife, really. Its metal was still bright, though it had to be really old. It wasn't blunt to the touch, but it wasn't sharp either, yet it cut through metal like it was soft cheese. A noble bought it from a merchant for a considerable sum, and I never saw it again. I've a sketch of it somewhere. The sorcery on it ... I've never seen the like, and I don't think I ever will again. It had edges ... not of this world."

Aldric wasn't entirely sure what she meant, and he didn't want to know. Sorcery such as that was beyond him.

"The settler that came here—do you think he's genuine?" he asked.

"I expect you'll find out when you get to where the settlement's supposed to be. Which means, instead of sightseeing, we'll have to spend the time until you leave working on your sorcery."

"But—"

"No excuses. If you get injured out there and I could have done something to prevent it, I'll be annoyed."

"Annoyed? Is that all?"

Soki's eyes glittered, and she smirked. "Maybe more. Pour

yourself some tea, and we'll start right now."

Aldric did as she suggested. Already, things were growing complicated, and he couldn't be sure what he'd face out there in the wilderness. When situations became desperate, he couldn't deny sorcery came in handy.

"I can't stay long," he said. "I have to be up at first light to arrange mounts and gear."

Soki cleared her throat, then glanced at him, and away. "Only a few lessons, I promise. Then you can relax. Stay the night. I'll wake you before dawn."

Aldric's heart beat faster, and his throat tightened. He could get to like it here. Perhaps he'd finally found a place where he could settle down. But cursed as he was, did he deserve it? And would his Church let him stay? "I'd enjoy that," he said.

Soki leaned over and their lips met.

~ ~ ~

Aldric buckled his khopesh belt around his waist, then realized he hadn't put his boots on yet. He cursed quietly, glancing at Soki, who was still asleep. Except she wasn't. Her eyes were open, and she began to laugh.

"Were you sneaking out before I woke?" she said.

"No. I just wanted you to rest. I would have woken you to say goodbye. Today I'll be busy organizing our departure."

Aldric was a little uncomfortable, he had to admit. Some in the Church saw relationships as a sign a priest wasn't fully devoted to the faith. And Aldric knew any relationship he had would be intensely scrutinized. It was bad enough the Church interrogated him constantly because he was a sorcerer; add in a sorcerer lover, and they'd submit him to even more intense grilling.

Rubbing her eyes, Soki snuggled further under the quilt. "The ward I cast woke me at the same time as you. It's still warm in bed though. Maybe you should come back. Would it be so bad if you didn't leave until later?"

Aldric looked down at his bare feet. He wanted to stay, but …

"I can't," he said reluctantly. "The sooner we leave for the settlement, the sooner I'll be back. And I don't know if I can trust this mercenary, Niklaus. I need to make sure the men we've been given can do the job."

Soki threw off the covers, stood up and stretched. She was completely naked. Her skin shone in the light of the sorcerous lamp. Aldric felt his face flush. He looked away, then cursed himself for a fool and turned back to openly delight in her body.

She laughed warmly at his attention, then slipped a nightshirt over her head.

"I'll help you with your boots," she said. "Then you can get to work while I go back to bed. And, Aldric, please be careful."

He met her eyes and nodded. "I will. This mission will be over before you know it."

## CHAPTER SIXTEEN

# ANOTHER INVITATION

THIS MISSION WAS ALREADY turning into a headache for Aldric. In a brief moment of self-pity, he longed for the vastness and solitude of the wilderness, where he felt more at home than in a bustling city, dealing with other people.

After acquiring mounts and saddles, he'd traced Niklaus to a blacksmith's, where Razmus had said the mercenary was buying weapons. Except as far as Aldric could see, Niklaus hadn't purchased anything. The mercenary was speaking heatedly to an older man.

For a change, it was Niklaus who was agitated, and the man he spoke to was calm and collected. He was long in the tooth, but carried himself well, his weight spread evenly across both feet. His dark eyes scanned the crowd in the street even as he listened to Niklaus. A slightly curved sword swung low from his left hip, and the thumb of his right hand was casually hooked into his belt— ready to draw the sword if necessary. There was a wiry hardness to the man and a wariness. *He always expects a fight,* Aldric thought. *And expects to win.*

The man shook his head, and Niklaus raised his eyes to the sky, then ran a hand through his hair. Negotiations weren't going too well, then.

Aldric crossed the busy street, catching Niklaus's eye as he approached. The mercenary waved him closer.

"Tell him, Aldric. There will be danger aplenty on this trip. Not just Dead-eyes, but other creatures too." He turned his head and winked at Aldric.

"I saw that," said the man.

Aldric wasn't sure what to say. Niklaus's words implied the man didn't want to join them because the mission wasn't dangerous enough. And it seemed the two men knew each other already. He settled for: "I'm Aldric. A magister of the Five."

The swordsman gave him a short nod. "You can call me Bryn. Niklaus here tells me you're going to babysit some settlers. People that can't even fight off some Dead-eyes."

"But there's more!" Niklaus said. "A lost ruin! Riches beyond—"

"I'm not interested in riches," interrupted Bryn. "I did a lot of spending when I was young, and it wasn't all it's cracked up to be. I'm after a challenge. Thought you'd be the one to provide it, but seems I was wrong."

"A whole tribe of Dead-eyes, Bryn. Plus whatever's leading them. It was luck that I found you here, and luck will make you rich."

"Probably just a smarter Dead-eye," said Bryn. "Though there aren't many of them. I think I'll look elsewhere. There's rumor of something dangerous stalking trappers to the west."

"Maybe it's a Dead-eye leading them," Niklaus said. "Maybe not. Over the centuries, other beings have used the Dead-eyes for their own purposes. It could even be a wraithe!"

Aldric turned his head sharply to Niklaus, but the mercenary was looking at Bryn. He couldn't possibly know about Aldric's encounter with the wraithe in the wilderness. It had to be a coincidence.

"And think of the ruins," Niklaus continued. "There'll be

something inside guarding the treasures. There always is."

Bryn grunted, unimpressed, fingers tapping the pommel of his sword. "You can't guarantee anything."

Aldric saw the pommel was made of cast silver in the shape of a hideously disfigured face with the tongue sticking out. The hilt was covered with tanned sea-ray skin: the choice of many a master swordsman for its excellent grip. If Bryn was as good as Niklaus seemed to think he was, he'd be an asset to their team. But Aldric sensed Niklaus was fighting a losing battle.

"I don't know what you're after," he said to Bryn, "but there are no guarantees anywhere. What we'll be doing is dangerous, and there's a chance—a small one, admittedly—that we'll have to face stronger powers."

Bryn's pale eyes regarded him. "You've been told to go by your Church?"

Aldric nodded. "I'm usually sent to sort out difficult situations."

The swordsman turned to Niklaus. "And you're here on the Lady's request?"

The mercenary's face was studiously blank. "Yes. I believe so."

"Well," Bryn said, "this stinks to the abyss—your two faiths teaming up. This isn't a walk in the park, no matter what they've told you."

"I've worked that out already," Aldric said. "I think we both have."

"Hmm," Bryn said. "I'm in. Whatever's going on, I think it'll turn nasty."

Niklaus grinned. "That's the spirit! Now, get your gear together and meet us at the old haggle yard on Locust Street. Do you have a horse? Good, we're leaving tomorrow. We'll provide all food and lodging, plus a decent bonus."

"Fifty gold royals now. Another fifty when we're done," Bryn said.

Aldric shook his head. A hundred golds? They could hire at least fifty men for that and still have change.

"Done!" Niklaus said.

Aldric felt his temper flare. How could Niklaus agree so readily to such an outrageous sum?

"I'll get your coins," the mercenary continued. "Now, if you'll excuse me, I need to arrange supplies, and there's some business I have to attend to. Aldric, you've got the mounts? Bryn has his own."

Aldric nodded, keeping his temper in check. "Yes. I've organized them. There are six of us so far." Hopefully Niklaus wouldn't hire anyone else.

Niklaus's eyes narrowed. "That brute chopping wood, what's he like?"

"He can handle himself. Oh, I forgot to tell you. A woman turned up after you left—one of your Church's priestesses. She wants to join us."

Niklaus sneered and looked about to spit, then thought better of it. "Bloody meddlers," he said vehemently. "Think they know everything. I'll deal with her." He stormed off without a farewell.

Aldric's mind was still reeling at Niklaus agreeing to pay a hundred gold royals to Bryn. "Why would Niklaus pay so much for you?" he asked the man cautiously, then held up a hand. "No offense, but that's a lot of coin."

Bryn smiled and tapped a finger on his sword's pommel. "Not so hard to believe if you know Niklaus. He doesn't care for coin, or many other things. He'd spend a fortune to have someone he trusts who's decent with a sword guarding his back. And he wants the company too: he doesn't like boredom. He could have used the coin to hire a few dozen fighters, but then he'd have the headache of looking after them."

Aldric exhaled hard through his nose. He'd prefer a dozen good men to one extraordinary one, but it was Niklaus's money, not the Church's, that was paying for Bryn. Well, it couldn't be helped. It seemed Niklaus would do whatever he wanted, Aldric's views be damned.

"How long have you known him?" he asked Bryn.

"He's an odd one. I've known him for years, and *of* him for decades. I move from town to town, looking for challenges, and we've worked together a few times here in the north. Some treasure hunting. Some mercenary work."

It seemed vague descriptions were all Aldric would get out of Bryn. "He's a good fighter, then?"

"Good?" Bryn laughed. "He's one of a kind. Trust me, Magister, you don't want to be on the wrong side of Niklaus. He's the best I've ever seen. Go against him, and he'll put you down, sword or no sword, sorcery or no sorcery. And your faith won't help you either. I've seen it. He's a demon in human form, or so some say."

"Those that have faced him?"

Bryn laughed evilly. "No. They're all dead."

## CHAPTER SEVENTEEN

# TRUTHS AND CHAINS

KURIO WOKE TO A stench she'd hoped never to smell again: burned flesh, overlaid with something sharp. The abhorrent odor seemed to have substance as it forced its way into her nostrils and mouth and into her lungs. She blinked, trying to focus. She shook her head, and a fresh wave of agony overcame her. Her hair covered her face, and she realized she'd been strung up by her arms and was hanging in the middle of a dimly lit room. Her feet dragged on the floor, and her arms had lost all feeling. Sweat trickled down her face and onto her lips. She sucked at it greedily before she could control herself. She was thirsty, her mouth as dry as a desert.

She raised her head slowly, to avoid any more pain. The filthy space was lit by a motley collection of lamps that cast a muted yellow glow over a number of tables and vats and containers, all covered with years of grime and gods knew what else. More light came from a brazier in one corner. Hot coals glowed orange, and rusty metal bars poked from them, their ends wrapped with leather strips.

Kurio didn't want to inspect the devices closely, but her eyes were drawn to a table that held a collection of metal implements. Unlike the rest of this shithole, they were bright and shiny.

Someone cared for them.

*I'm in a lot of trouble.*

She stood, wobbling slightly, and wriggled her body, hoping to get blood circulating into her arms so they weren't completely useless. As they began to regain feeling, she gasped. Bloody hells, they felt like they were on fire! She whimpered, waiting for the throbbing to subside. A trail of blood flowed down each arm, caused by the edges of the iron manacles cutting into her wrists. They were closed with a lock, not riveted shut, which was something, she supposed. Separate chains ran from them up to a pulley system bolted to the ceiling.

When she thought she could move a bit more without passing out, she took stock. She had none of her weapons and didn't know where she was or who had captured her.

On another table, jars and vials caught her eye. Underneath the table lay pale shapes that were probably teeth and splinters of what was maybe bone. From somewhere that might have been a few rooms away came a long, low, moaning wail.

*Big trouble.*

Metal squealed behind her, and she jerked around, unable to control her breathing. "Who are you?" she gasped.

Through a broad oak door walked a squat man wearing a leather apron. He might have been a blacksmith with those muscled arms covered with cuts and burn marks. But she knew he wasn't.

He leered at her with pale gray eyes and shook his bald head. "Didn't think you'd be awake yet."

Kurio became aware of how her position tightened her clothes against her body. She took a few deep breaths to calm herself as the torturer scuttled over to the brazier. He stamped on a foot-bellows to the side and pumped vigorously. The coals flared and hissed, spitting sparks into the air. Apparently satisfied with the heat, he moved to the table with the shiny implements and paused, one finger tapping his lips.

"Listen," Kurio said, desperation in her voice. "There's been a misunderstanding. I'm sure we can clear it up. Whatever you think I've done, I didn't. Please, you have to believe me. And if I have something that's yours, take it." She knew she was babbling, but couldn't stop herself. "I don't know where this stuff comes from. I'm just a fence. I resell stolen goods. I don't make it my business to know what they are, or read ... whatever might be on any papers or in books. If you just let me go, I'll disappear, and we can both forget this happened."

The torturer snorted. "Not likely." He picked up something the length of a finger that looked like a cross between a miniature sickle and a corkscrew. He smiled at her. "I have some special tricks for the ladies. They talk right quick."

Kurio's heart hammered in her chest. "We are talking! Fetch someone in charge, and I'm sure this'll all be cleared up."

"I ain't no dog," he growled. "Fetch this, fetch that." He spat on the floor.

She'd accidentally prodded a sore spot. "All right. I'm sorry. Of course you're not." She thought furiously, eyes on the bright, sharp instrument gripped in the sinewy hands. She could see this was a man who enjoyed his work. "I have information—"

"And I'll get it out of you."

"There's no need for that. I'll tell you ... your boss everything I know. I can't bear to think of myself maimed. I'm vain, you see."

He took a step toward her. "You won't be after I'm done with you."

Kurio licked sweat from her lips. *That's it, come closer.*

"Who holds your leash, I wonder?" she goaded. "Someone who doesn't mind working with scum like you. Do you bark when they call?"

He smiled thinly, but a red flush traveled up his neck, and the pulse there throbbed. He pointed the implement at her face and moved slowly toward her. Kurio flinched, as he expected her to, and jerked her face to the side. Feeling had returned to her arms and hands, and now was the time to act if she had any chance of surviving.

"Know what this'll do to you?" said the torturer.

Kurio wrapped her hands around the chains attached to her manacles. "No," she said, and jerked herself up, taking her weight on her aching arms.

A fleeting look of shock came over the torturer's face as she jumped and attempted to wrap her thighs around his neck. He slashed at her reflexively, and she kicked the implement out of his hands. It clanged to the floor, and as he bent to pick it up, she managed to kick him in the head.

He staggered, and she wrapped both legs around his neck. She locked her legs and squeezed her knees together. Her thighs pressed against his throat, gripping tight. She imagined his neck was a watermelon in a vise.

"Gah!" The torturer's face turned purple. He clutched her legs, desperately trying to pry himself free.

"Know what this'll do to you?" taunted Kurio.

His fists pounded her thighs, and she twisted violently, jerking him off his feet. She cried out in pain as she took his weight along with her own, but gritted her teeth until she could think again.

"It'll bloody kill you," she growled.

Panic flooded the torturer's bulging eyes. He whimpered and redoubled his efforts. He managed to get his feet under him and thrust himself upright. Agony flooded Kurio's arms as their combined weight almost ripped her wrists off, the manacles slicing into her skin.

The man staggered, and for an instant she thought he was going down, but he emitted a strangled moan and ran toward the wall. Kurio cried out as the chains tightened and the manacles gouged her wrists. Pain exploded. She bit her tongue, and hot metallic blood filled her mouth. Her shoulders burned, and her hands went numb. Warm crimson rivulets flowed down her arms as the torturer backed up a step, then jerked forward again and again.

*Shit. Shit. Shit. I can't—*

The man's feet slipped from under him, and he went limp. His eyes rolled into his head.

*Just a little longer …*

When she was certain he was dead, she let her legs go slack. Standing unsteadily, she spat blood from her mouth. It splattered onto other dark stains on the floor. Her eyes grew hot, and tears of relief flowed.

She took a few moments to suck in deep breaths, then shuffled over to the implement the torturer had dropped. She squeezed it between her feet and, moving carefully, rolled it so it rested on the top of her right boot, then flicked it into the air. She caught it on the first try and grinned.

It only took a moment to pick one lock, then use her free hand to pick the second. *Separate chains. Amateurs.*

She stood there, blood dribbling from her lips, sweaty and dirty, with a dead body next to her, and wondered what to do next. She had no idea where she was or who had captured her. What she did know was that she had to escape and, if possible, grab her equipment. The Skanuric paper she couldn't care less about now. They could have it, and good riddance.

The door swung open to reveal a man and a woman. The man was broad enough to block the doorway, and short enough that the woman's head peered over his close-cropped brown hair. He wore clothes of an expensive cotton weave, and a sheathed short sword dangled from his leather belt. The woman's long blond hair was tied up in a bun, and she wore traveler's leather pants and a thick linen shirt. Kurio hazarded a quick glance at their feet. You could tell a lot about a person from their footwear. He wore light leather boots, scuffed but obviously a swordsman's, while her boots were stained and worn—with a concealed blade.

The man frowned as he took in the dead torturer, Kurio's fresh blood splattered on the floor, and the implement in her bloody hand.

"Ah," said Kurio, brandishing the curved implement and wondering if she had time to grab another. "I was just leaving."

"No," the man said in a deep gravelly voice. "You're not."

The woman pushed past him into the room. "For god's sake, Mellish, you left her in here with Govert?"

Mellish shrugged. "Supposed to be his day off. How was I to know he'd decide to play torturer? The room was just supposed to scare her." He prodded Govert's body with his toe.

"Well, it looks like she's scared enough," said the woman.

"You don't care I killed Govert?" said Kurio.

"He did a job for us," the woman said. "There are plenty more deviants willing to replace him."

Kurio sidled around both of them toward the open door. She was almost there when she noticed two guards outside, both wearing boiled leather armor and carrying weighted blackjacks. She couldn't get past four of them. Not through the narrow corridors of a building she didn't know the layout of. She sidled the other way instead, toward the brazier.

"Don't try to run, my dear," said the woman. She flashed perfect white teeth at Kurio. "You've caused us enough trouble already."

*She's doing the talking,* thought Kurio. *Which means she's in charge. Mellish is only muscle.*

"You've got your paper," she said. "Now let me go."

The woman shook her head. "I'm afraid it's not that simple."

*It never is.*

"My name is Zarina," she continued. "And we need to know what you know. We want to know who hired you, where you delivered the cube, what you know about your employer, and what you know about us." She waved a hand around the room. "Although Govert is replaceable, I think you can see this room exists for a purpose. We try to avoid using it, but some people are ... recalcitrant. Are you recalcitrant, Kurio?"

Bloody hells, they knew her name. She shook her head, trying to project willing cooperation, and lowered the metal implement she still held in front of her. "No, no, not me. I'll tell you everything."

Willas and his weird friend Gannon could go to the hells for all she cared. It wasn't as if they'd worry about chasing her down if these people were after them, would they?

She took a deep breath. "A man named Willas hired me, a nobleman. He was sick, if that matters? I think he's dying."

"That's their style," growled Mellish.

"Hush," said Zarina. "Go on, my dear."

"Willas knew the layout of the building, gave me a diagram. He also knew about the Sandoval locking mechanism. He needed someone to crack it, was asking around the locksmiths. Word found its way to the Night Shadows, and I heard about it from an acquaintance. And for the hard-to-crack locks, I'm the one you want."

"But you didn't crack it," said Zarina. "You merely knew how it opened."

"Details," said Kurio dismissively. "Should I continue?"

Zarina raised her eyebrows. "Please do."

"When I took the cube—whatever it is, I don't know—I saw the paper and grabbed it. It wasn't part of the job, but it was obviously valuable, so ..."

"So you thought you could sell it," said Mellish.

She shrugged. "Maybe. Well, yes, in the beginning. But after I saw the writing was Skanuric, my curiosity was piqued."

"You recognized the writing?" said Zarina sharply.

"Yes. I'm not an idiot. There was another man with Willas when I delivered the cube. I'd never seen him before. He was … handsome. And big. Wore mail of some sort under his clothes."

Kurio wasn't telling them the whole story. You should always hold on to some cards.

"Could be anyone," said Zarina.

So they didn't know about Gannon. Did that mean he really was only a researcher? No. Somehow, Kurio knew he was the key to the whole affair.

She sighed. "There's something else. But I need assurances."

Mellish strode to the brazier and pumped the foot-bellows with regular strokes. The coals roared to life, glowing yellow. "Until we can replace Govert, it looks like I'll have to do the job."

Kurio dropped the torturer's implement and held her palms toward him in a gesture of submission. She knew when someone else held all the cards. "There's no need for that. He wore an odd ring, gold. It had a square face divided into four smaller squares. Each contained a Skanuric rune."

Mellish and Zarina looked at each other.

"You," Zarina said eventually, "are one lucky thief."

Mellish grunted. "Lucky they didn't kill you on the spot to cover their trail. Now, details, woman. What exactly happened? And what else do you know about the man with the ring?"

Kurio spilled it all: how she'd been contacted by the Night Shadows for the job; how much she'd been paid; where Willas lived; her encounters with Gannon, and the demons in his secret basement room; even that Gerret had waylaid her, and she'd had to kill him. She figured they probably knew about the dead thief already. When she'd finished, she felt exhausted. She'd been knocked about and needed rest. The blood on her arms had dried and stuck to her skin like glue.

Zarina looked perplexed, as if wrestling with a decision. She glanced at Mellish, then said, "What do you know of Nysrog?"

"Never heard of him. Is he a baker?"

"You've a smart mouth on you."

*So I've been told.*

"I don't know any Nysrog. Sounds like a foreign name. Is he a foreigner?"

"Do you believe her?" Zarina asked Mellish.

He nodded slowly. "She has no reason to lie. She knows that if we find out she's misled us, we'll have her back here and will pry the truth out one way or another. She's told us all she knows. Let's end this." He drew his sword.

"Wait!" screamed Kurio. "I told you the truth!"

"Mellish!" said Zarina. "We don't just kill people for no reason."

"We have good reasons," he replied.

"I swear it was the truth," said Kurio. "By all the gods I know. And any others I don't know about."

Mellish began to laugh. "The look on your face!" he said between chuckles.

Kurio's remaining strength drained from her, and she sagged to the floor. At least someone was enjoying themselves.

"We had to be sure," said Zarina.

*A practiced deception. Very funny.*

Kurio closed her eyes. "Please," she said, hating the note of surrender in her voice. "Just let me go."

"I'm afraid we can't do that," Zarina said. "You know too much."

Kurio slumped even more and held her head in her hands. "What now?" she asked, voice trembling.

"Now," Zarina said, "we get you cleaned up. Then we tell you more about what's going on. Then you decide to help us. We can use someone with your talents."

"What if I don't want to help you?"

Zarina laughed. "I'm afraid you don't have a choice."

~ ~ ~

Mellish and Zarina guided Kurio past the guards and down a long corridor. There were a lot of closed doors on the way. They came to a stone staircase leading up; Zarina went first, with Mellish pushing Kurio in the back when he thought she was moving too slow. They took her to a small room without much furniture. A few buckets filled with water sat next to an empty copper bathtub. A table to the side held towels and a brush. Mellish left and locked the door behind him.

"Strip," said Zarina.

"You first," replied Kurio.

"Do you have to make everything so difficult? You're filthy and stink like a lathered horse. And by the way, your wig's askew. Which isn't surprising given what you've been through."

With her head clearer and the threat of torture or death removed, Kurio decided to scale down her opposition and see what these people were all about. They weren't going to kill her—at least not just yet—and that meant she should play meek and mild and put them at ease. With any luck, she'd find her gear, and a little extra for her trouble, and make a hasty exit. Her trusty crossbow would be difficult to replace, and it was an expense she couldn't afford at the moment.

"All right," she said, removing the wig. She ran her fingers over her short-cropped hair, then jerked them away, realizing she'd probably just rubbed grime from the torture chamber into it. She grimaced with disgust.

"Hold your wrists over the bathtub," Zarina said. "I'll wash the blood off; then I've something to help heal the cuts from the manacles."

"You're too kind," said Kurio, with as much sincerity as she could muster.

Zarina scooped jugs of water from a bucket and poured it over

Kurio's forearms, wrists and hands, while Kurio rubbed gently at her wounds and hard at the blood on her arms. Her wrists were abraded raw and stung like a bastard.

Over at the table, Zarina opened a jar and used her fingers to take out a greenish ointment that looked like it was made from algae. "This will work quickly to numb the pain. I'm sure you'll be as good as new in a few days."

She spread the floral-scented ointment over Kurio's wrists. Immediately, the aching ebbed to a dull throb. Kurio closed her eyes with relief. Now the pain was almost gone, she realized how tired she was.

"Thank you," she said, meaning it.

"You're welcome."

Kurio felt Zarina slide something cold and metallic around her neck, and there was a snick as a lock clicked shut. Her eyes snapped open. Gone was Zarina's friendly demeanor. Instead, she was hard-eyed and stern-faced.

"I'm sorry," she said. "But it's for the greater good."

"What the bloody hells is this?" Kurio tried to pry the necklace off, but it was too tight. Then she felt it undulate, and her hand recoiled involuntarily. "What is this? What have you done?"

It felt like a flat band of metal, but there was a *wrongness* to it. It had moved, for gods' sake!

Zarina backed away. "Calm down."

"I bloody won't! What have you done?"

Those hard eyes again. "What I had to. You know too much. We need to ensure we can control you."

"Control me? You could have handed me a few royals and never heard from me again!"

"I couldn't take that risk. And your talents will come in useful. Be thankful you're not dead and floating in a canal. Now, strip and wash yourself. I'll bring some fresh clothes. And you'll get your gear back."

Kurio's hands clenched into fists, so hard her knuckles ached. "And what's to stop me leaving?"

"This." Zarina's eyes flashed, and she uttered a few words in a language Kurio didn't understand.

The pain came slowly at first, as if creeping up on her. In her legs and arms and her pelvis. She frowned and tried to ignore it. If she'd had a dagger, it would have been buried in Zarina's heart.

"What have you—"

Agony slammed into her, like white-hot daggers piercing her organs. Kurio heard herself gasp. Her hands clutched at her sides, digging into her flesh as if she could rake the pain free. She cried out, a wordless scream, and fell to the cold floor, where she writhed helplessly.

Her defenselessness filled her with rage. Pain she was familiar with, but this sorcery was something different. Harder. Sharper. Crueler.

The agony subsided. She clutched at her clothes, palms sweaty.

"That was but a fraction of the pain I could make you feel," said Zarina.

Kurio couldn't uncurl from a fetal position. Breathing was almost impossible.

Without warning, the remaining pain dispersed. Kurio kept her eyes closed and tried to move. Her grip was weak, and try as she might to sit up, she couldn't. She pressed her right hand to the floor and raised her body slightly. Shifting a leg, she managed to get it underneath her rear, then pushed herself to a sitting position with the remains of her strength.

A fraction of the device's strength had incapacitated her. She didn't want to think about what else it could do to her.

"I'm sorry I had to do that," said Zarina. Her voice sounded like it came from the room next door.

"You're a bloody bitch," Kurio spat.

"I wanted you to realize I'm serious. This isn't trivial, what we're doing. The fate of the world might depend on us."

"Leave me out of it."

"I'm afraid I can't. You're already involved."

Kurio drew a shuddering breath. "I'm all right now. Thanks for asking."

She shivered, and Zarina wrapped a soft blanket around her shoulders. Kurio thought about rejecting it, then reconsidered. She needed the comfort it offered.

She sat there on the floor in silence. Zarina didn't speak, seemingly content to let Kurio recover and contemplate what had just happened. There wasn't a way out of this that she could see, other than to go along with whatever Zarina wanted while looking for any opportunity to gain the upper hand.

"What is it you want from me?" she said, and it struck her to her core that these were the exact words she'd spoken to Gannon not so long ago.

All she wanted was to keep her head down and make enough royals to become the richest person in Caronath. Was that too much to ask after her shitty life? But it seemed now she'd been forced to offer herself, and her services, to two different people.

## CHAPTER EIGHTEEN

# COMPLICATIONS

ALDRIC WOKE SUDDENLY. THEY'D blown out the lamps before going to sleep on his last night in Caronath, but enough light came in from Soki's window for him to see outlines in the darkness: the large bed, the desk against the wall, a wardrobe and a dresser, and Soki's form next to him. Her scent lingered in the air, an expensive fragrance of orange and apple, and her bare flesh pressed against his, hot to the touch.

But that wasn't what had woken him. It was as if his wards had been tripped. With a quick check, he determined they hadn't been. What, then?

He slipped out from under the quilt. Soki stirred but didn't wake. Her wards hadn't been disturbed, or she'd be wide awake too. That was a good sign, wasn't it?

But for some reason, Aldric felt nervous. The shadows around the room seemed to have weight, or were hiding something. His hand reached for his khopesh hanging from a bedpost. He stood, gripping the hilt tight, and half-drew the blade. Dampening his breathing, he remained motionless and listened.

The wind in the trees outside. The faint groan of timbers. A skittering in the ceiling.

Aldric relaxed. A rat, he guessed. Maybe that was what had

woken him.

Still his unease remained. He drew the rest of his blade and placed the scabbard on the bed. He rubbed the back of his neck. Something wasn't right; he could sense it. Not through his sorcerous wards but ... through the god's mark?

The thought shocked him. His divine power could only be used to heal. What was happening? Usually the power of the Five inside him was a calm, gentle thing; but now it roiled and coursed like a raging stream.

Timbers in the ceiling creaked, as if a weight descended on them.

Aldric shook Soki's shoulder. "Wake up!" he whispered urgently.

Soki looked up at him blearily. "What?" she mumbled.

A crack split the air above them. Dust and wooden splinters rained down, showering the bed. Aldric grabbed Soki's arm and yanked her from under the covers. He dragged her to the floor, throwing himself on top of her before she could react.

A black shape broke through the hole in the roof and landed on the bed with a crash. It looked like a Dead-eye, but wasn't. Spindly limbs protruded from an emaciated body, but instead of the usual pale skin, this thing was mottled and dark gray. Its fingers ended in sharp black talons. It opened its fanged, lipless mouth and keened—a grating wail that chilled Aldric to his soul.

The air hummed as both Soki's and his dormant wards erupted into spheres, sparks flying where they overlapped. Aldric cursed and leaped away from Soki before their shields overloaded and became useless. He jumped between her and the creature, flicking a quick glance at her to make sure she was all right, and brought his blade up.

"Sorcerer," the thing hissed at Soki, then sneered at Aldric.

It charged and was upon him before he could fend it off. Its sticklike arms passed through his shield like it didn't exist. Claws ripped at his flesh, scoring long gashes across his chest. He dropped his blade and grabbed the thing's forearms, twisting them away, but it fought with immense strength. It forced him back, and he fell, the creature on top of him. He grunted as it pinned his arms to the floor. It loomed over him, leaning closer. A dark purple tongue like a serpent's flicked between the gash of its fanged mouth.

Soki screamed cants. Glittering streaks erupted from her outstretched hands, but somehow *bent* around the creature. They scored across the bed instead, leaving charred lines and sliced timbers. Her words trailed off in shock.

Aldric groaned and tried to push the creature off. But for all its thinness, it was *heavy*, as if made of iron. He couldn't move it. Sorcery was useless, and the thing was too strong for him. What else could he do?

He reached for his god's power and felt it suffuse him. He could keep Soki alive, and perhaps she could escape. Then maybe he could stay alive long enough to think of something.

As the warmth of his god's power bubbled through him, the creature screamed in agony. It let go of him suddenly, flesh hissing and bubbling, charred skin leaking crimson. He wasted no time and kicked out with both feet, managing to thrust it away from him.

Soki lunged at the creature, Aldric's blade gripped in both hands. Metal bit deep into its neck, and blood spurted. A savage snarl escaped as it turned to face her.

Aldric leaped and wrapped his arms around its emaciated torso. Smoke poured from its skin where they touched. It wailed, a penetrating scream that almost deafened him. They grappled, its monstrous strength against his muscles, staggering around the room, crashing into the dresser and wardrobe. He hung on, barely, sweat and blood making his grip slippery. He tangled his leg between its thin limbs, and they tumbled to the floor.

"Kill it!" he yelled as they writhed and jostled for position.

Soki stood with the heavy blade in her hands, looking frantically between Aldric and the creature.

"Don't worry about me," Aldric shouted. He felt his grip slipping, the might of the creature too much for him.

"Shit, shit, shit," Soki said, and thrust the khopesh's pointed tip toward them.

Sharp steel sliced Aldric's skin, burning like fire, but most of the blade sank into the creature. It screeched, jaws snapping and body squirming. With a burst of strength, it broke Aldric's grip and threw him aside. His head slammed into the wall, and the room swam before him.

He shook himself and saw the thing advancing on Soki. She waved his khopesh in front of her, muscles trembling with the weight of it, her eyes wide and frightened. She wouldn't be able to hold it off.

Aldric reached for his god's mark and threw power at the creature, as if he were going to heal it. The beast clutched its head and wailed. Aldric launched himself at its back, thundering into it. They tumbled to the floor. Soki stabbed the creature again and again. Aldric fended off swipes of its talons, but still they gouged his skin.

Soon, its flailing weakened, and he felt his strength begin to overpower it. He twisted it onto its stomach and immobilized one of its arms behind its back. Soki stood over them and brought Aldric's blade down hard into its skull. The creature gurgled and became still. Aldric jerked himself away from its bubbling hide. Its skin was on his arms and hands, hot and sticky.

"Are you all right?" he asked Soki.

She nodded, eyes still on the steaming creature, which was leaking blood across her floor. Her face dripped sweat, as did Aldric's whole body.

"What is it?" she said.

He had no idea. It was like nothing he'd ever seen before or read about. "I don't know. But sorcery didn't stop it. Only you stabbing it and my god's power saved us."

It was something like a Dead-eye, but clearly more developed and with vastly different abilities, immune to sorcery and able to penetrate wards. There was only one explanation: it was meant to kill sorcerers.

He looked at Soki and saw from her scared expression she'd realized the same thing. It hadn't been after him; it had come to kill Soki.

His khopesh dropped from her fingers and tumbled to the ground with a clang. "If you hadn't been here …"

Aldric clasped her cold, trembling hands in his. "It's over now. It's dead. Besides, you killed it, not me."

A wan smile lit her face, but was quickly replaced with a grim expression. She kneeled near the creature, peering at its blistering skin. "I didn't know your god's power could be used like this."

"Neither did I. I've never heard of this happening before."

He winced and pressed part of his shirt over a particularly deep gash in his chest. Soki's eyes widened, as if she had only just realized his torso and arms had been scored by the creature's talons.

"Can you heal yourself?" she asked.

Aldric tried to smile wryly, but his lips only twisted in distress. "No. That's not what Menselas allows. His power is to help others, not yourself."

"That's stupid," Soki said as she rushed to her dresser. She poured water from a pitcher into a bowl and tore strips of cloth from some shirts in a drawer.

"It's the way it is," Aldric said. He fell quiet while Soki cleaned and bandaged his wounds, providing whatever help he could manage. It would be enough to stop the bleeding until he could find a priest who'd also been touched by his god. When she was done, he rose to his feet, grimacing in discomfort. "I'll go to my Church. They'll heal me."

Soki prodded the corpse with her foot. "It's lucky you were awake."

"It moved through your wards without disturbing them?"

She nodded.

"Mine as well. But something woke me."

"Maybe it was your god."

Her words made Aldric's heart beat faster. He tried to control his quickened breathing. "I've … I've never felt Menselas before. I have his mark, but … only those higher up claim to have felt him directly."

Soki arched one eyebrow. "Claim?"

Aldric shrugged.

"Well," she said, "if you ever speak to him, thank him for me."

They laughed, and the tension in him eased slightly.

"I'll have someone from the Church collect the corpse," he said. "They'll want to examine it."

Soki shook her head. "No. I'll do that. I'm curious as well. All of my power and … I was helpless against it."

"Far from helpless. You killed it."

"All my life, I haven't feared anything," she said slowly. "Not since I knew I had the dawn-tide and dusk-tide powers and could shape them. The terrors normal children have … I didn't. But now … I'll need to learn to defend myself."

"Someone tried to kill you," Aldric said, putting words to what they hadn't spoken. "Or something. Can you think of anyone who'd want to do that? A rival perhaps?"

"No! There's no one." Soki rubbed her arms and glanced at the hole in her roof. Through the rupture, stars shone in the night sky. "It's this mission of yours, you know. It has to be. Your Church wants me to examine whatever you bring back from the ruins. And someone obviously doesn't want that to happen. You need to be careful. Watch yourself. I'll hide out for a time. Close up shop, and stay somewhere else."

The thought of leaving Soki alone after an encounter like this churned Aldric's innards with dread. "I'll make sure you're guarded."

She waved away his offer. "I'll hire my own people. I don't trust your Church. Not after this. Only they knew they'd hired me."

"Soki—"

"Don't," she snapped. "The priests are just like any other men, and you know it. Someone has a loose tongue, and it almost got both of us killed."

That wasn't fair, and she had to know it. It was fear talking.

A gust of wind whistled through the opening above them. Aldric shivered and noticed Soki doing the same.

"Let's get dressed," he said. "Then we'll move this thing out of here."

By the time Aldric and Soki had moved the corpse and cleaned up, it was only a few hours until dawn. The creature's gray skin was coarse and leathery, not unlike sea-ray skin, but thicker. Where the god's power had touched it, it had burned away. Aldric had been glad to wrap the body in a cloth and drag it down the stairs to a table in Soki's cold cellar. His wounds continued to pain him, and one had reopened.

"I'll find someone to patch the roof in the morning," said Soki.

She promised she'd be able to find out why the creature was immune to sorcery, but he had his doubts. She was one of the finest sorcerers he'd ever encountered, but this ... It was outside her expertise. She was confident she'd work out how it ticked, because she *had* to. Right now, she was vulnerable without the sorcerous protection she relied on. It had to deeply scare her.

~ ~ ~

At the church, Aldric kept out of sight as best he could and made his way to the healers. One was always on duty in case there was an emergency during the night. He cautioned the priestess to silence, stating he was on official business for the archbishop, and she saw to him with a bare minimum of questions.

A short time later, he entered the building on Locust Street. Of Razmus, Priska, and Stray Dog, there was no sign. Presumably they were sleeping in some of the many side rooms. But Niklaus sat at one of the tables. He was drinking already, or was that still? A half-empty bottle stood on the table. As Aldric approached, Niklaus drained his cup and poured himself another measure. It was a spirit, not wine.

In front of him was a tattered book open in the middle to pages filled with an erratic script. Aldric recognized the language as Skanuric just before Niklaus closed the book with a puzzled expression on his face. Could Niklaus have arranged the attempt on Soki's life? It didn't seem plausible, yet someone had. And whoever it was could control creatures Aldric had never heard of before.

Niklaus looked up at him.

"It's early," Aldric said. "Haven't you had enough?" The words came out harsher than he'd intended.

Niklaus sneered. "I don't tell you how to eat and piss, do I?"

He kept his eyes on Aldric and drained his cup, as if daring him to say more. Aldric ignored the challenge and slid into a chair on the other side of the table. He placed his khopesh on his lap, making sure he could draw the blade in a moment.

Niklaus noticed his position, and his eyes took in Aldric's haggard state and the dark stains on his hands and arms. "What happened?"

"Something attacked me. You wouldn't know anything about it, would you?"

Niklaus's eyes narrowed. "No. What's *something*?"

"It was like a Dead-eye, but different. Harder, stronger."

Aldric kept the detail of its immunity to sorcery to himself. He had no idea who could be trusted. Perhaps no one.

Niklaus pushed his cup across the table. Aldric shook his head.

"Drink. It'll calm your nerves."

Aldric sighed, but took the cup. He drained it in one swallow. Harsh liquor scalded his throat, and he coughed. His eyes watered. "Holy Menselas, man. What is this stuff?"

"Something cheap. It's good to remind yourself of your past sometimes. So, this not-Dead-eye, did your sorcery work on it?"

Aldric froze. "You bloody—"

"It wasn't me. I told you that already."

"Then how do you—"

"I've seen some things over the years."

So had Aldric, but nothing like this. And though he'd been educated by the best tutors his Church's coin could buy, he'd never heard a whisper of creatures related to the Dead-eyes. "And you expect me to believe you had nothing to do with it?"

Niklaus shrugged. He took the empty cup and poured himself another drink, lounging back in his seat. "I don't care what you believe. I've told you the truth. Take it or leave it. I didn't have to mention what I know at all. Your lady friend—she's uninjured?"

Aldric fumed, but he wouldn't get to the bottom of this by arguing with Niklaus. "Yes. We were lucky."

"More than that, I'd say. The ones I've seen were hard to take down."

Niklaus didn't know that Aldric's divine power had damaged the creature, then. A fact best kept secret.

"Where did you see these creatures?" he asked. "Who, or what, controlled them?"

"A power. One of the old races. A wraithe. We had a ... reckoning."

Aldric uttered a choked laugh. Niklaus was claiming he'd

fought a wraithe and lived. Then Bryn's words echoed in his ears: *He's a demon in human form, or so some say.* And: *They're all dead.* A chill swept through him. The deeper he was sucked into this mission, the less he wanted to do with it.

"You'll have to tell me the story sometime," he said.

"Bah. Same old: a fight, and someone lost. Not me. But I didn't kill it either. Anyway, this creature—it's a cousin of sorts to the Dead-eyes. Very rare."

Aldric glanced around the room, almost expecting someone to be spying on them, so remarkable was the knowledge they shared. "Who do they serve?"

"Anyone who can give them what they want."

"And what's that?"

"Why, sorcerers, of course! They eat them. Their power, at least. It's like a drug to them, highly addictive."

"It focused on Soki at first. Maybe I was too small a fish. Where did you see one?"

"In a city. Somewhere south." Niklaus frowned. "I can't remember the name. It was hot and sticky." He made to drink from his cup, hesitated, then placed it gently on the table. "Perhaps I've had enough for now." He looked Aldric in the eye. "Can you heal memories?"

"What do you mean?"

"If someone can't remember something, can you bring it back? Heal their mind?"

Aldric shook his head. "I've never heard of anything like that. What I do is purely physical. Perhaps I could take a look?"

"No. It doesn't matter."

Aldric could tell Niklaus wanted the subject dropped. "What else do you know about this creature?" he asked.

It had almost killed Soki. It would have if he hadn't been there. Holy Menselas, he didn't want to leave her alone now.

Niklaus gave him a serious look. "Something between the

Dead-eyes and the old races. Maybe it was a mutation once; or maybe it was bred, changed by sorcery."

Aldric ground his teeth. "You're not serious."

"I am." Niklaus leaned forward, resting one arm on the table. "There are more things in this world than anyone will ever know. From the Dead-eyes to the wraithes, to the gigantic metal cube the wanderers live in out in the wastes. Hells, man, even here the ruins are unknown, unexplored. There are things inside that would make your skin crawl and maybe even cause your god to flinch. One man can't know everything. I've been alive long enough to at least realize that."

His tone made Aldric pause; it was dark and melancholy. Perhaps it was a front Niklaus put on. Although so far, Niklaus hadn't been the type to put on airs or even to deceive him. In fact, he'd been brutally honest.

"What kills them?" he asked, testing the mercenary.

"Steel. Nothing else that I know of. They're stronger than Dead-eyes, but not as quick."

Aldric remembered how the creature had overwhelmed him. He was naturally fit and trained to keep himself in shape, but he'd been like a child against it—until Soki had injured the thing. He rubbed his eye and thought about how easily Soki could have been killed.

"We need to get started as soon as we can," he said. "The quicker we leave, the quicker we'll be back."

Niklaus grunted. "I agree. This Stray Dog is coming along?"

"Yes."

"Strange name. Melodramatic sort, is he?"

Aldric shrugged. "Hiding from his past maybe. But I judge him to be a trustworthy fellow. And he'll be good in a fight."

Niklaus chuckled. "You also judge your Church to be trustworthy, yet here you are. Here *we* are."

Aldric wouldn't have this mercenary questioning his Church.

No matter how skilled with a blade he was, Niklaus couldn't understand the concept of devotion to something greater than himself. But all he said was, "My instincts are good. We leave at dawn, as planned. What about this priestess of yours?"

"She's not mine. And she's a high priestess. She's coming with us."

A high priestess. Aldric couldn't believe it. What was she doing joining their mission? Nothing good, he warranted.

"Is she going to be a problem?"

Niklaus hesitated. He toyed with the bottle of spirits, rocking it gently back and forth on the table. "No. She's foisted herself on me—on us—for her own reasons. I don't know what they are, but I'll find out. Then there'll be a reckoning."

*What a mess.*

"Just be ready in a few hours," Aldric said. "And I'd stop drinking if I were you."

Niklaus chuckled. "If you were me, you'd never stop. I'll be ready. I'll catch an hour's sleep in one of the rooms upstairs. Worry about yourself—you look like you'll have trouble resting. Oh, and we'll pick up Bryn on the way. He has an … engagement at dawn."

Aldric frowned. "Isn't he working for us now that you've paid him?"

"He's just keeping his skills sharp. It won't take long."

"Just make sure he's ready," Aldric said, and made his way outside.

His face was hot as he fumed at the debacle this mission was turning into. His own Church keeping him in the dark. Niklaus's Church using both the mercenary and a high priestess to try to get what they wanted.

He looked into the sky. Dark clouds were sweeping in from the east, and even the light of Chandra and Jagonath together wasn't bright enough to penetrate them. Rain was on the way. He sighed.

Not the best weather to set off in, but he couldn't worry about that.

Right now, knowing he wouldn't be able to sleep, a visit to Etia was in order. He'd put off returning after his fruitless discussion with Hannus. But now, before he left Caronath, he felt he had to at least inform her that he was leaving. And perhaps seek her guidance.

~ ~ ~

He trudged up the last few yards of the hill on which *Rafic-ur-Djasir* stood. The rough obsidian seemed darker than black, as if it ignored the light of the stars and the moons.

He drew in a sharp breath when he realized no finches perched on the temple. He cast his gaze about, trying to spot some of the red birds, but to no avail.

Offerings still littered the ground around the pyramid's base: a jumble of foodstuffs and bowls of liquids, along with the ghoulish mummified animals.

There was no sign of the little girl either, but he hadn't expected to see her this early in the morning.

He made his way through the shadows around the base of the pyramid to the section where the door had opened before. "Etia!" he called, then again when there was no response.

Silence was the only reply.

He waited a while in the chill early morning air. Eventually, he placed a hand on the stone. It was warm to the touch. Hopefully, Etia still lived. She would need assistance if she was to arrest her decline and remain protected from the Tainted Cabal. But there was nothing he could do if she refused him entry, or to speak with him.

Aldric made his way back down the hill with the uneasy sense he was missing something important. He wondered if it would cost him his life.

## CHAPTER NINETEEN

# UNCERTAINTIES

WOODEN SHUTTERS BANGED IN the wind, and the flimsy curtains billowed. Moonlight shone across the polished wooden floor. Niklaus didn't remember opening the windows. In fact, he'd made sure the latches were tightly locked in case someone who wanted him dead climbed through. He squinted in the semidarkness, hand reaching for his sword hanging in its scabbard over the bedpost. He stopped, eyes widening.

A silhouette stood just inside the window opening, lit from behind by the cold white sliver of Chandra shining through a break in the storm clouds. His eyes traced the outline of her sensuous curves, lingering on the feathered wings that loomed over her head. She was here. Sylva had come to reward him. It was only the fifth time he'd seen her.

Niklaus drew his hand away from *her* sword, breath catching in his throat. Heat rose to his face and swirled down to his groin. A brush of air caressed his bare chest, carrying with it a strong scent of leather overlaid with musk and spices.

She stood there for long moments, unmoving, yet enticing. Then, with silent steps, she padded toward him. Her dress was nearly transparent, revealing as much as it concealed, offering him tantalizing glimpses of her curves. Her not quite nakedness sent a delicious shiver through him.

Sylva Kalisia climbed onto the bed and sat astride him, her movements as graceful as a panther, her weight pressing his hips deeper into the mattress, the tops of her feet resting lightly on his thighs. Her delicate dress rippled in the breeze, molding to her sensual body. Stretching to either side, her wings blotted out the moonlight, covering him in her shadow.

Niklaus scarce trusted himself to breathe. His heart hammered in his chest, and his mouth was dry. He dared not move, but the temptation to grab her, to roll her over, and press himself against her was almost overwhelming.

Her slanted violet eyes traveled over his face and body with a feral shamelessness that stopped his breath. She leaned over, and the tips of her midnight hair brushed across his face. She gripped his shoulders, her nails digging into his flesh, and dragged her silken hair over his tingling skin. Both hands pressed him down, and he railed against the constraint even as he reveled in feeling her full weight on him, longing for the touch of her sex against his.

A sound like a snap of cloth as her wings flapped once, sending cooling air redolent with her scent across his skin. There was something animal about her—heat and smell and closeness—that spoke to his soul. He couldn't think straight. Where their flesh touched, he burned with an intensity that both aroused and frightened him. He groaned wordlessly. The pressure in his groin intensified to the point it was almost painful. He ached for her. How could his heart hammer so hard?

Her long silken hair dragged across his chest as she moved across and down his body. The coolness of her palms trailed across his sweaty chest. He reached for her, and his calloused hands pressed against firm breasts, her dark nipples hard. He wanted to take her, thrust deep into her fiery core. He would make her beg for mercy!

She dissolved into nothingness, like evaporating mist. His hands closed around empty air. Her tinkling laugh sounded in his ears, close yet far away, filled with delight and promises and lust. Without seeming to move, she was now beside his bed. Her silken hair brushed across his naked torso again. Her breath blew hotly into his ear. Her burning lips brushed his skin.

"There are forces arrayed against us," she purred. "The world hangs in balance. Beware the ruin. The Tainted Cabal seek to bring forth a final cataclysm."

A rush of cold air as she backed away.

"Don't go!" he pleaded.

She floated backward to the window, a mischievous smile playing across her deep red lips. Fabric snapped as a strong gust of wind blew through the opening. The curtains billowed, draping her. Niklaus blinked. When the wind subsided and the curtains dropped, Sylva Kalisia was gone.

Niklaus woke, gasping for air. The window was still closed and latched. Sweat soaked his body and dripped down his sides onto the bedsheets. He cursed, struggling to sit up. His manhood throbbed painfully, as hard as rock. His limbs trembled, cold with sweat.

The goddess had touched him, promising unearthly delights and power. She watched over him with her divine love.

He lay back down and covered his aching loins with the blanket, but sleep never came. His skin prickled, alive to the promise of her touch. His member remained hard. His ears tuned to the darkness. Hoping for her return.

~ ~ ~

Zarina was staring at Kurio from across the room while engaged in a heated argument with Mellish. The barrel-chested man must have come in a hurry, as sweat darkened the armpits and collar of his linen shirt.

When Mellish paused, Zarina scowled and rubbed the back of her neck. She beckoned to Kurio, who hurried to obey. The woman was cold, ruthless, and cunning—and, if Kurio trusted her instincts, desperate.

The memory of the pain still lingered, making her scared and timid. But underneath, in her very core, was a kernel of hatred that gave her strength.

"What haven't you told us?" Zarina demanded. "Speak, woman! This is no game. If the demons triumph, we'll all be corpses. Or worse."

"N-nothing," Kurio stuttered. What was worse than being a corpse?

"Do you want more pain?" Zarina threatened.

Kurio felt her bowels loosen and clenched her muscles tight. She licked her dry lips, thinking furiously.

"Maybe ... I just remembered ... there's one thing. After Gannon told me his research had been destroyed, he said there was a ruin that had recently been found. A passing comment, as if of no importance. Something about the Churches investigating it. That's all I know. I swear."

"That matches what I've—"

"Shush, Mellish," Zarina said softly. She stared at Kurio for a few long moments, then shook her head. "We have no choice."

"That's what I've been saying," Mellish agreed. "If both the Cabal and the Churches are interested. And with what we know ..."

Zarina nodded. "We cannot pass up this opportunity. I'd have liked to wait until we could summon more of our people, but even the closest are too far away. You're all we have, Mellish. I can't join you, not with the Cabal's activity in Caronath to keep an eye on." Zarina's voice sounded almost anguished. "We have to make sure the artifact is in our possession. And if we can give the Cabal and the Churches a black eye while we go about it, all the better."

Although Kurio had no idea what they were talking about, it didn't take a savant to guess they wanted to gather royals and power for themselves. After all, that was what everyone wanted, wasn't it? Kurio did, except now she also wanted to be free of this abominable sorcerous band around her neck, and for Zarina and Mellish to die bloody deaths. People like them, who would do anything to achieve their goals, were as bad as the evil they claimed to oppose.

"I'll prepare my gear, then," Mellish said. "Our purpose is true. Anything is justified."

"Some betrayals are … hard," Zarina whispered.

Kurio couldn't keep the sneer from her face. She ducked her head, hoping they hadn't seen her expression. They justified betrayal and murder and torture.

"The thief has to come," Mellish said.

Kurio jerked her head up. "What? No."

Zarina laughed in the way of someone who thinks a child has said something foolish. "Why do you think Gannon was interested in you? Why do you think we've kept you alive rather than slitting your throat and dumping you into a canal?"

Kurio considered replying it was because they were good people, but she knew this wasn't true. "I … I have skills?"

A snort from Zarina. "Do you think it was chance you were employed to steal the cube? You've been a puppet all along. That artifact was created by the demons and their depraved followers long ago. It was kept secure so no human could touch it. Only a demon can handle it safely, or someone with demon blood."

"But … I touched it. So did Willas."

"Yes. And Willas is dead. His skin blackened and erupted with pustules. In the end, he begged for death. It was a relief."

*Bloody hells.* Kurio frantically examined the backs of her hands, her arms. Her heart pounded in her chest. "Am I dying? Is there a cure?"

"You're not going to die, silly woman. Haven't you figured it out by now? You have demon blood in you. That's why you were manipulated into stealing the cube. That's why Gannon is interested in you. That's why we have to control you. That's why you're going with Mellish."

*No, it isn't possible.*

She recalled her glimpse of wrinkled yellow-skinned limbs, blood-covered hands, fangs, finger-length horns protruding from heads and backs. That wasn't her. She wasn't a demon.

"That's ... My family aren't demons. Not my mother, nor my father. And neither am I."

Zarina's voice grew even harsher. "When Nysrog was in this world, he brought other demons through the veil. Vile creatures that cared nothing for the sanctity of human life. They gorged themselves on the flesh of men, women, and children. They raped and defiled, performed unspeakable acts. They sowed their black seed and took mankind's into themselves. Demons gave birth, as did a very few human women, and brought forth atrocities. Our organization has hunted their descendants, those of contaminated blood, for centuries. We aim to cast the demon spawn from this world." She paused, then added, "Your mother gave in to her base desires. She fucked someone with demon blood, someone other than your father. Its seed spilled into her, and she gave birth to an abomination. You."

"No ..."

"Did your brothers and sisters treat you differently? Did your uncles and aunts scorn you?"

*They beat me. They abused me. Hated me.*

"It's not true!" Kurio screamed. But it could be. It explained so much. Her eyes grew hot, and tears flowed. She couldn't stop them.

"They didn't know about the demon blood," said Mellish. "Much lore has been lost over the millennia."

"Shut up!" screamed Kurio. She clutched her stomach and curled into a ball on the cold floor.

"Your eyes are a giveaway," Zarina said. "Demon blood manifests in many different ways, but a common one is different-colored eyes. You tried to conceal it because you were hiding from your family. Another thief found out, and he had a loose tongue. So you killed him."

Kurio sucked in deep breaths between sobs. Her nose ran with snot. The hard floor pressed into her side. *Bastard. Tainted. Killer. Abomination. Demon.* She couldn't quiet her churning thoughts.

Something prodded her back. A boot. She felt Zarina's menacing presence looming over her.

"We need you for a small task, one you're uniquely suited to. There aren't many abominations left these days. Unfortunately for you, you won't survive it."

*We'll see about that,* Kurio thought. She would see Zarina and Mellish dead, and their plans for her could go to the hells. She would survive, and in the end, they would be the ones who died. A vision came to her: Zarina's blond hair tangled in her fingers, her throat slit, blood on Kurio's knife. Mellish lying next to the woman in a pool of crimson. It brought a brief smile to her lips, and her sobs lessened in intensity.

Other thoughts pushed themselves to the front of her mind. What effect had her nature had on the choices she'd made through her life? And what about her attraction to Gannon? Was that the demon blood inside her talking?

## CHAPTER TWENTY

# LEAVING

ALDRIC RETURNED TO LOCUST Street and set about readying the horses he had acquired. They weren't particularly good quality, but wouldn't let them down. Luckily the storm he'd seen approaching had been short and sharp, leaving the streets and air a little cleaner.

He'd just about saddled all the horses when Razmus appeared, shortly followed by Priska, their breath steaming in the cold air. Before long the rest of the group arrived, mostly bleary-eyed and sleep-addled. By contrast, Niklaus was bright and enthusiastic, bustling around and checking the cinches Aldric had tightened.

Stray Dog came out bearing a tray of steaming mugs and handed them around. Aldric took a sip of the cream-colored liquid. It was hot, with a bitterness masked by honey. It reminded him of a morning drink popular in the south, but this one was rougher. After a few swallows he felt more energetic.

Neb eyed his mug suspiciously, while Priska's hands wrapped around hers for the warmth. The priestess Niklaus had allowed to join them stood to one side, her face lost within her hood.

"Niklaus," Aldric said, "you'll have to lead us to Bryn."

He hoped the side trip wouldn't take up too much time. It wasn't long until full-dark, and they needed to make good speed to reach the settlement. An hour saved on the road was another hour they could spend preparing the settlers for the next Dead-eye incursion.

The mercenary nodded and mounted one of the horses. He was wearing a black wide-brimmed hat to shade his eyes and keep the sun off his face and neck. Despite his claim he'd spent a year in Caronath, he was clearly used to traveling.

"All right," Aldric said, raising his voice. "Everyone mount up. The horses are all much the same. We've a short stop to make"—he glanced at Niklaus—"then we'll be on our way."

Niklaus led them through the streets of Caronath. Only a sporadic few windows showed any light at this hour. They passed a brightly lit bakery with steaming bread piled on stalls set up outside, and Priska bade them wait while she purchased a few loaves.

As the pale light of dawn edged across the city, they arrived at a large parkland. Gravel paths spread in all directions, and there were groves of trees and reed-lined manmade lakes. Somewhere, a duck quacked, swiftly echoed by its fellows. On an open expanse of short-cropped grass nearby, two groups of people were gathered.

Niklaus called a halt, and Aldric spotted Bryn standing in front of one of the groups, dressed in thin pants and a shirt despite the chill. The swordsman brandished his blade and went through a short form before turning to nod to someone behind him.

A man stepped out from the opposite group, also wielding a sword.

"This shouldn't take long," Niklaus said.

A white-haired priest of Nayysur moved to a position between the two groups. He clutched a leatherbound book in one hand and scales in the other and was flanked by four guards of the Caronath Watch. Nayysur, the god of justice and wisdom. Was this ...? Aldric's chest tightened.

He turned to Niklaus. "This is a duel. What has Bryn done?"

Niklaus waved a hand. "He's filling in for someone else. It's the done thing these days. Some nobles quarreling over a woman. I wouldn't get excited about it."

Aldric clenched his reins in anger and shifted in his saddle. On the one hand, it wasn't his business what Bryn got up to when not directly under his control. But on the other, if he died today, they'd be one man short. And there was no time to look for a replacement. He cursed under his breath and glanced around at the others. He'd better say something, or they'd think Niklaus was in charge.

"We'll wait for Bryn," he said. "If he makes it."

"He'll make it," said Niklaus wryly. "The man he's pitted against is named Ziran. He's fairly skilled, or at least what they think is skilled around these parts. But he's no match for Bryn. That's the benefit of being a stranger in town. Shame there isn't someone taking wagers."

"This is someone's life you're talking about," Priska said.

Niklaus gave her a lingering look, then glanced away without saying a word.

Bryn and his opponent began circling each other. Ziran was tall and rangy, and his arms were corded like a laborer's. He must have spent a great deal of time training, Aldric thought. His mouth was stretched into a grin, and his movements were jerky, almost erratic. Perhaps it was meant to disconcert his challenger.

By contrast, Bryn looked relaxed. He stood with his feet firmly planted and sword raised high, only shifting position when his adversary's movement forced him to turn to remain facing him. His slightly curved blade moved marginally, its edge always toward Ziran.

Ziran's blade flicked out, faster than Aldric could have countered. Bryn glided fluidly backward a step, dropping his blade. Ziran's steel missed him by a few inches. Bryn hadn't even attempted to block Ziran's strike, just let it pass harmlessly in front of him.

"Hai!" Ziran shouted, and lunged forward, feet sliding over the dew-wet grass. He aimed a cut at Bryn, and this time sparks flew as Ziran's strike transformed into multiple attacks, low and high, from both sides and the front. Steel clanged on steel. The onlookers cheered and jeered.

Ziran jerked back. A stillness fell over the two duelists, Bryn breathing evenly while Ziran panted. And then Ziran fell to his knees. A pained look came over his face, and a hand clutched at his torso. It came away bloody.

Bryn relaxed, sword dropping to his side. He bowed to Ziran.

Aldric hadn't even seen Bryn strike.

"Gah," said Ziran, and toppled over. Men rushed to his side while those supporting Bryn raised a dandified young man to their shoulders.

~ ~ ~

They were a hundred yards outside the north gate of Caronath when Soki appeared behind them. Her horse was lightly lathered, which spoke to the speed she had ridden through the city, trying to catch up. Dust billowed in her wake as she rode along the dirt road between cultivated fields. Aldric's heart pounded at the sight of her riding her spotted mare as if born in the saddle, her hair flying wildly around her.

Bryn, Niklaus, and Razmus turned their mounts and rested their hands on their hilts.

Aldric raised his hand. "Peace. I know her."

Niklaus scowled. "Seems a little late for a farewell."

As Soki neared them, she steered toward Aldric, and he couldn't help but smile. Although part of him wondered with dread why she'd come after them.

"Aldric," she said breathlessly, "I'm sorry. They told me I had to come." Her mouth twisted with distress, and she fumbled with a saddlebag. She drew out a letter sealed with crimson wax and held it out to him. "Your Church sent me. I owe them a favor for something they did for me some time ago. When I went to see them about that job they asked me to do, they told me to join you. I don't think they—" She broke off and gave the others a sideways look. "Anyway, the letter is from Archbishop Hannus."

Aldric saw that the envelope of expensive bleached paper was fastened with the seal of the Five. He smiled at Soki, relieved there wasn't something wrong. "I assume this tells me to take you along?" he said wryly.

After the attack last night, he wasn't sure if she was still in danger. He'd feel better knowing she wasn't left behind to defend herself if one of those strange creatures made another attempt on her life. Then another thought crept into his mind: had his Church sent Soki to watch him? He didn't think she would do that, but … what did he really know about her?

Soki nodded. "I couldn't say no. And they also offered me unprecedented access to study the Church's artifacts."

"Having you with us eases my mind," he said. "It will be good to have the support of a sorcerer of your caliber."

He saw Priska's head jerk up, and she stared at Soki. If she'd been paying attention, she would have sensed Soki's mark earlier.

"Another sorcerer?" Niklaus said. "And a good one. Excellent." He looked at Bryn. "She'll disarm any traps on those treasure chests, eh?"

Bryn snorted with amusement. "If she can do that, she's welcome. But that's another person to split the loot with. If we find any."

Aldric shot the swordsman an angry look. Once, toward the end of his training, he'd been taken on a mission to investigate an ancient burial site deep in the Great Southern Mountains of

Ealysia. His mentor, Magister Ketil, had paid mercenaries and a sorcerer to accompany them, with promises of riches if they successfully traversed the rugged terrain and survived the savage creatures found there. Their companions had begun bickering among themselves as soon as they'd left, and on the twelfth day there was a scuffle, and a woman knifed a scruffy-looking youth. The lad died that night despite Aldric's best attempts to save him. All over gold they hadn't seen yet, which might not even exist. Aldric remembered wondering at how the mere thought of gold could cause such trouble to those who valued material possessions. And he remembered the sorcerer's cold, knowing smile. Afterward, Ketil had told him that everything was a test. "Menselas chooses our path for us, but it is up to us to make correct decisions and show ourselves worthy in the god's eyes. Gold is a temptation for lesser men and minor gods."

However, despite Bryn's apparent enthusiasm, Aldric had the feeling the swordsman didn't care as much for coin as he showed. It was an act, and one that was well practiced. Bryn was here for his own reasons.

"I don't rob graves or ruins," Soki said flatly. She looked Bryn up and down, eyes resting on his sword. "Or murder people."

"Must be nice," Bryn said, "to be born with a talent that means you don't have to work."

Soki's face darkened, her eyes narrowing.

"Enough!" Aldric said. "Lady Sokhelle Pearello is here by order of my Church. She is to be treated with respect. Both of you, no snide comments and no antagonizing each other. We've a job to do, and I won't let us fail because of infighting. We need to trust each other."

"Trust a sorcerer?" said Bryn.

"They're not all bad," Niklaus said. "This one looks decidedly lovely."

Aldric felt his face grow hot, tried to fight it, and failed. "She is not to be trifled with, Niklaus."

"I can speak for myself, Magister Aldric." Soki stared at Niklaus and drew herself up. "Almost all men and women cannot see what I can. They cannot understand the power I can wield with my mere thoughts and words. They assume"—she glanced at Bryn—"that because I was born a sorcerer, the exercise of that power requires very little work or sacrifice. Those that do not understand, belittle. I live and breathe sorcery, and I'd wager I've spent more time, blood, and sweat practicing than either of you have with your swords. Because sorcery isn't just what I do, what I'm good at. It is who I am."

Niklaus shrugged. "Good to have you along. Just try not to give too many speeches."

He turned his horse and continued along the road. Bryn did the same. Inside, Aldric fumed at their disrespectful attitude to Soki.

"All right," he said gruffly, voice raised to carry to the others. "Let's keep moving. If you have any questions, keep them until the next rest break."

Later, Soki rode her horse alongside Aldric's.

"You did well," he told her with a smile.

She grimaced, then exhaled a deep breath. "I find it easier to establish myself in the beginning. It saves complications later on. And speaking of complications … you know we can't continue our relationship while we're on this mission. We need to be circumspect."

Aldric nodded reluctantly. He'd already come to the same conclusion. It would only complicate matters and could lead to the others questioning his decisions. He'd just have to put his feelings aside for a few weeks. He could manage that. At least, he hoped he could.

"I understand. And I agree. Out here in the wilderness, any distraction could be fatal."

"Well, that's a bit melodramatic, but we need to make this job as easy as possible—for us and for everyone else." She hesitated, glancing at him sideways. "This man, Niklaus … there's something I have to tell you."

"You know him?" Aldric asked.

"No. But the other day when I said I couldn't see the mark your god has placed upon you, it wasn't quite the truth. I cannot see it, but for one as attuned as I am to sorcery, I can sense … something."

Aldric's chest felt tight. "Are you saying the god's mark is sorcery?"

Soki shook her head, biting her bottom lip. "No, it's not quite—" She broke off and shifted in her saddle. "For hundreds of years, scholars and sorcerers have wondered about the gods, and there are many theories. No one knows the truth. But back to Niklaus … He also bears the mark of a god. Which one, I couldn't say."

"Sylva Kalisia," breathed Aldric. "I thought he was just a mercenary they'd hired. But he's not involved with their faith in any way—at least, not from what he's said or his actions. Perhaps he's deceiving me."

"Perhaps. Or you could be right in your initial assessment. People don't always follow the path set out for them. Like you, for instance."

"I follow the will of Menselas."

"Do you? Or do you follow what the priests tell you to?"

Aldric couldn't hear any more of this. He put himself under enough scrutiny and second-guessed himself and his Church far too often. This mission wasn't the time or the place to examine his life.

"I do the will of the Church. For now, it has to be enough."

He turned his face away from the look of pity Soki gave him.

"I only brought this up," she said, "because nothing is ever black and white. Your Church knows more than they told you, or me."

"You don't trust me to do what's right?"

Perhaps she didn't. And without trust, could there be anything more between them?

Soki shook her head, laughing softly. "I trust you to do what you *think* is right."

*She sows doubts in my thoughts already.* Aldric felt the walls he'd built around himself crumbling, and they hadn't been on the trail a day.

He urged his horse ahead, not wanting to see or talk with Soki any longer. He must remain strong, blot out any doubt, and adhere to the tenets of his faith.

## CHAPTER TWENTY-ONE

# A WINDING ROAD

ALDRIC KEPT TO HIMSELF for a time, which allowed him to examine everyone in the group. Razmus and Priska rode close together. The ex-soldier sat his mount well, as did his daughter, both obviously accustomed to traveling. When he wasn't talking to Priska, Razmus kept his back straight and head high, eyes scanning the trees to either side of their path. Priska kept her cloak wrapped tightly around her body, as if it protected her from something. Her long black hair spilled over her collar and hung to the small of her back. Her skin was ivory and free of blemishes. Luckily, the tall trees kept out most of the sunlight else she'd have to worry about her skin burning, Aldric thought.

Niklaus rode ahead of the pair with Neb. Without the settler, they'd have been hard-pressed to find the valley where the settlement was located. At the base of the mountains, the hills and forest paths were numerous and almost a maze. Neb led them through the forest, keeping an eye on the position of the sun when he could. Their progress was good, but the settler insisted they had some way to go yet.

Occasionally, Niklaus looked back over his shoulder at the rest of them, and his gaze lingered on Priska every time. Aldric sighed.

This was a serious mission, and they could ill afford bad blood between the group over a woman. If Niklaus did anything other than look, Razmus was sure to react.

And without proper training, Priska wouldn't be much help to the mission. Aldric wished she'd remained behind in Caronath. Not that he begrudged her closeness with her father, but the others might see her as a burden. Someone they had to babysit.

Bryn rode like he'd spent much of his life in the saddle. Aldric thought there probably wasn't much the man didn't do well. His sword was always within easy reach, and his restless body couldn't keep still for more than a few moments. All day, he switched positions within the group, sometimes trailing behind for a while before slowly edging up to the front, past Niklaus and Neb. Sometimes, he even left the trail and made his way through the trees on either side. Often, he stretched and occasionally dismounted to walk his horse. Aldric thought that Bryn was keeping himself warm and limber, ready for anything, and decided it was a good idea in the northern forest and hills. He began his own limbering regime as they rode.

Stray Dog was different to Bryn, but both contained a suppressed violence that hid at the edge of awareness; although where Bryn was restless, Stray Dog was calm and relaxed. The hulking black-skinned man carried axes in cleverly designed sheaths strapped across his back, one handle protruding over each shoulder. He also carried a large knife in a belt sheath. Most surprising were the mail shirt and hard leather pants he wore, both of excellent quality. He hadn't responded when Aldric had asked where he'd got them.

The priestess who had pressed Niklaus into letting her join them remained cloaked and hooded. She didn't speak to anyone and kept to the back of the group. Aldric had noticed a disturbing amusement in the shape of her mouth, as if their whole mission entertained her. It got his back up, and though he didn't care for her, he needed to know more about her. The only thing he'd been able to get out of her so far was her name and title: High Priestess Valeria.

Soki flitted among the group, chatting amicably and making sure to introduce herself to everyone. She spent longer with Priska and, from what Aldric could see, looked upon the young woman with sympathy. And no wonder. For a sorcerer of Soki's talent and training, Priska's plight must have cut deep. It could have been Soki herself if she'd followed a different path.

Aldric flicked his gaze away whenever he caught himself watching Soki. They'd both agreed to keep the mission uncomplicated. But when they were back in Caronath … The thought put a smile on his face.

~ ~ ~

On the second day, Aldric noticed that Valeria was spending time with Priska. For her part, Priska seemed to enjoy the attention: she and Valeria chatted amiably for long periods. Aldric urged his horse closer, approaching from behind, wanting to overhear some of their conversation. He wasn't proud of the strategy, but he didn't trust Valeria for one moment.

"Of course, she's a goddess that all women should worship," Valeria was saying. "Please, ask me anything."

Priska mumbled something that Aldric couldn't catch.

"Our Church's reputation comes from disgruntled men who believe women should be their slaves," Valeria replied. "We don't exist to serve. The goddess Sylva Kalisia venerates women and gives her priestesses power to defend themselves. And men hate this. Why would the goddess care if you're a sorcerer? Women of power are valued and exalted above all others. Once this is over, you should—" Valeria turned to regard Aldric with cold eyes. "Is there something you want, Magister Aldric?"

Aldric shook his head and urged his mount to a trot. "Just passing. I want to talk to Niklaus. I hope the pace we're setting isn't too hard for you?" The question sounded lame to his own ears, but it was the first thing he'd thought of.

Valeria practically sneered at him. "We're not weak. Worry about the others, especially the sorcerer Sokhelle. She looks a trifle delicate for hard travel."

"I'm sure she'll appreciate your concern," Aldric said.

He realized that Valeria saw Priska as an asset and was doing her best to persuade the young woman to join her faith. It really wasn't any of his business, but he still thought it opportunistic of the priestess.

*Whatever happens will be the gods' will,* he told himself. But on this irregular mission, among strangers, somehow the words were unconvincing.

~ ~ ~

Each dawn, all three sorcerers would leave the camp to replenish themselves with the dawn-tide. At sunset, only Soki and Priska partook of the dusk-tide. Aldric kept his relic hidden away too, preferring to wait for a more private place to continue his study of the gem, and the history and secrets it revealed.

Shortly before sunset on the fourth day, they came to a clear stream, and Aldric decided they might as well make camp for the night. There was a patch of sand on a nearby bend that would make for a comfortable bed, and they'd wake to sunlight for once rather than the oppressive gloom of the forest.

As he called for them to stop, Bryn emerged from the thick brush, holding up a couple of pheasants he'd bagged with a bow and arrow. Razmus and Stray Dog went hunting for firewood, as they'd done each previous evening.

Priska handled her talismans, her lips moving soundlessly as she recited tables and formulas to reinforce her sorcerous training. Soki stood close, observing everything she did with a watchful gaze. Aldric did similar exercises every evening to keep the calculations fresh in his mind. But Priska would have to stop with hers and begin different ones if she was to be retrained.

The high priestess perched on a fallen log, hands clasped in her lap.

"Are you going to help?" Bryn asked curtly, standing so close he loomed over her.

Valeria sneered up at him. "No."

"Do you think we're your servants? You expect us to do all the work and cook you dinner?"

Aldric was about to intervene when Valeria rose to her feet. "Are you not a gentleman, Bryn? Do you not respect women and those who serve a higher power? I can cook if you like, but I guarantee you won't like the results."

Her words brought a laugh from Priska.

"Those who don't work don't eat," Bryn said with a sneer, and turned his back on Valeria.

The priestess sank down to her seat without another word.

So far, with everyone else pitching in, Valeria's attitude hadn't been a problem. But Aldric knew it wouldn't take long for someone to do more than just comment, and the situation would come to a head. He'd probably have to use sorcery then, to keep people apart. Letting it play out would only make things worse.

He dug a shallow pit in the sand and peeled strips of tinder from a branch, piling them up until Razmus and Stray Dog returned with the wood. He took a pot from one of the supply horses' saddlebags and poured in a prepared mix of vegetables and mushrooms. His Church had been generous with equipment and supplies, and they had enough of these meals to last for a few weeks if necessary. After that, there were dried beans and whatever they could forage and hunt. But the settlers would feed them, he was sure. It was the least they could do.

He half filled the pot with water from the stream, placed it next to the fire pit, and looked around. Valeria was watching him, her pale gray eyes visible in the fading light. Aldric smiled at her, then busied himself butchering the pheasants. The wild birds were lean, but fragrant from the plants they ate, which would flavor the dark meat. A quick roast, and they'd be done.

Razmus and Stray Dog returned before he'd finished, both depositing a load of wood by the fire pit. Soon they had a blaze going, with larger logs burning down to coals they could cook on. Aldric let Stray Dog take over roasting the pheasants. He had a knack for campfire cooking.

Aldric looked around for Niklaus and located him about fifty paces downstream on another patch of sand. He'd stripped off his shirt and was bare-chested, performing sword exercises with a long branch he'd trimmed of twigs and bark. He moved slowly, deliberately, not at all like the forms Aldric had been taught.

He approached Niklaus, his boots crunching over the smooth river stones. The mercenary stopped when Aldric was close, the branch extended in front of him, both arms at full stretch. His build was somewhere between Bryn's and Stray Dog's: cut muscles without being too lean, as if he exercised frequently. Aldric saw with surprise that Niklaus's torso was scar-free. There wasn't a single wound on his chest or back, unlike Stray Dog, who bore the marks of battle and violence.

Aldric weighed Niklaus up, wondering if he could take him in a fight. Niklaus moved well, was confident, and his reach exceeded Aldric's. Realistically, he probably wouldn't stand a chance against the mercenary ... not without sorcery.

"Something you want?" Niklaus said evenly. His skin was sheened with sweat, though he wasn't breathing heavily.

"This priestess of yours is going to be a problem," Aldric replied. Best to be blunt.

Niklaus uttered a soft laugh and lowered the branch. He stuck the tip into the sand and left it standing on its own. "She wouldn't take no for an answer. If we'd left without her, she'd have followed us, so I said yes." He shrugged. "It was the easiest thing to do."

Aldric fought the urge to sigh. "What good is she? What skills does she have?"

"She believes the goddess wants her to join us. She said she was shown signs."

Niklaus walked toward the stream. Aldric hesitated, then followed.

"What signs? Can she fight? Or will we have to protect her as well?"

Niklaus bent and cupped water in his hands, splashing it over himself. "Ask her yourself. She's not my priestess. But I will say this: just as you have been touched by your god, she has to have been touched by mine."

Although he'd studied long and hard under many tutors, Aldric had only heard vague whispers about the powers the Lady Sylva Kalisia bestowed on her priestesses. Unlike the Five, whose power usually manifested as healing—though those touched by the other aspects had different powers—the Lady's power was associated with pain, both physical and emotional. How that benefited anyone, Aldric couldn't begin to guess.

"Why did you say no to her at first?" he asked. "Didn't your Church send you on this mission? Don't you answer to the priestesses?"

Niklaus ran water over his short hair and shook his head like a dog. "I ... do what I want. I represent the Lady, that's true. But her priestesses have no hold over me."

Aldric frowned. What Niklaus said didn't make sense. "What do you—"

"That's all you need to know. The High Priestess Valeria is

here on her own business. What that is, I couldn't say."

*Holy Menselas. What a mess.*

"Do you think," Aldric said, taking a risk, "that she's after whatever is in the ruins?"

Niklaus wiped water from his skin and trudged back to his branch. He tugged his shirt over his head. "You're a smart man. What do you think?"

"I think," Aldric said slowly, "that this mission is a shambles. We need to—"

"No. We don't *need* to do anything. We're here to kill some Dead-eyes and investigate the ruins; then we head back to Caronath. That's all."

Aldric couldn't leave it alone. Didn't Niklaus want to know what was going on? "Your priestess might have other ideas."

"She can do what she wants. She's not my responsibility."

"Keep telling yourself that," Aldric said.

He left the mercenary and made his way back to the camp. Stray Dog had butterflied the pheasants, and the flattened birds were tied to sticks and roasting above the coals. Steam rose from the pot, and bowls and spoons had been set out. Neb bustled about, moving rocks and stones and wood and leaves so they'd have a clear patch for the campsite.

Aldric nodded his thanks to them both and went to see to his gear, giving himself time to think. He went through the motions of checking and rechecking his saddle and belts and weapons. Valeria was an unwelcome addition to the group, but if she stayed out of the way, she wouldn't be a problem. That, however, was unlikely. Archbishop Hannus had ordered him to explore the ruins and bring back anything he found. Valeria likely had the same idea. Shaking his head, Aldric checked his khopesh for rust before oiling it.

Next, he grabbed his belt pouch containing his talisman and approached Priska. He couldn't put this off any longer. Her expression was hopeful, almost causing Aldric to decide against what he was about to do. Who was he to try to teach someone sorcery? Especially someone like Priska, with her stunted pathways. His unease of his own power was so intense, sometimes he almost hated it himself. It had marked him for life and torn him away from what he'd been born to do: heal for the Five.

Taking a deep breath, he mastered his emotions and gave Priska a brief smile. "After our meal, I'll go over some things, begin to teach you what I can. But it's not going to be easy."

Priska nodded gratefully, a lock of hair falling across her face. "Thank you. It's been so long … I'd almost lost hope."

"No," Soki said from behind Aldric. He turned. "I'll do it," she added.

He nodded, relieved Soki had taken the task off his plate and that Priska would have a far more knowledgeable teacher.

"Sokhelle, I cannot thank you enough," said Priska. "To learn under you is a privilege. I'll do anything you say."

Soki laughed gently. "No, don't do that. Think for yourself, reason, evaluate my lessons, ask questions."

Under Aldric's tutelage, it would have taken years for Priska to recover, if she ever could. Learning from Soki, he imagined she might recover in a year or so. However, she still had years of frustrating work and failures ahead of her, and would need deep motivation and a strong will to come out the other side a fully functioning sorcerer.

Priska nodded eagerly. "I know it will be hard. My Covenant went down the wrong path, and retraining myself out of years of exercises and instruction will be difficult, but … I want to do it."

*I want the power* was what Aldric heard. And who could blame her? Though he was a reluctant sorcerer, to others, like Soki, it was their life, their dream. He knew what it was like to want something so badly you couldn't think about anything else. For Priska, there was a chance she'd achieve her dream with hard work. His own dream had been taken from him as soon as he became a sorcerer.

# CHAPTER TWENTY-TWO

# CHERISH

ALDRIC WOKE, HIS THOUGHTS groggy. He scrabbled for the hilt of his sword before realizing his defensive wards hadn't been triggered. After the encounter at Soki's the other night though, he wasn't taking any chances. He'd asked Soki to set up another type of ward every night before they slept, attuned to both of them. One that warned if anything larger than a child moved outside their camp. It was this ward activating that had woken him.

He looked around at the indistinct shapes of his companions. Two were missing. Niklaus and Valeria. *What are they up to?*

Taking care not to make any noise, he threw off his blanket and sat up. Bryn's eyes glittered in the dark. They'd opened as soon as Aldric had moved. Aldric peered to where Stray Dog lay, but the big man's back was to him. Soki sniffed and turned under her blanket. She didn't seem to think the alarm was anything to be worried about.

Aldric tilted his head and listened to the night. Insects hummed and clicked, and somewhere south an owl hooted. He made out a shape downriver and squinted. He couldn't be sure, but it looked like Niklaus had returned to the sandy stretch he'd practiced sword forms on, and next to him stood Valeria. They were talking in low tones.

If Aldric wanted to eavesdrop on their conversation, it was dusk-tide sorcery he needed. He had avoided using it, as if it might stain his soul, but his dealings with Soki had shown him it was only his reticence to handle a metaphorical darkness that stood in his way. Was this why Menselas had guided him here? To show him his foolishness?

He searched his memory for the words and calculations he'd been taught long ago. Mumbling to himself, he rehearsed them in his head and then whispered a cant. Sorcery flared—dusk-tide, oozing through his mind like shadowy oil. Sounds grew louder, sharper. Aldric could hear every word Niklaus whispered as if he stood right behind him.

"What do you expect to find here?" the mercenary asked Valeria. His tone was polite, formal even.

"Don't you know?" The priestess uttered a soft laugh. "No, I suppose you wouldn't. You're just her tool."

It was Niklaus's turn to chuckle. "Don't mistake your own desires for hers. Others have walked that path before, and I can tell you, they've regretted it. If you're here for personal glory, I'd reconsider your plan."

"I am one of her touched. The Lady wants me here. I've seen the signs."

"Is that so?" drawled Niklaus.

"How dare you question me!" hissed Valeria. "I bear her mark. I am her high priestess. You're only a sword that—"

"Careful now. I'm here because she wants me to be. You're meddling. I don't like that."

"What you don't like doesn't matter."

"Doesn't it? It seems to me, High Priestess, that what I dislike matters very much." There was an unspoken threat in his tone.

After a long pause, Valeria said, "We don't have to be at odds. If we work together, this mission will go much more smoothly."

"For you maybe. You're forgetting that I don't care about what you want. I only care about her. She directs me. And if you try to put your wants ahead of hers, you'd better watch yourself."

"Our Church could be so much greater!" Valeria whispered. "Think about what we could achieve if we weren't treated like some minor religion. If our priestesses had more influence, people would flock to us! The other faiths would have to acknowledge us as a power to be reckoned with. We'd be able to—"

Niklaus's soft laughter grew louder and cut off her words. "You're traveling a dangerous path. As I said, you should think long and hard about whether you're confusing your wishes for hers. Others have done so, and it didn't turn out well for them. The Lady will know what you do. Count on it. As for me ... if she directs me to help you, I will. Until then, you're on your own."

Sand crunched underfoot, and Aldric looked up to see Niklaus's shadow coming toward the camp. Valeria was still, as if considering his words, which took Aldric aback. Niklaus had suggested the high priestess was guilty of placing her own goals above those of her goddess. In other parts of the world, he would have been strung up for his temerity.

The mercenary entered the camp, and Aldric saw that even for the brief talk with Valeria, he'd buckled on his short sword and wore his longer sword across his back. He held his metal cane in one hand and rested it on his collarbone.

As Niklaus passed by Aldric, he leaned over him and said, "Never use sorcery to eavesdrop on me again."

~ ~ ~

The day was overcast, but the rain stayed away. Aldric missed the patches of sunlight that usually dappled the forest's floor. Without the sun, their path became darker and more threatening. Bryn still ranged around their group, but the others unconsciously drew closer together, their mood subdued. Except for Soki, who gazed around as if nothing could hurt her.

Ahead of Aldric, Niklaus talked animatedly with Stray Dog, who didn't say much, just gave an occasional nod or shake of his head. The high priestess with questionable motives rode next to Priska again today. From the look of things, she and Priska were talking, though so softly Aldric couldn't hear what they said.

Razmus rode up beside them, and Priska frowned at him, while Valeria kept a smile fixed on her face.

"Perhaps you should spend less time with this *priestess* and more time with Sokhelle, learning sorcery," Razmus told his daughter. "It's what you've always wanted, isn't it?"

"I have time for both, Father. And please don't tell me what to do. You've interrupted our conversation, which is rude."

Razmus glared at Valeria, but slowed his mount to let the two women move ahead. He trailed behind them as if he were a spare wheel, giving them disapproving glances they were unlikely to see through the backs of their heads.

Aldric couldn't blame Razmus for disapproving of Priska's choice of friends. The others didn't know what he did after eavesdropping on Niklaus and Valeria. The priestess was touched by her goddess, just as Aldric was by Menselas. But what powers that gave her, he couldn't say.

Ahead of Niklaus and Stray Dog, Neb came trotting back to the group, a grin plastered across his face. "Almost there!" he crowed, and twisted in his saddle to point to the west. "Between those two hills is where we want to go."

Aldric couldn't see anything different about the surrounding forest, but so far the old settler had proved knowledgeable about the terrain, and they'd eaten fresh meat and root vegetables every day because of him.

Niklaus stood in his stirrups and peered westward. "I don't see any smoke. So maybe we're here before the Dead-eyes."

Neb's expression twisted in fear.

"Pants-pisser," Niklaus said callously, and Bryn snorted in amusement.

Aldric urged his mount forward and shot Niklaus a stern look. "I'm sure everything's fine," he assured Neb. "Remember, they don't gather in numbers unless it's full-dark."

"Aldric's correct," said Soki. "To attack a settlement in numbers, the Dead-eyes will wait for an auspicious time. What is it called, this settlement of yours?"

Neb took off his battered hat and scratched his head. "Yes. Of course." But his eyes still flicked left and right. "The town is called Cherish—the original settlers voted on the name. In Cherish Valley."

Niklaus chuckled and shook his head while Bryn grimaced.

"We'll quicken the pace from here," Aldric said. "Neb, lead the way as usual. We'll make sure Cherish is safe as soon as we can."

Neb gave him a grateful smile.

The others urged their horses after Neb. Taking one last look behind him, Aldric joined the back of the group. *The settlement is all that matters,* he thought. *Leave Niklaus and Valeria, and Hannus, to their games.*

His job was to keep people safe and make sure they survived. Anything else was secondary. Even the ruin.

~ ~ ~

A valley of verdant lushness extended for miles to the north between the hills. Sunlight broke through the clouds, and a bright sliver of silver snaked into the distance: a river. A short way into the valley, the trees had been cleared, and ramshackle dwellings spotted the landscape. Wood smoke plumed from chimneys, and somewhere a dog barked. To either side of the settlement, fields, both freshly plowed and filled with crops, showed the settlers were eking a living from the forest.

Far in the distance, more trees had been cleared, and cattle, sheep, and goats grazed. By the stream, a mill wheel turned, powered by the flowing water. The mill's first floor was constructed of stone, the only building that had been made to last. Another large building was half built, but judging by the weeds growing from the dirt inside, it had been abandoned. If the settlers feared the Dead-eyes, they also had other concerns, Aldric guessed.

A few people were visible in the mostly deserted settlement: a woman carrying buckets from a well, children running between houses, a short man pushing a wheelbarrow full of tools. Perhaps everyone else was working in the fields or cutting wood in the forest.

Aldric noticed the remains of a burned building to the east. Charred timbers jutted into the air, and chickens pecked among the ruins.

"Was that there before?" he asked Neb.

The settler followed Aldric's extended arm. "Aye. The Dead-eyes did it. Knocked over an oil lamp. Family got out, but they lost everything."

Neb trotted his horse toward Cherish, and everyone trailed after him.

Niklaus moved his horse closer to Aldric's. "We've arrived at the asshole of the world," he said. "I'd hate to die here, torn apart and defiled by Dead-eyes." He looked over at Stray Dog. "How about you? Fancy dying here with the farmers and their dirt?"

Stray Dog gave Niklaus a blank look and shrugged. "That's not going to happen."

Niklaus chuckled, as if Stray Dog had said something amusing. "No, I suppose not. But if they've got some beer or spirits, plenty of food, and maybe a pretty girl or three, they might make it worth my while to save them."

Aldric shook his head in disgust, while Stray Dog rode away after Neb.

"No sense of humor," muttered Niklaus.

"Maybe he doesn't find you funny," Bryn said.

Priska snorted. "I'd wager not many do."

Niklaus placed his hand over his heart. "You wound me, fair maiden."

"She's no one's maiden," growled Razmus; then his eyes widened as Niklaus and Bryn burst out laughing.

His daughter gave him a withering look, and Soki shook her head. Even Aldric had to hide a smile.

"That's not what I meant," Razmus said. He shot Niklaus a dark look before following in Stray Dog's dust.

Priska glanced at Valeria, who shrugged. "Never mind him, my dear. Fathers will always try to shelter their daughters. And sometimes that love can smother."

Holy Menselas, managing these people was worse than herding cats, Aldric thought. And now they'd have the settlers to deal with as well.

Neb cantered into the settlement and waved his hat in the air. His shouts echoed across the fields, and the few settlers in the street looked up. One pointed past Neb toward Aldric and the others. The settlers dropped whatever they were carrying and scurried inside their houses. In moments, the street was empty. Even the children had disappeared.

"A fine welcome indeed," Niklaus said, and laughed loudly.

Aldric scowled at him, wondering if people despised him everywhere he went. Immediately, he felt guilty at the thought.

"Hello!" cried Neb. "I'm back. I've brought warriors with me!"

In the distance, a door slammed shut. Then only silence greeted him.

Aldric urged his horse forward, and his companions followed. Neb's shouting grew louder as they approached, then trailed off.

Metal screeched to their right as a door opened a crack. Two children poked their faces out. A woman shouted at them, and the door closed quickly.

Bryn cleared his throat. "Where's the inn?" he asked Neb, face deadpan.

Stray Dog snorted as he suppressed a chuckle.

Neb jammed his hat on his head. "Most are out in the fields and the mine. That's why no one's here." He cleared his throat. "When they all get back, there'll be a proper welcome. And there's no inn. You'll stay in the meeting hall, which is next to the mayor's house."

"You have a mayor? In this place?" Soki said. "Well, we'd better go meet him, then."

Neb drew himself up. "You have. It's me. That's who's the mayor. But my place isn't big enough for everyone."

"Of course," Aldric said, attempting to head off any disparaging comments about the arrangement. He would prefer a separate room, but they'd make do. "That's fine. Whatever is available will do."

"As long as there's something to drink," Niklaus said.

"And eat," added Stray Dog. "I'm starved."

They all were, having skipped the midday meal, as Neb had said if they did, they'd reach the settlement before dark.

"Ah, we don't have a lot to offer," said Neb, wringing his hat in his hands like a chicken's neck. "But you're welcome to what we can spare."

Niklaus gave Aldric a sharp look, a smirk on his face. Aldric ignored the implied criticism, though he heard it loud and clear: *These settlers want us to fight and possibly die for them, yet they begrudge us food.*

Aldric helped people—it was what he did—but it never ceased to amaze him how some people wanted things both ways. In this case, the settlers wanted their problem with the Dead-eyes solved, but they didn't want to have to deal with the type of people required for the solution: rough men who killed for a living, and sorcerers, who they likely had a superstitious fear of. Aldric understood their dilemma and even why they were so afraid. They wanted a simple life, free of troubles. But the Dead-eyes, and now Aldric, had brought violence among them. He didn't think the settlers would give them a warm reception, and he worried about the reaction of the others.

"We can meet the rest of your people later," he told Neb. "For now, find us somewhere to put our gear and stable the horses."

Neb looked at Aldric, his face pale and a worried crease in his forehead. "They don't mean nothin' by it. They're afraid. Life is tough out here. Making a new beginning, scratching a place from nothing, isn't easy." He coughed a laugh. "And now the Dead-eyes have … We go to bed afraid, and we wake afraid. And not just because of the Dead-eyes."

Soki gave Neb a reassuring smile. "We understand."

Neb led them to a large building that turned out to be a sort of common hall: log walls, joins packed with clay, supported a shingle roof already graying with age. A large iron triangle hung from the front veranda, along with an iron beater.

The group dismounted and tied their horses to rails in front of the hall.

"Take your gear inside," Razmus advised. "We don't want to come out, and it's all gone."

"Here now," Neb protested. "We ain't like that. In a community like this, we look after each other."

"I like to take precautions," Razmus said. "And we aren't part of your community."

Aldric sighed and raised his voice: "Do as he says. I don't want any misunderstandings while we're here."

Grumbling greeted his words, but the others began unloading their saddlebags. Lugging their gear, they followed Neb inside. It was dark and cold, and Neb bustled over to a long bench against one wall and sparked a lamp alight. Using the flame to light other lamps, he soon had five going, which he positioned on shelves about the room. There was a round stone fireplace in the center, made from river stones and fired clay, with a flue above. Surrounding it were benches and stumps for seating, and not much else. The floorboards were wide, rough-sawn timbers.

"It's going to be cold at night," Soki said, "with the wind coming in through the floor."

"We might have to sleep close to each other," Niklaus said, smiling at her. "For warmth."

Aldric felt his face flush, even though he realized Niklaus was baiting him.

"I'm sure we'll make do," replied Soki.

"Get a fire going, Neb," Niklaus said. "It's as cold as a Dead-eye's—" He broke off and coughed, glancing at Priska.

"He's not your servant," Stray Dog said. He dumped his gear by the door and moved to a pile of wood stacked close to the fireplace. He drew a knife and began stripping wood for kindling.

Razmus followed his lead after storing his own gear next to Stray Dog's. The others did the same, with Neb bustling around them as if he were an innkeeper and they'd hired his whole place for the night.

He was nervous for some reason, Aldric thought.

"Put your things there, High Priestess," Neb said to Valeria. "That's right. They'll be safe. Now, I'll get a drink for everyone."

He hurried over to a barrel near the bench, ladled water into wooden bowls, and passed them around. Priska, Stray Dog, Valeria, Bryn, and Soki accepted theirs with thanks and drank deeply, as did Aldric, parched after the day of traveling. Razmus looked at his suspiciously while Niklaus screwed his nose up and didn't accept his bowl.

"Water?" he said contemptuously. "Where's the beer? And

how about some food while you're at it?"

Neb pushed the bowl toward Niklaus. "Water's all we have. When I gather the settlers to come and meet you, I'll have them bring some food. But we—"

"Don't have much," finished Niklaus. He waved away the bowl. "I saw the fields of barley, and from the looks of things, you've been here a few years. Don't tell me someone's not brewing beer."

"And how about some tea?" added Valeria primly. "A hot drink would be nice."

"I agree," Soki said. "It'll chase away the cold."

Neb backed away and returned the bowl to the bench. "I'll get the others. I ... ah ..." He shuffled hurriedly out the door.

Aldric shot Niklaus a dark look. "Go easy on him. And the rest of the settlers." He looked around at the others. "They've had a hard time with the Dead-eyes, let alone eking an existence out of—"

"They wanted wolves to protect their flock from other predators," Niklaus interrupted. "And now the wolves have come to save them, they're scared. Well, you needn't worry—this wolf isn't going to eat any of them. But the least they can do is feed us properly and give us something stronger than water. Am I right, Bryn? Dog?"

Stray Dog kept stacking sticks in the fireplace, but shrugged his boulder-like shoulders.

Bryn sniffed. "They'll hide the good stuff. What do you expect? Bloody peasants."

Bryn's complaints were wearing thin, and Aldric caught himself reaching for his dusk-tide repository, the beginnings of a cant on his tongue. Hastily he withdrew from his power and clamped his mouth shut, horrified that his anger had caused him to lose control. And not only that: his subconscious thought had been to use sorcery against Bryn—dusk-tide sorcery. *Menselas forgive me.*

"They need our help," he said instead, "but they don't have to like us. These are people not used to violence, and they're living in fear of the Dead-eyes. We should be reassuring them, easing their minds. Not giving them a whole new set of problems."

Stray Dog sparked his tinder, and flames licked about the wood, causing it to crackle and steam. Smoke rose to the roof. Some disappeared out the flue, but the rest gathered in the highest point like a heavy mist.

Niklaus stared at it and sighed. "I see they didn't bring a builder with them."

Priska laughed, then covered her mouth with a slender hand.

Aldric realized he was still carrying all his own gear and stacked it beside the rest. The break gave him time to cool down and order his thoughts. When he'd arrived in Caronath, he hadn't been prepared to be sent off into the wilderness with a bunch of strangers, and on a mission that grew more dubious the longer he thought about it.

*A few weeks at most,* he told himself. *Then I'll be done here and be back in Caronath, with Soki.*

He returned to the fire to see Stray Dog had filled a battered kettle with water and placed it next to the blaze to boil. Valeria was rummaging around in her saddlebags and pulled out a metal container.

"What's that?" asked Priska.

"Tea," Valeria said. "I'm sure the settlers will have their own brew, likely made with local plants and wildflowers, but it'll be harsh and probably not very tasty." She patted Priska's hand. "Trust me when I say mine will be much better."

Priska smiled at Valeria, but Aldric felt a tinge of unease. Was Valeria finally thawing out toward them, or was this a front she was putting on? Even Niklaus didn't trust her. She had to be here for the ruins.

Aldric rubbed the back of his neck, trying to stave off a rising headache. His thoughts turned, reluctantly, to Soki. She was here at the behest of his Church. Didn't they trust him? Or were they expecting the group to encounter a threat only a powerful sorcerer could overcome? It angered him that Hannus, or Hierophant Karianne, kept him in the dark. And just when he'd been given the relic by Roald.

Stray Dog placed a few more logs on the fire, then moved the kettle closer. Niklaus wandered around the room, poking at things and sniffing at the dust. His sword was still strapped to his back, and the tip of his cane tapped the thick timber floor with each step. Priska chatted softly with Valeria and Soki about tea in its various forms, if what Aldric caught of their conversation was anything to go by. Bryn sat next to Razmus, sharpening his sword with a whetstone, while the ex-soldier mended a torn seam on a leather jerkin.

Aldric took a seat by the fire and warmed his hands.

The kettle boiled, and Stray Dog used two sticks to take it off the heat.

"Where is Neb?" asked Niklaus, now beside Aldric.

Aldric realized quite some time had passed, and the settler hadn't returned. He stood. "I'll go look for him."

"Don't bother," Niklaus said, striding toward the door. "The sooner we get this over with, the better."

He jerked the door open and ducked his head to avoid cracking it on the lintel. Aldric rushed after him, unsure of what Niklaus was about to do. If he barged into settlers' houses and riled them up, it would make their job all the more difficult. Aldric needed to stop him before he made a mess of things.

Night was approaching fast, and the settlement was dark and washed out. As Aldric's eyes adjusted to the dimness, a loud clanging assaulted his ears. Niklaus was striking the metal triangle, the beater in his hand a blur. The cacophony echoed around the settlement. Soon, Aldric heard shouts of alarm and doors banging.

"Dead-eyes!" yelled Niklaus, continuing to beat the triangle. "Dead-eyes are coming! Grab your weapons! Grab your chickens! Dead-eyes are here!"

The rest of their group filed onto the hall's veranda. Priska and Razmus looked around nervously while Valeria smirked. Stray Dog took one look at Niklaus, shook his head, and went back inside. Bryn leaned against the wall and placed both hands over his ears.

Settlers came screaming and yelling out of their houses. Some carried children, their eyes wide with fear, while others bore flaming torches and makeshift weapons. Women dragged bundles they thought too valuable to be left behind, and some older children helped an old woman with a cane as she struggled toward the hall. A few people ran from one house to the next, shouting in alarm and peering into the forest surrounding the settlement.

A crowd came toward Niklaus, who had stopped beating the triangle. Aldric's ears rang even after the noise ceased. More than a few of the settlers waved rust-spotted swords. Neb was with them, brandishing a staff, alongside a man who held a dagger small enough to be used as a fruit knife.

"Is that a scythe?" asked Valeria, indicating another settler.

"I think so," said Soki.

The skinny man waved the farm implement in the air, as if Dead-eyes had wings and he was fighting them off.

Aldric walked slowly toward the panicking mob, quietly seething at the ruckus Niklaus had caused. This was no way to introduce themselves, especially since the settlers were already wary of them. He held his hands out, palms facing them.

When they didn't settle, he took a breath and yelled, "Quiet! Calm down! There are no Dead-eyes. It was a false alarm."

Like water draining from a leaking pitcher, the hubbub slowly died.

Neb stepped forward, helped by a few shoves from the other

settlers. "What's going on? Where are the Dead-eyes? Who rang the alarm?"

"I did," Niklaus said, stepping forward to stand beside Aldric. "Don't be afraid. No Dead-eyes are here."

"The clanger is for emergencies!" Neb shouted. "Look what you've done! You've scared everyone."

Niklaus laughed without mirth. "We've come all the way from Caronath to help you, and look at you! Pants-pissers, hiding in your houses. Is that the welcome we deserve? I ring the alarm, and you run around, arms flapping." He waved his arms wildly and laughed again.

"That's enough!" Aldric said. "They're right to be scared. Of the Dead-eyes and of us."

He walked toward Neb, who was eyeing him and Niklaus and the settlers uncomfortably.

"Have everyone return to their homes," he told the old settler. "Then bring the food you promised. It's the least you can do."

Neb flashed Niklaus an angry look before turning back to the crowd. "False alarm! Everyone go home. No, not you, Shand. You come with me to get some food for these ... the people the Churches have sent."

Aldric and the others watched as the settlers shuffled away, casting frequent glances over their shoulders. Soon, they'd all disappeared back into their houses. Neb was left with a slim young girl who looked to be about fourteen. Her freckled face was dirty, and her brown hair looked like it had been hacked off at the shoulders with a blunt knife.

She and Neb hurried over to a storage barn close by and returned a short time later bearing a basket each. Inside the building, they unpacked their contents onto the table: loaves of hard bread and packages of greased paper tied with string. To Aldric, it looked like preserved food, not the fresh produce he'd been expecting. And going by the grumbles coming from Niklaus and Bryn, he wasn't the only one to notice.

"What is this?" he asked, pointing to the packages.

"Dried meat. Some dried fruit. The loaves are good if you toast slices from them."

Stray Dog looked at Neb like he'd sprouted an extra head, while Soki pursed her lips.

Niklaus was right, Aldric realized: the settlers wanted help, but they also wanted them gone. And while they were here, they would feed them the poorest food they had.

He placed a hand on Neb's shoulder. "Neb, this will do for tonight. But tomorrow, we'll expect better."

Shand glanced at him, then quickly away again, and stopped unwrapping a package that smelled of dried fish.

"I told you," Neb said. "We don't have much."

"I understand. But this is unacceptable. We're here to help you and the other settlers. If we feel you don't want us here …"

There was a sharp hiss of indrawn breath from Shand. Neb frowned at her and shushed her with a gesture.

"Your Churches told you to help us," he said. "You can't leave until we're safe."

"Looks safe here to me," said Bryn from beside the fire. "You all look like you're doing really well." He stared at Neb until the settler looked away.

Aldric squeezed Neb's shoulder, trying to reassure him. "We're all tired. I'm sure in the morning we'll feel better. After a decent meal."

Neb nodded. "I'll see what I can scrounge up tomorrow."

Niklaus snorted.

"Good," Aldric said. "Then that's settled. We'll do our best to sort out the Dead-eyes for you as quickly as we can. Then we'll be gone, and things can get back to normal. For everyone."

Aldric wasn't sure he believed that himself.

Neb nodded curtly and gestured to Shand. "Come on, girl."

"I'm not a girl," Shand said.

Neb grabbed her arm and dragged her to the door. Her protests faded as they went outside, and the door closed behind them.

"Ungrateful bastards," muttered Bryn.

Valeria shrugged. "What do you expect from a bunch of provincials."

Priska was poking the various packages. She wrinkled her nose as she touched the dried fish, a bony freshwater variety from the look of it. "Ugh, this stinks."

"Enough complaining," Aldric said. "Neb said he'll provide better in the morning. For tonight, eat what you can, and get some sleep."

After a few slices of toasted bread and some dried mutton washed down with water, Aldric felt better. But from the sour looks of his companions, it would take a lot for the settlers to redeem themselves tomorrow. *One step at a time*, he thought.

He spread his bedroll against a wall and settled down to sleep. By the fire, Priska and Valeria conversed in hushed tones. Aldric worried about Valeria's influence on the young woman. He wondered if he should somehow separate them, perhaps guide Priska to Soki instead so she could start unraveling Priska's defective knowledge of sorcery. But he needed rest.

And he still had his own duty to fulfill: to use the relic to glean some knowledge, some insight, from its random visions. That, at least, would be something.

# CHAPTER TWENTY-THREE

# JOURNEY OF TEARS

THEY'D SECURED KURIO TO the horse, and Mellish had said his goodbyes to Zarina. Then he'd spirited her out of Caronath under the cover of night.

Her hands ached from clutching the reins, but try as she might, she couldn't loosen her grip. Along with the tight metal band around her throat, her wrists were manacled and locked to an iron ring on her saddle. The metal abraded her already raw skin, and her wrists stung with every step of her horse. Her mind swirled, seldom settling on a single thought as they flitted inside her head like mayflies. *Willas. The metal cube. Gannon. Demons. Zarina.*

"Where did you learn to ride?" Mellish said contemptuously, breaking her distracted reverie.

"I didn't."

Her thighs and rear ached abominably. She was city born and bred, and her nose itched and ran from the wilderness around them. The air was strange: unpleasantly thin and tasteless without the fragrant dust of Caronath.

"That explains it. Likely honest animals would fear you, demon."

"My name is Kurio, and I'm no more demon than you are."

Mellish leaned to the side and spat from his horse. "Zarina said you are, and that's good enough for me."

"Good dog," muttered Kurio.

"What's that?"

"Nothing."

She could see the stock of her crossbow poking out from the saddlebag behind her. So they'd at least packed all her gear, not that she could see Mellish letting her use it. Not under any circumstance. She understood why they'd secured her so well, because she'd kill Mellish the first chance she got. At the moment though, even if she strained, her weapon would still be two feet from her hands.

"Then shut your mouth," he said. "We've days of traveling yet, and I don't want to listen to your constant whining."

The rest of the day passed in a blur, Kurio lost in her thoughts, vaguely aware of not stopping for a midday meal. Mellish shoved a canteen made from a hollowed-out gourd into her face, but she drank little of the water, not caring if she spilled any.

Trees went by. The horses clopped across rivulets and streams. Birds sang. Bugs hummed in chorus. Eventually the light grew dim, and Mellish called a halt. She noted he buckled on his sword as soon as he dismounted.

Kurio winced at the ache in her back. She slid out of the saddle, and agony flared in her legs and hips. She cried out in pain and fell to the ground. As she lay there, fingers clutching the soft earth, weeping softly and cursing the gods, Mellish led her horse away.

Too bone-tired to care, Kurio watched as he set up camp. Bedrolls for the both of them, a fair distance apart, and a single blanket. There were plenty of sticks and branches close by—one thing the forest was good at providing—and she was never out of his sight as he gathered enough for a fire. He built a structure of sticks above a pile of bark and some fungus he'd found, then struck an alchemical stick, which flared brightly before settling down to a flame. He lit the tinder, and soon the campfire was ablaze. The light of the fire, its warmth on her face, gave Kurio some hope.

"Won't someone, or something, see it?" she croaked, then coughed. Her throat was dry; she hadn't drunk enough water.

There was a canteen with the cooking supplies. She struggled to her feet and, fumbling with her secured hands, managed to swallow a mouthful.

"Talking again now, are we?" said Mellish. He placed another branch on the fire.

"You told me to shut my mouth."

"I'm sure that's not the first time you've heard that."

Swallowing a sharp retort, Kurio took another swig of water. This one went down easier as her throat recovered.

"Most men ask me to open my mouth."

The words felt bitter on her tongue, but she was desperate. If there was any way she could get Mellish off guard, she had to try it. She wouldn't go so far as to lie with him—the very thought repelled her—but if she could get close enough, with his thoughts on her body and his ardor clouding his mind …

"I won't be touching you, demon."

Kurio frowned. "You seriously believe I'm a demon, don't you?" She settled cross-legged in front of the fire, massaging her aching thighs with the balls of her palms.

Mellish didn't answer, just began preparing a meal of bread and cheese. Kurio groaned. Mellish was obviously no cook, and days of eating only bread and cheese would leave her constipated. She watched as he also brought out dried prunes and salted plums.

"You think of everything, don't you?" she said.

"Eat. Drink more water. Sleep. We'll be at the ruins in no time. We've been researching them for years. If the stupid settlers hadn't stumbled upon them, we'd have looted them undetected. Just do what you're told. And once this is over, you'll be free."

Kurio didn't think that was true, and Mellish's half smile as he said it confirmed her fears. Was she quick enough to stand and kick coals over him, then subdue him? Maybe the coals part, but her manacled wrists meant she wouldn't have a chance against him one on one.

"Zarina told me I'll likely die," she said.

Mellish remained silent, and his refusal to reply unnerved Kurio. He really did think she wasn't human.

"You didn't answer my question," she pushed. "Won't our fire be seen? Aren't there Dead-eyes and all manner of creatures in the wilderness?"

Mellish snorted and spat a wad of phlegm into the flames. Kurio wrinkled her nose.

"You only have to fear me," he said. "The Dead-eyes are unlikely to bother us until full-dark, and we'll be safe by then. If anything else approaches, I have a few surprises and some wards they'd have to get through. Nothing out here is strong enough to breach them, except maybe a powerful sorcerer or a wraithe."

He gnawed on his bread and cheese like a rat and likely spoke of his wards to deter her from an escape attempt. Kurio shivered. Wraithes were the villains of many a childhood story. "They don't exist. Wraithes, that is."

Mellish bowed his head, as if he felt the weight of a painful memory. "There aren't many left, and they usually stay within their steel-walled city. They only come out for specific purposes, and they are prone to violence. So if you do see one, beware."

"How come you know so much about them?"

"My order has many books. There's much to learn, and unlearn, of our history."

"What order is that? The Order of Kidnapping Women? The Glorious Knights of Torture?"

She thought she'd get a rise out of Mellish, but he simply gave her a flat stare.

"We're called the Order of the Blazing Sun. Mock us if you must, but we have been active for thousands of years. We fight and kill demons. Most importantly of all, we oppose the Tainted Cabal."

"The what?" said Kurio, feigning ignorance.

"Followers of the demon Nysrog."

Kurio tried to spread her hands. Couldn't. Her manacles clinked together. "You'll have to forgive me," she said. "But I've never before heard of demons or your order."

Okas had mentioned Nysrog and demons, but she'd thought he was deluded.

Mellish placed a salted plum in his mouth. His jaw worked, as if he chewed cud. For long moments he didn't speak; then he shrugged. "We pit ourselves against the Tainted Cabal. The sorcerers who follow Nysrog and seek the demon's infernal power for themselves. A few were given immortality—a fragment of their soul shattered free and bound forever. They work to return the world to darkness."

"It sounds dreadful."

Mellish gave her a sharp look. "It would be. But we have stopped them. So far. There aren't many of us, but we persevere."

"Why do you need me?"

Mellish shoved a plate filled with dry bread, cheese, prunes, and plums at her. "Eat," he said, then removed a thick book from his gear and began to read.

Kurio looked despairingly at her meal, then broke off a hunk of bread and some cheese and chewed slowly. Her horse, a brown mare, whinnied and shifted its feet, tugging at the rope securing it to a tree. Kurio finished her food, got up from the fire, and approached the beast, whispering calming words. Her hands smoothed its coat, patted its side, and it nuzzled her arm.

"I think the horses are thirsty," she said. "Have they been watered? There isn't any around here. Why didn't we camp by a stream?"

"The last water was hours ago," said Mellish with a shrug. "We should cross a stream tomorrow morning, with any luck."

"Don't you think that's unkind? The horses need water. We can spare some."

"We need the water for us. They're only animals. They'll survive."

Kurio shook her head at his casual cruelty. He didn't give a whistle for the horses.

"You said you had wards. So you're a sorcerer?" she asked.

If he was, she knew she'd likely never escape. With only a word, her bones could be flamed to charcoal, and her blood boiled.

To her surprise, he shook his head. "No. We've gathered items of power over time. Some are useful."

*Scavengers then. With an overinflated sense of importance.*

"By 'we', I take it you mean the Order of Imprisoning Women?"

Mellish rose to his feet so quickly Kurio flinched.

"You think this is amusing?" he snarled. "We go to save the world. You'd best remember that and cooperate."

"I'm manacled," Kurio said with venom. "And collared by this sorcerous torture device, in case you've forgotten."

Rage filled Mellish's face, and his mouth twisted into a sneer. "Oh, I haven't forgotten. And you won't either. It's time for another demonstration. After this, you'll obey me, demon, and you'll know what's coming the instant you disobey or try to escape."

His hand moved to an object secured to his sword belt. It looked like a bronze turtle, with gemstones dotting its shell.

"Mellish," Kurio said meekly. She'd pushed him too far. "Please. I—"

An immense weight crushed her. She buckled, felt stripped and trampled. Darkness and vertigo assailed her, and she groaned. Agony tore at her with searing tendrils. Her skin and flesh felt immolated by fire.

Strangely, through all the pain, she sensed another presence … Somehow it gave her hope. She clung in desperation to an inner kernel of herself, knowing the agony was an illusion. Her body and mind were whole. She would survive this.

Yet her endurance waned. She was, after all, only human. Her mind went blank. There was nothing, a void as insubstantial as fog.

Then sound came to her, tearing at her ears. "Wake up, demon."

She lay facedown on the ground, pressed into the damp earth and leaves. Her mouth tasted of bile. She shivered, too weak to move. She tried to breathe, and the air tore at her throat like razor-sharp knives.

"Get up," Mellish barked.

Kurio struggled to her knees. "You're an asshole," she grated.

Mellish was sitting by the campfire. An alchemical globe hung from a chain around his neck, shedding light on the tome he studied. The book was a handspan thick, bound with dark leather and a flap lock. Her gaze was drawn to the turtle on his belt. The evil relic that controlled her collar. No, not her collar. Theirs.

A hostile glare from Mellish. "Did you enjoy that, demon? Our history tells of demons that take pleasure in pain."

"My name is Kurio." She crawled away from the horses until she was close to the fire again. "So tell me, Mellish, how many demons have you killed? Ten? Twenty? Hundreds?"

"Seven. Their spawn are scattered. Hard to track down."

"Like me? Women … or children? Did you kill children, Mellish?"

No answer. Only a clatter as he threw a stick on the already blazing fire. She'd take that as a yes.

"Am I spawn?"

"Yes."

"To be slaughtered like an animal?"

"Yes."

"Look at me!" she shouted. "I'm a woman. I'm human!"

"No. You're not human at all."

"You deceive yourself! I am human born and human raised. If there is any demon blood inside me, it is weak or nonexistent. I don't have powers …" She trailed off. She *did* have powers of a kind—her talent. She ignored her rising fear and continued. "I don't hunger for human flesh. For blood. I'm not a monster."

"But you are. You are diseased, a scourge upon this world. Our tenets dictate that demons and their spawn must be eradicated. The smallest drop contaminates the whole, so there can be no leniency. No mercy. I've seen darkness. We're the bulwark against it. The defenders. The saviors. If we fail in our task, darkness will consume the world. Night … will be endless."

*No*, thought Kurio, *you are the demons*. Whatever crusade Mellish and Zarina were on, it had twisted them. They were cruel, monstrous. Heartless. Any indignity, any cruelty, any *murder*, was justified. She knew then that she had to get away, or she would die.

"How do you know I have demon blood?" she asked.

"You weren't harmed by the cube."

"I didn't touch it," she lied. "I used calfskin gloves."

"You lie," Mellish spat. "Your kind are treacherous. Deceivers."

"Is there another test? I'll prove I'm no demon."

Mellish laughed cruelly. "There's another test, and you'll face it soon enough. Then you'll join your kind back in the hells. And good riddance."

Kurio fell quiet, not wanting to antagonize him further. She reached up to touch the collar around her neck. Zarina had used the collar to cause her pain, but she hadn't needed another object to do so, like Mellish did. Zarina was a sorcerer, but Mellish wasn't. That fact gave her a glimmer of hope.

Kurio couldn't help herself. She glanced at her crossbow again.

"I see you looking at it," Mellish said.

Kurio suppressed a sigh. "It's good workmanship. I just wish I'd paid extra for the sea-ray-skin grip. Have you ever used a sword with a sea-ray-skin hilt? Your grip will never slip, no matter how damp your hand is."

"My hands don't sweat. It's my opponents who fear me."

"They don't? Sounds like a demon talent to me."

Mellish returned a quiet chuckle. "So eager for another taste of pain? I can accommodate your desires."

"No, thank you. What are you reading?"

"Information on demons. A history of my order."

He placed the book, open, on the ground. She could see the pages were covered with tiny text and illustrations.

"You can read?" she said before she could stop herself. She managed a fake smile. "I'm sorry."

"We're knights. Our Order has—"

"You're not bloody knights! You're deranged! You torture people, and you've imprisoned me with this"—Kurio tugged at the metal collar around her neck—"arcane shackle."

Mellish gave her a thin smile. "We only torture demons and those that serve them."

"But that's ... Argh! You stupid oaf! Can't you see I'm human?"

"Get some sleep," he said curtly. "We'll be starting out before dawn. I want no more of your talk tonight."

Fuming, Kurio wrapped herself in the blanket against the chill of the night. She knew better than to argue with Mellish when he'd made his mind up. His thoughts ran a narrow path, and he wasn't easily swayed. No doubt it was an aptitude Zarina found useful.

Mellish wasn't the brains of their little outfit. If little it was. The sorcerer Zarina was in charge. Killing Mellish would only be the beginning. She took a deep breath, tasting cold air on her tongue.

She would have to be careful. Others she'd seen on a path of vengeance always ended up broken or dead. But she was different. Her talent set her apart. And now ... perhaps her blood.

## Chapter Twenty-Four

# Sketchy Plans

THE MORNING AFTER THEIR arrival, Aldric watched as Niklaus drew a map of the village and the surrounding area in a patch of earth he'd swept clear of leaves and twigs. Stray Dog, Razmus, Bryn, and Soki stood with Aldric around the crude map, while Priska wandered in a circle, gazing at the houses about them. She looked on edge for some reason and kept glancing at Razmus. If she and her father were arguing about something, now wasn't the time, Aldric thought.

All of them were munching on soft rolls filled with a sticky, preserved fruit mixture. Neb had dropped a basket of the rolls with them a short time ago, before stomping off muttering about bringing some of the settlers back with him to listen to their plans for defense of the settlement.

"Hills here," said Niklaus, scratching curves in the dirt. He peered toward the edges of the valley to the east and west. "And cliffs here." He marked lines on both sides of a cluster of boxes—the settlers' houses.

Aldric squatted beside the diagram and pointed to the eastern cliffs. "Neb said the Dead-eyes came from the east. So they have a way down the cliffs. Maybe there's a trail. There are bound to be crevasses and rockfalls they can negotiate."

Niklaus nodded and placed the tip of his stick on the hills even farther east. "And they have to come from here. Or at least pass through, if their tribe is in the mountains."

"Why wait around here?" Bryn said. "We should hunt them down and kill them. Maybe we'll be lucky, and they'll be led by a wraithe."

Aldric suppressed a shiver. He had no desire to encounter another wraithe. It seemed Bryn had come along to test himself; he didn't care about the settlers.

"No," Aldric said firmly. "We can't risk it. Full-dark is soon, and if the Dead-eyes attack Cherish while we're out searching for them, it won't go well for the settlers."

Bryn chuckled. "That's understating it. They'll be slaughtered."

Aldric clamped down on an outburst. The swordsman would be worth a hundred untrained settlers when it came to fighting, so he didn't want to put him off side.

"We have practically no time," he said instead. "We have to train the settlers as best we can and organize some defenses before we do anything else. The Dead-eyes won't attack in numbers yet, but some could be out scavenging for food and might be tempted by the settlement. Or maybe they'll send a few scouts."

Bryn rolled his eyes. "Good luck getting these fools to wield a weapon properly. I still say we hunt the Dead-eyes. It's stupid to wait here. How about you, Niklaus? What do you say?"

Niklaus looked at Aldric. "The magister is right, I'm afraid."

Bryn groaned, and Stray Dog chuckled at the swordsman's irritated expression.

Out of the corner of his eye, Aldric saw Valeria approaching. The priestess stopped short of joining them, took Priska by the arm, and drew her a few steps away. She bent close to Priska and whispered. Priska laughed, then shook her head.

"We can't wander off," continued Niklaus, "until we're sure the settlement will be here when we get back. The Dead-eyes are unlikely to return until full-dark, but I've seen them attack in numbers at other times. When they were pushed."

Aldric stood, grateful for the mercenary's backing. "Defending the settlement is a priority," he said. "We need some barricades, and the settlers should set up a watch. If we find the trail the Dead-eyes are using to get down the cliffs, we can stop them in their tracks."

Stray Dog cleared his throat. "I don't think the settlers should hide in their houses. They're too spread out." He placed a large finger in the middle of the map. "We can build some barricades here, between the houses—create a defensible area big enough for all the settlers. That way, when the Dead-eyes come, they'll have a safe haven."

"If they huddle behind a barricade, it won't do them any good," Priska said from behind Aldric. "The settlers don't want to ward the Dead-eyes off. They want them killed or driven away, never to return."

"But it'll keep them safe while we fight," Aldric said. "It's a good idea."

"Perhaps we should go further," Niklaus said. "There won't be too many Dead-eyes, so we could use the barricades to funnel them into a killing space where we can outflank and slaughter them. The settlers can help by keeping the Dead-eyes penned with spears. If we don't have to worry about the settlers running around in a panic like last night, we'll be free to hunt the Dead-eyes that burst through or scale the barriers."

Bryn barked a laugh. "I like your thinking, Niklaus. Keep the sheep penned while the wolves roam free. There's one problem." He held out his hands, palms up. "These hands weren't made for manual labor. I'd rather let sharptooths in the sea strip the flesh from my bones than put down my sword to pick up an axe."

"Nothing wrong with axes," grumbled Stray Dog. "I've built a barricade or two in my time. I can organize the settlers and get the work started. It's mostly just cutting down trees and tying them together."

"The settlers will do the hard work," Niklaus said. "That's what they're used to."

Reluctantly, Aldric nodded. "Niklaus is right. It's their village, and I'm sure they want to save it. We're more valuable training them to fight. We can arrange shifts. A few of us will oversee the building of defenses, while the others can train the settlers with weapons."

Stray Dog scratched behind his ear, then examined his fingernail. "The settlers won't want to leave their fields and other work."

"Too bad," Aldric said. "It's only a few days, and better a slight delay than being dead."

"What about sorcery?" asked Priska. She'd come close to Aldric's back, and her words were pitched low, as if for him alone, but not soft enough the others hadn't heard.

"Yes," Niklaus said. "What about sorcery? Can't you find the Dead-eyes and destroy them from here?"

Aldric shot the mercenary a dark look. From the twinkle in Niklaus's eyes, he realized the mercenary knew exactly what sorcery was capable of and why what he'd suggested couldn't be done. He'd asked the question because it would be in the others' minds. But even Soki wouldn't be able to do what Niklaus had suggested, though there were legends of sorcerers who'd done much more. And in his relic dreams, Aldric had seen what the ancient sorcerers were capable of.

"That's something only the greatest sorcerers could do," he said. "And I'm far from an adept. We'll have to kill the Dead-eyes with cold steel. If there's anything more powerful directing them, we'll rely on Sokhelle. I'm sure she has a few tricks up her sleeve."

Bryn sniffed, and Stray Dog nodded thoughtfully. With any luck, the question of sorcery wouldn't come up again.

Menselas must have had a reason for gifting him with both the god's powers and the stain of sorcery. But his reticence to use the dusk-tide forces severely hamstrung his abilities. Perhaps this was why he was reconsidering after so many years of aversion?

Priska moved to Soki's side and looked at her with a pleading expression. "When will we train again?"

"Tonight. I promise."

"Why not now? I've learned so much already in such a short time."

"We're about to be attacked by goodness knows how many Dead-eyes," Soki said sharply. "We have to see to the settlers' safety first."

"If I know more sorcery, I'll be better able to help them."

"Enough!" Soki snapped. "If this is your attitude, maybe I should discontinue your training." She glared at Priska before her expression softened and she took a deep breath. "I don't want to control you. I'm not here to be a nursemaid. I'll teach you for a little longer, but then you're on your own. You'll either survive, or you'll succumb to your growing arrogance, and someone will take matters into their own hands."

Priska's mouth drew into a tight line, but she nodded to Soki.

Valeria laid a hand on Priska's shoulder. "Sokhelle is jealous of your talents," she said, loud enough for them all to hear. "When we get back to Caronath, come and see me. My Church could use someone of your abilities."

"Don't try to corrupt her," Soki said. "Once I'm done with her training, she'll be able to make her own decisions. But until then, she's mine."

"It was just a job offer," said Valeria. "Once you've discarded her."

"Enough," Aldric said. "You must put your differences aside while we're here."

Training another sorcerer, Soki could handle. At least until Priska unlearned enough to start down a more efficient path of logic and calculations. Then … well, Aldric would decide if that happened. If Valeria was trying to entice Priska to join her Church, then perhaps Aldric should intervene. No good would come from Valeria, of that he was certain. The Lady Sylva Kalisia was mysterious to him, an unknown, but having dominion over pain and suffering told a story all its own.

Niklaus chuckled. "I thought sorcerers were rare, but there's three of you here! We're truly blessed with an abundance of talent. And all for some Dead-eyes." He raised his eyebrows. "It makes you think, doesn't it?"

Soki gave Niklaus a sharp look, and Aldric had to concede he had a point. Three sorcerers, at least two people touched by their deity, and a few extremely skilled warriors, all in the one small group.

"Here's your friend," Niklaus said, looking over Aldric's shoulder.

Aldric turned to see Neb scurrying toward them, his battered hat on his head. Accompanying him were three children with bandaged arms or legs, and a young man with his arm in a sling. Trailing behind them came Shand, who wore a clean skirt today and looked like she'd washed her face.

"Magister Aldric," Neb said, "we need your help. These children cut themselves on sharp rocks when they decided to climb a cliff and a section gave way. And young Alvar here broke his arm chopping down trees the other day. He was careless, and one fell on him. I only just found out, and his mother is distraught. Can you heal them here, or do you need somewhere special? A holy place? There's a clearing just inside the forest where people go to pray, with idols for a few different gods. You could—"

Aldric held up a hand, and Neb's chatter stopped. "Inside your common hall is fine. It'll be comfortable there."

"Good news travels fast," Niklaus said with a mocking smile.

"You go look after the settlers, Aldric—heal their cuts and bruises, and kiss them goodnight. We'll work on some defenses and training. Hopefully three days' training will be enough so they don't skewer each other. Maybe they'll have a chance against the Dead-eyes."

~ ~ ~

Valeria refilled Hazel's cup with tea. The porcelain was glazed a light blue and was almost delicate. Probably one of the elderly matron's family heirlooms. Three young women sat around the table with them, all dressed in their best clothes, if she didn't miss her guess. The rest of the cottage matched the old woman's appearance: worn, haggard, faded.

The girls drank from cups or mugs they'd brought with them. Hazel's tiny house lacked basic comforts as well as space.

"I'm sorry about the quality of the tea," Valeria said. "Someone took a bag of my best leaf, and I've had to stretch what I have left. It's not too bad though, thanks to the tea you found in the back of your cupboard."

"I don't know how long it was there," said Hazel in a trembling voice. Her wrinkled hands rested in front of her on the thick table.

*Years, probably.* Valeria smiled and sipped from her cup, twin to Hazel's.

"Never mind," she said. "We'll make do. That's what the men expect, isn't it?" She chuckled self-deprecatingly, as if there was nothing they could do to change their situation. Hazel had been easy to influence and jumped at the opportunity to host a gathering.

*Small steps,* Valeria reminded herself. These women were like sparrows, come to peck at the seeds she had sprinkled. A sudden move would startle them into flight. But if she was lucky, there would be one among them who had enough backbone and fire to be useful to her goddess; and Valeria could test her for signs she'd been touched by Sylva Kalisia.

The goddess's power was bestowed in what at times seemed a haphazard manner. Valeria herself had been unaware of being chosen from so many other girls in her village, until one night, when she was outside taking in the beauty of the moons, a woman had approached her. A priestess of the goddess.

So far, in Cherish, Valeria hadn't seen any of the girls drawn to the moons, though she made a circuit of the tawdry settlement. Still, the moons were only slivers at the moment, with full-dark almost upon them. And she probably wouldn't be here when the moons were full, which was the best time to search for potential priestesses. She'd have to follow Niklaus wherever he went after they'd dealt with the Dead-eyes. For better or worse, she'd hitched her wagon to his.

"Priestess Valeria?"

"Oh, I'm sorry, what was that?"

"Tell us again about your goddess," the straw-haired woman gushed, "and what she does. Forgive me but ..." She glanced at the young women to either side of her. "We heard rumors she worships pain and suffering."

"The goddess worships nothing," said Valeria smoothly. "She is a goddess, after all."

The women chuckled.

"My guess is you've been told a version of the truth far removed from reality. Probably twisted by your menfolk."

Valeria didn't hate men herself; they were useful tools. But that was all they were. They thought with their members and their blades and couldn't be trusted with complex tasks. Which was one reason she was fascinated by Niklaus. Why would the goddess choose a man to be her Chosen Sword, rather than a woman?

"Life," Valeria continued, "is pain. Hazel will tell you this."

The old matron nodded her scraggly head. "It's true! From

birth to death, we experience pain."

"Exactly," said Valeria. "What people have warped in their desire to denigrate the goddess is merely a reflection of our lives. Pain grounds us, teaches us, and brings forth life."

One woman, the youngest, Shand, shifted in her seat and frowned into her mug of tea. Valeria noted that she hadn't drunk any yet.

Shand cleared her throat. "How do you become an acolyte of the goddess?"

*Ah*, thought Valeria. *Now we're getting somewhere …*

# Chapter Twenty-Five

# Sparks

IN SANSOR, THE MAIN city of what many ignorants termed the "heathen" realm of Kaile, settlers who braved the wilderness to carve out another slice of earth for humanity were revered for their courage and toughness. More warriors than farmers, these settlers lived in squalid conditions until they could be sure the area around the land they'd claimed was relatively safe, as there were many creatures out in the wilderness that didn't hesitate to dine on human flesh. Only then would they build more permanent structures and bring out livestock and their loved ones. To them, the settlers of Cherish would seem weak and stupid. But to Niklaus, there wasn't much between them. Neither knew the reality of what lurked in the remotest parts of the wilderness, nor the horrors the land they coveted had already witnessed. But Niklaus knew. Firsthand.

He checked on Stray Dog and Razmus, who had managed to erect a few barricades already. The walls, comprised of saplings no thicker than his forearm, were shoulder-high and so makeshift there were many gaps, some wide enough to stick his hand through. But the barricades didn't need to stop arrows, just Dead-eyes.

The Dead-eyes' spindly limbs and fingers enabled them to

scramble over anything, but the barricades would at least slow them down. And hopefully draw them into the funnel Stray Dog was creating, where, they all hoped, the settlers would be able to skewer or bludgeon the creatures to death.

"It's just digging holes and securing the logs," Stray Dog said in response to Niklaus's surprised look. "And the settlers have been working hard. It's amazing how motivating the fear of death can be."

As Niklaus watched, four settlers pulled on ropes to raise another barricade between two buildings. When it was upright, another three men shoveled dirt into the holes the main pillars rested in. After the dirt had been tamped down, two more men secured the barricade with wet rope to supporting timbers.

"More rope there, Alvar," Stray Dog called. "We don't want the Dead-eyes pulling it down, do we?"

"No, sir!" enthused Alvar, a young man wearing a woven straw hat. He wrapped more of the hemp rope around the support, showing no sign his arm had been broken recently.

"That'll do," Stray Dog said, and Alvar leaped down from the barricade and sauntered over. Niklaus could see his face and neck were sunburned, and he had the corded muscles of someone who spent a great deal of time doing manual labor.

"When do I get to use a sword?" he asked.

"Never," Stray Dog replied. "Tomorrow you'll drill with club and spear. That's all we have time for."

"Alvar!" yelled an older man who'd helped pull on the rope. "Come over here."

"My father, Tokash," said Alvar, and shrugged. "He doesn't want me talking to any of you. After we kill the Dead-eyes, will you teach me how to swing a sword?"

"How about axes?" said Stray Dog.

Alvar looked disappointed. "I already know how to swing an axe."

Niklaus laughed. "Not like Stray Dog you don't."

A shadow loomed between them, and Alvar twisted around as Tokash's hand grabbed his shoulder and jerked him backward. The man scowled at both Alvar and Stray Dog, then cuffed Alvar upside the head.

"You heard me! Get over here and keep working, or else the Dead-eyes will kill everyone because of you. Do you want that on your conscience?"

"No, Father, but I—"

"Enough! You're a disobedient boy." Tokash smacked Alvar in the head again.

Alvar cringed and stepped away, eyes tearing up, the side of his face a bright red from the smacks. The man raised his arm again, but Stray Dog clamped a massive hand around his forearm.

"I think he's learned his lesson," Stray Dog said, "don't you?"

"Keep out of this," Tokash snarled, "or I'll—argh!"

His face contorted in pain, and his knees bent as Stray Dog twisted his arm.

"You won't do anything," Stray Dog said. "And if I see, or hear, you've hit Alvar again, you'll answer to me."

He released his grip, and Tokash staggered away, one hand massaging his arm and elbow.

"Alvar, go with your father and help the others out," Stray Dog added. "We don't have a lot of time. Get back to work. I want to see another two barricades up before sunset."

Alvar gave Stray Dog a mock salute before scampering off in the direction of a heaped pile of saplings. Tokash glared at Stray Dog, then scurried back to the settlers, who'd stopped working to watch the exchange.

"You seem to have everything in hand," Niklaus said dryly.

How the settlers treated each other and this type of manual work didn't interest him. He'd seen enough battlefields to be intimately acquainted with defensive works and the carnage they could cause if planned well.

Stray Dog shrugged. "It's easy enough. Once we told them what we wanted, they got stuck into it without complaint. They're good people. Hardworking. Not afraid of sweat and a few blisters."

"Don't get too friendly. They might be dead soon."

Dog glanced in the direction Alvar had taken. "Not if I can avoid it. Don't you have somewhere to be?"

Niklaus glanced toward another group of settlers, who were being led through a series of drills by Razmus. They were using poles with sharpened points, not all of them straight, and stabbing what looked to be a scarecrow.

"Yes," Niklaus said. "Thank you for organizing the barricades. Sometimes I'm not good with people."

"That's because you're an asshole."

"You see what I've seen, and it leaves a mark." Deep in the wilderness, the Dead-eyes were the prey. And there were some areas the Dead-eyes feared more than any and refused to tread.

Niklaus left Stray Dog and Razmus to the settlers.

~ ~ ~

After an early dinner of bland, dried foodstuffs and watered-down beer, Niklaus got up to leave the meeting hall. By then the sun had gone down, and he avoided talking to the others as they came in to eat. He tried not to catch the eye of the settlers he passed—an old woman carrying firewood, and a young boy with a chicken dangling from one hand.

Crickets chirped in the long grasses by the river, seeking mates. In the mud and reeds, frogs croaked, doing the same. Niklaus sat atop a boulder close to a rickety bridge crossing the river. The ground underneath his boots was sandy and covered with patchy thin grass. Willows grew around him, tall and black in the night, leaves rustling in the wind. Far above, stars twinkled, and the occasional bat flew past. Both moons were low tonight and mostly obscured by the walls of the valley, leaving Cherish in darkness.

*Almost full-dark,* Niklaus thought. *Soon the Dead-eyes will come. I wonder who will survive the onslaught.* If some of their party or the settlers met a gruesome end, it wouldn't bother him any. Their self-righteous chatter and good intentions wore thin after a while.

Spotting a millipede hunting for food, he dragged the tip of his cane along the sandy soil, creating a thin, shallow trench. The millipede crossed the line and immediately began convulsing. Niklaus watched it writhe until it died. The worm of Ak-Settur's venom was potent, and even just a trace was deadly.

Niklaus looked back at the settlement. Smoke poured from chimneys, and light from windows. He caught the sound of laughter on the wind, a voice raised in anger, and, faintly, a gentle song. He was finally alone, away from the forced intimacy of strangers. He breathed deeply, savoring the chill air sweeping down from the frozen north.

He should visit Margebian, the Witch of Winter, again, up in those frigid mountains. It had been some time since he'd seen her, and he knew she got lonely. When had he visited her last? He couldn't recall, but remembered her delight when he'd brought her some tea, though even that memory was hazy. She'd probably finished it by now. Sometimes he wondered why she hid herself away from the world, and other times he knew all too well why.

Leaning his head back, he rested it on the cold, hard pommel of the goddess's sword. Sometimes, if he closed his eyes, he could feel her presence in the steel. He turned his head from side to side slowly, rubbing his scalp on the pommel. His thoughts turned to the mask hidden with his gear: one piece of the Armor of Divinity. Along with his journals it was too valuable to leave behind in Caronath. If he could unearth more pieces and Eckart's research bore fruit, then he could be with Sylva.

To his right, footsteps approached along the beaten path. He sighed. Sometimes he almost envied Margebian her solitude.

Priska, he decided, from the cadence of the steps and the stumbling hesitation when she was close enough to see his outline.

"Ah ... Niklaus?" she called tentatively.

*As if she didn't know.*

"Yes, my dear. You shouldn't be wandering in the dark on your own. Aren't you worried there might be Dead-eyes about?"

"I'm with you now. Besides, Sokhelle has taught me a few things. She's extremely accomplished. My other teachers were ... not like her."

Priska came closer, and Niklaus saw she'd brushed her hair so it hung artfully, framing her striking face. Her shirt was unbuttoned so low it would be unseemly in polite company. *So that's how it is.* Overconfidence in her newfound sorcerous abilities had the young woman reveling in her power and eager to take risks.

Though the girl's skin was pale instead of dusky, the rest of her appearance was so close to his goddess's, it was uncanny. Surely it was a coincidence? Or was he losing his mind, finally, after all these centuries? The holes of accumulated memory loss had reached a tipping point, and soon he'd be nothing more than a puppet of the goddess, a shell devoid of meaningful memories.

The thought of being alone with Priska filled him with both dread and anticipation. His hands trembled. Suppressing a curse, he cast her from his mind. Whatever she was, she was no goddess. No one could match the perfection of the Lady.

"Does your father know you're out here?" he said roughly.

Priska shook her head, then brushed hair from her eyes. "He's busy talking with Stray Dog. That man scares me. Aldric is boring, Bryn just wants to bed me, and Valeria is so nice to me I think she is either hiding or wants something. Sokhelle suggested I go over what I've learned, so I snuck outside." She shivered melodramatically and wrapped her arms around herself. "Is there room on that rock for me? It's cold tonight."

Despite his reservations, Niklaus couldn't deny he was drawn to Priska. He shifted to his left. "There is indeed. The wind is from the north, and it's brought the ice of the glaciers with it. It's as cold as Margebian's heart."

When Priska sat next to him, her hips and arm brushed against his, and he felt her warmth through their clothes. His pulse quickened, but his reluctance remained. He had patchy memories of real relationships he'd had; all of them ended badly when his lover grew old and he remained the same. Only the goddess was unchanging.

"Do you think she's real?" asked Priska.

For a moment he thought she meant the Lady, but she couldn't read his mind.

"The Witch of Winter?" he said.

She nodded. "I think she's a myth. Made up to frighten children into obedience."

Niklaus shrugged, making sure to brush his shoulder against hers. "Perhaps. There are many wonders in this world. And horrors too. Only last year, a band of adventurers set out from Caronath to confirm Margebian's presence among the glaciers. A month later a few survivors straggled back, frostbitten and haggard, wasted from starvation. They said they'd seen her, Margebian—a hoary woman with sky-blue eyes and wings of silvered snow."

Niklaus suppressed a laugh. *Hoary.* Margebian wouldn't like to hear herself described so.

Priska snorted. "Fools. They should have taken a sorcerer with them."

"They did. He was the first to be slaughtered. You see, she's part demon, or so they say, and employs their peculiar brand of sorcery. She knows the secrets of both dawn-tide and dusk-tide sorcery too, after centuries of research and experimentation."

"With all that power, why does she hide away?"

"Perhaps she's sick of people. It happens."

Priska tilted her head and gave Niklaus a saucy smirk. "I think you're teasing me. Trying to scare me like a child. But I'm not a child, and I don't scare easily. The Gray Hand Covenant taught me things. Terrible secrets. I know sorcery Sokhelle doesn't. If she did know ..."

Niklaus fixed Priska with a penetrating stare, but she was looking away, pretending to be interested in the running water. He knew she was alluding to summoning creatures from the abyss. Priska would be greatly surprised by his knowledge of such things—but nothing cemented a bond like a secret shared.

"Tell me more," he said. "I'd like to get to know you better."

Uttering a gentle laugh, Priska leaned forward, her long raven hair swaying. The movement caused her shirt to open slightly, revealing more skin and the curve of a breast.

"Well, not all knowledge has been lost," she began.

"Priska!" yelled Razmus. "What are you doing out here? And with him!"

She leaped to her feet and looked around guiltily.

Niklaus watched as her father strode angrily toward them. *I could do without this tonight,* he thought. *But these two have been on the precipice of an argument for days. Best they get it over with.*

"She's her own woman," he told Razmus. "She's not your little girl any more."

Even in the darkness, Niklaus fancied he saw Razmus's face go red. The man spluttered and stood there trembling, hands clenched into fists.

"I don't need your protection," Priska said. "Father, please, just go back inside."

Her eyes flicked to Niklaus in embarrassment, then away again. He saw how her chest rose and fell as she drew deep breaths.

"Priska, heed my counsel," Razmus said. "Come back with me. It's cold out here. You can work on your sorcery inside, where it's warm."

Priska's eyes flashed with anger. "I won't hide any longer! Finally, after all these years, I don't have to. Sokhelle will teach me, and I'll leave my broken, stunted past behind."

Razmus cursed. "You're still young, still learning. I understand you feel you've been cooped up for too long. But you need to be cautious. And this man—he isn't right for you."

"I'll decide who's right for me!" shouted Priska. "I've spent years trailing after you. A burden. Agreeing with everything you say. Ashamed of what I'd become. Of my failures."

"We were together," Razmus said. "Side by side." His expression was poised between fury and sadness. "I want the best for you."

"And now I have it. You don't need to look after me any more. You can live your own life."

"You are my life."

That seemed to give Priska pause. "No," she said eventually. "You're *weak*. And you needn't be. I realize it now: I've held you back. Well, you can stop worrying."

Niklaus cleared his throat and stood. "Perhaps I should leave. This is a family matter."

"Yes, it is," snarled Razmus.

"No," said Priska. She grabbed Niklaus's hand. "We were just talking. Is there something wrong with that, Father?"

*Bloody hells.* Niklaus racked his brain for a way to escape the drama. As he did, he noticed movement in the long grass. An animal? And something else … no, someone else, hiding …

Razmus stamped closer, face and mouth twisted with anger. He pointed a trembling finger at Niklaus. "Keep your hands off her. She's too good for the likes of you."

*Too ordinary and predictable actually. But a pleasurable substitute for a short time.*

Niklaus disengaged himself from Priska's grip and spread his hands. "I was out here alone. I didn't seek her out."

"You're tempting her, you whoreson! If I find out you've touched her, I'll—"

"What?" Niklaus said, a coldness to his words. "You'll what?"

Razmus kept silent, glaring.

"Pants-pisser," Niklaus said.

"Father! You have to stop!"

The shadow in the grass surged toward them, followed by two more. They resolved into thin, pale shapes. Priska screamed, stumbling as Niklaus shoved her aside. A blur of white flashed through the space she'd recently occupied.

Niklaus drew his short sword and slashed at the creature's torso. An inhuman wail sounded as his blade bit into flesh. He left it to die, then leaped at the oncoming Dead-eyes, considered using his cane on them for fun, then discarded the idea—the others would know they'd been poisoned, and the card up his sleeve would be revealed.

Slavering, fanged mouths came for him, and his steel moved in glittering arcs. He slashed down through the collarbone of one, pivoted, then cleaved the third through its neck. To make sure they were dead, he speared their scrawny bodies, blade piercing their hearts. One mewled and attempted to drag itself away. Niklaus stabbed it through the back.

He looked around, searching for signs of more Dead-eyes. There were none. Only three of them, then—a scouting party. Probably saw them sitting by the bridge and thought they were easy pickings. The Dead-eyes were always overruled by their brutal appetites.

He glanced at Razmus, who had managed to fumble his dagger from its sheath only after Niklaus had dispatched the creatures.

Priska lay on the ground, staring in horror at the stick-limbed

Dead-eyes like she'd never seen one before. Their pale skin shone, even in the darkness of the night.

"Keep your eyes open!" he told Razmus.

The ex-soldier nodded and scanned the night.

Niklaus wiped his blade with grass, then sheathed it. He offered a hand to Priska, who took it gratefully. She rose to her feet and brushed dirt from her clothes.

"What happened to your sorcery?" he said mockingly. "I thought Sokhelle had taught you things."

"I ..." she stammered. "They surprised me."

"Foolish girl," snapped Razmus. "You're trying to run before you can walk."

Niklaus had to agree. If she was halfway competent, she would have known the Dead-eyes were out there and blasted them to ashes. Well, maybe not blasted them. Only a very few sorcerers were that accomplished.

"Never mind," he said, flashing Priska a reassuring smile. "I'm sure you'll do better next time. There'll be plenty of Dead-eyes for everyone soon." He released her hand. "Excitement's over. You two go back to the settlement. Boring Aldric will want to know what's happened. I'll stay here and scout around."

Looking aggrieved and casting wary glances at Niklaus, Razmus complied, beckoning to his daughter. Priska seemed so shocked by the attack, she submitted to her father's request to go with him to warn the settlers and their group.

Niklaus watched them go until their backs were swallowed by the darkness. "You can come out now," he said.

A cracked laugh issued from behind a tree twenty yards away. Valeria appeared and walked slowly through the patchy grass, seeming almost to glide. Though her expression was calm and unconcerned, her eyes flashed daggers at Niklaus.

"That slit isn't worth your time," she said.

"Jealous?" Niklaus replied, hoping to rile her. He'd initially marked her as Matriarch Adeline's, sent to keep an eye on him, but she seemed to have her own agenda. As long as it didn't interfere with his, she could do what she wanted.

"Hardly. I can offer so much more. But I'm worried she and her father will be a problem. They're so … provincial. She has some talent for sorcery, but she'll need a lot of discipline if she's to serve the goddess."

Valeria lifted both hands and pulled back the hood of her cloak. The silver chains securing her braids glinted, and her dark painted nails looked like claws.

"I can handle them," Niklaus said.

"You'd better," Valeria said flatly.

"Priska is exploring her newfound power and the freedom it provides from the shackles her father has placed on her. She's nothing to me. As for Razmus … he'll regret insulting and opposing me."

"We can't have any dissent in our little group, can we?"

"Precisely. We should have left them both in Caronath, but these idiots were forced upon me." Valeria probably didn't realize he included her in that comment.

She chuckled throatily, as if she knew something he didn't. "She does look a little like the Lady, does she not?"

Niklaus stiffened before he could stop himself. "No one looks like the goddess."

"I see your desires, Niklaus, as if they were written on a page in front of me. You might as well reach for the moons."

"You know nothing of my desires. Best you remember that, if you want to stay alive."

"We both know you won't kill me. You *can't* kill me. I'm one of her high priestesses, and you're her Chosen Sword. We both serve her. And if Sokhelle tries to stop me fulfilling the goddess's wishes, she'll find out how weak she is compared to divine power. Sorcerers! Always convinced they have the upper hand. Light counters light. Dark counters dark. They don't like to remember they are feeble. Sokhelle's pitiful wards will crack and crumble against the power the goddess has bequeathed me."

"How melodramatic. I'm sure Sokhelle will be mortified to find her talent and hard work count for nothing when fighting someone with no talent who's been handed her power on a plate."

Valeria hissed. "You mock me. Just as well you're Sylva Kalisia's chosen, or you'd feel my wrath."

"I don't desire to feel anything of yours."

That was Valeria's problem, Niklaus decided: she lusted after things. Power. People. And if she couldn't obtain what she wanted by guile or force, she destroyed it.

The priestess visibly hardened, then she laughed softly. "You will. The goddess ... it may be her plan. What I do know is that whatever Aldric's Church is after, we must take it for ourselves. Together we will forge the goddess's Church anew! You, the anvil, and I, the hammer."

*Interesting.* If the goddess wanted more, she would have it. However, who was he to assume *her* will? Was he here to help Valeria or to stop her? He wasn't sure that Valeria didn't serve herself first and the goddess second. And she was in for a shock if she thought she could get away with her plan of raising the goddess's Church from its current position.

Niklaus shivered in a particularly icy blast of wind. He hunched his shoulders and indicated they should head back to the settlement. "Come, it's full-dark in two nights, and the Dead-eyes were scouting the village. It looks like the Lady wants us to earn the gratitude of these defenseless settlers."

The inky sky towered above them, and the pitch-black cliffs surrounding the valley seemed to brood, dark and hollow.

~ ~ ~

Razmus rubbed his aching eyes and yawned. He hadn't managed much sleep after his fight with Priska. She was too headstrong! Why wouldn't she just listen to what he had to say and heed his advice?

He looked around in the gray predawn light. No one else had risen yet, and he'd decided to slip outside before he had to make small talk with anyone and head off to begin the early morning training. It was refreshing the settlers didn't grumble about such an early start, like his soldier colleagues used to: as farmers they were accustomed to getting up at the crack of dawn.

Smoke poured from the chimneys atop the nearby houses, though only a few had lights on inside. But right now, he found it hard to care about the settlement. Priska's rejection had left him empty inside. After all their time together, he couldn't comprehend why she was acting this way.

He made his way to the cleared space where he'd been drilling the settlers with sharpened sticks and whatever other weapons they could lay their hands on. The straw-stuffed dummy had been ripped to shreds and lay on the ground at the base of its pole. A raven was hopping around it, a few stalks of straw in its beak. When Razmus approached, it flew off into the closest tree. As he watched it go, Razmus was surprised to see one of the settlers— the heavyset miller named Drusst—perched on a log. He was eating a sweet roll, both cheeks bulging like a bullfrog's.

Drusst nodded and shoved the remaining half of his roll into his mouth.

Razmus nodded back, but decided not to go over. He wasn't in the mood for conversation. Besides, the settlers had left their sharpened poles lying all around the place. He began to pick them up and stack them to one side, thoughts wandering back to Priska.

*It's not like she's never rebelled before. Gods knows she's had a hard life, and sometimes she needs to let off steam. But now isn't the time.*

It was all Niklaus's fault for trying to bed her with no thought other than getting his wick wet. And Valeria's too, for filling Priska's head with tales of a woman's rightful place in society and how her goddess valued women over men.

He saw Valeria going with three young women and an older one into a house. No doubt getting her claws into them. Maybe she'd leave Priska alone now …

And that sorcerer too, Sokhelle. Razmus paused. Maybe he was being too harsh. Sokhelle was teaching Priska to better control her powers. A dream of his daughter's, he knew, and one they'd thought would never come true. Damaged as she was, and without a Covenant willing to take her in, Priska had resigned herself, however bitterly, to never reaching her full potential. Now that had changed.

Behind Razmus, Drusst cleared his throat. "Want me to help? Or should I start on the drills we went over yesterday? The others will be here soon. I brought some fresh bread." He gestured to a lumpy sack a few yards away.

"You're not milling today?" asked Razmus, throwing more poles onto the steadily growing pile. Drusst had shown more promise than the other settlers. If he wasn't so fat, he'd have had potential as a soldier. Not that he'd shown any interest … Razmus paused. For settlers to get so fat, they must have more food and beer than they'd been willing to share.

"Only the bare minimum of other work until we see off the Dead-eyes," said Drusst. "Mayor's orders."

"Fair enough."

Where was Neb, Razmus wondered. The old man had left in the middle of drills yesterday and never returned.

Drusst's toe nudged the dismembered scarecrow. "Should I put this back together? We'll need something to practice on."

"No need. Today we're sparring with each other."

The miller's eyes brightened and he licked his lips. "Really? At last." He picked up a pole and leaned on it.

Two more settlers joined them: Lavst, a thin boy who Razmus thought probably wasn't shaving yet, and Uvagen, a burly man with a bushy beard and short hair who looked like a blacksmith or lumberjack.

"Get a pole, lads," Drusst said loudly. "We're fighting each other today."

"I'm no lad," said Shand as she strode up to the training area. She'd joined them for a short time yesterday and hadn't done too badly considering her lack of height and slight build.

Nervous laughs eased the tension slightly. They knew what they learnt here would be used very soon, and the specter of the next Dead-eye attack hung over them.

"Aldric can heal anyone who gets injured," Razmus said. "You did well yesterday. I'm proud of you all." Razmus thought that in another life Drusst might have made a good warrior.

He realized he was. The settlers were all working hard, learning skills they might only use over the next day or so, and never again. But if your life was on the line, it gave you an incentive to focus. "But I've noted a few problems and today we'll work on everyone's weaknesses."

Lavst and Uvagen grabbed poles and squared off. Shand sat in the dirt to the side and pulled a dried apple out of her shirt. She bit into it with relish, as if expecting a fine show from Lavst and Uvagen.

"Go through the attacking and defensive forms first to warm up," said Razmus. "Then we'll spar until the others arrive."

"Why not longer?" asked Lavst. "I'm sure the others'll want to have a go—"

"Because you won't be taking on the Dead-eyes one-on-one," snapped Razmus. "That'll just get you killed. You stay together, shoulder to shoulder, and you fight as a unit. If you don't, you'll die. Understand?"

Uvagen nodded, a grim smile on his face.

Lavst swallowed. "I do," he said. "I'm sorry."

Razmus ran a hand over his tired eyes. "No, don't apologize. I shouldn't have been so harsh, but this is serious. You're all doing your best, and that's all I can ask for."

A slow smile crept across Lavst's face, and he motioned for Uvagen to join him in sparring.

Razmus turned to pick up a pole of his own and found Drusst hovering closer than was comfortable. He took a step back, noting that Drusst had a fake smile plastered across his face and was shifting his weight from foot to foot. *What now?*

"Something you want to say, Drusst?"

"Er ... the high priestess that came with you?" He'd pitched his voice low so the others couldn't hear.

Razmus nodded, frowning. He hoped this wasn't trouble. "What of her?"

"A few of the men are upset. Yesterday she was preaching to the young women, telling them all sorts of nonsense. Some of the girls are enamored of her and her high-class ways, and they're talking of traveling to Caronath to join her Church. She's stirring up trouble, and we want her to stop. Things are hard enough here without filling the young folks' heads with ideas."

Suppressing a sigh, Razmus gave Drusst a curt nod. "I'll talk to Aldric, see if he can rein her in. After all, we're here to help, not create discord. But if she's only preaching, there probably isn't much he can do. People are free to choose for themselves."

*One rule for the settlers and another for Priska,* thought Razmus. But Priska was his daughter, and he only wanted what was best for her.

*As the settlers want for their daughters.*

CHAPTER TWENTY-SIX

# OLD TALES AND NIGHTMARES

KURIO HEARD THE SCRAPE of a boot on earth. Leaves rustled. Something hovered over her. She turned onto her back in a panic, flinging the blanket aside.

Mellish stepped back from her, one hand on the hated turtle. His gray eyes were the same as always—hard and mocking, tinged with disgust.

A pale light shone faintly to the east. The campfire had died and was nothing but ash. A cold wind blew, cutting through her shirt. Kurio lurched to her feet, seeing that Mellish had already packed their—his—gear, and the horses were saddled. She must have slept through his preparations. And no wonder: her joints still ached from the agony he had sent coursing through her again last night.

He made a game of it. At night he tortured her; and during the day, trepidation haunted her, even though it could have been pleasant riding through the forest. She knew what was coming when they stopped. And Mellish enjoyed her dread. Reveled in it.

*Demon*, he'd whisper to her as she writhed.

*Cursed.*

*Abomination.*

Kurio put on a brave face and went about the business of

tugging her boots on, then walked over to the fire and picked up the scrap of bread her captor had left for her. She squatted by the ashes, pretending they were still warm, and gnawed on the dry, coarse breakfast. It was all she'd get until midday. At least he left her to eat without troubling her.

The farther away from Caronath they rode, the meaner Mellish became. As if whatever chains that bound him to Zarina and their cause loosened, and he revealed his true self. Her wrists crusted with dried blood, the accursed sorcerous collar around her neck, Kurio silently cursed all the gods and goddesses she could remember.

"Hurry up, demon," Mellish said.

Kurio rose without speaking and hastened to her horse. It huffed and nuzzled her arms as she patted its neck.

As she was about to mount, she heard Mellish's tread behind her and felt his fingers entwine into her hair. He gripped it hard until it pulled at her scalp. "We're almost at the settlement," he whispered into her ear, so close she felt his breath on her skin. "Remember to behave yourself when we're there. And don't speak. You're my mute assistant and bedfellow."

Kurio remained silent, bracing herself for the cruel wrench she was sure would come. But his grip loosened, and the tug did not eventuate. She seized the chance to mount her horse, which moved her out of his reach. Looking down into his cruel, piglike eyes, Kurio almost spat in his face. He looked smaller from up here. Diminished.

*I must kill him*, she thought. *But how?*

He had too much power over her. If she took the smallest step toward him, made the least threatening gesture, a fire of agony and screams was sure to follow.

*The pain goes, doesn't it?*

*Or does it become a part of me, stain my soul?*

*If I'm a demon, do I have a soul to be stained? Or am I already damned?*

Kurio rubbed her arms to warm them in the biting dawn air, but nothing would lessen the chill inside her heart.

~ ~ ~

The sun had passed its zenith and was descending. They hadn't stopped to eat the entire day, though Kurio had seen Mellish reach often into a saddlebag for something to chew on, probably dried meat. He didn't offer her any. It didn't matter. She'd passed from hunger to a point where she couldn't care less if she ate or not.

This far into the wilderness, the air was even thinner, and Kurio's nose itched. She had to sniff to stop it running. She studied her captor. Short brown stubble covered his face now, and the expensive shirt he'd worn in Caronath had been replaced by one of a tougher, more serviceable weave.

His hand moved to touch the turtle at his waist, and Kurio flinched and almost cried out before she could stop herself. Mellish laughed, obviously having heard her gasp of fear. It wasn't the first time he'd made such a feint, and his cruelty made her cringe.

She turned her gaze to the forest around them. Monotonous trees and drab bushes and hardly any wildlife, except for a few lizards basking in the remaining sunlight.

*I wonder what the range is on his little turtle?*

She slowed her horse a touch, letting the distance between her and Mellish grow imperceptibly. She hung her head to seem as if she was dozing in case he turned to look at her. Occasionally she opened her eyes a slit to see how far she'd fallen behind and if Mellish suspected anything. All she had to do was get far enough away and keep running. Right now Kurio couldn't see any other way.

Mellish rounded a bend in the trail. Kurio's breath caught in her throat as he and his horse disappeared behind the thick trunk of an ancient tree. She hauled on her reins to turn her mount and urged it in the opposite direction as quietly as she could.

*Bloody hells. There's no point doing this half-heartedly.*

She dug her heels into her horse's flanks. "Go, go go!" she whispered urgently.

Her mount's pace increased to a trot. A shout came from behind them, but no pain.

"I'm free!" she said, laughing, relief flooding through her.

Agonizing fire lashed her nerves. She doubled over, retching as her stomach twisted into knots. But in the blaze of agony, she imagined a presence there with her. Strangely, it offered comfort, understanding.

The pain redoubled, and Kurio fell sideways, off her mount, and slammed into the earth.

The next thing she knew, Mellish stood over her.

Kurio groaned. Her head ached, and her shoulder throbbed from her fall.

He stared at her, expressionless. "For your kind, there is no escape."

~ ~ ~

The day sank toward dark, reddening the trees of the forest, and Mellish led them slowly, searching for a suitable place to camp. Kurio caught the occasional glimpse of the turtle when his horse turned to follow a bend in the trail.

Night was coming. Pain was coming.

She shivered, and a whimper escaped her lips before she clenched them tight against her weakness. She thought back to the times she'd felt a comforting presence in the midst of her suffering. Maybe she was going mad.

Mellish halted his horse, and Kurio looked up into her

tormentor's eyes. Mellish smiled a dishonest smile at her. "Are you well, demon?" His tone was that of inquiring after an old friend.

He was too far away to spit on. And though she knew she would have paid for it in full, and then some, she would have done it. Despair tugged at her. Hate sank its poisoned fangs into her heart. "Piss on you," she snarled. It wasn't much of a curse, but she was frightened. She could scarcely control her trembling.

Mellish only laughed, a sound without mirth.

They kept moving and came upon a rocky area where the trees and undergrowth thinned out. Only then did Kurio realize they'd been riding up a slight incline for some time. Many of the trees amid the granite outcroppings were stunted and twisted. Pines held a smattering of needles, their bare trunks diminutive.

The light faded, and they rode a path among warped trees in the twilight. Mellish went carefully, keeping his eyes on the surrounding forest. The trees thinned to nothing, giving way to a clearing of flat rocks surrounded by tufted grass. Aged bones poked from the grass on one side of the space. At the far side, blackness. A cliff edge.

"We'll camp here," he said. "Must have taken a wrong turn. We'll have to go back to find a way around."

A vision came to Kurio of Mellish tumbling over the cliff to be dashed on sharp rocks below.

She gathered her courage against the coming night and dismounted, stumbling on loose gravel. When she looked up, a dark figure stood at the edge of the clearing opposite the cliff. It had appeared as if from nowhere, without a sound or betraying movement.

A curse from Mellish; a frantic scrabbling as he drew his steel.

The figure—a man, it had to be, he was so tall—remained motionless.

"Who goes there?" Mellish shouted. "Reveal yourself. Stop skulking in the shadows."

His right hand brandished his sword while his left shook his alchemical globe. Holding it high, he waited until its glow brightened to cast a thin radiance across the clearing. His mount stamped skittishly, and he struggled to control it with his knees.

Kurio edged nearer to her horse and gripped the saddle. The stranger was cloaked, a hood obscuring his face. Beneath the fabric, she caught the telltale glint of mail.

The sound of Mellish's harsh breathing was broken by a deep, resonant voice speaking a fluid language Kurio didn't recognize.

But evidently Mellish did. He answered tentatively, as a toddler would, as if searching for each word before speaking.

When he'd finished, the stranger remained silent. His hood moved as he shook his head. Eventually he spoke again, this time in Nan-Rhouric, the old but common tongue of the north. "What do you do here?"

"Begone, wraithe!" shouted Mellish. "Your kind isn't welcome here."

Kurio swallowed and clutched her horse's reins. A wraithe? Mellish seemed sure it was one of the old race. According to the old folktales, the remnants of their civilization were supposed to be in hiding. Kurio swallowed a mouthful of spit and clutched her horse's reins.

"Be careful who you command, mortal. Cause offense and you will be slapped down." The words were spoken casually, as if the wraithe were bored, but with a certainty born of strength.

Mellish licked his lips. "We only seek to camp for the night. We didn't know this area was yours."

"Mine? This barren place? Only mankind claims ownership. You cling like babes because your lives are so short."

"We …" began Mellish, a tremble in his voice, "we'll go, then. Demon, mount your horse."

Kurio scrambled to obey, though she wasn't sure staying would be any worse. Perhaps she should let the wraithe take her. How dreadful would it be? Would it enslave her? Or kill her? Would that be so bad?

"We'll leave now. If you attack or follow us, I'll destroy you," Mellish said.

At that, the wraithe's head jerked as if stung. Sneering laughter came from it. "You, destroy me? You bear no mark, no catalyst, nor are you a manipulator. You cannot even illuminate your way without a toy."

It barked a harsh word, and a globe as bright as the sun formed in the air, hovering far above them. It gave off a dazzling radiance, banishing darkness and stretching shadows around them in a circle. *Sorcery,* realized Kurio.

"You bear relics of old," said the wraithe, "which give you false confidence. But you merely found them. Like the scavengers you are."

Mellish glanced around as if looking for reinforcements, eyes wide, fear written large on his face.

*So this is the end,* Kurio thought and closed her eyes. *It's a relief, really.*

"I'm warning you," Mellish said unconvincingly.

"Go," the wraithe said. "Mankind will be annihilated soon, and the world will forget you."

Kurio's eyes snapped open. "No," she whispered. "You're supposed to kill us."

The wraithe tilted its head toward her. It had heard her plea. But it did nothing.

"No," she repeated. "No!" She realized she was crying, hot tears trailing down her cheeks.

"Move, demon!" Mellish snapped, sheathing his sword. "Do you want to die? Move!"

He tried to turn his horse around, but it fought him, unnerved by the stranger and the incandescent light. He twisted in the saddle to keep one eye on the wraithe.

"He-yah!" yelled Kurio at the top of her lungs. She urged her horse forward, jamming her heels into its sides, aiming straight for Mellish. *He thinks I'm a demon. I'll show him one.*

"What the—"

Her horse shied away, too late. It crashed into Mellish's, and there was a snap like a breaking branch as his leg jammed between the horses. Mellish cried out, and his globe tumbled from his grasp. Kurio turned her mount, thinking to run. But she still wore the collar, and Mellish held the hated turtle. There was no escape. Only death would free her. His, or hers.

Yanking at the reins, she yelled again and rode at Mellish. He was bent over the neck of his horse, clutching its mane. Shattered bone poked from his pants leg, and he wheezed raspingly.

On the other side of the clearing, the wraithe hadn't moved a muscle.

Kurio rammed Mellish again, aiming for his broken leg. They collided with crushing force. Mellish cried out as his mount was thrown sideways. The horse scrabbled for purchase on the stone, but its hooves slipped, and it tumbled over the cliff.

Mellish screamed all the way down. There was a massive thud, then silence.

Kurio's breath came in harsh gasps, clouding the air in front of her. Her limbs trembled, and her stomach churned. Bile rose, and she swallowed it.

She glanced at the wraithe. It remained silent and ominous.

*I have to see. I have to confirm he's dead. If he survived ... I'll finish him off.*

Blood pounding in her ears, Kurio dismounted. Her knees buckled, and she clung to her saddle to stop herself falling. A moment passed. Two. Forcing herself to move, she staggered to the cliff. She stood on the edge, dizzy with relief, fearing she might lose her footing and plummet to her death as well—but she had to know if Mellish was dead.

All she could see was blackness. There was no sound save the moaning of the wind, her heavy breathing, and the occasional flap of the wraithe's cloak.

Ignoring the creature, Kurio cast around for Mellish's alchemical globe. She tossed it over the edge and heard its glass shatter on the rocks below. Light spilled across granite, throwing shadows and illuminating Mellish's twisted corpse. He'd been thrown clear of his horse. Both were unmoving.

She staggered with relief. More tears flowed, hot and salty. She wiped her eyes, hating herself for her weakness.

With an effort of will, Kurio pulled her eyes from Mellish's broken form and examined the wraithe. It still hadn't moved, hadn't spoken.

She took a tentative step toward it, holding out her manacled hands. "What do you want with me?"

It moved slightly, mail clinking. "With you? Nothing."

Kurio sobbed with relief. "Then why are you here? There's no one for miles around. This wasn't a coincidence."

"I was … drawn here. Pulled from my task."

"And what task would that be?"

"I am to prevent. Failing that, to witness."

That didn't make any sense. "Witness what?"

"The coming of the Seventh Cataclysm. Another downfall of mankind. Perhaps their end." It shrugged. "Perhaps."

Kurio felt cold fingers of dread clutch at her. "You hate us. You hate humankind."

There was a long silence. "Hate is … insufficient."

"Am I … Can I live? Am I free to go?"

A nod of its hood. "You are free, demon. The Dead-eyes will eat your companion after they have defiled his corpse."

Kurio fancied she heard satisfaction, or pleasure, in the wraithe's words. She drew herself up, feeling her strength returning. She was free. All she had to do was climb down the cliff and retrieve the turtle from Mellish and whatever else she could salvage.

But ...

"Am I?" she asked the wraithe. "A demon? Do you know?"

Though she could only see darkness inside the hood, Kurio felt the wraithe's eyes upon her. "Yes," it said. "I see their blood in you. In your face, in your essence."

The clearing spun. Kurio fell to her knees in despair. Biting her lip, she stopped herself from sobbing, from showing weakness. She tasted copper: her own blood.

"You do not fear me?" the wraithe said.

Kurio managed to shake her head. "No. I've ... had enough of fear, of pain."

The wraithe circled her kneeling form. "Do you wish me to decide for you?"

It was offering to kill her. A release. An end.

"No," she whispered.

"Good. Some demons—a rare few—are able to make their own decisions; they are not driven by their base desires, their demon instincts. You demonstrate that your blood does not master you; you will not exult in degradation. You will make a name for yourself."

Kurio shifted her weight. A sharp rock pressed into her shin, and she decided to stand. "I just ... I just want to return to Caronath. I want my life back."

As she said it, she knew her world would never be the same.

She raised her still-manacled hands and rubbed her burning, tired eyes. When she looked up, the wraithe was nowhere to be seen. The incandescent ball hanging above her winked out, and darkness flooded in.

Kurio drew a deep breath, then approached the cliff edge. The climb down in the dark was terrifying and gritty, but also glorious. Mellish was dead.

She moved as quickly as she dared, her hands scraped and bloodied by the granite, remembering the wraithe's promise that the Dead-eyes would come to defile and then eat Mellish's corpse. Finally free from the collar's torment, she had no desire to die out here in the wilderness.

At the cliff bottom, the illumination from the globe's alchemical fluid was fading. She spat on Mellish's face, then rifled through his clothes. The turtle first. This close, she could see the gems were embedded into each segment of its shell, and it clasped a ring of curled wire in one of its feet. Carefully avoiding touching the gems, she clipped the turtle to her belt with the ring. Then she rummaged through Mellish's pockets until she found the key to her manacles. She unlocked them and threw them as far as she could into the darkness.

He had a pouch filled with royals, which she pocketed, though she decided not to bother taking his sword or other gear. She still had to climb back up the cliff face with aching and stinging palms. Luckily, her crossbow and her own gear were in her horse's saddlebags, or they might have been damaged in the fall.

Kurio almost thanked the gods, then spat again. None of them had helped her when she needed them. She was done with them.

She stuffed a tinderbox with alchemical matches and some of the dried meat and cheese into her shirt, then fingered the orichalcum amulet Mellish wore. In the fading light of the globe, the metal seemed to glow red, and she could just make out hundreds of tiny Skanuric runes etched into the piece. Perhaps this was what the wraithe had meant when it said Mellish bore relics of old? Kurio shrugged and slipped the amulet over her head. She tucked it under her shirt, where it nestled between her breasts, warm against her skin.

The large book Mellish had been reading caught her eye. She scanned a few pages filled with minute writing and strange illustrations of creatures, probably demons, and objects, and cities, and fortresses. It was heavy, but she decided to take it. She undid a few buttons and shoved it inside her shirt. It would be awkward to climb with it, but doable.

Ascending was easier, as always, though she had to stop frequently to rest and to adjust the book where it dug into her ribs.

At the top, she paused to catch her breath and rub her aching hands. Her horse regarded her with uninterested eyes and went back to cropping the grass.

The settlement was supposed to be close by. All she had to do was make her way through the forest safely to find it. Once there, she could recuperate and buy provisions and begin the journey back to Caronath. She wanted no part of Mellish and Zarina's business with the ruins the settlers had found. The sooner she was back in the city, back where she was comfortable, the better. And then Zarina would pay.

Her fingers touched the collar around her neck. She could pass it off as jewelry until she found a sorcerer to rid her of it.

Lights twinkling in the distance caught her eye. Kurio stood and squinted. It had to be the settlement down in the valley. She laughed with relief. Surely she'd reach it tomorrow, but for now, she needed rest. Her body ached, and her mind was scrubbed raw by emotion.

She unloaded her haul and gathered armfuls of wood. Then she built up a large fire, lighting it with a strike of an alchemical match. Soon, it blazed hot, crackling and cheery.

Kurio checked her gear in her saddlebags to make sure it was all there. Then she unsaddled her horse and tied it to a bent tree.

Laying out her bedroll, she snuggled under her blanket, face to the fire. It was comfortingly hot on her cheeks and forehead. She closed her eyes and, for the first time in days, drifted off to sleep almost immediately.

She woke at dawn, sweating under the blanket, the fire's coals still warm. The air was bitter and crisp on her face, stinging her cheeks and causing her nose to drip. Far away in her consciousness was a faint glimmer of terror, just beyond her grasp. She vaguely remembered the formless ills that had harrowed her dreams and shivered. But they faded to nothing with the coming of dawn.

She tossed the blanket aside and rose, stretched her stiff limbs and aching hands. It was a new day, and the sun seemed brighter now she was free. She raked fingers through her short, tangled hair.

"Hello, Kurio." A rich voice, thick and sweet.

She jumped and turned. Behind her stood Gannon, full lips smirking, an amused glint in his bright blue eyes.

What was he doing here? How had he found her? Her mind froze. She couldn't speak. Couldn't think.

"I'm so glad I caught up to you," he said, then muttered a few words in a foreign tongue she didn't understand.

Kurio felt a cold breeze brush across her skin, and the heat of blood rushed to her face. Bloody hells. Her heart pounded beneath her breasts; her eyes drank him in like she was a giddy adolescent. She tore her gaze away, embarrassed at her reaction. Her thoughts coalesced, then scattered again before settling.

"You came to save me?"

He had chased Mellish all the way from Caronath, just for her. Never before had she felt something with such strange certainty.

# CHAPTER TWENTY-SEVEN

# ANCIENT REVELATIONS AND FRESH WOUNDS

SIAN SCREAMED. MARTHAZE STARTED awake at the sound, scrabbling for his dagger. He was sure he'd left it close by—couldn't find it. He moved to Sian and held her shoulders. Her body trembled, her breaths short and sharp, the blanket fallen to her slender waist. She pushed him away and stumbled to her feet, arms folded against the chill night air.

"Sian?" he said. "What is it?" Had she been attacked by something, a sorcerous intrusion invisible to his eyes?

Around them, a few other priests and sorcerers stirred, but none came to see what the commotion was about. They were all fatigued from their exertions of the last few days. The demons and their human worshipers had renewed their assault in an attempt to break out of the ring surrounding them, which slowly tightened.

"Go back to sleep," Sian said. "It was only a dream."

There were tears in her voice, and he felt sorry for her, though she was a cursed sorcerer. They all suffered nightmares now. An inevitable consequence of the mind-numbing horrors they'd seen, of the hardships they'd endured for years. The war had lasted far longer than anybody had expected.

He returned to his ragged blanket; it was all he had left. But Marthaze gave up searching for sleep long after Sian had found it again. He shivered, breathed an oath, then rose quietly. There was no solace to be found in sleep these days. There hadn't been for many a year.

Far in the night-shrouded distance, glittering lights flickered— the Covenants going up against the Tainted Cabal's sorcerers. He knew Sian grieved for her lost colleagues, as did he for the fallen priests and priestesses. The Covenants bore the brunt of the fatalities: always on the front lines, scouring the earth with arcane cants, slaughtering dozens of the demon's fell army. Seven out of every ten sorcerers had been killed already, leaving only the strongest, the most puissant. The most dangerous.

Marthaze found himself on the edge of the camp. Watchful sentries noted his approach, but let him be. Often, those who'd had their fill of slaughter just walked away, even though they walked to certain death at the hands of the monstrous horde. The sentries knew better than to try to stop them.

One distant illumination shone brighter, redder, than the others. Marthaze knew this to be the Grandmaster of the Evokers, whose sorcerous might eclipsed that of the Grandmasters of the other Covenants, and who had in her possession the potent Chain of Eyes. How exactly the artifact worked Marthaze didn't know, not wanting anything to do with the sorcerers and their godless power. He watched the lights flit to and fro like fireflies above the infernal mass, trailing glittering arcs of destruction. Beneath them, demons and humans died in their hundreds: flesh and bones scorched, limbs severed, heads cracked like eggshells.

After a time, the Grandmaster's bright light dimmed slightly. Dawn was approaching, and the assault would lessen while the sorcerers replenished their reserves by the light of the rising sun.

As the Grandmaster came closer, Marthaze was able to discern an individual shape within the glow she emitted. A silken robe covered her slender form, and she glided across the churned and bloody terrain as if walking were beneath her. He sensed the sentries stiffen as she approached, no more comfortable with their allies than he was. But if it meant defeating Nysrog and the Tainted Cabal, the lesser evil could be tolerated. At least, for a time.

A hundred yards from Marthaze and the sentries, the Grandmaster's radiance winked out. She dipped, then, as if her sorcery failed her, and fell toward the smoking corpses carpeting the ground, then recovered and resumed a steadier descent.

When she landed ten paces away, Marthaze could see just how tired she was. Eyes bloodshot and red-rimmed; limbs and torso thin from lack of food and insufficient sleep; cheeks gaunt, sweat-drenched hair plastered to her scalp. She passed a skeletal hand across her face in weariness. Around her neck hung an orichalcum chain festooned with green cat's-eye chrysoberyls: the Chain of Eyes.

One of the sentries, bolder than the others, offered his arm for the sorcerer to lean on. "Grandmaster Shalmara," he said, awe in his voice, "may I escort you to your tent?"

She bowed her head slightly and accepted.

Aldric sat bolt upright, the ancient memory jolting him awake.

Niklaus was standing nearby. "A few more Dead-eyes were scouting the settlement," he said. "I killed them."

Aldric shrugged off his blanket and rubbed his eyes. The relic was still in his hand. He shoved it into a pocket. "What time is it?" he asked, thoughts sluggish as he tugged his boots on.

Shalmara. The same sorcerer who was currently the Grandmaster of the Evokers? How could it be? The idea was inconceivable.

"Almost midnight," Niklaus said. "I didn't think any more would come after last night, but there'll be more on the way. Maybe tonight. Definitely tomorrow when it's full-dark."

"Send out Stray Dog and Bryn—"

"Already done."

Valeria sat next to the smoldering fire, making tea, as if there weren't more productive things to do. Of Soki and Priska there was no sign.

"Good," Aldric said to Niklaus. "Where are Sokhelle and—"

"Also outside. Apparently they couldn't wake you."

Aldric buckled on his khopesh. He left a hand on the blade's hilt, the familiar feel calming his nerves. "Take me to where you killed the Dead-eyes." Three Niklaus killed last night, and now more. If the Dead-eyes could afford such losses, how many did they number?

Niklaus grabbed two legs of roast chicken as they left, as if they were going on a picnic.

He led Aldric out of Cherish toward the stream. There was no sign anywhere of others from their team. Aldric assumed they were out scouting; and Soki and Priska were using whatever sorcery they could to try to find out if there were any more Dead-eyes close by. Even in his worn-out state, Aldric's skin tingled. It happened whenever Niklaus was near, as if he brought with him a violence that something deep inside Aldric reacted to—his animal mind responding to a perceived threat.

The dream sat uneasily with him: Shalmara, the Grandmaster of the Evokers, battling the demon lord Nysrog's army. It couldn't have been the same woman he knew, could it? He thought back to his meeting with Shalmara in Nagorn City. She was old, almost a mummified corpse come to life. And the scar around her neck, along with her asking if he'd found the Chain of Eyes … it wasn't just a coincidence, he was sure.

But if she had somehow extended her life, did it really matter? She was on their side; he'd seen her fighting the infernal demons. Still, his thoughts were distracted and scattered, and now was no time to search for answers. He kept his hand on his khopesh and a cant of protection on his tongue.

Niklaus led him to five lifeless bodies near a bridge over the stream.

"What were you doing out here?" Aldric asked.

The mercenary glanced at him, then toed one of the spindly Dead-eyes. "It would be peaceful here, if it weren't for us and the Dead-eyes," he said, waving a hand at a nearby cornfield. "This valley is a good location. The earth is fertile, and there are plenty of trees in the surrounding forest for timber. There are even fish in the river, which runs deep. They've made a nice little place for themselves. The Dead-eyes may be more than they can handle, but they're not entirely defenseless or totally lacking weapons. Ask yourself, where did the settlers get them from?"

He offered Aldric a chicken leg. Despite the situation, Aldric accepted it. There might not be time to eat later. He looked over the fields and back at the settlement, remembering how some of the villagers had come out clutching swords when Niklaus had rung the alarm.

The answer was obvious. "Bandits," he said.

"And the food they gave us initially—scraps, whatever was about to go off, and stale bread. The settlers want the Dead-eyes gone, and they want us gone. Labor for these people if you want. Help to protect them. But know that they see us as nothing more than expendable muscle. If we die, they'll just ask for more of us. And your Church will send another in your place. So heal all you want, but remember your mission. Kill some Dead-eyes and investigate the ruins."

Aldric swallowed a final mouthful of chicken and tossed the stripped bone into some long grass. "And what will your Church do if you die?"

Niklaus shrugged. "I don't know. I don't really care." He grinned. "It hasn't happened yet, though death has been close more times than I care to remember." A frown crossed his face, and he grew somber, thoughtful. "Tell me, Aldric, does your Church spy on your activities? Perhaps question people about where you've been?"

The change of subject startled Aldric. "No," he said, too quickly.

His Church did keep tabs on him; because he was a sorcerer, they treated him differently to other priests. There had been that one time in Kyuth ... he'd stumbled across a nest of skorn: scaly-skinned, vicious creatures, half-lizard, half-dog, with jaws able to crack bone. An underworld boss had brought them in and tried training them as guard dogs and to menace others. What the thugs hadn't realized was the skorns' rudimentary intelligence meant they couldn't be controlled or caged for long. They'd turned on the criminals and ripped them to shreds before escaping into the city's sewers. After Aldric had hunted them down, killing every last one, a local woman came to him with information to sell. Priests of Menselas were asking after him, wanting to know what he'd been up to, where he'd gone, who he'd visited.

"They check up on me sometimes," he admitted to Niklaus. "But there are forces out there that could sway even the most steadfast worshiper. Everyone has a price. For some it's gold. Others might find themselves swayed by a woman or other reward."

*Have they asked Soki to watch me? Surely not ...*

"I've known many men, and you're one of the rare ones," Niklaus said. "You're confident there's nothing anyone could offer you that would sway your loyalty. But you're wrong. There's always something."

"I serve Menselas, and he has blessed me with talents."

"Like being a conduit for his divine healing?" asked Niklaus.

"Among others." Though Aldric was often undecided whether to number sorcery among his talents.

"Every man has his price," repeated Niklaus. He bent and

wiped his fingers on a patch of dry grass, then straightened. His penetrating eyes studied Aldric. "You don't want to be here"—he waved a hand around them—"on this mission. You want to heal. To put down your sword and live a cozy life taking care of those who come for help. Maybe settle down with a good woman. Start a family."

"I do what I'm good at and go where my Church directs me."

But Niklaus's comments stung. Because he was right. *Always I do what I'm told, no matter how much I'm reviled for being a sorcerer.*

"And you?" he asked the mercenary. "Don't you want to stop fighting?"

"Me? I can't put down my sword. After so long, it's what I am."

Aldric kept his gaze on the blackness surrounding them, squinting so as not to miss any movement. "What do you mean? You aren't forced to fight, and you don't lack for coin. You could retire; lay down your sword and do something else."

Niklaus shook his head and chuckled softly. "No, my path is set. Just as you serve your god, I serve my goddess. Each in our own way."

"Through violence? Killing?"

"Not always, but … often."

A killer. That was all Niklaus was.

"Then it seems our ways are opposites," Aldric said dismissively.

He expected the mercenary to be offended, but Niklaus merely laughed. "Not so different. You've killed for your Church. I can see it. And not just Dead-eyes and creatures in the wilderness or in the ruins. Men. Women."

"I … I was forced to," Aldric protested. "I often had no choice."

He became aware he'd mimicked Niklaus's response.

"Not so different then, you and I. At least I'm honest with

myself."

Aldric bridled at Niklaus's words and tone. But the mercenary's face was pensive, as if he were lost in thought.

"One day I will lay down this sword," he continued, "if my plans come to fruition. But you … your god has marked you, and you want to heal people with his power. You've spent a lot of time with the settlers, healing them, looking after them. It's … admirable. But your Church only tolerates you. You will never find peace there."

"I will," Aldric said, with more confidence than he felt.

Niklaus shrugged. "You need to be free. Not of your god, but of your Church."

The statement made Aldric suspicious. Was Niklaus trying, clumsily, to make him lose faith?

"The Church is my god's instrument in this world," he said. "They are intertwined. I'll never be free of the Church, not after everything they've done for me. And I'll never be free from my god. I wouldn't want to be."

"Gods are free of other gods. But I think you're mistaken. The Church isn't the instrument. You are. As is everyone else your god has marked. The Church is just an organization."

Images from Aldric's childhood came to him: the wonder of his first healing, and his parents' delight; the look of awe and reverence on the priests' faces when he was tested. He knew he owed the Church a debt he couldn't repay.

"I disagree," he began, but was interrupted by a wild clanging sound, faint but distinct.

"The alarm," said Niklaus. "The Dead-eyes are back."

He took off down the path. Clutching his sheathed blade, Aldric rushed after him, stumbling over the rocky ground, heedless of the bushes scratching his bare arms.

A woman's scream reached them. Shouts of alarm and panic rang out.

Aldric urged himself to greater speed, his chest burning, his mouth dry. Niklaus continued to get farther away, seeming to glide across the ground without stumbling over rocks and roots. A jagged branch snagged Aldric's shirt, dragging him to a stop before he tore himself free.

He skidded around the corner of a house into a chaotic scene lit only by a sliver of Chandra. Spindly limbs attached to shrunken bodies flashed everywhere. Dead-eyes. A settler lay unmoving on the ground, blood pooling under him from shredded arms and torso. His face had been sliced open until it was an unrecognizable mess.

On the other side of the square, Stray Dog and Bryn herded a group of women and children toward a nearby house. Pale-skinned Dead-eyes came at them with their high-pitched keening and growls, to be met with steel and death. Stray Dog hacked at the creatures with his axes while Bryn thrashed with his blade. Milky blood splashed across the ground.

Niklaus was nowhere to be seen. Neither were Soki and Priska, Razmus and Valeria.

Aldric whirled as something white flashed to his left. Razor-sharp claws came at him, and he batted them away with his still-sheathed blade. He jerked to the left and drew his khopesh in one swift motion, slashing at the Dead-eye. The crescent blade carved into its chest, and it collapsed, flailing, its boiled-egg eyes never changing between life and death.

More snarling faces came out of the shadows. He cut two down before they realized he was there.

The alarm had stopped ringing. Aldric glanced around. Were there other settlers in danger? He couldn't see any more. Stray Dog and Bryn were standing with Dead-eyes lying prone around them, cloudy blood seeping into the earth.

From somewhere in the distance came a chorus of piercing howls. Others joined in until the sound echoed around the valley, drowning out everything else.

"Bloody hells," shouted Bryn. "How many are there?"

"Stay together," Aldric yelled, backing toward them while keeping his eyes on places the Dead-eyes might appear from. "Don't split up. Where are Soki and Priska and the others?"

"Don't know," growled Stray Dog.

Dead-eyes rushed around the corners of two houses, as if they'd been hiding there. Bryn cursed and hurried to stand at Aldric's left while Stray Dog positioned himself to the right. The creatures' fanged mouths shrieked as they grew closer, then they were upon the three men, dirt-crusted claws extended.

Aldric cut at the thin bodies, their movements almost too quick to counter. He jerked back as a clawed hand lunged at him, then slashed with his blade, shearing through a skull. The Dead-eye slumped to the ground. Another went down as his blade cleaved its breastbone.

Bryn's sword flashed again and again as he danced among the Dead-eyes, leaving injured and dying in his wake. He fought silently, while Stray Dog grunted with each swing of his axes, severing limbs and hacking Dead-eyes into the ground.

A new pack of Dead-eyes leaped at Aldric, too many to counter. Claws raked his arm, and his dormant wards erupted. Sorcery shielded him in its globe, repelling the razor talons. He stumbled back, arm burning from the cuts, and tripped over a fallen Dead-eye. He landed heavily and rolled to his feet to see the Dead-eyes that had attacked him lunging at Stray Dog.

The big man's axes chopped at the creatures, breaking spindly limbs and smashing into torsos. But there were too many. Slavering mouths latched onto his left forearm, and Stray Dog bellowed as fangs plunged deep into his flesh. His right-hand axe hacked at more Dead-eyes, but his left waved wildly as the creatures savaged his flesh.

Aldric stepped toward him, but Bryn was there. His blade cut shining arcs through the air, and the Dead-eyes mauling Stray Dog lost their lives to cold steel. Cloudy, viscous blood pumped onto the dirt from their limp bodies.

Stray Dog dropped an axe and began prying away the jaws still embedded in his arm, which was a mass of shredded flesh. His blood dribbled onto the ground.

"I'll cover you!" shouted Bryn.

More Dead-eyes were coming, hurtling from the shadowy gaps between houses. As Aldric sprinted toward them, he released his sorcerous shield, and the golden glow vanished. He shrugged off the weariness of the draining sorcery. Better to conserve his strength in case he needed it.

Dead-eyes raced at him, shrieking with vicious delight. Six—no, ten. Damn it, there were too many. Cursing, Aldric fumbled with the talisman at his belt and structured a sorcerous calculation. Spit thick in his mouth, he reached for his dawn-tide power and uttered a cant just as the Dead-eyes reached him. A blast of energy exploded outward from him in a circle. The Dead-eyes flew backward, knocked off their feet.

Aldric, stumbling with exhaustion, managed to lurch forward and hack clumsily at the few that were still alive, dispatching them before they recovered.

Where were Bryn and Stray Dog? He glanced back to see both of them fighting more of the Dead-eyes. Stray Dog's arm streamed with blood, but he held his second axe again. Bryn was grinning as he effortlessly laid about him with his blade, no Dead-eye coming close to him without losing a limb or its life. There must have been at least twenty of the creatures lying lifeless in the dirt, and still more came.

A fresh group rushed at Aldric as one. He backed away, looking frantically for a wall, something to guard his back. A Dead-eye leaped at him ... Aldric shouted savagely, plunging his blade into its chest. He yanked his khopesh free and steadied himself to face yet more of the creatures racing toward him. He scanned the darkness behind them. Were there still more streaming into the settlement?

A violet light erupted around the pack of Dead-eyes, tracing a perfect circle on the ground. The creatures stopped in their tracks, as if hitting an invisible wall.

Aldric sensed a commingling of dawn-tide and dusk-tide sorcery emanating from his right. There, standing atop one of the houses on its gently sloping roof, was Soki. She shone with arcane brilliance to his sorcerous sight. Power he could never hope to command flowed through her, guided with exquisite control.

She reached out a hand, twisted it, and spoke a cant Aldric didn't understand. The Dead-eyes in the violet circle screeched. Their skin smoked, and they collapsed as one, wailing and thrashing in the dust. Orange flames erupted from splits in their flesh as their bones burned with fierce intensity.

The reek of charred flesh made Aldric gag. He looked away, to the shadows, and saw the remaining creatures' egg-like eyes reflecting the light of their blazing companions. Yelping cries echoed around the valley, and the Dead-eyes turned and ran.

Soki nodded grimly, then slid to the edge of the roof, threw herself off, and landed lightly on her feet.

"Are there any more?" Aldric asked her. She would know; her sorcery was far greater than his.

She closed her eyes, whispering words too low for him to hear.

"They've gone," she said eventually. "Somewhere to the east." She hesitated. "There are many more of them out there."

Of Razmus, Niklaus, Priska, and Valeria, there was still no sign.

~ ~ ~

*So,* thought Niklaus, *they are coming from all sides.* He bared his short blade, leaving *her* sword on his back. It was too sacred to be dirtied by the blood of these foul creatures.

He moved out of the open and ran along a wooden wall. To his left, a door slammed shut and a bolt drove home. Frightened faces peered from between curtains. Ahead, a woman with tears running down her face herded a group of seven children toward another house, presumably more secure. The Dead-eyes had come sooner than expected and the barricades still weren't ready.

Where were Soki, Priska, and Razmus? He didn't much care if Valeria lived or died, but if she was able to draw on the goddess's divine power, as she claimed, she could look after herself. The high priestess wouldn't use her abilities to protect the others, of that he was certain.

Glancing around the square, Niklaus saw a wagon and a stack of barrels against the wall of a house. Nothing they could use in their defense. A streak of white flashed behind a row of bushes. *Bloody Dead-eyes.* For him, it was like fighting sheep, but the creatures would likely be a problem for the others.

He spun around a corner and into the path of two Dead-eyes. He leaped, snarling savagely. A quick thrust, and his blade drove through the eye socket of one; then he cut the second from shoulder to navel. Niklaus kept running, yanking his blade free with a sucking noise.

He heard a scuttling to his right and ducked his head as a Dead-eye flew at him from atop a stack of crates. A wrist flick sent his short blade slicing through its scrawny neck, and its head landed in the dirt, gushing milky blood.

Frightened screams came from all around—the settlers cowering in their homes.

He almost spat at the cowards, but instead raised his voice. "Razmus! Where are you?"

An answering shout came from somewhere ahead, beyond the last of the poorly built buildings the settlers had raised out of the dirt.

Niklaus increased his pace, putting down another three Dead-eyes that were unlucky enough to cross paths with him. He raced along a track toward another stream. Valeria stood with her back to an old tree, watching Razmus grappling with two Dead-eyes. A bad idea, considering their claws. Razmus's arms and back were drenched with crimson, and his sword was nowhere to be seen.

*Fool! Always carry more blades than you think you'll need.*

As he came closer, Niklaus saw Priska kneeling beside the priestess. She clutched a talisman in her hands, fingers roaming over the sorcerous aid as she prepared a cant.

Niklaus was ten paces from Valeria when a sudden urge to plunge his sword into her back came over him. His short blade swung out, ready to strike—but he stopped himself. *Not now. Too obvious.* Besides, he didn't know what she was really up to yet, so her death would have to wait, as annoying as it was to have her here. And if the goddess wanted her high priestess dead, she would show him a sign.

His shining blade passed within a hand's breadth of Valeria as he dashed past.

"Save my father!" screeched Priska as soon as she saw him.

A third Dead-eye rushed at Razmus, and Niklaus thrust his sword into it. The blade stuck in its chest, and though he twisted and pulled, it remained stuck between two ribs. He let it go, grabbed one of the Dead-eyes savaging Razmus by its sparse matted hair, and yanked it off him. He twisted its emaciated neck, which broke with a sharp crack, severing its spine. That should give Razmus some respite. He dropped the lifeless corpse, then stepped on the Dead-eye that had his sword wedged between its ribs. He grasped the hilt and heaved, and this time the blade slid free. He plunged it into the back of the last Dead-eye Razmus wrestled with, then hauled the corpse off him.

"Thank you, thank you," gasped Razmus. He stared at the blood coursing down his arms. "I need help. Please."

"You should have been faster," Niklaus said. Everyone always wanted something.

Priska rushed over to Razmus, obviously having abandoned whatever sorcery she was trying to perform. But her hands drew back from staunching her father's wounds.

Niklaus sighed. A stunted sorcerer, and squeamish too.

A shadow flickered at the edge of his vision. He peered toward it, but it was gone. *The Lady Sylva. What does she want to show me?*

He spoke to Priska, aware of Valeria edging closer. "Find something to bind his cuts. Tear your clothes, if you must."

He turned his back and strode to where he'd seen the shadow. In the darkness, something large rustled through bushes. It emitted a deep-throated growl.

*That's no animal.*

Niklaus felt his arms tingle with anticipation. He held his short blade out, tip toward the sound, and advanced slowly.

A shape barreled out of the shadows. Spindly-limbed and gaunt, it looked like a larger Dead-eye, except with black and gray mottled skin. Knife-like talons protruded from its hands. It was similar to the creature Niklaus had killed so many years ago and the one that had recently attacked Aldric and Sokhelle, according to the priest's description. To encounter one was a rarity. But two in so short a span of time? That pointed to a powerful agency behind the creatures. Who was their master, and what did they want?

The creature hissed, then emitted a wail through its fanged mouth.

Niklaus shrugged his shoulders to loosen them.

The creature charged, talons extended. Niklaus dodged and weaved, avoiding each swipe. A slice of his short blade across its stomach, and he leaped back, frowning. He hadn't felt the usual sensation of blade parting flesh. *Steel should have—*

The black Dead-eye came at him again. Its assault was furious.

Niklaus dodged its knifelike talons, parried—and felt his wrist twist as his blade was almost wrenched out of his grip.

He stumbled, shocked at the creature's iron strength. A wild slash surged toward his head, and he let his momentum drop him to his knees. The claw whistled over him, brushing his hair.

He rolled away across the dirt, breath hissing between his teeth, then leaped to his feet, chest heaving. His short blade weaved glittering arcs as he dodged and parried the creature's furious attacks. Each time he blocked, it was like striking an iron bar. Niklaus deflected its swipes, swaying away as one came too close and rushed past his face. He thrust, and his point jabbed into the creature's chest like it was striking hard wood.

*Blood and damnation. Sorcery of some kind protects it.*

He countered fast enough to kill a human five times over, but although his assaults struck home, they couldn't penetrate whatever protected the creature.

*This is … different.*

Niklaus ducked and ran, creating some breathing space and luring the thing away from the others. He crouched slightly, sword close to the ground.

The black Dead-eye stood there, mouth open. A hissing sound came from it in short bursts. It was laughing at him.

"I kill you," it said, the words guttural but recognizable.

Niklaus parried another swipe of its razor talons. "Not likely," he said, breathing heavily. But if his blade couldn't injure it …

Its purple tongue darted from its gash of a mouth, as if tasting the air like a snake. Its eyes flicked over Niklaus's shoulder.

*It's not after me,* he realized. *Who, then? Aldric? Most likely Sokhelle, as she's a sorcerer. And the other creature was after her.*

Dropping his short blade, Niklaus swung *her* sword from his back to his hip and drew. Growling, the black Dead-eye rushed him, and he arrested the creature's swipe with a ringing parry. He flicked the blade and gave a feral grin as it parted flesh, and the creature whimpered.

*Not used to pain, are you? Well, here's some more.*

He slashed at it viciously, the blade carving glowing lines in the dark. The creature whirled its arms around in a harried defense— and Niklaus's sword sliced hunks from its flesh. He hammered it again and again, and the creature stumbled back, off balance.

He cut deeply into one of its legs, then, as it fell to its knees, he severed its arm. The creature flailed its other arm frantically, screeching.

*Huh, it bleeds crimson like a human.*

With a two-handed slash, he cut its head off. Its remaining arm and legs twitched feebly as gouts of blood sprayed across the dirt before slowing to a trickle.

Sweat running down his face, lungs burning, Niklaus looked around for signs of more Dead-eyes. *None.*

He kicked the black creature's corpse savagely and stared into its lifeless eyes. *What are you? And who controlled you?*

"Magnificent!" gushed Valeria.

Niklaus closed his eyes for a brief moment.

"Let me see it!" she implored. "I must touch it!"

There was no doubt what the priestess referred to. Niklaus backed away from her and sheathed the goddess's blade. It was already sparkling clean, the Dead-eye's blood absorbed into the steel.

"No. Not until I know what you're up to and if you further her plans." He bent and picked up his short sword.

"Of course I do! How dare you question me."

"Look to Priska," Niklaus said.

The young woman was by Razmus's side, speaking soothing words through her sobs. Valeria ignored Niklaus, so he approached the girl instead.

"Priska, the danger has passed. But sometimes the Dead-eyes poison their talons. Razmus will need healing. Go and fetch

Aldric. Quickly now!" With Priska gone, he could do away with Razmus ... if he desired. But what did his goddess want? Did she want Razmus dead so Valeria could sway Priska?

Priska nodded, her eyes red, face tear-streaked. She backed away, uttered a sob, then ran toward the settlement.

Niklaus squatted beside Razmus and supported him into a sitting position. Razmus shifted his weight, coughing weakly.

"I've never ... heard of Dead-eyes poisoning their claws," he croaked.

"They don't, but she needed something to spur her away from here."

Niklaus had almost let Priska dither over her father until it was too late to create this opportunity, but something stopped him. With Razmus gone, Priska would become more malleable in Valeria's hands, and Niklaus was loath to aid the priestess. He would have to let Razmus live. For now.

# CHAPTER TWENTY-EIGHT

# AFTERMATH

ALDRIC WALKED THROUGH THE carnage with Soki at his side. The Dead-eyes' bleached blood seeped into the ground, leaving dark trails and patches. Their limbs looked even thinner than when they were alive.

Bryn had taken off his shirt and torn strips from the fabric, bandaging Stray Dog's gashed arm. "Not a single villager came to help," he snarled, spitting into the dirt.

"They're frightened," said Stray Dog. "Mice don't fight cats."

"The Dead-eyes are hardly as dangerous as cats to mice," scoffed Bryn.

Stray Dog shrugged. "To the settlers, they are. Not everyone is born a warrior."

"Bryn, find the others," Aldric said, kneeling beside Stray Dog. "And make sure the settlers are all right. Bring any injured here to me."

Soki placed a hand on Aldric's shoulder. "Don't exhaust yourself," she warned.

He shrugged free from her grasp and placed his hands over the rent flesh of Stray Dog's arm. Warm blood oozed between his fingers. Stray Dog flinched with pain.

"Let me," Aldric said.

His brief flashes of sorcery had taken a lot out of him, but this was what he'd been born for. He closed his eyes and opened himself to his god's power, feeling it flow into and through him. He gloried in its warmth, bathing in the serenity it brought him.

First things first: the muscles and tendons had to be knit. One part of Aldric's will bent to this task while another examined the bone to make sure it was whole. It was scored in places from the Dead-eyes' sharp claws, but nothing too bad. Underneath his hands, he felt the flesh ripple and squirm like a carpet of snakes. Somewhere, as if from far away, he heard a gasp.

Aldric concentrated. Skin next. He drew the flesh close to the bone together first, fusing it, forcing the muscle to grow. A trickle of sweat slid down his forehead and into his eye. He ignored it. Next came the outer layer of skin, which was more elastic and easier to set.

When he was sure the muscles and skin were mostly reconnected, Aldric reluctantly let go of his god's power. He shuddered at the feeling of loss, wanting to reach for it again. With a great effort of will, he stopped himself and opened his eyes. Stray Dog's arm looked whole, albeit crisscrossed with new hairline scars.

The big man grunted. "Thank you," he said gruffly, clenching and unclenching his hand, eyes roaming over his patched-up skin. "Brings back memories."

Aldric remained kneeling in the dirt. Niklaus was right: Stray Dog's wound had drawn him, as nectar drew a bee. He'd wanted to heal him. *Needed* to.

Aldric was relieved that Stray Dog hadn't asked questions about his healing ability. *He's seen it before,* he realized, remembering the scars on the man's chest and back. Maybe he didn't care. Maybe the dog had been trained well.

Aldric immediately chastised himself for the uncharitable thought. Stray Dog deserved better than that from him.

He staggered wearily to his feet, almost overcome with exhaustion. If he'd used more sorcery against the Dead-eyes, he might not have had the strength for the god's work. As it was, he felt drained. For the briefest instant he felt a surge of jealousy as he recalled the power of Soki's sorcery and how she'd remained energetic and sprightly afterwards. It had hardly affected her.

He quickly quashed the sensation. But ... if he had more power, he could do more good. And he wouldn't be as physically drained, which would leave him more able to handle his god's gift flowing through him.

A sudden coldness filled Aldric. Sorcery was anathema to the Church of Menselas, and for the first time ever, he was wishing for more of it. It was Soki's influence ... Was this how corruption started? Aldric had seen what became of sorcerers who tried to channel more power than they could handle. Some were left withered and misshapen; others died and became mere puddles on the ground.

Voices came from all around—the settlers shouting at each other through the walls, asking if the fight was over. Some had used the barricades for defense, as planned, but most had hidden inside their houses. *Mice trapped in cages.*

"Aldric," screamed Priska, rushing around the side of a building, sobbing uncontrollably, "it's my father—he's hurt."

"Where is he?"

Aldric held her arms, but she collapsed against his chest, and he had to take her weight. Soki raised her eyebrows at him.

"Come on," he said to Priska. "We mustn't waste time."

She pushed away from him to stand on her own two feet. "This way, this way." And she rushed off north, toward the stream that ran along the northern side of the settlement.

Aldric followed with Soki. He couldn't keep up with Priska, who had dashed off without looking back. He stumbled with fatigue a couple of times, and Soki jammed her shoulder into his armpit to steady him.

"You're exhausted," she said crossly when he mumbled his thanks. "Don't push yourself too much. You're no good to anyone if you're unconscious."

It didn't take long before they came across Razmus. Priska kneeled over his still body, sobbing and wailing. She pressed her face to his, heedless of the blood smearing her clothes and skin.

Niklaus and Valeria stood a respectful distance away, while Bryn and Stray Dog had followed behind Aldric and Soki.

"He's lost a great deal of blood," Niklaus said, moving closer. He crouched down and placed his hands on Priska's shoulders. "But Aldric's here now. Razmus will be all right."

She nodded, wiping her eyes with the palms of her hands. "He can't die ..." She shook Razmus's body, as if to wake him from sleep. "I don't know what I'd do," she said between sobs. "He's always been there for me. Always."

Aldric kneeled next to her. He took in the deep gashes across Razmus's arms and chest and the amount of blood around his body. The ex-soldier's face was pale, and his lips blue. Without hesitating, Aldric let Menselas's power suffuse him again. By the end Aldric was trembling, and his vision swam. But Razmus's breathing was deep and even, and some color had returned to his face.

"He'll need rest," Aldric managed. "And get some broth into him."

He staggered upright and would have fallen if Stray Dog and Soki hadn't grabbed hold of him.

"Thank you!" Priska said.

"You need rest too," Soki said sternly to her. "We're taking you back."

After her father's brush with death, Aldric knew the girl would be fragile and vulnerable. Valeria had her confidence, and Aldric didn't trust the priestess further than he could throw her.

"Look after Priska," he told Soki, adding close to her ear, "She's spending too much time with Valeria."

Soki nodded. She bent and drew Priska to her feet. "Come," she said gently. "We'll get you back to the settlement to clean you up. You and Bryn can help me carry Razmus."

Priska allowed Soki to draw her away. Bryn lifted Razmus, his elbows crooked around the ex-soldier's armpits. Soki and Priska took a leg each, and they slowly carried Razmus toward the settlement.

When Aldric was sure they couldn't hear him, he said, "There were far more Dead-eyes than I'd expected before full-dark."

Niklaus sneered, jerking his chin in the direction of the village. "Bloody settlers lied to us, to your Church. And it's not just the Dead-eyes—you should see what attacked me."

He gestured to a large form on the ground about twenty paces away. It was so dark now that if Niklaus hadn't pointed it out, Aldric might have missed it. He pushed Stray Dog's helping hands away with a word of thanks and stumbled over to it. His breath caught in his throat. A black-skinned Dead-eye, but larger, more vicious. It looked to be the same kind of creature that had attacked him and Soki.

Niklaus kicked something, and the creature's head rolled closer to the body. "I don't think it was after me though, was it, Aldric?"

*Soki. Another of the creatures had come to kill her.*

"What is it?" Stray Dog asked. He prodded the creature with his boot. "I've never seen anything like this before. And I've seen many things."

"Another mindless monster," said Valeria. "But it was no match for the sword of—"

"Enough of your nattering, priestess," snarled Niklaus. "Round up the settlers—whoever's brave enough to come outside now. And find Neb. Bring him here, to me. He has some explaining to do."

Valeria drew herself up, eyes flashing with anger. "Why should I? I don't take orders from anyone."

Despite his fatigue, Aldric felt his blood boil at her words. They had a mission: to protect the settlers. And they needed to be a team to get the job done. *We've only been here a few days, and already Razmus has almost died. He would have if I hadn't been here.*

"You do what we say," he told her, voice hoarse with exhaustion, "or you go back to Caronath. We don't have room for someone who doesn't pull their weight. So you either swallow your pride and find Neb and any other settlers who are about and bring them to us, or you can leave in the morning. It's your choice."

Valeria opened her mouth to speak, but shut it when Niklaus took a step toward her. "Go. Do as he says. Stray Dog, you go with her."

Valeria sniffed, then turned her back and walked away. Stray Dog looked at Aldric, shrugged, and followed her.

Aldric squatted next to the headless corpse. Concerns and suspicions beset him. It was no coincidence, the appearance of another of these creatures. This mission—to protect the settlers, drive off the Dead-eyes, then investigate the ruins—was getting ever more complicated. And far more dangerous.

"We'll have the settlers dispose of the Dead-eyes," Aldric said. "And this thing ... Soki—Sokhelle—will want to study it. It makes sense to know your enemy."

Niklaus grabbed the creature's head by its wiry hair and looked behind its ears. "My blade was useless against it," he said, his eyes flicking to Aldric, then away. "At least at first. It was protected by sorcery. You'd know more about that than I do."

The creature had cuts all over its body. Its arm had been severed, like its head.

"Then what happened?" Aldric asked.

"I have a few tricks up my sleeve."

Aldric narrowed his eyes. "Then you should share them. Such knowledge would benefit us all if we run into another of these things."

"Not this trick."

"Do you want to return to Caronath with Valeria tomorrow?" Aldric's tone was hard.

Maybe this wasn't the right time to confront Niklaus. Then again, there might never be a better one. Niklaus stared for long moments at Aldric. He looked as if he might be calculating the cost of revealing a secret, or perhaps what dark deed he'd have to do later to preserve it.

"The priestess won't be leaving us," Niklaus said eventually. "She'll follow orders from now on. And I told you before: steel can kill these creatures. There was no trick. Whatever sorcery protected it, it failed."

He spoke with confidence, as if Valeria had agreed to obey his commands. And he hadn't risen to Aldric's baited question.

"We've been attacked by two of these creatures now," Aldric said. "That's not a coincidence."

Niklaus nodded. "I agree."

"You said that someone—or something—always controls them."

Aldric remembered the wraithe he'd encountered in the wilderness on the way to Caronath. It had warned him that humans meddled with things best left alone. Aldric had assumed it meant sorcery, but what if it had meant the ruin? That was the only thing he could think of, of any significance. Yet, at this point, they hadn't entered the ruin, so why send the black Dead-eye against them? Unless it was a preemptive strike?

"Something doesn't want us here," Niklaus was saying. "It was content to let the settlers stay until they found the ruin."

What was so important about this ruin? Something significant enough to warrant both Aldric's presence and a representative of

Niklaus's goddess. It wouldn't be the first time his Church had kept him in the dark.

"I think," he said slowly, "whatever it was counted on the Dead-eyes driving the settlers away. When that didn't work, it sent them in greater numbers. And then this creature. And it seems the only thing here worth protecting is the ruin."

"I agree," Niklaus said, and shrugged his shoulders. "We should check it out."

Aldric stood up. "Whatever happens, we have to get rid of the Dead-eyes once and for all. We can't have them attacking the settlement. And we certainly don't want them here when we're investigating the ruin."

Niklaus rolled the head closer to the body. He wiped his hands on a tuft of grass and stood, kneading the small of his back. "Kill Dead-eyes—that's something we can all do. Except Razmus apparently." He chuckled.

*An especially poor joke,* thought Aldric. Then again, what could you expect from a mercenary?

"We need to bury the Dead-eyes," he said.

"We should just cart the Dead-eyes away from the settlement," Niklaus said. "Leave them to rot near where we think they're coming from. Might deter them from attacking again."

"We'll do it," Aldric said. Though he didn't particularly like the idea of leaving the monsters to rot, it might prove effective.

~ ~ ~

"Do you have a smaller knife?" Soki asked Neb. "Maybe a fruit knife? Anything with a finer blade will do."

She wiped her hands on a rag, leaving a stain of clotted blood and yellowy ichor. The stench of the creature was almost overwhelming, and Soki had to breathe through her mouth in order not to gag. An arcane globe she'd created cast a bright light around the room. A small fire gave off some warmth, but its illumination was insufficient for the work she had to do.

From his spot next to the door, Neb opened one eye a slit, then squeezed it shut again. "Maybe the widow Hazel will have a fruit knife. She was wealthy once and brought some fancy plates and utensils with her. It's still dark, but she might be up—doesn't sleep much these days. Oh gods, can we bury or burn the creature soon? We'll never get the smell out of the wood."

The dark-skinned Dead-eye lay on a table Soki and Neb had dragged to the center of the room. She had peeled back the creature's chest to reveal its ribs, and removed its organs, which sat in various wooden bowls next to the corpse. They didn't have much time before full-dark, so sleep would have to wait.

Soki tapped her bloody knife against the table and bent over to examine the body cavity. "I didn't get a chance to open up the one we killed in Caronath. All of its organs are similar to a normal Dead-eye's, except larger. It must be related. Fascinating."

A strangled sound came from Neb. "When will you be finished?"

"Soon, if you get me the knife I need."

Neb exited the shack and slammed the door behind him. The building shuddered, and dust drifted down from the beamed ceiling. Soki waved her hands to try to stop it settling on the corpse.

She hadn't been able to find a catalyst on the creature, so it wasn't able to use sorcery. Still, some creatures had innate abilities, like demons. Niklaus had said it was immune to his steel, for a while at least. But that couldn't be an innate talent, as it wouldn't fail at a crucial time. Which meant someone else was shielding it.

The realization sent a chill through her, and she dropped the knife on the table and stepped back. The creature in Caronath had tried to kill her, which meant it was likely this one had been sent on the same mission. She shuddered as goosebumps rose on her skin and managed to stop herself from rubbing her arms and wiping blood over them.

Without warning the door opened. Soki uttered the first few syllables of a cant, then stopped as Shand stepped inside. The girl was carrying a pile of sticks and a hessian bag, which hopefully held the fragrant herbs Soki had asked for.

"Here you go, Lady Sokhelle," Shand said, placing the bag on the floor next to Soki.

She moved to the dust-covered fireplace, dropped the sticks, and began setting a fire.

"Thank you, Shand."

The girl looked wild—maybe because of her shorn hair—but she was helpful and curious. Her clothes were in worse condition and dirtier than those of the other settlers Soki had seen, and her belt was a length of frayed rope around her slender waist. Either she was very poor, or no one looked after her properly. Soki resolved to question Neb later once the Dead-eyes had been dealt with. Maybe she could do something to aid the girl.

With a few strikes of flint and steel, Shand had a small blaze going in no time.

"Get some of those herbs on it straight away," Soki said. "And don't skimp. There's no reason to put up with this stench if we don't have to. I shouldn't be much longer. If you'd like to go now, I'm sure Neb will—"

"I'd like to stay," Shand said as she threw a handful of dried herbs on the fire. With a jump, she perched on the edge of a side table, her eyes never leaving the creature. "Why is its skin darker than the other Dead-eyes? What does it eat? Do you think—"

"All good questions, Shand." If the girl could stomach watching her slice apart the creature, Soki had no issue with letting her stay. "It is bigger than any Dead-eye I've seen, though it seems to be of the same species."

"The same what?"

"That means it could breed with the regular Dead-eyes."

Shand grimaced and wrinkled her nose. "Eww! That's disgusting!"

"The creatures have to breed, just like everything else. Nothing lives forever."

Though some lived an inordinately long time, like wraithes. Soki's breath caught in her throat. Old histories and legends told of wraithes that led tribes of Dead-eyes, treating them as slaves, forcing them to labor in their mines and build their cities. Was a wraithe involved here? Aldric said he'd encountered one in the wilderness ... but that was on his way to Caronath. Still, it was worth questioning him again about the encounter.

At the same time, she could work on persuading him to use his dusk-tide power more often. He had hamstrung his sorcery, and it angered her more than she admitted to him. The most potent cants combined dawn- and dusk-tide power, and Aldric couldn't afford to limit himself. One day, his life might depend on his mastery of the dusk-tide. She wouldn't have his death on her hands just because he was stubborn.

There was a knock on the door, and Neb entered. He held out a slim knife to Soki. "Matron Hazel says it's an heirloom. Looks just like a fruit knife to me."

The knife was a solid piece of silver, with a patterned handle. "I'll wash it thoroughly," promised Soki. "Did you tell her what I require it for?"

"No. I thought it best not to."

Shand snorted, earning a frown from Neb.

"I have other work to do," he added. "Shand, I need you—"

"The Lady Sokhelle wants me to stay," lied Shand. "In case there's anything she needs help with."

"Oh, that's all right, then."

Neb kept his eyes on the dissected creature as he backed out the door. When it closed, Shand let out a soft laugh.

"There was no need to lie," Soki said. "I was going to ask you to stay anyway."

Shand shrugged. "I didn't know that. And besides, following Neb around all day is boring." She rolled her eyes and pretended to yawn. "You're different to Valeria."

Soki paused, the fruit knife hovering over the creature's eyeball. "In what way?"

"She doesn't do anything. She just talks and drinks tea. The other girls think she's a princess in disguise, as well as being a priestess of the moon goddess. She says her goddess values women above men and gives powers to her priestesses. Can you imagine it? Like sorcery, only better."

What was Valeria up to? Was she planning to build a temple out here in the wilderness, or merely preaching to the settlers? Or was she stirring up trouble?

"Such power is rarer and limited compared to sorcery," Soki replied. "But yes, it is often stronger for specific tasks."

"She said sorcerers don't like the Lady Sylva's priestesses because they're jealous."

"That's not right. When did you speak to her?"

"She met with a few of us at the widow Hazel's."

"I suppose they're interested in the big city and what life is like there. I can tell you it's not all it's cracked up to be."

"I didn't think so, but they're stupid. Most of them anyway."

"What are you interested in, Shand? What do you want?"

The girl pursed her lips and hung her head so her hair covered her face. At first Soki thought she wasn't going to answer; then she said in barely a whisper, "I'm interested in learning things. The truth—about everything. And I want a mother and father, but that's not going to happen."

A lump rose in Soki's throat. Maybe she could do more than furnish Shand with new clothes. After they'd dealt with the Dead-eyes, she'd ask Neb about taking the girl with her back to

Caronath. She could do with someone to help around the house and at the shop.

"Thank you, Shand, for being honest." Soki placed the tip of the fruit knife just under the creature's eye. "What I'm going to do now," she said, applying pressure until the tip sank a knuckle-length into the skin, "is remove its eyeballs."

Shand leaned forward eagerly.

# CHAPTER TWENTY-NINE

# CONFRONTATIONS

ALDRIC HAD DONE THE best he could to heal the wounded in the settlement, then collapsed into his bed. Except sleep hadn't come. He'd given up after an hour and joined the others who also couldn't sleep.

On the other side of the room, Stray Dog sat cross-legged on his bedroll, oiling his axes. Niklaus said Bryn was out scouting the perimeter of the settlement and checking the defenses. The fight with the Dead-eyes, combined with Razmus's grievous injuries, left a dismal pall over the company, and Aldric didn't know how to dispel it. Along with the injuries among the settlers there had also been one death—a young man who wasn't scared enough of the Dead-eyes and whose excitement at seeing warriors swinging swords had overcome his common sense.

Aldric checked on Razmus. The former soldier was in a deep sleep, which was good. It would aid his recovery. Beside him was a bowl half full of broth and a spoon. Good, someone had been feeding him.

Aldric poured himself some hot tea, then grimaced at its feeble taste.

From her seat by the fire, Valeria saw his expression and gave a faint laugh. She looked mournfully into her own cup.

"Yes, the flavor is … delicate. Some thieving settler stole a bag of my best leaf, so my supplies are running low, and I'm having to stretch every pot. And the settlers, goddess bless them, refuse to share their own supplies. *Oh no, we don't grow tea; we make do.* Liars. They gave me shaved roots and bark instead."

The goddess's blessing sounded more of a curse the way Valeria bestowed it.

Aldric grunted. "As long as it's warm."

The night was the coldest yet as an icy wind blew from the north.

Valeria patted the seat next to her with a gloved hand. "It's warm over here."

Niklaus's chuckle broke Aldric's awkward pause.

Valeria's expression darkened, and she stared daggers at the mercenary, who ignored her and went back to his exercises.

*Valeria's nothing next to Soki,* Aldric thought. He looked away from Valeria, suddenly afraid she might see his thoughts on his face. "It's full-dark tomorrow night," he said, eager to change the subject.

"How positively enlightening," Valeria said mockingly. "And here I thought you were an idiot."

"Where are Sokhelle and Priska?" he asked.

"Out practicing sorcery, one would assume," Valeria said. "Leave them be, Aldric. You can't follow Sokhelle everywhere like a dog after a bitch in heat. It's getting uncomfortable for everyone."

He should have gone outside as soon as he'd abandoned his attempt to sleep. Then he wouldn't have to deal with Valeria. "The Lady Sokhelle is teaching me sorcery, along with Priska. I don't have to justify my movements to you, or anyone."

Too late Aldric realized he'd just done exactly that.

"Do you think sorcery will help you?" Valeria placed a hand against her mouth and gave a dry cough. "It didn't help Razmus, the poor man."

Aldric opened his mouth to reply, but was interrupted by Soki calling him from outside the meeting hall. He leaped to his feet, eager to be done with Valeria and her malicious streak.

Soki was right outside and grabbed his arm as he emerged. She pulled him around the side of the building, to where Priska was waiting. The young woman was staring at the cliffs to the south. Behind him, Aldric heard the door open again as others followed him.

"There!" Soki said, pointing. "A light."

"I think it's a fire," Priska said. "But we saw a brighter light at the same spot earlier."

"That was dawn-tide sorcery," said Soki.

Priska looked at her sharply. "You could sense that? From here?"

"It couldn't be anything else," Soki said. "But yes, I sensed it. It was ... strange. I've never felt anything like it before."

"That's not good news," Aldric said.

"A fire?" Niklaus said from behind them. "That's why you dragged us out here? It's as cold as Margebian's tits."

"Niklaus!" said Aldric, shocked at his crudity. "There are women present."

The mercenary gave a mock bow. "I apologize to all the women present. Sokhelle, Priska, Valeria, and yourself."

Aldric rolled his eyes, feeling heat rise to his face. Valeria, who'd just appeared from behind Niklaus, gave a throaty chuckle.

"Can you work a divining?" Aldric asked Soki.

"Can I?" She flashed him a wry smile. "Of course. But you'll owe me."

"Anything," he said, with a smile of his own. "If it's within my power."

Soki instructed Priska to hold her talisman in one hand. "Another lesson for you. Hold my hand with the other, and I'll guide you through the process. You'll be able to feel what I'm doing. It's night, so we'll use dusk-tide power. There … do you see the currents of the night? Gather your questions, bind them, and send them forth."

Aldric knew what Soki was doing technically, but the complexity of such sorcery was beyond his meager abilities. He knew that Priska wouldn't be able to follow the entirety of what Soki was doing either; she was just along for the ride.

With his sorcerous sight, he watched arcane forces gather around Soki … a twisting darkness, a solidity of shadows.

"A woman," whispered Priska.

"Yes," confirmed Soki. "What else?"

"I … She's injured. Hurting. There's … No, I'm sorry. I've lost it."

"It'll become easier with practice," Soki said. "Now … a woman … lost … in pain … but there's also relief. She has … power. There are sparks of potent sorcery around her. Three of them. Someone died close by, not long ago."

Aldric swallowed. More complications. "Did she kill them?"

Soki frowned. "No," she breathed after a time. "A fall. From a cliff." Her breath caught. "There's something else … a presence … a being … ancient … insane."

"What is it? Is it close by?"

"No. There is a man close though." Soki shook her head, then opened her eyes. She blinked repeatedly, as if to clear them. "It's gone."

"We should go and find them," Aldric said. "It's not safe out there with the Dead-eyes."

"They've made it this far," Soki said, "so they're not unskilled. Besides, I think they must already be on their way here. There's nowhere else close by. But I can check occasionally in the hours before dawn."

Aldric nodded his agreement.

"Excellent!" Niklaus said, clapping him on the back. "We'll get some sleep and see these people tomorrow. Whoever they are."

~ ~ ~

The next day, after partaking of the dawn-tide to replenish his repository, Aldric pressed the settlers and his group to greater urgency in preparing for full-dark. Luckily, the fight with the Dead-eyes the previous night gave the settlers impetus.

Stray Dog and Razmus—who had declared himself fully recovered—and a work crew of settlers dragged the stick-limbed corpses some distance from the settlement, leaving them to rot in the sun. Burning wasn't an option, as the creatures' flesh gave off a putrid smoke. Besides, they wanted the crumbling carcasses to frighten off live Dead-eyes.

Aldric warned Razmus not to overexert himself, as he'd need another few days to recuperate, but the ex-soldier waved away his concern.

"I'm not a baby," he said gruffly. "I need to get back out there and take the settlers through their drills. A few are coming along nicely, especially the miller, Drusst. But there are others who could still use a bit of guidance. I don't want them panicking once the Dead-eyes get here."

"All right, but stay in the shade, and just order them around. I'm sure you can manage that."

The morning passed quickly, with Soki informing them the man and woman were headed toward Cherish. Aldric worked side by side with the settlers to finalize the barricades. Stray Dog seemed to get along well with the villagers, especially a lad named Alvar.

"Tell the woodsmen we don't need any more logs," he shouted to the younger man during a well-earned break. "It's too late now to begin erecting more barricades. We need them back here to help out."

"Yes, Stray Dog, sir," Alvar said, and scurried off in a puff of dust.

"We should stop soon anyway," Aldric said.

Stray Dog nodded. "They'll be no good to us if they're too tired to wield a weapon. We should give them a few hours' break before nightfall."

"Good idea. I'll make sure Razmus and Bryn do the same."

Aldric made his way to where the settlers were going through drills. He passed Niklaus standing at the opening between the barricades through which they hoped to funnel the Dead-eyes. The mercenary hadn't been much help with the laborious preparations, but come full-dark when the Dead-eyes attacked, Aldric knew he'd be worth his weight in orichalcum.

To his eye, the settlers' drills didn't look too sloppy, though their long sharpened poles were unwieldy and tended to tangle, especially when Razmus had them change direction. Drusst the miller seemed to be taking a lead role and harangued the men as much as Razmus did.

To Aldric's surprise, Bryn moved among the settlers, offering advice, showing them how to better position their feet and hands.

"They'll do, but we should rest up soon," said Razmus when he saw Aldric. He was sitting under a tree on a three-legged stool, with the remains of a meal of bread and cheese on a plate beside him.

"That's what Stray Dog suggested," Aldric replied. "And I dare say the scarecrow could use a break. I think they've gone through a few."

Razmus chuckled, then stood and stretched his back. Aldric saw him hide a wince of discomfort from his recently healed wounds.

"With any luck they won't see much action, and then this will be all over," the ex-soldier said, a strange mix of anger and confusion playing over his face.

No doubt he was worried about Priska.

"Sokhelle is a good person," Aldric said, trying to allay his fears. "She'll look after Priska and teach her well."

"It's not Sokhelle I'm worried about. It's that damned priestess and Niklaus."

"We'll be back in Caronath soon, and Priska will be too busy studying sorcery to have much time for anything else."

Razmus grunted, looking unconvinced. "You don't have any children, do you?"

"No, but I have a younger sister."

"Then you should know what I'm talking about. These days, young women are too headstrong by far."

Aldric thought of Kittara. He should have been there for her, but he'd been too busy. He shook his head. Now wasn't the time for self-recrimination. He'd write to her and try to guide her as best he could.

"Priska will be fine," he said to Razmus, and nodded toward the settlers. They had stopped their drills and were squinting at the sun, clearly anxious about the oncoming full-dark. "They should stop now and spend some time with their families. It may be the only time they have left."

Razmus bellowed at Drusst and the other settlers, telling them they could rest after another hour. One young man approached Aldric to ask him to heal a shallow gash along his side from the tip of an errant sharp pole. Aldric obliged, though it weakened him. Afterwards, he made his way back to the meeting hall. As he stepped inside, he saw Valeria bending over his belongings.

She straightened when she heard the door open, a guilty look flashing across her face. As she saw Aldric, her expression changed to one of triumph.

"What have you been hiding from us, Aldric?"

She raised a hand, and he realized she held the pouch

containing his relic.

"Give that back right now! Are you a thief as well as a … a …"

"A what? A priestess of a degenerate goddess? I know what you priests of Menselas"—she sneered the name—"think of us. It's written all over your face."

She tossed Aldric the pouch. He caught it and checked inside to make sure the relic was safe.

"Keep your hands off my belongings," he warned. "And everyone else's."

"I sensed something, but only now just pinpointed it. Do you think it makes you special? How far have you delved into the memories?"

Aldric paused, his jaw clenched. How did she know? The relics were a secret of his Church, weren't they?

"You know nothing about it," he said.

"I know that wisdom that is borrowed, not earned, can be dangerous."

"If I catch you going through my things again, I'll swear I'll—"

"What—kill me? What would your precious Sokhelle think of that? Oh, I know you two are intimate. It's plain to see for one trained as I have been. Be careful this mission doesn't get one of you hurt."

Blood rushed to Aldric's face, and he took a step toward Valeria, fists clenched. Part of him knew he'd lost control, but he was sick of holding himself back. "Is that a threat?"

He raised a hand and reached for both his dawn-tide and dusk-tide power, wishing for Valeria to give him an excuse to lash out. The smallest thing, and he would—

He cried out as agonizing fire lashed his skin. It dug deeper, into his muscles, and he sank to his knees, vision blurred with tears. His stomach rebelled, and he swallowed bile. The room swam around him, and he keeled over sideways.

When the torture subsided, he found himself curled into a ball on the floor. He breathed deeply, managed to gather himself and roll onto his back.

Valeria stood over him, face expressionless. "I don't threaten," she said softly. "That was just a taste of what I can do. Don't ever raise a hand to me again, or you'll wish you'd never been born. Do you understand?"

Aldric groaned. He felt like he'd been beaten to a pulp by a gang of burly men.

"Do you understand?" she repeated.

"Yes," he croaked.

"Say you're sorry."

"What?"

"Say. You're. Sorry."

Valeria was unhinged. Maybe she always had been. Or perhaps whatever the priestesses of the Lady Sylva Kalisia went through had made her crazy. After all, Sylva Kalisia was the goddess of pain and suffering.

"No," he said, bracing himself. "I won't."

Valeria let out a laugh. "So you manage to find your balls when pushed. Maybe it isn't too late for you." She turned and left.

Aldric remained on the ground for a few minutes, fuming at Valeria, then got up and poured himself a cup of tea. The kettle had been left to keep warm by the side of the fire, and the tea was dark and murky. He grimaced at the bitter taste and ate a stale sweet roll to counter it.

Valeria was a problem. He surmised she'd used her goddess's power on him; and just as his god's power healed, hers caused pain.

"You're driving yourself too hard," Soki said behind him.

Aldric turned to find her almost close enough to touch. She'd entered the building unnoticed while he worried. Her cheeks were pink, as if she'd just scrubbed them, and her dark hair was freshly braided with the interwoven colored strings of her clan.

Unconsciously, his hand reached out to her before he remembered their agreement. He jerked it back and gave her a guilty look. She didn't need to know what had happened between him and Valeria. She had enough to worry about.

"It's hard, I know," she said, amusement in her brown eyes. "But it's almost full-dark, and this will soon be over. With the rest of our group, we should be able to deal with the Dead-eyes with relative ease. The settlers have done a good job erecting the barricades, and they'll fight for what they've built here. We're well prepared this time."

He knew she was right, and nodded. But he wondered if his troubles would end with the settlers. One thing was certain: he wouldn't let Hannus push him into another mission like this one, even though the consequences of disobeying the archbishop would be severe.

"I'm more concerned about Razmus and Priska," Soki said. "Now he's healed, they're back to fighting. She's too headstrong, too eager to rush ahead with her training. It may be dangerous, and I fear she'll get worse before she gets better. Razmus's near death hasn't tempered her behavior."

"I'm confident you can control her. She looks up to you. She'll see reason. And when we're back in Caronath, you can keep her too busy to get into trouble."

Soki's expression softened. "Maybe. She's been through a lot."

She offered Aldric her hand, and, after a moment of surprise, he grasped it.

"I know you think I'm a powerful sorcerer," she began. He made to interrupt her, but she placed a finger to his lips for the barest instant. "And compared to you, I am. I don't mean to cause offense, but I know how you revile your sorcerous abilities. Only … there are greater powers than sorcery." She uttered a nervous laugh, and her brow creased. "Listen to me, I'm rambling. What I mean to say is your god has touched you, and through him you have immense power over the body, over healing. I can sense that Valeria is also touched by her goddess. And her power could well be superior to mine. I have trained hard and pushed myself to my limits, and, I think, come close to the capabilities of the sorcerers of old. But I cannot defeat a goddess."

Aldric regarded Soki thoughtfully. He debated telling her about Valeria overcoming him, but something held him back.

*Tomorrow,* he said to himself. *It'll all be over tomorrow.*

"You're wondering what Valeria's plans are; why she's here," he said. "And you're warning me that if it should come to a confrontation, you might not be able to withstand her. I agree. Let's stay out of her way."

Soki almost looked vulnerable as she regarded him with tenderness.

"It might be a stretch to say she'd attack me," she said. "But she's an unknown. And I hate unknowns."

Aldric sighed. "She's not here to protect the settlers from the Dead-eyes. Nor is she a companion to Niklaus, although they share the same goddess. I believe she's here for the ruin. I should have realized it from the beginning. Holy Menselas, I hate being kept in the dark. Hannus and Valeria can go to the hells, both of them."

"It won't be over after the Dead-eyes," Soki said. "Then we'll have to deal with the ruins, and Valeria."

Aldric shook his head. "One thing at a time. Protect Cherish first; then I … I mean we … can worry about Valeria."

"It's another worry for you. I'm sorry."

Aldric smiled and shrugged. "You can make it up to me when we get back to Caronath."

Soki clasped her hands behind his head, drew him down, and placed a kiss on his cheek. Then, quick as a cat, she bit his ear playfully.

"Ow!" he exclaimed.

She danced backward. "I can't wait for Caronath." She turned and, just as she was about to exit, said over her shoulder, "Be wary, Aldric Kermoran. I'd hate to lose you."

And she was gone into the fading sunlight, the door swinging shut behind her.

~ ~ ~

Aldric buckled on his khopesh belt and checked the relic again. The memories of one of the high priests of the Five from thousands of years ago was irreplaceable. Useless to anyone but a priest bearing the god's mark, but still there were collectors of curiosities who'd pay a good deal of royals for such a treasure. Valeria had obviously sensed it, from what she'd said, and couldn't contain her curiosity.

His questing fingers found the hard lump inside the pouch, felt the silver wire surrounding it, and he sighed. With the attack on Soki and then leaving Caronath as quickly as possible, he hadn't thought again about the archbishop's request to borrow the relic. But after the revelation about Grandmaster Shalmara, he needed to use the gemstone again as soon as possible.

Outside, dark clouds covered the sky, moving swiftly from the south. Aldric considered going back inside for his coat, but thought he'd grow warm enough with some sword forms to work out the kinks.

He asked an elderly woman with a bent back and a broad-brimmed hat woven from straw where he might find the others of his group. She was shuffling off to the fields, carrying a hoe in one hand and a walking stick in the other. She directed him to the cliffs a few hundred yards away. Aldric arrived in a bad mood, having stewed over Valeria's actions the whole way.

Then he spotted Bryn and Niklaus playing cards at a makeshift table. Each had a pile of copper coins in front of him, along with a tin cup, and empty bottles were strewn on the ground. A sheet of canvas stretched over a sapling framework protected them from the sun. Aldric felt his blood boil. Did they think this was a holiday? They were here to protect the settlers, not drink and gamble while they ordered them around.

"What in the hells do you think you're doing?" he raged at them.

Bryn glanced at Niklaus and spread his hands, as if it was the mercenary's fault. "Just a few games of Malice. It's better with five players, but it helps to pass the time."

Niklaus raised his eyebrows at Aldric, then took a sip from his cup. "Calm down. Things are well in hand here. Pull up a—"

"Why are you sitting around instead of training the settlers? It looks like a gambling den here. How much have you been drinking?"

Niklaus stood with a slight wobble. His cane was propped against his chair, Aldric saw, and his sword was strapped to his back.

"Anyone can teach them to poke a stick," the mercenary declared. "We need to be fresh for when there's fighting to be done. Besides, you've been doing what you want rather than helping."

Blood suffused Aldric's face. "I've been overseeing preparations and healing injuries among the settlers. And you're not resting, you're getting drunk!"

Niklaus waved a hand in dismissal. "You've left us to do the work while you indulged yourself, so don't complain if things aren't being done to your liking."

Bryn glanced at Niklaus as if he thought he'd crossed a line, but didn't say anything.

*So Bryn also thinks I've indulged myself*, Aldric thought. The settlers had needed his help. But ... perhaps he shouldn't have exhausted himself healing them. Still, that didn't make lounging around and drinking and gambling acceptable behavior.

"Stray Dog doesn't need any more timber," Aldric said. "It's the settlers that need the most help now. You should both be training them."

"Might as well try to train a monkey to wield a sword," sneered Niklaus.

Aldric suppressed an annoyed sigh. "They need all the help they can get. They're terrified of the Dead-eyes, and they're doing their best."

"We should have gone to find out where the Dead-eyes are coming from," said Niklaus.

"The settlers told us where the ruins are," Bryn told Aldric. "We should go and take a look now, while there's no action. There could be treasure there. Riches beyond your wildest dreams." He laughed.

"I don't need riches," said Niklaus. "I'll settle for a night with Priska once this is over."

Bryn sniggered lewdly, and Aldric felt heat rise to his face. Maybe it was his humiliation at Valeria's hands, but he couldn't let this pass.

"Don't come between her and Razmus," he told Niklaus. "They have enough problems without you interfering. You may have saved Razmus from the Dead-eyes last night, but don't push him, or me, too far." His hand moved to his khopesh hilt.

"I wouldn't," warned Bryn. "Not if you like your guts inside your belly."

Niklaus chuckled. "It was just a joke. Here, Aldric, have a drink."

He filled up an empty mug and handed it to Aldric.

"Three is better than two for Malice," Bryn said, gathering the cards into a pile. He began shuffling them, though seemed to be having trouble focusing. "Shit!"

Cards sprayed from the deck—and somehow Niklaus caught

them all in midair. One moment he was still, and the next his hands held the spilled cards.

"Damn it," Bryn said, staring at the cards he was still holding.

"Here you go," said Niklaus, his tone dry. "Shuffle them back in." He stood and checked his weapons. "Go and prepare for these new arrivals, Bryn, while Aldric and I check on the defenses again. I don't think you're in any condition to help at the moment, and we're expecting the visitors soon."

Aldric nodded at Niklaus, ignoring Bryn. "Let's go."

# CHAPTER THIRTY

# ADDITIONS

A FEW HOURS PAST midday, Aldric, Soki, Niklaus and the others watched as two riders approached Cherish from the south. The settlers had all made themselves scarce.

As the distance between the groups closed, Aldric noted the woman, riding ahead of her companion, was slight of build, with dark hair cropped short. The man was obviously a warrior, tall and broad-shouldered. He rode with the hilt of his sword close to his right hand and wore mail underneath his clothes. To Aldric's sorcerer-trained eyes they appeared normal, but to scry them to find out more about them would mean using dusk-tide power.

"Is either of them a sorcerer?" he asked Soki. "At this distance I can't tell."

She shook her head. "No. Unless they're extremely skilled at hiding it."

"Well, that's something." Aldric rolled his shoulders, which were stiff and sore. His head was fuzzy from not enough restful sleep. Not just the stress of the mission, but his use of the relic. And he really needed more time to recover from the exertions of his healing.

The woman rode awkwardly, seeming unused to horseback,

and looked haggard and her short hair stuck up in spikes. In contrast, the man rode smoothly, at ease and relaxed. As they neared, he urged his horse ahead of the woman's and halted it when still twenty yards away. He was clad in worn traveler's gear—thick pants and shirt, and a sturdy brown coat—though they were of surprising quality.

Aldric heard Bryn shift and glanced back to see him gripping the hilt of his sword, knuckles white, and staring at the big man. Stray Dog had also noticed and had a frown on his face.

"You know him, Bryn?" Aldric asked.

Bryn hesitated, then shook his head. "No. But I know a dangerous man when I see one."

Stray Dog grunted at Bryn's assessment.

Niklaus chuckled. "There's dangerous, and then there's dangerous."

"Greetings!" called the newcomer. "What town is this?"

His voice was strong and syrupy, and Aldric could see his bright blue eyes and chiseled features. He heard Soki mutter her approval, and Niklaus laughed again.

Aldric swallowed his annoyance and stepped forward. "This settlement is named Cherish," he said. "You're welcome here, both of you. The settlers are ... not the friendliest, but I'm sure they'll provide food and lodging for a few royals."

The man smiled and nodded. "Good. My name is Gannon. And this is Kurio. We need some rest. Especially my companion. She's had a rough time of it lately." His gaze traveled across the group, lingering for an instant on each of them. "This is a warm welcome."

Aldric heard the unspoken question in his words. Seven turned out to greet two travelers, if that was what they were.

"The settlers aren't as dour as Aldric here makes out," Soki called. "I'm Sokhelle."

"We have some tea brewing," added Valeria. "Not that it's very good. And we also have some questions for you."

Gannon dismounted smoothly and gestured for Kurio to do the same. She obeyed inelegantly and moved to join him, leading her horse. As they walked toward the group, Aldric found himself noting Gannon's similarities to Niklaus. Both had a fluid way of moving and a confidence that bordered on arrogance. He glanced at the man's sword hanging from his hip and saw it was plain and serviceable. Nothing unusual there.

The travelers stopped, and Gannon placed a hand on Kurio's shoulder. She frowned and glanced up at him, but didn't move away. Aldric saw that she wore a knife at her belt and a crossbow slung over her shoulder.

"Questions?" Gannon said. "About what? We're tired and hungry. Perhaps they can wait?"

"I'm afraid not," Aldric said. "We perceived sorcery last night from your location. And someone died."

"He was a pig," Kurio said. She ran a hand through her hair, and Aldric noticed red marks circling her wrist. Her hand dropped to touch a metal collar around her throat. "He tortured me. And if any of you get too close, I'll kill you."

"Now, now, that's no way to greet people, Kurio." Gannon turned to Aldric. "She's been through much over the last few days. Really, we just want to recuperate, and we'll be on our way."

"Recuperate?" scoffed Niklaus. "Then you've come to the wrong place. There's a horde of Dead-eyes about to descend upon us."

"I shouldn't think you'd have any trouble disposing of such pests," Gannon said. "Your little group looks more than capable of looking after itself and this quaint village."

"There was something else," Soki said. "I sensed a ... presence. An ancient being ... I'm not sure what exactly."

"Kurio," Gannon said, "perhaps you should tell them what happened to you and what you saw."

Kurio swallowed and nodded. "I was ... kidnapped," she began haltingly. "In Caronath. Some freak who ... I don't know what he planned for me, but ... it wasn't pleasant. He manacled my hands together. Kept me chained." She brandished her forearms at them. Her wrists were abraded raw. "Last night, in the dark, I ... freed myself."

There was more to this story, Aldric decided. She'd been kidnapped, yet she carried a crossbow and knife. Still, she might have stolen them from the man who was killed.

"He fell," Soki said. "Down a cliff."

Kurio's head jerked in a nod. "There was another who saw it. I think it was a wraithe. My ... captor called it one."

Another wraithe, and in so short a space of time, when Aldric had never before seen one? He'd put his encounter in the wilderness down to chance. But now he had the niggling thought that the meeting had been by design.

"What did it look like?" he asked.

"Frightening," Kurio said. "It kept its face obscured with a hood. It had powerful sorcery."

"So that's what we felt," muttered Soki.

"It spoke a language I didn't recognize. At least, it did at first. Then it switched to Nan-Rhouric. I'd thought the wraithes were myths. But ..." Kurio shrugged.

Aldric knew better, from his education, as would Soki. But to see a myth come to life must have been terrifying for this woman.

"Well, this 'old presence' you sensed is gone now," Gannon said. "Who knows what its purpose was? As for me, when I realized Kurio had been kidnapped, I trailed her and her tormentor from Caronath." He gave a wry smile. "Though it seems she didn't need my assistance. Such a talented woman. If I don't miss my guess, you have your own reasons for being here. Whatever they are, we won't stand in your way. Chance brought us here, and we'll leave as soon as we can."

"We could use an extra sword when the Dead-eyes come," Niklaus said.

"You're welcome to my help," Gannon said. "Fewer Dead-eyes will make for a brighter world. And that's what we all hope for, isn't it?"

"We'll be gone as soon as we can," echoed Kurio. "Maybe tomorrow. This fresh mountain air is already doing me good."

To Aldric, she looked pale and distraught.

"Then it's settled," Soki said brightly. "You're welcome here."

"As I said, there's tea brewing," said Valeria. "It's terrible, but you're welcome to it. Come, I want to hear more about this wraithe."

On the way to the meeting hall, Gannon traded small talk and banter with Soki, Bryn, and Aldric, and even managed to coax a slight smile from Priska. Niklaus was quiet, and as usual Stray Dog said nothing either. Inside, the newcomers settled by the fire, and Stray Dog added a few more logs to the coals. Valeria and Soki bustled around, and soon everyone had mugs of steaming tea to warm their hands.

"So you're the leader here?" Gannon said, his eyes meeting Aldric's, piercingly sharp. "You're a motley band, if you'll forgive my familiarity."

"My Church, and Niklaus's, sent a team to deal with the Dead-eyes plaguing the settlement," Aldric explained. "There's also a ruin close by, which I'd suggest you steer clear of."

"Of course," Gannon said. "I've heard terrible tales of the creatures that inhabit them, from the times before. And of what happens to foolish adventurers that attempt to loot them."

"I've heard some of the ruins are traps," Kurio added, surprising Aldric.

Gannon gave her a sharp look.

"Where did you hear that?" Soki asked curiously.

Kurio shrugged and took a sip of tea. "A scholar at the

university in Caronath. He said some of the ruins caused the cataclysms. It sounded unbelievable to me."

"You were right to be skeptical," Gannon said. "Valeria, my dear, could I please have more of that delicious tea?"

"I'd hardly call it delicious," said Valeria, jumping up to pour more for him. "But I did my best." She smiled at him, and he raised his mug to her.

"During my days in the wilderness chasing after Kurio," he said, "all I drank was pine needles steeped in water."

Valeria gave a mock shudder.

"Surely your situation wasn't that dire?" said Soki.

"A little poetic license," Gannon said, and the two women laughed.

Aldric didn't join in their merriment. The attitude of the two travelers to each other made him wary. Gannon acted as if they were old friends, yet Kurio looked at him all doe-eyed, and she sat so close as to be almost touching him. She looked fairly uneasy with everyone else though. Perhaps her behavior was a result of all she'd been through since her abduction.

~ ~ ~

The rest of the afternoon passed quickly, with Aldric, Niklaus, Bryn, Stray Dog, and now Gannon going over maneuvers with the settlers to ensure they were clear about what they needed to do. Last night's incursion had happened when they were disorganized, and they didn't want a repeat of the confusion.

They ran through the spear drills again and showed the settlers how to wield pitchforks against the fast-moving Dead-eyes. But with any luck, Aldric thought, the settlers would only have to clean up the Dead-eyes the experienced warriors missed, or those that breached the defenses. Soki's and Priska's sorcery would help on that account, by shielding the barricades to further deter the creatures.

By the end of the afternoon, most of the settlers were in a foul mood after being sworn at by Niklaus and Bryn.

"Enough!" called Aldric. "We all need to rest. Everyone, go home, and catch a couple of hours sleep if you can; then we'll meet just before sunset. It'll be a long night, but gods willing, you'll all make it through. Then the threat of the Dead-eyes will be gone."

There was worried muttering among the settlers.

"Did you think this would be easy?" Niklaus shouted at them. "One night! That's all you have to get through. Do you have the balls to last one night?"

The settlers left scowling, clutching their simple weapons as if they were talismans.

"A surly bunch," remarked Gannon. "I would have thought that with the Dead-eyes coming, they'd welcome having you around. Although a few like that Drusst fellow seem to have taken a shine to you."

"Bloody farmers," said Bryn. "Sheep who fear the wolf, then when they find another wolf to protect them, they fear it too. Dirt grubbers. No thought to the future." His eyes flicked to Gannon, then away.

"It is best to consider your future," said Gannon. "At least I find it so. Age creeps up on you, doesn't it?" He laughed softly. "As warriors, our strength is fleeting."

"None of us are old men yet," snapped Bryn.

"But we will be," Gannon said. "That's my point. Time wearies every man."

Niklaus shrugged. "Most warriors don't get to take their last breath lying in bed."

"This talk is too maudlin for me," Aldric said, turning away. "I still need to see what sorcery Soki and Priska have come up with for the barricades before I can rest."

He was tired, and the reality was, he still didn't know who he could trust. If he was honest, everyone was an unknown foisted on him by his Church.

On the way back to the meeting hall, Gannon clasped Aldric's arm. "I need a quiet word," he said. "Away from the others."

"What is troubling you?" Aldric asked.

To his surprise, he found himself with a cant at the ready. Was it coincidence that Gannon and Kurio had arrived in Cherish just before full-dark? Or something more sinister?

Gannon remained silent until the others were out of earshot. When he turned to Aldric, his expression was one of pure misery. A flock of birds erupted from trees to swarm the sky, their shadows flickering over the fields.

"How much danger are we in?" he asked. "I have to know."

Aldric shrugged. "Not much, I hope. We've prepared as best we can, and we have a few skilled warriors and sorcerers to fight the Dead-eyes."

Gannon nodded and clasped his hands together as if nervous. "It's Kurio I'm worried about. When she was taken, I was beside myself. I felt physically sick. But I didn't let my fear control me. Instead, I asked around and was lucky. Coin loosens tongues."

Aldric waited, not sure why Gannon was confiding in him.

"I discovered that she'd been taken north from Caronath, and again I was lucky—I caught up to them a few days later. But by then, it was all over. Kurio had rescued herself."

"You care for her," Aldric said softly. It made the stranger less of an enigma. His distress at Kurio's fate showed he was as vulnerable as anyone. For it was clear to Aldric that he loved Kurio.

Gannon nodded, still not meeting Aldric's gaze. "I'll fight alongside you," he said. "I've killed a few Dead-eyes in my time, and another blade might make all the difference. I want to protect Kurio, and the settlers of course. I just ... I wanted you to know why I'm here, my motivation. You can count on me."

He looked up then, his bright blue eyes piercing Aldric's.

"Good," Aldric said. "I understand how it feels to care for someone, to want to protect them."

And once the Dead-eyes had been dealt with, Gannon and Kurio would travel back to Caronath and leave the rest of them to finish up the mission.

"Is there someone back in Caronath waiting for you?" Gannon asked. "Family?"

Aldric shook his head. "I have no wife. My role with my Church keeps me busy, and I travel often. My family is far away, in a village just outside Nagorn City."

"You're a long way from home. It sounds like you lead a hard life. When you're back in Caronath, you should come to my home for dinner. I'm a decent cook, and a taste of family life will do you good."

"I'd like that. Thank you."

"So, no siblings?"

"I have a sister, Kittara. She's growing up too fast—she's headstrong."

Gannon chuckled. "As we all were at that age."

"I guess. She chafes at the fact she has to help on the farm."

"Well, I'm sure she'll settle down, like all adolescents. She's ... not a sorcerer like you?"

Aldric frowned. "How did you know?"

"Your talisman. It's a giveaway."

"So it is. No, my sister isn't a sorcerer. And at her age, I don't think she'll manifest any power."

"Such things can happen though. At least so I was taught," Gannon said.

Aldric was surprised by the reply. Gannon must have had a good education to know this fact. Then again, his costly clothes and erudition showed he'd grown up wealthy, so perhaps it wasn't so astonishing.

"It's rare," he admitted. "A long time ago, it was less so."

When Nysrog's demons had somehow pushed people with latent sorcerous ability into fully functioning sorcerers. It was one reason they'd gained so many followers. The lure of arcane power was great among the weak-willed and a reward few had thought possible.

"I'd better get back," he said to Gannon. "Thank you for confiding in me. I appreciate it."

"It's the least I could do. It seems we're all in this together."

~ ~ ~

The sun descended inexorably, and the dusk-tide washed over Aldric. Usually he preferred privacy, but didn't want to wander outside alone as full-dark approached. He gave a violent shudder as he reluctantly availed himself of its resonance, replenishing his repository. He might need all the power he could muster for the fighting ahead.

"Are you all right?" Kurio asked him.

He'd not even noticed she was in the room. His gaze seemed to slide right over her unless he concentrated. Perhaps it was because she was so still and covered by blankets.

Aldric gave her a reassuring smile to cover his surprise. "I'm fine. Just a chill. So tell me, what do you do in Caronath?"

She gave him a sidelong look. "I find things for people. It doesn't pay much, but it keeps me in food and shelter."

"I guess what I'm trying to ask is, can you look after yourself when the Dead-eyes come? That crossbow: did you take it off the man who kidnapped you?"

He noticed her hand stray to touch a strange turtle figurine attached to her belt. "Yes. It looks well made," she said. "I thought perhaps I could sell it."

"If you don't mind," Aldric said, "I could heal your wrists. It won't take long and only a little power."

"I ... I'd like that."

"And your collar ... Did he put that on you? There's a blacksmith here. Perhaps he could remove it?"

"Perhaps." One of her fingers tugged at the metal band. "Do your healing, then. But don't expect any favors."

Blood suffused Aldric's face. "I wouldn't ... I won't ask anything of you."

"I'm sorry. I'm a bit prickly at the moment."

Taking Kurio's hand in his, he found it firm and hard, as if she wasn't used to a sedentary life. Her palms were abraded and red.

"Breathe," he said. "Stay calm, and let Menselas flow through you."

"What?"

"My god. My power to heal comes from him. Just as other gods and goddesses gift power to their priests and priestesses."

"And demons? Where do they get their power?"

Aldric involuntarily squeezed her hand before he caught himself. "What do you know of demons? You mean the man who ..."

"Tortured me? Of a sort. It doesn't matter."

Menselas's power washed through Aldric. Warm, calm, joyful. Strangely, he could not apply it to Kurio, as if something about her repulsed the god's power. He delved deeper to find the cause of the resistance. Her blood ... it was tainted with something he'd never seen before.

Menselas's power suddenly surged, and the cuts and redness on Kurio's wrists diminished, then faded to old marks. Her palms smoothed, and she gasped.

"There," Aldric said gently. "Isn't that better?"

She jerked her hand from his. "Yes. Thank you."

Weariness settled over Aldric. He shouldn't have healed this close to the Dead-eyes' incursion. But Kurio had pain in her eyes, and she'd been through so much.

"When you're back in Caronath," he said, "if you need help, with anything, look for me at the Church of the Five."

Kurio nodded, not saying anything.

"I felt something," Aldric said cautiously, "in your blood. There's something amiss."

She glared at him, eyes hard, and snapped, "Mind your own business." Then looked away, sullen and distant.

"Aldric!" called Niklaus from outside. "Neb wants you!"

Aldric squeezed Kurio's shoulder. "I'm sorry. You'll be fine. It'll all be over by morning."

~ ~ ~

As more of the strangers returned to the hall, Kurio felt uncomfortable among a growing crowd. She escaped to a nearby stream and took her time washing. She didn't have a change of clothes, so had to put her dusty and sweat-stinking shirt and pants back on, but at least she felt more human.

*If human I am …*

Remembering Aldric had noticed the turtle on her belt, she transferred it to a pocket, then walked around the settlement—Cherish, they called it—looking at the wooden defense barricades, with a funnel to guide the Dead-eyes into a cleared space. Although most of the settlers were resting, a few were being drilled by the middle-aged man named Razmus and Bryn, a wiry swordsman who moved gracefully. His bearing and ease with his slightly curved sword spoke volumes: she knew a killer when she saw one. As she strolled past, she noticed his silver sword pommel was carved with a hideously disfigured face. Not to her taste, but most men thought details like that fleshed out a picture of themselves they wanted the world to see.

Kurio had the figure of a boy and wasn't wearing skirts, but that didn't stop the settlers from staring at her and making comments. They were used to seeing the same women day in, day out, she thought, and the sight of someone new had made them forget their manners. Eager for solitude, she filched two apples from a passing cart, tucked them into her shirt, and scrambled up the side of a building and perched on its roof.

The apples were deliciously tart and full of flavor, but the view was uninspiring. Farmland and crops, animals and trees. Settlers hurrying from building to building, preparing for the Dead-eyes as if an entire army was about to invade their shithole in the woods. Somewhere behind her a woman shouted, and something thumped against the side of the building.

Kurio nibbled on the apple core. There was a time soon after she'd run away from her parents when an apple core would have been a luxury. Not that she'd gone hungry, but rats and pigeons were far more plentiful than fresh fruit.

"Fancy meeting you here," a woman said.

Kurio turned to see the severe-faced priestess standing on the roof, her skirt hitched up to reveal slender ankles that were so white they mustn't have seen the light of day for quite some time. What was interesting was that Kurio hadn't heard her climbing up, which would have been a feat in that skirt.

"Are you a sorcerer?" she asked.

"Oh, goodness, no. There was a ladder close by, and I politely asked for assistance from some of the young men avoiding work."

Kurio snorted in amusement. That explained the shouting and the thump. "Careful up here," she said. "It's getting dark. What do you want?"

"So blunt," Valeria said.

She gingerly shuffled along the sloping roof and sat down next to Kurio, arranging her skirt over her legs. Her nails were painted a dark purple. This close, Kurio could see her clothes were made of quality cloth, and she had silver chains braided into her long hair. Priestessing must pay well.

"Aren't you helping with the preparations?" Kurio asked.

"I've done all I can. Now it's up to the warriors and settlers to defend the place against the Dead-eyes." She shrugged. "It won't be hard, and then we can investigate the ruin."

"What ruin?"

The ruin was why Mellish had brought her all the way out here, but Kurio wondered why it was of interest to Valeria.

Valeria stared at her for a long moment. "You really don't know? Never mind, then. Tomorrow, you and your friend can be on your way. He's quite attractive, isn't he?"

Kurio half shrugged. "Some women would say that."

"Well, I did say that," said Valeria. "But I'm not here to talk about him. Does he know about your necklace? About the pain it can cause you?"

For an instant, Kurio couldn't breathe, her chest tight. It took a few heartbeats for the sensation to pass. When it did, she tossed the remains of her apple core off the roof, aiming for, and missing, an old man in stained, rough-spun clothes. Wiping her hand on her pants, she felt for the turtle in her pocket to make sure it was still there.

"What do you know about it?" Her words came out softer than she'd intended.

"I know it was stolen from our church, one of a few. The thieves had no idea what they were taking. How you come to be wearing it, I couldn't begin to guess. But I can imagine what you've been through. When you escaped, did you take the triggering artifact? It's in the shape of a turtle."

"No," said Kurio automatically.

"It was the man you killed, wasn't it, who gifted you with such pain? You must have a talent or knowledge he wanted to use; otherwise why put the collar on you. What is it?"

Kurio didn't like that the priestess had figured out so much about her. And calling the agony of the collar a "gift" was absurd.

"I could tell you," she said, "for enough coin."

"How about I remove the collar instead? My Church will pay a handsome sum to get it back."

It didn't require much thought to agree. She hated the collar. Hated Mellish and Zarina for forcing it on her. Her only regret was that Mellish's death had been relatively quick.

"Remove it, please," she said. "But I'll return it to your Church myself."

"You'll have to. It has tasted your pain now." Valeria reached up to touch the collar. To Kurio's surprise, it tingled and warmed, then opened with a metallic snick. She pulled it free and held it in her palms. It looked so innocuous, so plain, for something that caused such agony.

"What was it like?" asked Valeria.

"Wearing the collar?"

"No. The pain. I've heard it's exquisite."

Kurio stared at the priestess. She must be mad. Maybe everyone was, even Kurio herself. "It was … intense."

Valeria's fingers trailed across the thin metal, and she leaned close. "During the pain, did you sense her?"

Kurio drew away. She had thought she'd felt someone, but it had been a hallucination caused by the agony.

"Who?" she asked.

"The goddess. The Lady Sylva Kalisia." Valeria clasped her hands together. "I see you're reluctant to talk about it. Perhaps you'll be more amenable tomorrow."

She made to rise, but before she left, words tumbled from Kurio. "His name was Mellish, the man who used the collar on me. But he's dead now. I killed him."

"Good. Was there anyone else?"

Kurio nodded. "A woman. Zarina. She was the one who put it

around my neck. They said they belonged to the Order of the Blazing Sun."

"Ah ... I have heard of them. They're diminished, but still manage to make a nuisance of themselves. Thank you for that information. I'll notify my Church when I return to Caronath. This woman—did she happen to be wearing an amulet made from orichalcum? One with tiny Skanuric runes etched over its surface?"

Kurio had to stop her hand from moving to touch the amulet where it rested between her breasts. She shook her head slowly. "Sorry."

Valeria released a heavy sigh. "Are you sure? It would look something like this." She drew out an amulet from under her shirt. It looked exactly like the one Kurio had taken from Mellish. "It was also stolen from us. Only high priestesses wear them, and they ... bestow certain benefits."

"I didn't see anything like that," Kurio said.

"Well," said Valeria, "ask for me when you bring the collar back to our church."

She smiled at Kurio, then gingerly made her way back down the roof to the ladder.

Kurio returned to looking out over Cherish and beyond. She had a creeping suspicion that more had passed between her and Valeria than she was aware of.

And had she really sensed a goddess in the midst of all that pain?

# CHAPTER THIRTY-ONE

# BLOOD AND SORCERY

FULL-DARK DESCENDED ON CHERISH. Chandra, usually the first moon to rise, stayed below the horizon, as did the red orb of Jagonath. Only a milky band of stars crossed the pitch-black sky. The background hum of the night was abnormally quiet. Without the moons' glow, nocturnal animals didn't come out to hunt. Even the crickets were silent.

In long-forgotten ruins and crypts, this was the time the undead rose. And in the wilderness, the Dead-eyes were at their boldest and most ravenous.

They came shortly before midnight.

Soki sent incandescent globes spiraling into the night, slicing away the darkness and bathing the areas outside the settlement in radiant light. One globe would have exhausted Aldric, but Soki sent one after the other, explaining the calculations and methods of their creation to Priska between complex cants. Aldric couldn't help but gape in awe at her skill.

The settlers crouched behind the barricades, fearful and trembling. Some cried out in admiration at the spectacle of Soki's sorcery of such power they'd never witnessed, bleaching the night. But most were too scared to do more than mutter imprecations and grip their weapons in white-knuckled hands.

Aldric positioned himself between two buildings in one of the openings they'd left, with Niklaus, Bryn, Razmus, and Stray Dog around him. From here they could see where the Dead-eyes were more numerous and position themselves to take the brunt of the attack.

Valeria had disappeared, likely hiding somewhere until the fight was all over. Gannon had volunteered to stand by the hall with Kurio for support, to reinforce any settlers who looked to be in difficulty.

A few settlers cried out and pointed. Others howled in terror. Someone threw a spear over a barricade; it landed barely twenty paces away.

In the distance, pouring down the cliff sides, came the Dead-eyes. Not dozens, but *hundreds*. More than the trees of the forest. Carpeting the fields like a plague of locusts. White flesh, stick limbs, fanged mouths, and a thousand staring boiled-egg eyes. A mass keening wail erupted from the creatures, knifing the air with inhuman hunger. Driven by some primal urge as old as time, they had come to feast on flesh, to crack bones for their soft marrow, to defile and desecrate.

"Shit, shit, shit," hissed Bryn.

"The barricades will be useless," Stray Dog said flatly.

He was right, realized Aldric. There was no way they'd be able to hold the barricades. No chance they'd kill all of the Dead-eyes and leave Cherish unscathed. There were simply too many of them.

"Get back!" he shouted to the settlers. "Back to the houses!"

"Which houses?" yelled Drusst, the miller. His eyes were wild, mouth twisted in fear.

Aldric didn't know. He hadn't planned for this. Where had they all come from? He'd never seen or heard of this many Dead-eyes attacking before.

"It doesn't matter," shouted Niklaus. "We'll protect the retreat and clear the streets. Just run!"

"Bryn and Stray Dog, form a line with us, and we'll give the settlers time to escape," Aldric said. "Soki!" he yelled. Sorcery, his nemesis, was the only force that could save them now.

"I see them!" she answered from somewhere behind and above them.

Aldric turned and saw that Soki and Priska had climbed onto a roof, their feet planted on either side of its peak. Soki snarled a cant, and Priska followed her lead. Dawn-tide and dusk-tide sorcery combined, a potent, complex mix. Globe after globe appeared above Soki, each burning with furious layered-orange intensity. Moments after they materialized, they arced through the air with an earsplitting howl. Priska's globes were smaller and wobbly, but they too darted away from the now chanting sorcerers to land outside the settlement. There was a sudden glare and a muffled detonation. The trees cracked like twigs, and Dead-eyes were blown sideways. Some tumbled lifeless to the ground while others clutched at gaping wounds. Some flamed like burning torches, screeching in their incomprehensible tongue. Still more flinched and ducked, crawling on their bellies.

Another globe struck. Then another. A rain of fire and death fell upon the horde of Dead-eyes, a sorcerer at the height of her power scorching the earth with furious cants.

The Dead-eyes thrashed and cracked and burned in the dozens. Their wails and screeches intensified into an incoherent roar. But still more of the creatures came, scrambling between trees, among rocks, clambering around the devastation. A pale tide of rushing inhumanity.

The first one clambered up an outer barricade, clawing at the recently hewn logs, a silhouette lit against scourging arcane energy. Then, like a breaking thunderstorm, they came as a deluge of howling maws and scrabbling talons.

"Hold the line!" Aldric shouted. "Watch your back!" Where

were Gannon and Kurio? He couldn't see them anywhere.

"Bloody hells," growled Stray Dog, his twin axes weaving as he readied himself.

"Goddess damn you, Niklaus," Bryn said through clenched teeth. "There'd better be treasure after we've slaughtered these maggots."

Razmus's face was grim, his eyes constantly flicking to Priska and back to the approaching Dead-eyes. "I'll stand with the settlers," he said. "If I'm there, they'll be less afraid. I'll make sure they don't run."

He dashed off to the group of settlers waiting by the killing ground behind the barricades.

Aldric drew his khopesh, the silvered blade shining in the gloom. "He's right. We need to protect the settlers and the women and children."

"Like hells!" Bryn snarled. "We need to hole up somewhere too!"

"Scared, Bryn?" Niklaus laughed. "I didn't pick you for a pants-pisser! Run, then!" He drew his short sword in his left hand, his cane tucked into his belt.

Dead-eyes flowed over the barricades, their spiderlike stick limbs creating a grotesque backdrop.

Niklaus took a step forward and reached for his chest strap. In one swift movement, the sword on his back swung down to his hip, and he drew the blade. It shone like moonlight on a river. Aldric saw sorcerous runes stamped on the first third of the steel and caught a glimpse of a winged woman.

"Watch your own backs," Niklaus said, then raced toward the horde.

Bryn and Stray Dog both looked at Aldric. *Holy Menselas, we should remain together.*

"Stay here," Aldric commanded them. "Niklaus!" he shouted.

Small orange globes landed among the creatures inside the

barricade—Priska's sorcery—while Soki's more potent spheres continued to rain down outside the settlement. Aldric knew Soki wouldn't risk using her deadly sorcery so close to them, so she was doing as much damage as she could before resorting to finer arcane weavings.

The first of the Dead-eyes struck at Niklaus. They moved fast, gangly limbs slashing and pointed teeth chomping. Niklaus moved faster, his blades a shimmering blur, his long sword leaving a swathe of light in its wake. Dead-eyes engulfed him. Their crazed faces shrieked, and their milky blood sprayed all around. Niklaus stood firm, an immovable rock. The mercenary's ability was unmatched. Nothing would get past him. He was an anchor they could all tie to.

"Let's go!" Aldric cried. "To Niklaus."

He, Bryn, and Stray Dog rushed to join the fray. Aldric slashed with his khopesh, battering the snarling faces all around. They fell, wailing, only to be immediately replaced. Soon he and his companions were slipping in mud formed from the creatures' blood. Stray Dog's axes weaved and hacked, his face sheened with sweat. Bryn danced and leaped in a vicious display of skill.

But they'd done little to stem the tide.

Niklaus surged forward a few steps, but Aldric noticed the Dead-eyes were slipping past them, ignoring the bulwark of death they'd created.

"The settlers," he gasped, and coughed against the gut-wrenching stench of gore.

He glanced behind to check on Soki and Priska. Both were surrounded by spherical shields that repelled the few Dead-eyes that climbed onto the roof. Soki raised her hand and shouted a cant. Sorcery blasted along the roof and swept three Dead-eyes to the ground.

Niklaus's laughter reached Aldric. The mercenary's blades blurred in an intricate dance of steel, felling several more Dead-eyes.

"They're thinning out here," Aldric called to him. "They're avoiding us. They know we're the danger."

Screams and terrified shouts sounded as Dead-eyes fought their way inside the houses. Two homes were alight, flames licking across their roofs. Aldric didn't know whether the settlers were using fire to fight the Dead-eyes, or if the creatures had knocked over lamps or cooking fires. A group of women and children ran from one of the burning houses, escorted by a few men. He recognized one of them as Alvar, still in his noticeable straw hat.

"Alvar!" roared Stray Dog. "Get inside!" Blood dripped from numerous cuts on his arms.

Other settlers milled around, filled with terror. One woman screamed continuously, her shrill cries rising above the tumult.

A Dead-eye leaped out of the darkness to cling onto a man's back, its pointed teeth latching onto the nape of his neck. Alvar beat at it with a club, to no avail.

"Damn it," snarled Stray Dog, then broke into a sprint toward them.

"We need to retreat!" Aldric shouted, panting hoarsely.

A Dead-eye lunged at him, and he felt a burning pain as its talons opened a gash along his forearm. He slashed his crescent blade through its skull.

A strangled cry came from Bryn, and Aldric saw him press a palm to the mangled cloth and flesh of his thigh. They were vastly outnumbered. No matter their skill, they couldn't last against this many Dead-eyes for long. Their injuries would accumulate, and eventually they'd all fall.

Two more Dead-eyes leaped at Aldric. He spoke a cant of protection, and they bounced off the sphere of sorcerous energy that suddenly surrounded him.

Niklaus hacked one of the creatures into the earth, and Bryn skewered the other.

"They should be running scared," Bryn said. "Why aren't they?"

Aldric realized Bryn was right. After such slaughter of their kind, the Dead-eyes usually ran. They must be being directed ... presumably by a wraithe.

Bryn parried a clawed hand and thrust his blade into the creature's chest. Fangs clamped around his ankle, and he cried out. Aldric slashed his khopesh down and severed the head from the spindly neck. Bryn swore as the jaws stayed clamped to his boot. He kicked the air a few times until they dropped off.

Only Niklaus remained unscathed. Not a single Dead-eye had been able to penetrate the deadly sphere his steel traced.

~ ~ ~

Stray Dog had managed to escort the group of settlers to another house, but the occupants weren't opening up. Three of the settlers carried the now unconscious man with the bloodied back, whose head lolled. Dog's axes hacked into another Dead-eye as it came at them, the sharp blades making short work of its gangling form.

"Open the bloody door!" shouted Dog. He hammered on it again before giving up.

Three more Dead-eyes came at the group, and Alvar joined Dog to fend them off the settlers. Stray Dog dropped one axe and latched onto a white leg before it disappeared into a broken window. He yanked the Dead-eye half out and hacked into its back until it was still.

A woman's screams came from inside the house. Dog looked around and saw no Dead-eyes were close to him, but more were racing toward the settlers close by. Stray Dog leaped at them and hacked viciously, claws raking his arms before he sent another two Dead-eyes lifeless to the dirt. Then he saw Alvar facing off against three of the creatures. It was too many—

"Alvar!" he roared, and pushed between two settlers to get to the boy and the three Dead-eyes.

Alvar thrust his sharp pole at one, which jumped back, but he wasn't quick enough to stop the other two coming at him from either side. They jumped at him, clawing and biting. Alvar cried out, dropping his pole and punching and kicking while the Dead-eyes savaged him.

Stray Dog leaped at them, axes thudding into white flesh. He screamed wordlessly, hacking at the Dead-eyes until they dropped.

Stray Dog fell to his knees and cradled Alvar's inert form. "Aldric!" he screamed. The priest could heal Alvar. But even so … Stray Dog could tell the boy was injured beyond saving. There was nothing he, nor anyone, could do.

*Too late.* Tears streamed down his face. *I'm too late. As always.* Too late to save his son, which was why he'd had to leave his wife. He couldn't face her after.

~ ~ ~

*The sooner I'm gone from this goddess-awful place, the better,* thought Valeria.

A snarling Dead-eye rushed toward her, and she let loose with her goddess's power. The creature howled like a dog run over by a wagon and writhed on the ground.

Valeria gritted her teeth against the pain; a reverberation of what she'd caused the Dead-eye to feel. The goddess's gifts came with their own attachments, one of them being her gifted priestesses felt a portion of the agony they inflicted. It had made for some interesting times during her training, when she and her fellow acolytes had tested each other to see who could withstand the most pain.

Frightened faces peered at Valeria through a window of Matron Hazel's cottage—some of the young women she'd been grooming for the goddess. One of them waved, a gesture Valeria didn't return. She glanced up at the roof of the cottage, where about a dozen Dead-eyes were tearing at the shingles. It wouldn't take them long to force their way inside. She wracked one with her goddess's power, though at this distance it took a few moments to take effect. The creature danced a strange jig on the roof before falling off and crashing to the ground, where it twitched feebly.

A surge of weariness washed over Valeria. She'd had to use the goddess's power more than a few times and she was reaching the limit of her abilities. She couldn't afford to save the women, and perhaps that was Sylva Kalisia's will. Cherish had proven a barren ground for women suited to following the goddess. They were just too plain and unintelligent. Apart from Shand, who'd tried to hide her contempt for the other women her age, and failed miserably. Valeria wondered briefly where the young woman was during the attack.

Screams rose from Matron Hazel's cottage as the Dead-eyes broke through the roof. The stick-limbed creatures tore at the edges of the hole, sending shingles and thin timbers flying. Then they squirmed through and disappeared from sight. Within moments, blood smeared the glass as the Dead-eyes sated their hunger.

*A waste of time,* thought Valeria. *I shouldn't have bothered, and just focused on Niklaus.*

She turned her back on the cottage, almost out of energy. She needed to get out of the fray—if she could just get back to the meeting hall until the excitement was over.

~ ~ ~

Razmus shoved his makeshift spear into the open mouth of a Dead-eye. It made a gurgling noise and clawed at the shaft. He twisted and gave the pole another shove, then jerked it back. The Dead-eye fell lifeless to the ground, adding its milky blood to the rest seeping into the earth.

Around him, the Dead-eyes' corpses were two and three thick as the brave settlers did their best to weather the savage onslaught. To Razmus's left stood Drusst and to his right was Uvagen, their shoulders touching as they stood with the settlers and created a wall of spears to repel the Dead-eyes.

Wild-eyed settlers yelled between gasping breaths. Not used to fighting, let alone mass combat such as this, their nerves were worn thin. But fear held them in place. Fear of dying, and fear of their families being killed.

"Hold the line!" Razmus shouted. "And hold onto your knives!"

Each of the settlers held a blade in their right hand, a backup weapon in case any Dead-eyes got close. Where had all the Dead-eyes come from? It wasn't natural. There had to be at least four tribes fighting together, when usually they kept to their own hunting grounds.

Dozens of the creatures came at their spear line, shrieking and howling, their sightless eyes somehow able to see, claws tearing at the settlers. One broke through, dodging panicked spear thrusts, and was stabbed with knives before it could do more than take a chunk of flesh from a young man's leg. Lavst, Razmus realized. Lavst collapsed, creating a break in the spear line.

"Get him out of there!" shouted Razmus. "Close the line or the Dead-eyes'll get through!"

Lavst was dragged clear, and the settlers bunched together to close the gap. Razmus hoped they'd somehow get Lavst to Aldric. But with the chaos the night had quickly descended into, he doubted it.

More snarling Dead-eyes came at them. Razmus and Drusst and Uvagen thrust their spears again and again and again, piercing chests and guts and throats.

A despairing cry rose from their left, and Razmus saw the line collapse as a wave of Dead-eyes overran the settlers. Neb, who was in charge of the left, was borne to the ground by three Dead-eyes that tore at his head and shoulders with talons and fangs. Men and women fell beneath pale-limbed creatures, who savaged flesh and lapped at the blood.

"There's too many," said Drusst.

"Fall back!" Razmus ordered. "Put your backs to a wall or we're all lost."

Some of the settlers raised their spears and turned to flee.

*Damnation!* "Get those spears back down!" Razmus roared.

But it was too late.

A stream of Dead-eyes pelted toward Razmus, limbs flailing. Before he could react, they flowed like a white wave over the terrified settlers.

Uvagen broke the line and rushed to reinforce them.

"No!" Razmus shouted.

Their defensive formation had been broken, and now it was every settler for himself. Uvagen disappeared under countless Dead-eyes, his spear swinging wildly.

Razmus grabbed Drusst's arm and shoved him toward a house behind them. "Get as many inside as you can. I'll hold them off."

"But—"

"Do it!" He gave the big man another heave and turned back to the oncoming Dead-eyes.

As the first came at him, time seemed to slow. Razmus thrust his spear through its stomach, then tugged his weapon out. Blood spilled along with ichor. But more savage mouths replaced it, each wailing like the damned, baying for flesh to sate their appetites.

Someone stood at his left, guarding his vulnerable side. The girl, Shand, her mouth drawn into a thin line.

"Get out of here," said Razmus.

"No."

Razmus was about to order her to leave when more Dead-eyes attacked. He thrust his spear into them, fighting alongside her. Thrust again. Two more down.

Razmus stepped to the side and swiped at a Dead-eye that had managed to get close. His shaft connected with its head with a sickening crunch, but as it fell, another latched onto his arm. Needles of pain shot through him as its pointed teeth sank to the bone. His hand lost all feeling and the spear slipped from its grasp. He shoved his knife into its throat, but the Dead-eye wouldn't let go and dragged him to the ground.

*No. Priska, where is she?*

Agony flared in his leg as another Dead-eye swiped its claws and left three long gashes.

*Gods, where is Priska? Is she safe?*

Razmus saw Shand screaming as Dead-eyes latched onto her arms and legs. Her crimson blood spilled to the earth and she fell.

Taloned hands held him down as more and more Dead-eyes gnawed at his flesh. Razmus twisted, trying to squirm out of their grasp. To no avail.

*Priska ...*

~ ~ ~

The creatures still clambered over the barricade, but none rushed toward them. Instead, they split into streams, racing to all parts of the settlement. A yawning pit opened in Aldric's stomach. He had failed to protect Cherish. He glanced around, desperately seeking a solution, at the same time knowing all was lost.

They were cut off from the rest of the settlers.

He saw Razmus disappear under a tide of Dead-eyes before another wave came at him. He defended himself as best he could, using bursts of both dawn-tide and dusk-tide sorcery to protect them all when the avalanche became too much. His reticence to use the dark power had fled when he'd realized he'd failed.

"More Dead-eyes to kill." Niklaus laughed. "Neb's going to be pleased."

"Not if he's dead," said Bryn, wrenching his blade from a caved-in skull.

Bryn slipped on viscera, stumbling to one knee. A Dead-eye leaped over him and lunged for Niklaus, its claws raking down the mercenary's back. Niklaus pivoted, a snarl on his face as he rammed his short blade into the creature's chest.

They were going to be overrun, just like Razmus and the spearmen.

Aldric spoke a cant. Sorcery flared, and a globe surrounded them, pushing back the tide of Dead-eyes enough to give them a moment's respite.

Niklaus trod on a Dead-eye's leg to prevent it scrambling away while Bryn stabbed it through the eye. Bryn bent over his sword, chest heaving, face dripping sweat.

*Stray Dog,* Aldric thought frantically. *Where is he?*

He saw the big man twenty yards away, batting a Dead-eye aside, trying to keep it away from a corpse on the ground. Alvar, Aldric realized. More Dead-eyes threw themselves at Stray Dog, savaging his flesh.

All around, pale figures flashed through the night. Shouts and screams filled the air, and many of the houses were alight, casting a wavering orange glow across the settlement. Flickering lights and explosions continued to erupt around the perimeter as Soki and Priska wrought sorcerous destruction. Dead-eyes thudded against Aldric's ward and almost overcame it. He chanted a cant of strengthening, then tapped into a trickle of his dusk-tide power to maintain the sorcery.

"Where's Sokhelle and Priska?" Niklaus shouted. "We need them!"

"Too far away. They can't hear us over this noise." And if he didn't do something now, Stray Dog would soon be dead. Quashing his fear, Aldric reached for his dusk-tide power and felt its darkness suffuse him. He recalled ancient chants he'd learned from the Evokers but had never dared to use before. Dark power flowed through him, more than he'd ever used. He almost retched at its foul touch.

He spoke a few words, and a clap of thunder sounded. Dead-eyes flew through the air, emitting shrieks as they crashed to the ground, and their bones shattered. Aldric dropped his wards.

Niklaus gave a savage laugh, his face and clothes splashed with the creatures' pale blood. "That's better!" He rushed toward the mass of Dead-eyes that were brutalizing the settlers.

Aldric grabbed Bryn, who staggered beside him, almost spent, and they followed Niklaus. The mercenary's blades were already carving into Dead-eyes. Aldric's khopesh joined the fray while Bryn guarded their backs. Together, the three of them dispatched Dead-eyes, leaving a scene of devastation.

Only a few settlers survived, and they had terrible wounds that guaranteed a slow death. One man clamped a hand over his shoulder, his arm hanging by a strip of flesh. A woman crawled across the blood-soaked earth, clothes and skin shredded.

Razmus lay unmoving, his eyes staring. His throat was gashed open, and his chest was painted scarlet.

Stray Dog struggled to his feet, his arms and legs a mass of bites and cuts, all dripping blood. Aldric wondered if he would make it through the night. If infection set in to any of those wounds, he was sure to die.

"Razmus is gone, along with Shand," Niklaus said, almost gently.

"Poor guy," Bryn said. "He's been unlucky."

"I can heal—" began Aldric.

"There's no time!" said Niklaus. "You're no good to us if you keel over. More Dead-eyes are coming."

~ ~ ~

Gannon ushered Kurio inside the meeting hall when it was clear they faced a horde of Dead-eyes, not just a few dozen. He barred the door, cursing in a language Kurio didn't recognize.

She retreated to a corner and heard the sounds of battle outside the building. Howls and screeches of inhuman creatures. Sokhelle and Priska chanting, earsplitting wails of destructive sorcery answering their call. Light flashed through the shutters covering the windows. Aldric shouted orders. Settlers cried out in fear and despair. The clash of steel. The screams of the dying, both human and not.

Kurio looked at Gannon. He stood deathly still next to the fire in the center of the room, the flames painting him in flickering orange. He had undergone a remarkable transformation of character since turning up right after she'd killed Mellish. He was still suave and charming, but there was a coldness underneath. Perhaps it was because of their situation, out here in the harsh wilderness, caught up in this group's difficulties.

"There are too many," Kurio said to him. "We should find somewhere to hide." She rechecked her crossbow, making sure both quarrels were ready to be fired. Was this how it ended? She wanted to go to Gannon, to wrap her arms around him, rest her head against his armored chest, tell him that she loved him. But there was a hardness to him that kept her away: clenched fists, feet set wide apart, face like a thunderstorm.

He'd followed her into the wilderness to save her, and now he was likely going to die. No wonder he was angry.

Gannon turned his eyes on her and his expression softened. "Kurio," he said, "what's the matter?"

"I've killed us," she replied. "If it wasn't for me—"

"Nonsense. There is a way out of this, I'm sure. Now please leave me to think." Gannon removed a slender silver rod from a pocket and traced lines in the air, as if drawing symbols. He began to speak, strange words in a guttural tongue that made Kurio think of savagery and despair.

Sorcery? "What are you—"

"Shush. A few moments and I'll be finished."

Kurio shook her head. Gannon was a sorcerer? Or was the wand an artifact that gave him power? She retreated a step. What had happened? This man, she remembered loving him, but the feeling was rapidly dissipating like fog under the morning sun. She blinked, trying to make the miasma surrounding her thoughts disappear faster. Her breathing grew difficult. Now she saw him in a different light. He looked *soiled*.

Then clarity struck her to her soul. Her abnormal infatuation. Her unnatural trust.

Nausea filled her. She coughed and almost retched as her mouth filled with sour spit.

She had been tricked. Beguiled into subservience. Gannon had suborned her free will, made a slave of her desires, altered her memories. He didn't love her any more than she loved him. She pointed her crossbow at him. Hesitated. She wanted him to see—

Then abruptly she felt them. Outside the hall, somewhere. She swayed, then stumbled, head spinning. Multiple calls tugged at her mind, her heart. What were they?

She blinked again and reached out a hand to a wall to steady herself. Gannon. She'd been thinking about Gannon. His betrayal. Suddenly she feared him.

She tried to spring her crossbow lever, but her hand wouldn't obey her thoughts. Gannon turned to regard her curiously, head tilted to the side, as if she were a bug.

Part of her, she realized, would not survive what was coming.

"There," he said, "I almost lost you."

He spoke a few words and her thoughts were blown away as if on a breeze. What had she been thinking? Kurio saw her crossbow was pointed at Gannon and lowered it guiltily. He smiled at her and she returned it, basking in his affection. He had come all this way just to rescue her.

From outside came a harsh chant from many throats: *"Nar armathuk!"* and again, *"Nar armathuk! Aman-chalak!"*

"What's that?" Kurio said.

"Demons," replied Gannon. "It seems the Dead-eyes have other problems."

Someone hammered on the door.

"Open up!" screamed Valeria.

Gannon moved to the door and unbarred it. The priestess rushed inside, face glistening with sweat, eyes wide.

"Demons," she said breathlessly. "There are demons out there slaughtering the Dead-eyes."

"We know," replied Gannon. "Come, help us gather all the gear. We're getting out of here."

Kurio ignored the priestess and checked her crossbow. She frowned. Had she already done that? No matter. Whether Dead-eyes or demons, she was certain she and Gannon could fight their way clear. Then they would be free of this primitive settlement for good and could head back to Caronath.

~ ~ ~

The Dead-eyes kept coming. It seemed there was no end to them, and they fought savagely until killed or maimed beyond hope. Aldric, Niklaus, Stray Dog, and Bryn were covered with their milky blood. Aldric wiped some from his face, spitting the rancid taste from his mouth. They couldn't hold the Dead-eyes off much longer.

Some of the Dead-eyes were screeching and scrambling away

from the settlement, appearing harried and agitated. Many glanced behind them. Looking for direction? For their leader? No. Their inhuman faces were … filled with fear. Aldric's heart hammered in his chest. His pulse pounded in his ears. The Dead-eyes were fleeing for their lives.

"Aldric!" screamed Soki. "There's something else out there."

"Bloody hells," Bryn snarled. "What next?"

A dismayed cry came from Priska.

Soki's cants grew in volume and vigor. A cascade of fiery globes rained down from the sky and detonated, cracking and shaking the ground. A conflagration erupted, splashing trees with flaming goo, scorching their bark to black and their leaves to ash.

Barks and growls penetrated the gloom—not the Dead-eyes' howling shrieks.

White globes from Soki and Priska arced into the night sky, illuminating the settlement.

A figure leaped atop an outer barricade, perched there—a wrinkled, ocher-colored, scaled body. It held a Dead-eye's limb in one clawed hand. Its orange eyes punctuated the darkness, and fangs protruded from a gash of a mouth. Horns jutted from its head and back.

Aldric gaped. Was it … a demon? His knees almost buckled. *It can't be* … But he remembered the illustrations from his training, recopied from history to history over the millennia.

Another joined it. Then five more. Seven pairs of glowing orange eyes stared at them, as if waiting for a signal. They brandished strange wavy blades that ended in a double tip.

Outside the barricades, claws scraped against wood and stone. A scratching that rose above all other sounds. More demons. Of those he could see through the gaps, many had erect phalluses, and the mad glint in their eyes showed they hungered for more than food. A foul reek pervaded the air, like rotted breath.

One among those perched on the barricade, slightly bigger and darker than the others, rose onto two feet. In one taloned hand it held a rod of polished stone wound with strips of orichalcum. It raised the artifact high above its head and uttered a guttural phrase.

Every other demon took up the chant in unison, their combined voices amplified over the Dead-eyes' tumult: *"Nar armathuk!"*

The larger demon chanted again, slapping the rod into its other hand in time with its rasping voice.

*"Nar armathuk!"* chorused the demons in response, thumping their chests so hard the skin turned red.

*"Nar armathuk! Aman-chalak!"* they screamed.

Echoing chants came from all directions as more demons repeated the guttural words while waving their double-tipped swords above their heads.

"Blood and damnation. Demons," said Niklaus, snapping Aldric from his fugue.

"Abominations," Aldric said. His Church had taught him many secrets, but this was one he'd never thought to face.

Bryn flicked a glance at him. "Fight? Or retreat? They're not attacking."

"Yet," replied Niklaus.

Aldric looked back at the settlement. Some Dead-eyes still tore at doors and smashed through windows. Men, women and children screamed. Inert shapes lay in the streets, Dead-eyes tearing at their flesh.

Soki chanted, casting sparkling illuminations, searing Dead-eyes with coruscating fire. Burning waves broke over the creatures, charring flesh and bone. Many dropped in their tracks, wailing in agony, thrashing wildly.

But Soki's scourging fire wasn't enough. She looked at Aldric, tears of anguish running down her face, and shook her head. The

Dead-eyes had driven a wedge between them and the settlers. There was nothing they could do. And they still had to deal with the demons, a potent threat that required more skill than the butchering of Dead-eyes.

A specter of primal evil had arisen.

*We're surrounded,* he thought. *I've failed. My god put his faith in me, and I failed him.*

The demons' chanting had intensified; they were working themselves into a fury.

*Why now?* Aldric wondered. *Why here?* Someone must have summoned them. A follower of Nysrog? Fear gripped him, weakening his limbs. The Tainted Cabal were here.

Outside the barricades, Dead-eyes were being overwhelmed by the demons. Aldric guessed there were a few score of the infernal creatures, and the Dead-eyes either fled or were being slaughtered, though there was the odd pocket of resistance where Dead-eyes clumped together. Inside, some Dead-eyes milled around in confusion while others still ripped at the settlers' houses in a frenzy.

Someone among them had to belong to the Tainted Cabal, Aldric thought. Was it Gannon? Or one of the others? Aldric realized he scarcely knew anyone around him, even Soki.

"The settlement's lost," Niklaus said. "But the demons have given us a chance. While they're slaughtering the Dead-eyes, we'll flee."

Bryn was supporting Stray Dog, whose face was drawn. He hunched slightly so as not to stretch his wounds.

Priska lowered herself off the roof and came running up. Tears streaked her face. "Soki said you'd need help. Your sorcery isn't— oh, sorry. It's just that—"

"It's fine," Aldric said. "I'm sorry about Razmus. He was—"

"Aldric," said Niklaus, "we don't have time for this."

Tears coursed down Priska's face, and she hugged her waist.

"Where is Valeria?" Aldric said. "And Gannon and Kurio?"

Just then, Gannon burst out of the meeting hall, his sword swinging in wild arcs, slicing through any Dead-eyes in his way. *Holy Menselas!* The man had hidden inside and avoided most of the combat. So much for wanting to help them.

Behind Gannon came Kurio, aiming her crossbow with one hand, dagger gripped in the other. She put a bolt through one Dead-eye's throat and stabbed a second as it dodged a blow from Gannon.

Valeria poked her head out the door, clutching her cloak tight around her body. Aldric wasn't surprised she'd steered clear of the fighting.

"Bloody Dead-eyes," said Gannon as he approached, trailed by Kurio and Valeria. "Those poor settlers." His saddlebags were slung over his shoulder, and Kurio carried her backpack. "Are those ghouls? Why were they chanting?"

Kurio's eyes flicked to him, and she frowned.

"They're bloody demons!" Bryn snarled. "We should do the same—grab our stuff and hunker down somewhere defensible."

Aldric shook his head. "No. We stay. They're doing our work for us—look!" The demons were hunting the Dead-eyes and viciously killing them, but seemed to avoid their group. Why? "The demons aren't interested in us. We can still save some of the settlers."

"Stubborn fool!" Niklaus said. "We've done all we can here. Even if we had a score of soldiers, we couldn't hold them off. Not the Dead-eyes, and certainly not these demons. The settlement is lost. All the settlers are as good as dead already."

"What are the demons waiting for?" asked Gannon.

"I don't know," said Bryn. "And I don't mean to find out."

Aldric sensed deep wells of dawn-tide and dusk-tide approaching. Soki ran up to them, panting. "I couldn't do any more," she gasped. Tears ran down her face.

"I know. You did well," Aldric said. It couldn't be her. It just couldn't.

"Let's go, now!" Niklaus urged. "We have to punch a hole through their line before they turn their focus on us."

Dead-eyes and demons. Aldric couldn't have known there would be so many Dead-eyes, nor that demons would appear. Archbishop Hannus would make sure the destruction of Cherish would be held against him. As it should be, if they survived.

~ ~ ~

All about them, demons roared and snarled. Niklaus ducked and weaved between their flashing fangs and inhuman faces, laughing as the infernal creatures fell to his steel. *Her* steel. Blue sparks sprayed from his blade as he parried and knocked aside the demons' weapons. With each death, he moved farther away from the settlement. It was over; Cherish was lost. All that was left to do was to flee and survive. He realized he was shouting in Skanuric, his native tongue. Words of challenge, of defiance. Words of adoration and sacrifice to his goddess, Sylva Kalisia.

It mattered not if Aldric or Sokhelle understood him. They were insignificant.

One demon evaded his thrust, quicker than the others. A claw ripped Niklaus's arm, slicing his flesh. He punched the hilt of his short blade into its face, causing it to stagger, then sliced its throat. Purple blood spilled like wine from the gash and from its mouth.

Niklaus heard the grunts and shouts of his companions as they fought behind him. No doubt this was their first encounter with creatures summoned from the hells. Demons howled as they fell to Bryn's sword, to Stray Dog's axes, and Aldric's curious curved blade. He sensed bursts of sorcery from Soki, dawn-tide power commingled with dusk-tide. If an arcane attack had been aimed at him, *her* sword would have responded in kind.

He lunged, stabbing another demon in the gut. Its orange eyes clouded, but still its face snarled in rage. He kicked it and yanked *her* sword free. The demon's blood steamed and hissed, vanishing from the steel in an instant.

Suddenly the demons were gone, retreating into the darkness. The way ahead was clear. It was strange how quickly they'd withdrawn, but Niklaus wasn't one to spurn a gift. He could ponder why later. He sheathed his goddess's sword and wiped demon blood from his face. It tasted foul and left a purple smear across the back of his hand. He spat and looked behind him to assess his companions.

Sokhelle and Priska continued to throw sorcery at the demons as they withdrew. White and gold light carved through the darkness, and those it touched twisted and wailed, falling in burning heaps. Apart from a sheen of sweat from their exertions, both sorcerers seemed uninjured, though harried and ragged, close to exhaustion. Priska more so than Soki.

Stray Dog was down on one knee, panting like his namesake. His thigh was a mass of raw sliced meat. Bryn sported many cuts, but stood defiantly, staring at the mass of retreating demons. Sokhelle glanced at Aldric and smiled, while Priska licked her lips and gazed at Sokhelle in adoration. Gannon stood with Valeria and the girl, Kurio. His blade was unsheathed, but neither its steel nor his clothes bore the stain of demon blood. Someone had to protect the women, Niklaus supposed.

Aldric stood a dozen paces to the side, a sphere of dawn-tide sorcery shielding him. A demon lay dead at his feet, but his curved blade was clean. It was made from star-metal, Niklaus realized. Why would a priest of Menselas have a star-metal-forged blade? The only reason was to fight demons. Priest, sorcerer, warrior … Aldric wasn't here merely to protect the settlement. His presence was ordained, like Niklaus's. Aldric's god wanted him here. Niklaus wondered if Aldric realized it yet. Probably not.

Sweat mingled with blood trickled down Niklaus's face. He wiped it away and nodded at Aldric. In the distance, a dancing shadowy horde ravaged the settlement. He didn't care. It was obvious now why the goddess had drawn him here. Not just to examine the ruin, but to find out who, or what, commanded the Dead-eyes and the demons.

# Chapter Thirty-Two

# Ruin

NIKLAUS HEARD THE OCCASIONAL curse as his companions stumbled over the uneven ground and protruding roots. They were running along a beaten path toward the walls of the valley. The fetid stench of the demons had been replaced by loam and pine, and he breathed deeply, glad to be rid of their presence. He hadn't seen this many demons since the fall of Onsheruul, the Tainted Cabal stronghold, which he'd helped destroy many centuries ago.

They were the same as the ones he'd poisoned at the mansion. Matriarch Adeline had known about them too. Had more been summoned and followed Niklaus's trail to Cherish? Had he brought them here and doomed the settlers? Then again, he'd destroyed many a town in his time, so what was one more to add to his tally?

In the distance, screams sounded, despairing wails and shrieks of pain. Dead-eyes who hadn't been slaughtered yet. Captured by the demons, victims of their perverted cravings. These people thought the sight of Dead-eyes eating flesh and drinking blood was horrifying. Wait until the demons had their way with the settlers, copulating with women and men alike, alive or dead. Their hungers were hard to sate, and they had no conscience. The lower demons anyway. The demon lords and their ilk were mercurial, though mostly amoral. Nysrog himself was a twisted caricature of a demon, driven insane by a summoning gone awry. But his power was still felt millennia after he had been defeated and sent back to the hells.

He glanced back as Stray Dog stumbled, and Aldric and Bryn steadied him. They groaned as they supported his weight, but maintained the steady pace Niklaus had set.

As they drew closer to the cliffs, more and more rocks littered the trail. Their pace slowed; no one wanted a turned ankle or worse.

Sokhelle launched more of her burnished globes into the sky, their brightness sending the stars into hiding and blanketing the landscape behind them with a pure white radiance. And illuminating innumerable orange eyes.

Demons flitted between trees and rocks; and now they were closer, their infernal growls and shrieks became audible.

Priska looked like she was about to throw up. Her mouth twisted in horror and revulsion.

"Run!" Niklaus exhorted them all.

They urged themselves to greater speed, risking injury, desperate to make the ruin unscathed. Sokhelle and Priska sent faintly glowing spheres ahead to light their path.

"Where are we going?" Bryn said. "There's nothing out here."

"There's a ruin close by, isn't there?" Gannon said. "Does it offer sorcerous protection? It's certain death out here unless we find somewhere defensible."

"Gannon's right," Soki said. "But we have to get inside. These old ruins are notoriously difficult to enter. There are arcane locks and traps and possibly guardians to deal with. It could take hours."

"I can get us inside," Aldric said. "My Church ... we know a few tricks. And I have some knowledge of the guardians that inhabit such ruins. With three sorcerers, especially Soki, we shouldn't have any problem dealing with them."

Sylva Kalisia's words came to Niklaus: *Beware the ruin. The Tainted Cabal seek to bring forth a final cataclysm.* But was she being truthful or attempting to prevent him from realizing his utmost desire? Eckart had sensed a presence to the north, similar to the mask. Could it be inside the ruin?

A banshee wail split the night as Soki immolated one of the leather-skinned demons that came too close. Gannon flinched at the sound. For a tough-looking warrior, it was a strange reaction, Niklaus thought. Priska, immersing herself in her sorcery, also flung bolts behind and around them as the do-gooder priest Aldric hustled the others to a greater pace.

The path narrowed, and granite rocks underfoot gave way to sharp-edged boulders. Niklaus noted that Aldric, Bryn, and Stray Dog seemed to breathe easier now they had a modicum of protection on either side. But Aldric's face still held a stern, worried expression, while Sokhelle kept biting her lip and glancing behind them.

"There!" shouted Aldric. "Neb said the fifth cave to the left."

The hole was irregular, but nothing marked it as different to the others.

"Yes," Sokhelle said. "I can feel it. It draws me ... calls me almost."

*We've been herded here*, realized Niklaus.

What was inside the ruin? The goddess had sent him here, hadn't she, so she must know. Did Matriarch Adeline also know? She was the one who'd told him about the ruin. Had the goddess prodded the old crone? But he didn't like the idea of holing up inside some ancient ruin, hoping the Dead-eyes and demons couldn't get inside, and waiting until they left.

What were the chances the demons would leave? They had to be here for a reason. Nothing else made sense.

Inside, the cave was pitch black. Sokhelle's spheres of light seemed to struggle against the weighted darkness. She chanted, and the entrance filled with a nebulous, glowing shroud. Sparkles drifted over its surface like leaves blowing in a courtyard.

"That should stop the demons for a while," she said.

Aldric spoke a few harsh Skanuric words, sorcerous, so their meaning was lost to Niklaus, and another globe appeared, illuminating stone and revealing a wall of worked orichalcum farther inside the cave. Massive double doors stood twice the height of a man, polished to mirror brightness, unweathered by time. The walls to either side were banded with intricate carvings that showed almost lifelike mailed figures bearing swords and spears and shields, their hair rendered strand by strand, minute teeth in gaping mouths. There were demons too, with mottled skin and jutting horns, patchy hair and wicked limbs. An entire host of the creatures, some of which loomed over the rest, in battle with the armored men and women. And above them all, a brooding presence, a muscled giant with hard-scaled skin, taloned hands, and a spiked tail. Leathery wings jutted from its sinewy shoulders; twisted horns protruded from a ravenous head. Niklaus recognized the scene: a terrible battle from long, long ago.

"Nysrog," breathed Aldric.

"Guag-Arbela," said Niklaus, drawing a sharp glance from the priest. "The fearsome ancient battle that sent Nysrog back to the hells."

"An end to the madness," Valeria said. "That was over ten thousand years ago."

"Not an end," said Gannon. "From what we've seen tonight."

Aldric took a step toward the wall. "This ... war is still going on. That's all I can say."

Niklaus laughed. "Why not tell everyone the truth? The demon lord Nysrog was banished, but not killed. His corrupted sorcerers and progeny were wiped out, except for a few who realized they were going to lose and made an early escape. Since then, they've gathered power and insinuated their agents into the noble classes, governments, and merchant organizations in every country, with the sole aim of bringing back their lord, Nysrog. That is their greatest desire, the lust that drives them."

They were all staring at Niklaus. In all his years serving Sylva Kalisia, he had never found himself in a situation so fraught with uncertainties and hidden variables. He had the sense that far more hung in the balance than he realized. He debated whether to cut his losses and take his chances out there among the demons. He was fairly certain he could fight his way through the infernal creatures. Their focus was on the ruin and this group of misfits. But ... her hand guided him. The hand of his goddess. And if he was to prove himself to her, to show he was worthy of becoming her equal, there was no question of stopping now.

~ ~ ~

Aldric noticed that Kurio glanced sideways at himself and Sokhelle, but he didn't speak. *Couldn't.* For the secrets of his Church were not for others to hear. That Niklaus knew of them was more than troubling, and Aldric vowed to question the mercenary the next chance he got, away from the others.

"Well," Gannon said quietly, "it's a good thing we have sorcerers like Sokhelle on our side, then. And Churches like yours and Aldric's. But I've never heard of this Nysrog, either spoken of or in history books. So I think we're fairly safe."

"Myths and superstitions," said Valeria dismissively. "Tales of a primitive society."

"Whatever it is," Bryn said, "the orichalcum on that wall is worth a fortune."

"You'll die if you try to touch it," Priska said. "There are complex wards protecting it. I can sense them." She smiled gratefully at Soki. "I wouldn't have been able to before."

Aldric was impressed by her assessment. Priska had made rapid strides under Soki's tutelage, and he supposed her intense desire to undo her inferior training and embrace her talent had proven fierce motivators. Perhaps he'd been too hasty in dismissing her …

"The wards are powerful," Sokhelle confirmed. "I wouldn't attempt to break them without weeks of studying." She turned to Aldric. "This is where you come in, isn't it?"

He nodded slowly, his eyes still taking in the ancient battle and the frightening form of Nysrog.

"Aldric," Niklaus said, "it's your turn. You said you could get us inside."

All eyes turned to Aldric, and he felt the stirrings of unease. His job had always been to keep people out of the ruins, to keep them safe, and the horrors sealed within. Now he was about to crack one open and lead a group inside. They had been herded here; it seemed obvious to him now. But if they stayed outside, they'd be torn apart by the demons. They had to secure themselves inside the ruin. There was no other choice.

*Just for a short time*, he told himself. *Just until the demons leave.*

And then what? A fraught race back to Caronath, perhaps with the demons on their trail? Or perhaps the demons wouldn't leave, not with the knowledge that they were barricaded inside with nowhere to run.

The Tainted Cabal had to be behind the appearance of the demons. He glanced at Gannon and Kurio: newcomers who had preceded the coming of the demons and also the Dead-eyes. Were they part of the Cabal? Or innocent bystanders caught up in events beyond their control?

"Aldric!" Soki warned as something hammered into her barrier, sending ripples across its surface. "That was a rock. A big one."

Three demons resolved from the darkness outside and threw

themselves at the sorcerous ward, scratching at it with their talons, hammering with their fists and their two-tipped blades. More appeared until there were at least twenty of the slavering creatures attempting to breach the barrier.

Fanged mouths roared defiance, and from somewhere in the distance came the strange chant they'd heard in the settlement: "*Nar armathuk!*" The demons outside screamed it too and slapped their chests, some slicing themselves with their talons. The chant echoed off the cliff walls as the demons worked themselves into a frenzy.

"Your sorcery is a giant sign calling them here," Niklaus said dryly.

Soki scowled at the mercenary. "If it wasn't for my sorcery, they'd be pouring through the cave entrance. Care to try your luck fighting them off?"

Niklaus grinned and rolled his shoulders. "These are lower demons. I've fought worse. Far worse. I'd survive. Though I'm not sure about everyone else."

"Enough!" shouted Aldric. "Please. Can you put your differences aside for a moment? I have to concentrate."

Soki shook her head, but gave him a contrite look. Niklaus just shrugged and moved to the cave entrance, where Stray Dog and Bryn were standing.

"Lots of demons," Stray Dog said. He was favoring his injured leg, putting all his weight on the opposite limb.

Bryn nodded. "They're like a swarm of ants. Where are they coming from? I've never even seen a demon before."

"From the hells," Valeria said. "Or that's what I assume. Likely a sorcerer's summoning gone wrong. Sorcerers are always after greater power."

Both Soki and Priska gave the priestess a sharp look. Soki opened her mouth to say something, then apparently thought better of it.

Aldric thought of Priska's Covenant, the Gray Hand; they'd turned to summoning creatures from the abyss. Had Priska such knowledge? Had she done something stupid, energized by what she'd learned from Soki along with the greater control of her powers?

"That's what I've heard too," Gannon said. "Never trust a sorcerer. Present company excepted, of course."

Soki screamed. She placed a hand to her forehead and fell to her knees in the dirt.

Aldric rushed to her aid. "What is it?"

Priska helped him lift Soki to her feet. Her face was drained of blood, and her body trembled in Aldric's hands.

"There's ... something assailing me," she gasped. "Not sorcery. I don't know what it is. It's ... clawing at my shield, trying to tear it down." She screamed again, and her knees buckled. "Quickly, Aldric, open the ruin!"

Stray Dog moved to assist Priska in supporting Soki, and Aldric approached the orichalcum doors. He kneeled before them and rubbed his face, trying to banish his weariness. He took a deep breath and, with a whispered cant, awoke his sorcerous sight.

The doors glowed a pale rose, then brightened to a lurid purple as their sorcerous wards revealed themselves to him. Intricate, complex things, layer upon layer of barriers and traps. He suppressed a gasp. Far from the usual wards he'd encountered, these ones were an order of magnitude more elaborate. Whoever had created these wards was a master capable of the finest sorceries. Even Aldric's teachers, the best the Church could afford, paled in comparison. Whoever shaped these was possessed of a talent that dwarfed even Soki's. Only sorcerers from the age of Nysrog and before had the skill required to shape these wards.

He wiped his damp palms on his thighs. Holy Menselas, should he even open the doors? But if he didn't, they'd be ravaged by the demons.

He glanced at Soki, and his chest tightened at the thought of losing her. Of seeing her taken by the demons. Abused. He couldn't let that happen to her. She was special to him. He'd never felt this way about any woman before.

Aldric returned his attention to the abstract wards. He ignored the most potent ones—so puissant they shouted pain and death. Carefully, he reached for both his dawn-tide and dusk-tide energies and shaped them into a spike. Holding the forming calculations firm in his mind, he touched the talisman on his belt. Its algebraic markings confirmed his mathematical solution and gave him the mental space to let go of those patterns and to create others. The familiar rounded shape of the talisman in his palm calmed him, settling his thoughts. Aldric was suffused with power, filled with the certainty that his god guided him.

He sent his sorcery forth, searching for a unique ward. Centuries ago, his Church had stumbled onto the fact that these ruins were not meant to be sealed for all time. Though they were guarded by powerful forces and fell creatures, their creators had installed a back door of sorts. Once you knew it was there, it was possible to use arcane power to dissipate the wards, to create a window of safety through which you could enter and exit at will. Although these wards were far more complex than any he'd seen before, there should still be a back door to them. Or so Aldric hoped.

He rechecked his calculations, clenched his resolve, and drove his spike into the center of a ward located at the bottom left of the door. For a moment, nothing happened. Aldric breathed a sigh of relief that he hadn't been annihilated.

Then, with his arcane sight, he saw the swirling sorceries dissipate, coiling and compressing into churning knots.

He heard Priska gasp and knew she was seeing the result with her own sight.

Aldric wiped sweat from his forehead and turned to the others.

His gaze found Soki first. She stood immobile, a frown on her face, staring at the wards. Eventually, she nodded. She had seen everything he'd done, and now knew one of his Church's secrets.

Aldric wondered how much trouble he'd be in when he told Archbishop Hannus. And what the Church would do to Priska and Soki.

"What happened?" asked Kurio.

Valeria sneered at Aldric. "Did you fail?"

With a crack and a groan, the line separating the two doors split open a hair's breadth. Chill wind whistled through the gap, its force pushing the doors a few fingers wider. A faint violet glow shone through the breach. Violet scaleskin, and quite bright too, which meant the fungus had been absorbing powerful sorcerous emanations.

"Well done," Soki said, giving Aldric a wan smile. "A neat trick, and just in time. Let's get inside before the demons tear down my barrier."

Aldric couldn't help basking in her praise, though it was only a simple technique, not his skill, that had opened the ruin.

"The sooner we're behind those thick doors, the better," Gannon said.

"There could be traps," Aldric warned. "We can't rush in."

"Let him rush," Bryn said, nodding toward Gannon. "One less person to split the loot with if he trips something and kills himself. He's not part of the team."

Any further argument was stopped by an almighty creak as the doors opened wider. Aldric turned to see Niklaus with a palm on each, pushing with all his might. The whistling of the wind faded once the gap grew larger, and the air inside smelled stale, motionless for an age.

Soki spoke a cant, and two points of sorcerous light arced through the open doors. They floated upward and stuck fast to the stone ceiling, revealing a spacious room.

Niklaus strode through the doors. When nothing happened to him, the others rushed to follow.

Aldric waited until everyone was inside; then he took one last look at the depiction of Nysrog and followed. With Stray Dog's assistance, he pushed the doors together, and they closed with a thunderous clang of finality.

"Don't you have to reinstate the wards?" Kurio asked from behind him.

Aldric turned. He was surprised that she didn't seem at all scared or nervous. "They'll spring back into place themselves," he explained.

"And then I can release my barrier," Soki said. "I'm not sure I can maintain it much longer."

"What's all this frost?" asked Bryn. "It's as cold as a frost giant's tits in here."

Valeria screwed up her nose at the swordsman's comment. Niklaus gave a short chuckle.

Aldric examined the floor of the room. It was covered with what looked like baked paving bricks measuring two feet to a side. They were a gray so dark it was almost black, and each depicted a swirl of curved lines. Each pattern matched up with the one next to it, so the entire floor seemed a mass of tentacles. The pattern was at once beautiful and creepy. He'd never seen anything like it before in any other ruin.

"Healing first," Aldric said.

He bade Stray Dog and the others with injuries to sit, then opened himself to his god's power. Before long, their wounds had sealed over, and fatigue had drained from their tired eyes.

Aldric passed a weary hand over his own face as the last injury closed, but as he did, Menselas's power flared again, and he felt his tiredness vanish. He started in shock. That had never happened before. It was impossible to heal yourself using the god's power. Had Menselas himself reached down and banished Aldric's exhaustion? Why? Did the god want him ready for something?

Being healed by Menselas set Aldric's mind to skittering. It was a sign, and any other time Aldric would have rejoiced, but not here, not now …

Aldric thought again of the demons. Or perhaps there was danger inside the ruin. Hannus's directive to explore it had always sat uncomfortably with Aldric, but now … He held back the impulse to urge everyone to leave this place immediately and take their chances with the demons.

"What's that?" asked Priska.

Aldric saw that she was pointing farther into the ruin, to a series of broad paved steps that led down to another platform at the entrance to a second massive chamber. The platform was slicked with frost and growths of violet scaleskin, and to each side was a forty-foot drop. At the bottom, faintly lit by the scaleskins' luminescence, a gray misty membrane churned and seethed, like water under a pier, with an occasional white sparkle erupting from the film.

Thirty yards from the side edges of the platform, rising from the membrane, carved walls arced up and overhead. The carvings showed hordes of men battling demons—another representation of Guag-Arbela, the final battle against Nysrog. Armored knights fought alongside robed sorcerers, swords and staves raised to the heavens. Soldiers formed shielded tortoise shapes to withstand the demons and—Aldric's breath caught in his chest—fell sorcerers. The Tainted Cabal.

"I still can't believe that demons are real," said Bryn, mostly to himself. "The ones outside looked far more dangerous than the Dead-eyes. More intelligent, more vicious."

"I wouldn't worry about the minor demons," Niklaus said. "It's their masters you need to worry about. They keep themselves hidden, even now, after so long. They lurk like slugs under stones, offering temptations and rewards to the weak-minded."

"It looks to me," Gannon said, "as if there are demons of greater power alongside the humans that control them. See, there." He pointed at a mail-clad demon that towered over the others. "Does he not command them?"

"Ancient history," said Aldric. The sooner he was back to Caronath to report all of this, the better. His Church would ... he paused. What power did his Church have to stand against such creatures? He hoped they weren't relying on a handful of sorcerers, like himself, and some guards. Besides, Menselas's power was used for healing, not for fighting. Although ... it had helped Aldric to kill the strange Dead-eye.

"I'm going down the steps," Bryn said, pulling Aldric out of his thoughts.

"No!" Aldric said. "These places usually have guardians. We must be careful."

"You can see there's nothing here," Niklaus said. "But you're the expert, I suppose."

The platform continued into the chamber for twenty paces before it ended at a colorless veil of arcane power.

"There are more of those curtains further in," said Kurio, tugging at her short hair with one hand. "See? And there's something right at the end of the chamber."

Peering into the gloom, Aldric saw the platform extended beyond the first veil, but couldn't make out what Kurio had described.

One of Soki's sorcerous globes detached from the ceiling, shot down the stairs, and swerved upward to stick to the cavern's roof. "*Mursel ken-dur*," she chanted, and the globe burned as bright as a small sun.

Kurio was right. Beyond the first veil there was a second. And a third. And a fourth. And behind them all, Aldric could make out a cube shape. Some sort of coffer perhaps, waist-high, possibly made from metal. But each barrier clouded his sight further and details were difficult to make out.

Under the brilliant light of Soki's sorcery, he could see that the patterns on the baked pavers in front of the first veil were different from in the first chamber. And some were covered with what looked like Skanuric script.

"Well, Aldric," Niklaus said, "are we going to huddle here or go exploring?"

Aldric rested one hand on the hilt of his khopesh. There was no sign of a guardian, a Reaper, or anything more powerful. But still … this place troubled him. He kept expecting a monster to set upon them whenever their backs were turned.

"We should stay here," he said firmly. "We'll wait by the entrance until dawn, then see if the demons have gone."

"How will we know it's dawn?" asked Stray Dog.

"Soki and I will know. And Priska. The dawn-tide will find us, even here. It will be weak, but we'll feel it."

"This is ridiculous!" said Bryn. "There's no guardian. And there's something at the end of that chamber. Probably treasure! Worth a great deal to the right person. I'm going to take a look."

He began to descend the steps.

Gannon's mail clinked as he strode after him. "A quick look, then we'll come back and rest," he told Aldric. "We all need some sleep."

"I second that," Valeria said. "And I wouldn't mind some tea later. Priska, are you able to …?" She waved a hand.

"Yes," Priska said. "I can heat up some water."

"Then that's settled," said Valeria.

Kurio's toe traced a crescent line in front of the steps. "I don't like this place," she said. "And those sorcerous barricades—are they to keep us out? Or to keep something in? Or both?"

"Aren't you the least bit curious?" Gannon asked, looking at her. "And what danger could we possibly be in? We have not one but three sorcerers with us."

"That's right," said Niklaus. "Enough arguing. Let's go."

Against Aldric's misgivings, they all followed Bryn onto the platform at the bottom of the steps. The frigid air chilled Aldric's exposed skin.

"It's Skanuric," Soki said, examining the writing.

"What does it say?" asked Gannon.

Aldric swallowed and looked at Soki. She met his eyes, grimaced, and then shrugged as if to say, *It's up to you.*

"It's instructions," Aldric said, a reluctance to translate tugging at him.

Soki walked along the line of writing-covered pavers, head bowed as she examined them. "On how to breach the sorcerous barrier. Curious. Why create a barrier and then leave instructions on how to open it?"

The instructions were incredibly complex. Aldric's knowledge and skill weren't enough to decipher all of the workings. After the first few pavers, his comprehension failed.

"Could you open it?" Stray Dog asked Soki.

"Why not?" added Valeria. "I'll admit what's behind these four curtains has me interested."

Niklaus gave her a sharp look, but Valeria only shrugged.

"Don't tell me you don't all want to know too," she said. "We're walking where no person has for millennia. There's obviously something of value here. We'd be remiss if we didn't try."

"I'm afraid it's not going to be that easy," Aldric said. "The writing warns of multiple challenges and of sorcerous and divine power. And ..." He hesitated. "Demon blood. The meaning is unclear. Skanuric is difficult."

Niklaus cleared his throat and flashed Aldric an annoyed look. "What Aldric fails to mention is that the writing also speaks of the reward at the end."

"Niklaus," warned Aldric.

"It's hardly a trap," the mercenary countered. "It's just a vault, albeit an unconventional one. A sorcerer—or sorcerers—of great power created this to safeguard their valuables."

"And what valuables they must be, eh!" Bryn said.

"I can breach it," Soki said quietly, and all eyes turned to regard her. "At least, I think so. It's ... difficult, but won't require much dusk- or dawn-tide power."

"Do it," Gannon said.

Bryn and Stray Dog nodded their agreement.

"Wait," said Soki, "I'll work a divining first." She turned to Priska. "Would you like to try?"

Priska's mouth opened in surprise; then she nodded eagerly. "Yes! I won't let you down this time."

She took her talisman in her hand and whispered a cant. Aldric felt her dusk-tide energy flow, then form into complex patterns.

"Good," Soki told her. "You're coming along nicely. Now, frame your questions, bind them, and send them out."

This sorcery was complex, beyond Aldric. Perhaps he should make use of it more. After all, its influence hadn't corrupted Soki. Through his sorcerous sight, he could see the dusk-tide roiling around Priska, its shadows made material.

"There's something there," whispered Priska. "Something valuable."

"I knew it!" said Bryn.

"Hush," hissed Soki, then to Priska, "What else?"

"There's a tunnel ... stretching through the rock ... an exit, I think. I ..." Aldric saw the shadows around her disperse. "I lost it. I'm sorry."

Soki rested a hand on Priska's shoulder and smiled. "You did well. And it will get easier with training and practice."

"This is excellent news," Valeria said. "We can scoop up the treasure and leave this derelict place through the back door. We'll avoid the demons and be away before they know it."

"I don't think that's wise," Aldric said. "We shouldn't tamper with what's here. Better we wait the demons out."

"Oh, come on, Aldric," Valeria said. "You just want your Church to come back later and take everything for themselves!"

"That's not true," Aldric protested. "This place is dangerous."

"Yeah," Niklaus said with amusement. "We're all about to die." He looked around with an expression of mock fright.

Valeria and Priska laughed, as did Bryn and Gannon. Their mirth had a relieved edge, as if they needed an outlet after barely escaping death at the hands of the demons. Kurio didn't look amused; instead she glanced around at the ruin with a frown.

Aldric looked at Soki, hoping she'd agree with him.

She shook her head. "Valeria has a good argument. I mean, it's probably safer if we see what is in the chamber. As Gannon said, we have three sorcerers, and you have also been touched by Menselas. And Niklaus, Bryn, and Stray Dog are all skilled warriors." She spread her hands. "We have to at least try. If we succeed, we can discuss what to do next. If we don't, we'll just have to hope the demons leave. And I, for one, try not to rely purely on hope."

"That's decided, then," Gannon said. "Will this barrier take you long?"

"No," Soki said. "A few minutes."

Aldric moved back to the base of the stairs and tried to smooth his frown. This was why his Church kept the ruins sealed, so treasure hunters weren't tempted to risk their lives. And here he was, leading a group of people inside a ruin more powerful and disturbing than any he'd ever encountered before.

He recalled the carvings of Nysrog and the Tainted Cabal and wondered what specific dangers this ruin might hold.

# CHAPTER THIRTY-THREE

# GUARDIAN

NIKLAUS WATCHED AS SOKHELLE placed herself in front of the first veil. She looked back at Aldric, long raven hair sliding over her shoulder, and gave him a reassuring smile. He returned it, but when she directed her attention back to the sorcerous curtain, the priest's smile slipped from his face. The fool was probably feeling guilty the settlement and everyone in it had been destroyed. Niklaus wouldn't lose any sleep over it. People died every day.

But there was an oddness to this situation he disliked. It wasn't lost on him that the demons that had followed them from the settlement were similar to those he'd killed in Caronath. The Tainted Cabal had come out of hiding, and perhaps they'd found out he'd stolen the grimoire and come for him … But the Dead-eyes and the demons were at odds, he reminded himself. Which meant there were two players in this game.

He stood tall, stretching his back and rolling his shoulders to loosen them. This ruin was old and had probably been here long before Caronath was even a settlement. Niklaus had seen a few similar hoary places over the years, but had never considered entering one. The goddess had sent him here. Perhaps she knew what he was working toward, and this was a test before she allowed him to ascend and join with her.

Bryn chatted amiably with Priska, who seldom returned words of her own. The death of Razmus had to be weighing heavy on her. Stray Dog stood with Gannon and Kurio, the two newcomers, all three of them fixated on Sokhelle and what she was about to do.

Valeria sidled up to him. "There is power here," she said in low tones, "if we can take it."

Niklaus snorted. He had Valeria's measure. And if she continued down this path, the goddess would slap her down.

"Leave me out of your plans," he told her. "I go where and do what *she* tells me."

"I only want to bring her glory."

*Bring yourself glory, you mean.* "Enough, Valeria. Leave me be."

The high priestess slunk away to the rear of the group, a faint sneer on her lips and fire in her eyes. Niklaus returned his attention to Sokhelle. She was kneeling now, speaking cants as an arcane fog rose to surround her. Priska moved to stand just behind the woman, obviously entranced by what she was about to attempt. Aldric looked to Sokhelle when Niklaus felt the touch of dawn-tide and dusk-tide sorcery through the goddess's sword.

Soki's lithe body became partially obscured as she worked her intricate cants. His skin prickled with sorcerous ether. Lines scribed the air in front of Sokhelle: spectral pictograms and phantom schematics. Sorcery was skill. Sorcery was knowledge. Sorcery was intellect. And Soki was a master of all three. So potent were her weavings, he heard them crackle as they met the freezing air.

A hiss of breath escaped Aldric—a surge of jealousy? The priest didn't fool Niklaus, even though he was blind to his own desires. He hid behind his healing abilities and confined himself in the strictures of his Church. But the call of his sorcery was strong. However much Aldric forced himself to despise it, he longed to use the power, to make a difference. Niklaus almost laughed out loud.

"Ah ..." Soki whispered. Then she barked a series of cants, words torn from her throat in quick succession. A crack sundered the air, then a flash of brilliance.

When Niklaus's eyes recovered, the veil was gone. Behind it, the platform extended to the second barrier.

Soki stumbled to her feet, brushing at her knees. Aldric rushed to her side so she could rest her weight against him. She looked at him with weary eyes, then her red lips curled into a smile.

"I did it!" she said, and spun on her heels, hair flowing like a billowing skirt. She clapped her hands. "It was ... harder than I thought. I was stretched to the limits of my knowledge. If the next barrier is more complex, my guess is I'll fail."

"That's no way to talk," Bryn said. "Come on!" He strode past them, toward the next curtain.

The goddess's sword on Niklaus's back vibrated slightly, and he sensed a break in reality, a gate opening. Soki's globes winked out, and blackness came crashing down. Only the faint light from the violet scaleskins remained, casting their glow across the ruin. Ice cracked all around them as the cold intensified.

*A Reaper,* thought Niklaus. *No, something darker, pulled from the hells or the abyss.*

Before he could shout a warning, an elongated shadow plummeted from the ceiling. It landed heavily, and the pavers beneath it cracked. A faint, deep-throated singing sounded, with a low, intense resonance that shook Niklaus's bones.

With slow grace, a lanky figure rose from the floor to tower above them, twice the height of a man. It shook its head, as if confused at being woken from thousands of years of slumber.

A frigid mist rose from its exquisitely crafted armor of black metal that fitted like a second skin, and the two curved swords clenched in its fists. The creature's proportions were strange: long limbs with an extra joint; a cinched waist between slightly wider chest and hips. Atop its long neck was an elongated head covered with short bristly hair, and a pointed snout with needlelike fangs that dripped viscous saliva. Its eye sockets glowed a bright orange.

Niklaus drew the goddess's sword from its sheath and rushed the beast, hoping it wasn't fully awake yet and therefore vulnerable. Their only hope was to keep it distracted until Sokhelle and Priska could scourge it with sorcery.

Aldric shouted a cant and spherical wards sprang up around him. So the priest knew what it was too.

Niklaus thrust *her* shining blade at the thing's throat, but it scraped off without leaving a scratch.

Aldric's crescent blade rebounded off the creature's armor with a clanging sound, as if it had hit an anvil. Even star-metal was useless against it.

"Go for its eyes!" shouted Aldric. "Or its mouth!"

A good plan, if they could get close. But Niklaus had another idea. He backed up a few steps to give himself room, dodging sweeps of the creature's blades as it weaved a net of sharp steel around itself.

Kurio somehow loosed two bolts from her crossbow in quick succession. One struck just below the creature's eye and ricocheted into the darkness. The other disappeared into its maw, to no effect.

Gannon made a stand by her side, feet wide, sword held high, as if daring the beast to come at him.

Valeria raised a hand, but her sneering smile turned to dismay in an instant. Whatever she'd tried to do with her goddess's power had failed, Niklaus thought. She backed away.

Shrieking, glittering lines of sorcery erupted from Sokhelle and scoured across the creature's armor, leaving blackened smoky scars in their wake. But no blood poured from them, and Niklaus realized they'd barely scratched the surface of the tough metal.

Neither their blades nor sorcery could harm it.

The faint singing that came from the creature rose in volume and intensity.

Bryn and Stray Dog joined their furious assault. Bryn's sword bounced off the creature as he pounded it with manic cuts, to no avail. He backed away, eyes wide.

Stray Dog's axes had more effect. Each battering strike, propelled by his immense strength, dented and cracked the creature's armor. With a roar, Stray Dog flung himself into an overhead strike, but the axe shattered on impact.

Finally, the beast reacted. A lizard-quick strike of its arm sent Stray Dog crashing into a tangled heap. The creature leaped and landed on top of him, crushing his chest. The big man struggled even as blood frothed from his mouth, and lashed out feebly with his remaining axe. Its blade skidded across black metal.

His other fist hammered at the creature repeatedly, quickly becoming a bloody mess. The creature stomped its foot onto his rib cage with a loud crack. Stray Dog gurgled, his head shaking from side to side uncontrollably. His torso was almost split in two, and jagged shards of bone stuck out from his flesh. Blood sloshed across the floor.

The creature struck again, just as gracefully and quickly, hammering a limb into Sokhelle and Priska. Sparks erupted from their spherical shields as they absorbed the crushing force, but it batted them away, sending them tumbling across the floor.

His expression one of abject dismay, Aldric clutched his talisman, and Niklaus felt a massive surge of dusk-tide power. The priest uttered Skanuric cants, sending flames cascading toward the beast.

Niklaus and Bryn dived out of the way and scrabbled for safety. Furnace-hot air from Aldric blasted across them, singeing skin. Aldric continued to speak the dark sorcery, pouring his desperation into the cants. The light of his fire painted the beast and the chamber in pulsing yellow and red, joined by more of Sokhelle's coruscating lines as soon as she recovered.

The creature ignored the sorcery surging over it. "You are but a worm," it roared at Aldric, words resounding with immense strength. "A fool meddling in what he cannot understand. You have pulled me from my home. I am sent to destroy you."

"Flee!" Aldric yelled to the others. He ceased the cataract of fire, and his wards glowed brighter and seemed to split into two layers.

An instant later, the creature hammered a limb down on top of him, and Aldric's outer wards vanished completely as the stone beneath him buckled. His inner wards held, but were soon fractured by the immense pressure the beast was forcing onto them, cracking his arcane shield. Swaying with exhaustion, and face pale with fear, Aldric cried out more Skanuric words, probably attempting to create new wards with the dusk-tide power.

*The fool thinks he can withstand the creature.* Or maybe he was trying to give them time to escape. But where could they run?

Niklaus had survived incredible odds before, by the grace of the Lady Sylva, and he trusted in his own abilities and her guidance. He drew his cane and sprinted toward the beast, past Aldric's blurred form. He ducked and weaved—avoiding Sokhelle's glittering lines and the creature's slicing blades—and leaped high, cane held in one hand. He thrust it past the creature's gaping maw, deep into its throat.

The beast tossed its head, throwing Niklaus through the air. He landed with a crunch of bone; his chest felt like it was gripped in a slowly closing vice. Placing his hands on the ground, he pushed himself to his knees. The movement sent pain shooting through his body.

"Pitiful worm," the creature thundered. "My hide is iron. My—" It coughed and staggered to the side, then heaved up a torrent of green sputum.

It keeled over with a screeching wail, the skin of its face rippling, as if something moved beneath it. Its limbs twitched, muscles spasmed, then its black armor split along multiple lines. A foul-smelling greenish liquid gushed out, pooling across the pavers. Miraculously, the creature's chest ceased to heave, and it uttered a long, drawn-out sigh.

Niklaus levered himself to his knees. His chest ached, breath coming in agonizing, wheezing gasps. The creature had called him a worm, but it was the worm of Ak-Settur's venom that had killed it.

Aldric wiped sweat from his eyes and continued staring at the corpse of the creature from the abyss. He dropped his shields and backed away. Sokhelle rushed to him and clasped him in her arms. Everyone was shouting in relief or horror or amazement. Aldric squeezed Sokhelle's arm, then rushed to Niklaus's side.

"See to Stray Dog first," he managed to tell Aldric.

"He's gone. Menselas's divine healing is powerful, but it can't breach the veil between life and death to bring a soul back."

"A pity," said Niklaus. If it could, he might have a use for Aldric.

A tingling warmth filled him as his broken bones shifted and mended, and his bruised organs and muscles repaired themselves and filled again with blood. It was a curious, writhing sensation and not one he particularly enjoyed. At least there was no pain.

# Chapter Thirty-Four

# Blood Sacrifice

A LDRIC'S EYES DROOPED WITH weariness. He clutched at Niklaus's shoulder, then slumped to the ground. It was some time before he regained consciousness.

He groaned and moved his aching head slightly. "How long was I out?"

"An hour or so," replied Priska.

"We didn't want to wake you," Soki said. "You needed rest."

"And you look like you still do," added Gannon.

It sounded like they were at the other end of a long tunnel. Aldric opened his eyes a fraction, squinting at the harsh light of Soki's globes. He tried to move, but his limbs seemed made of lead. He drew in deep breaths to try to clear the fuzziness in his mind, then forced himself to sit up.

"How is Niklaus?" he asked.

"I've been better," the mercenary responded. He limped into Aldric's view, wincing at each step.

Most of the damage caused had been roughly cured, but Aldric could see he would require another round of healing before he was anywhere near back to normal. "I'll try again later," he said.

"Don't rush," Soki warned. "You almost killed yourself. And

you're no use to anyone if you're unconscious."

"I can survive like this for a while," Niklaus said. "I'm no stranger to pain."

Aldric nodded weakly and placed a hand on the ground to steady himself. Just sitting up made him feel fragile. He had no idea why his god had banished his weariness earlier, but not this time.

"I can mask the pain when I'm healing," he told Niklaus. "But any discomfort from unhealed wounds will return once I stop."

Soki and Gannon helped Aldric to his feet, and he nodded his thanks. Someone had covered Stray Dog's ravaged midsection with a flimsy scarf. Likely Soki or Priska.

Aldric looked at the massive corpse of the creature. It seemed to have shriveled a fraction, as if its insides had shrunk.

"Will you be all right to continue?" Gannon asked.

Aldric shook his head. "Are we really going on after what just happened? There could be more of those ... creatures." He turned to Niklaus. "What did you do to it?"

The mercenary shrugged, one hand on the hilt of his long sword, which hung by his hip again. "I happened to have a particularly potent poison with me. Since nothing else seemed to work, I decided to use it."

"Do you want to try to recover your cane? It's somewhere inside the creature."

Niklaus grimaced. "Not at the moment. Later, when I've recovered a little."

"I've never heard of such a strong poison," Gannon said. "Where did you obtain it?"

"From an alchemist," replied Niklaus. "To tell the truth, I wasn't sure it would work. He might have sold me something worthless."

Kurio came up to them, her eyes fixed on Niklaus. "Why would you need such a thing? Did you know you would be facing more than just the Dead-eyes?"

"I would ask the same question," said Valeria.

Aldric also wanted to know. Did Niklaus know more about the mission than he'd shared? And did Hannus know what was inside the ruin, but chose not to warn Aldric for whatever reason?

Niklaus's eyes narrowed. "I couldn't use the poison effectively against so many demons. And I carry such things precisely because they're effective in certain situations, like this one. You should be thanking me."

"Do you come across many creatures immune to sorcery and steel?" asked Gannon.

Niklaus ignored the question. "If Aldric feels well enough, we should continue."

Aldric didn't feel well enough. What he needed was a week's rest, preferably in a bed.

"We shouldn't go any further," Soki said. "Aldric's right. It's too dangerous."

"We've dealt with the threat," Valeria said. "We should go on. Losing Stray Dog was unfortunate, but we shouldn't lose sight of—"

"Unfortunate?" Aldric snarled. "He was ripped in two. He gave his life to protect us. And if I wasn't here, Niklaus would be dead too."

Gannon stepped between Aldric and the priestess.

Aldric realized he'd taken a step toward Valeria with his fist raised. Not only that; he was a hair's breadth away from using dusk-tide sorcery. He shied away from his repository, fearful of whatever cant he'd been about to speak.

"Any death is unfortunate," Gannon said, his voice even. "And Stray Dog was a good man."

Aldric nodded, not trusting himself to speak.

Soki placed a hand on his. "I can prevent any other creatures from materializing," she said. "Now I know what to look for, I'm confident I can disarm any triggers before they summon anything."

"See," said Gannon. "That's reassuring, is it not?"

"Let's get to work on this next veil," Niklaus said. "The less time we spend in here, the better."

~ ~ ~

Kurio's hand sought Gannon's as the group moved toward the second barrier. His grip steadied her; and there was something about him that stirred her blood and made her want to survive to be with him. Her other hand held her crossbow tight, the familiar weapon also giving her comfort. The shadows in this place unsettled her, though she was used to darkness. The ruin was cold and full of dangers. The sooner they were back in Caronath, the better.

She couldn't stop thinking about the demons either. Her mind flitted from one thought to another, seldom stopping. Their repellent appearance. Their savagery and depravity. Their hideous chanting, all the more terrible as it showed they were intelligent and had developed a culture of sorts. The demons were the worst aspects of mankind made manifest, ruled by base desires and hungers.

Demons. Everything came back to them. Ever since she'd met Gannon and discovered his research, the infernal creatures kept appearing. She'd put it down to bad luck. If she believed it would help, she'd donate a good amount of gold royals to any god that could change her luck. Or at least wipe the slate clean. But the gods played with all of their lives and didn't care.

The demons' blood was dark purple. Her blood was red. She wasn't a demon. But Zarina and Mellish, and the wraithe, thought otherwise. What was the truth? Would she ever really know?

Gannon squeezed her hand, then released it. Kurio found

herself already longing for his firm warmth.

"The patterns on the pavers," said Priska. "They change after each barrier."

Kurio realized she was right. As did the writing, although it was still Skanuric.

"It doesn't speak of sorcery this time," Aldric said, "but of power divinely gifted."

Sokhelle frowned thoughtfully. "Aldric, do you—"

"Not mine," he said. "It's nothing to do with Menselas. It talks of pain, of anguish." He turned, eyes seeking Valeria. "It speaks of the moons, of darker powers."

"And errant passions," Sokhelle added.

"Just as well I'm here, then," Valeria said. "Or you'd be stuck at this barrier."

Kurio couldn't hold herself back. "Well, that's fortunate." It was all too convenient. Couldn't these people see it?

"Yes," said Valeria. "But we're not through yet."

Kurio grunted softly. "I'm wondering what all these barriers are protecting. Someone's gone to a lot of trouble to keep this place secure." She frowned and looked at Aldric, then Sokhelle. "I take it one person couldn't have done this?"

"It's possible," replied Sokhelle. "If that person was chosen by the Lady Sylva Kalisia and was a proficient sorcerer."

"Someone like Aldric, except devoted to the Lady?" said Niklaus, and shook his head. "The goddess has no need of sorcerers in her Church. At least, I've never met one."

Kurio wondered then why she'd overheard Aldric and Sokhelle saying the priestess had taken pains to try to convert Priska to her cause.

"We shouldn't mess with this sorcery," she said. "Let's go back to the entrance, wait for the demons to leave, then head back to Caronath."

"Should Valeria investigate the barrier?" asked Gannon. "Or

perhaps her only talent is making tea?"

Valeria flashed him a look of pure fury. "Be careful what you say. My power is not to be made fun of. Nor is the Lady. You think muscle and steel are superior, but you're only a bag of meat—as Stray Dog found out."

"As are we all," said Niklaus. "Valeria, cease with the theatrics and get on with it. This place makes me uneasy."

Valeria clenched her jaw, but nodded curtly to Niklaus. She gathered her skirt in her hands and moved to stand in front of the veil. After a short time, she kneeled and began murmuring in a tongue Kurio hadn't heard before. It was throaty and liquid, alluring. Kurio found herself straining to catch every word, then noticed everyone else also staring at Valeria.

"The language of the Lady's Church," Niklaus said, startling Kurio and breaking her fascination.

"At least they did one thing right," Gannon said with a mocking grin.

Niklaus turned to regard him. "What do you mean?"

Gannon shrugged. "The Lady's Church has diminished over the years, is that not so? Sylva Kalisia's power wanes."

Kurio jumped as Valeria uttered a terrible shriek, as though it had been torn from the depths of her soul. Her arms were stretched out in front of her, fingers clawing, nails scraping on the pavers. Her whole body trembled, and she emitted another wail.

Sokhelle rushed toward her, only to be stopped by Niklaus, who moved swiftly to block her path.

"Pain and anguish are part of how the priestesses serve the goddess," he said. "Do not intervene, or things could go awry."

More words flowed from Valeria's lips, still throaty and fluid, but hurried too, and desperate. Her breath came in harsh gasps, and sweat dripped from her face, spattering the floor. She shrieked, the tendons on her hands bulging, as if she were clawing her way through the hard floor.

And the veil dissipated.

Sokhelle brushed past Niklaus, who now let her go. She rushed to Valeria. The priestess pushed the other woman's hands away. "Leave me," she snarled. A trickle of blood oozed from one nostril. She wiped at it with her hand, then smoothed back her damp hair. She coughed, then lurched to her feet and wobbled uncertainly. "Niklaus." She held a hand out.

The mercenary moved to Valeria's side, taking her hand and arm to steady her. Strangely, he looked unconcerned at her shaky condition.

"It is done," Valeria said. "It was ... an intense experience."

She breathed deeply and leaned further into Niklaus. He bore her weight and guided her over the line where the barrier had been.

Kurio looked ahead to the object the arcane shrouds were guarding. It seemed clearer now—a cube of metal about a yard high and covered with some kind of complex pattern too obscure to make out. Her eyes narrowed. "Is that ..." she said, then trailed off, biting her bottom lip. It looked like a larger version of the cube she'd stolen and delivered to Willas ... but that meant ...

She shrugged Gannon's hands from her shoulders and moved closer to the next veil. She needed time to think, but her mind felt sluggish.

"Is that what?" asked Priska.

Kurio shook her head. "Nothing." She glanced at Gannon, who returned her look with a blank expression.

Bryn slapped Niklaus on the back and hurried forward. "Two down, two to go!" he crowed. "We're going to be rich. I can feel it!"

Gannon laughed. "Royals can't buy you everything. Remember that."

"True!" said Bryn. "But when you're getting long in the tooth like me, you have to look to the future. Coin can buy almost everything. As for what it can't, well … you make what bargains you can."

"Some bargains can be hard to stick to," said Gannon.

Bryn glanced back over his shoulder. "I'm a man of my word." He rushed to the next veil and stared down at the writing on the pavers. Without looking up, he waved everyone closer. "Come over here. What do these say?"

To Kurio's eyes, the veil shimmered faintly. Wavelets of power swirled across it, creating the impression of a sky filled with stars reflected on water.

"It is Skanuric again," said Aldric. "It doesn't reference sorcery, but power divinely gifted. Not of pain and anguish this time, but of different aspects."

Priska pointed to one of the pavers. "This word—I recognize it from sorcery. It means 'five'."

~ ~ ~

Aldric felt his stomach sink. His hands trembled, and he clenched one into a fist and the other around the hilt of his khopesh to stop them. This barrier had been created by a priest of his Church. He didn't need his divine power to ascertain the fact. The Skanuric script spelled it all out: the Elder, the Mother, the Healer, the Warrior, the Hooded One. The five aspects of Menselas.

"Only one aspect is needed to break the barrier," Soki said from behind him. She moved closer and placed a hand over Aldric's clenched fist, giving it a reassuring squeeze. "The healer."

"So this one's for Aldric?" asked Bryn.

Niklaus grunted.

Bryn turned to Aldric. "What are you waiting for?"

"Let me think," Aldric snarled. He knew with certainty that whatever they found behind the veils, Valeria would strive to control it. She sought a resurgence of her goddess, and the pain and suffering of others meant nothing to her.

"It's all right," said Soki. "We've come this far." She smiled and squeezed his hand again.

"I have a bad feeling about this," Aldric whispered to her.

"So you're not even going to try? Even though Stray Dog gave his life to get us this far? And after what Valeria went through? Look at her, Aldric. She's still in pain."

He glanced over at the priestess. She was sitting on the floor, head held in trembling hands.

"So am I," he said, but it sounded weak even to his own ears.

"I may not like her," Soki said in a low voice, "but she went through hells to bring that barrier down. Mine was only a test of my sorcerous abilities; hers was a test of her ability to withstand intense pain. I think yours will be a walk in the park in comparison."

She seemed faintly disappointed in him, and he felt a tingle of blood suffuse his face.

"I'm not worried about that. I'm concerned there's something else going on here. It can't be a coincidence that each veil requires a different power to bring it down, and our group contains someone with that power."

Soki's eyes narrowed; then she shrugged. "What about the demons? Would your Church and Valeria's have chosen to work together if they'd known about them? I don't think so."

She was right, Aldric knew. But still … the situation filled him with a deep unease. They'd all been drawn here for a purpose. Someone had manipulated them. Was it divine guidance? Or something sinister?

There was a design here. A plan they were all part of. There was so much he didn't know. He might as well be fighting blind. Archbishop Hannus had wanted him to explore the ruins, but was that his primary consideration or only secondary? Perhaps Hannus was behind all of this. He'd sent Aldric to explore the ruin, after all, and ordered him to bring back whatever he found there, presumably employing Soki to examine the same artifacts. If Aldric had them in his possession, then he'd hold all the cards. If Hannus was corrupt, he needed to be stopped and cast out of the Church. Was this why Menselas had drawn Aldric here? If he pretended to fail at breaching the barrier, would he also be failing his god?

"Aldric," Niklaus said, interrupting his thoughts, "I think we should talk."

He'd left Valeria on her own, and the priestess was sitting on the floor.

"Leave him be," Gannon said. "He's worried the two women performed better than he can."

"Be quiet," Soki told him. "Aldric—"

"What are you waiting for?" interrupted Priska, echoing Bryn. "This is exciting! We're so close!"

"Who is going to remove the last barrier?" Aldric said loudly. No one else had any other powers ... that he knew of. Sorcery had been used, then Valeria's goddess's power, and now his was next. After that, what could possibly be the key? "You, Bryn, with your sword? Or you, Gannon?" He gave Kurio a hard stare. "Kurio, what is your hidden talent? Or Niklaus?"

No one answered for long moments.

Then Soki spoke. "I guess we'll find out soon—if you can disperse this barrier."

There was still a chance they'd fail at the last hurdle. At least Aldric could hope so. Swallowing his fear, he stepped up to the veil and awoke his divine sight.

Light pulsed across a fine knit of designs. *No, not a design. A mesh of power. It ... hurts, like a wound. Ah ...* Aldric wove his god's gift, and his palms began to glow faintly. He handled raw energy as though it had substance. It was a complex healing, and sweat beaded his brow as his fingers threaded patterns over the injured veil. If he made the wound whole, the barrier would dissipate.

It was a simple matter, in the end. Aldric concentrated and released his god's energies. The mesh flashed bright, becoming whole again. But only for an instant. Then it collapsed.

Aldric shivered. He'd done it. For good or for ill.

Bryn crowed, his delight echoing around the chamber.

Priska clapped her hands, and Soki gave Aldric a warm smile.

"Next one!" shouted Bryn as he rushed ahead.

Niklaus stood in front of Aldric and looked him in the eye. "We need to talk," he said quietly but forcefully.

"What about?" Aldric said. He was on edge as it was. Whatever Niklaus wanted, it could wait. Or could it? He was worried enough to hear him out.

"Don't you see? What are the chances of a group turning up and being able to breach all the barriers? Think, man!"

"I have thought. What if it's what my god and your goddess want? Have you considered that?"

Niklaus flinched. "I stopped trying to second-guess the Lady long ago. And I don't trust this Gannon. There's something wrong about him."

"Come on, you two," Bryn said. "Time for chatting later. What do these pavers say? Soki? Priska?"

Soki's gasp caused both Aldric and Niklaus to go to her. She was staring at one paver larger than the rest. Carved into its surface was a muscled manlike creature, with a spiked tail, leathery wings, and twisted horns. An image they'd seen before, on the doors of the ruin. Nysrog.

In its taloned hand, it held another demon's severed head, drops of blood splattering from it to the ground.

"What is it?" said Priska. "What does it mean?"

Soki looked up, dread in her eyes. "Aldric, could you please confirm the translation? There are a few words with double meanings, and some that scholars disagree on."

Aldric squatted to examine the Skanuric script, finger tracing some of the harder words. "This is 'blood'. And this one's definitely 'demon'. Though, this word ..." He hesitated. It had different meanings. The most common one was 'lethargy' or 'not caring'. And the next word ... to 'pierce the veil'.

"I think," he said slowly, "we need to kill a live demon as sacrifice."

## CHAPTER THIRTY-FIVE

# WALKING ON ICE

DREAD DUG ITS COLD claws into Kurio. Her chest tightened, and her breath came in shallow wheezes. The grip of her crossbow began to slip from her sweaty hands, and she alternated wiping her palms on her pants.

*No … it can't mean me … I'm not a demon … I'm not!*

She clung to Gannon's arm, trying to ground herself and ward off her rising panic.

He stroked her hair. "Calm yourself, my sweet."

"I …" she gasped, but couldn't continue. *Why am I here? I should leave. Run.*

She had watched the demons die beneath Niklaus's blades, their rabid savagery no match for his weaving steel. The muscled, slavering creatures had lunged at him, and he'd separated them from life quickly and efficiently, his swords blurring so fast they were shining curtains sending whips of blood arcing. Sokhelle and her protégée, Priska, had sent scintillating lines into the creatures, scouring their leathery, scaled skin, slicing and burning. And the sight of the demons being slaughtered had thrilled Kurio. She had *rejoiced.* She had wanted them all to die. But knew it wouldn't alter anything, change the truth of what she was. She was one of them in some shape or form.

The demons had foul desires; she remembered their lustful looks and erect members. They were mindless horrors, lusting after flesh and blood. Hatred personified; depravity writ large. She wasn't like those creatures. They repelled her. She'd gladly kill the foul things with no regrets.

She remembered the wraithe's words: *You demonstrate that your blood does not master you; you will not exult in degradation.*

Gannon gripped her arm, breaking her out of her reverie. "Stay close to me," he hissed softly. "Leave them to fight over what to do next. We'll be safer together."

She remembered the demons she'd seen at his house … He said they'd been killed by poison. Niklaus had killed the guardian of the ruin with poison.

"Gannon," she said, "the demons at your house. Was Niklaus the one who killed them?"

He smiled at her, though his eyes were guarded. "He has to be. I don't know who we've fallen in with, but we'd best be on our guard. Don't trust any of them."

He muttered a phrase under his breath, strange words in a language Kurio didn't understand. Her mind swirled, and she lost her train of thought. She was so tired.

She saw the sorcerer Sokhelle talking with Aldric, the priest who had been kind to her. Their hands waved as they discussed the final veil and its requirement of demon blood.

Sokhelle turned to speak to the group. "My interpretation is that we need both demon and human blood."

"There are dozens of demons out there, waiting for us," Bryn said. "But I'm not going back out to capture one." His pink tongue licked his lips. "We need a plan."

Kurio kept her mouth shut. How much demon blood did they need? Aldric had said the demon would die … What if they found out that demon blood coursed through her veins? But it didn't. Despite what Zarina and Mellish had said, and the wraithe too, she still couldn't believe it.

*Stop it,* she chided herself. *Stop being foolish. It's true.*

And if they found out, they'd sacrifice her. Everyone wanted to use her. How much blood did they need? Aldric had said the demon would die.

Perhaps she could slip away unnoticed … It might be the only way to save herself. Her hand reached up to touch Mellish's amulet—hers now—through her shirt. Somehow, it calmed her. Whatever properties it had, she wished it could spirit her away from here.

The only person who'd been truthful with her and treated her as she deserved was Gannon. He'd even chased after Mellish when he'd learned she'd been kidnapped. If that didn't prove he had feelings for her, she didn't know what would.

"There's more writing," Niklaus said, scuffing the floor with his toe. "Here. It mentions blood again."

Aldric peered at the script. "The demon and human blood must be bound somehow. I cannot fathom the true meaning—it's unclear."

A gasp escaped Kurio's lips before she could stop it. She felt the blood drain from her face, leaving it cold. "Let's leave," she said, voice trembling. "Nothing good can come of this."

"Now, now," said Gannon. "They've brought down three of the barriers. We can't just leave with only one remaining. Then any half-baked treasure hunter could lay their hands on the cache inside."

Kurio just wanted to be gone from this cursed place. From whatever was playing out in this godforsaken tomb. Caronath was where she should be, safe and snug in one of her boltholes. Not in a sorcery-riddled ruin in the middle of the wilderness, where she was completely out of her depth. *Give me a dark night and cobbled streets,* she thought. *With buildings all around, places to run and hide.*

She closed her eyes and calmed her breathing, which had

grown rapid and shallow. Then she did the only thing she could think of: she tried to use her talent. She emptied her mind and thought of clouds, then nothing.

Abruptly, to her surprise and dismay, a feeling of danger swamped her, far stronger than anything she'd ever sensed before. She felt as if she were falling, but when she opened her eyes, she remained upright, though her vision had a reddish cast, as if she looked through colored glass.

*This is new …*

The forms of the people around her were indistinct, their outlines blurred, and their voices were muffled, as if they came from far away. Where she knew Aldric stood was a shape that glowed golden, with an intense pearly curved slash at his hip. Sokhelle was both white and dark, swirling together; as was Priska. Niklaus shone silver, but his sword was as black as pitch. Bryn was red, Valeria a churning violet, and Gannon was a lurid green.

Her attention was caught by the coffer on the other side of the final veil: it bubbled with the faces of the damned. Leering and screaming, mouths open in wordless cries of agony.

*Danger*, her talent yelled at her. But it was more than that. Danger was too timid a word.

"Stop," she gasped hoarsely before she could help herself. Why was she seeing this? Had her talent grown stronger somehow?

*Run!* The thought was an old friend. She'd run from her tormentors as a child, had run from her family when their abuse became too much. And since then, she'd run from everyone who'd tried to get close to her—apart from Gannon. She'd been drawn to him.

*What am I doing here?* Kurio asked herself. Ever since acquiring the metal cube for Willas, her life had been driven by external forces. And now here she was, trapped inside a ruin protected by ancient sorcery, with a group of people who wanted her blood, even if they didn't know it yet.

Someone was laughing at her. A god or goddess—maybe all of them.

"We're so close. We can't stop now!" shouted Bryn. He stood in front of the final veil, his back to it. "Look how far we've come! There's treasure in that coffer. I can smell it!"

"He's right," Gannon whispered in Kurio's ear. "But what type of treasure, eh?"

Something smashed into Kurio's head, and her vision swam. She stumbled and felt the floor slam into her knees and hands. She tried to push the pain away—couldn't. She couldn't speak either—her throat wouldn't obey her. What was happening? Who had hit her? Gannon?

She reached up to grab his arm, but her own was leaden. Her whole body felt numb and lifeless, as if she were a wooden doll. She felt she was in the audience of a play, watching the actors perform their parts.

Gannon bent and stroked her hair before lifting her in his arms. Kurio still couldn't move.

*No,* she thought. *What's this about? Why is he doing this?* She willed her hands to bring up her crossbow. To no avail. *He's going to … he's …*

Kurio threw everything she had into her struggle to move, to break Gannon's grasp. The only effect was that her breathing became faster, causing her head to spin.

"Human and demon blood intermingled," Gannon said. "That will breach the final barrier."

With an almighty heave, he threw Kurio at the veil.

A thousand red-hot needles pierced her flesh—the collar's torture multiplied tenfold. It seemed to go on forever as she thrashed wildly—until her seared nerves and wounded psyche couldn't take any more pain, and for an instant she thought she saw a woman's hand reaching out.

Darkness embraced her and spirited her awareness away.

~ ~ ~

Kurio stuck in the arcane curtain like a fly caught in a spiderweb. Coruscating filaments arced across the veil, crackling and sizzling. Kurio screamed like the damned—an agonized wail torn from the back of her throat. Her limbs spasmed violently, and her spine arched so torturously Aldric thought it must snap. Smoke billowed from her clothes as they charred to ash, then the sorcerous tendrils went to work on her flesh, scoring deep red welts across her skin. Mercifully, Kurio blacked out, her head lolling on her limp neck.

How could Gannon sacrifice Kurio so cruelly? He recalled the strangeness he had sensed in her when he healed her hands—she must be part demon—which meant Gannon was Tainted Cabal.

"Bryn, your assistance, please," Gannon said, brandishing his sword.

Bryn drew his blade and moved to Gannon's side.

Niklaus cursed and stepped back, his short sword appearing in his hand as if by sorcery. Aldric drew his curved blade and prepared a cant on his lips, knowing Soki, and even Priska, would be doing the same. Valeria moved to the side and backed away.

"What is the meaning of this?" Aldric said. "Drop your weapons!"

"No," said Gannon flatly. "I don't think so."

"Drop your sword, Bryn," said Niklaus. "Or I swear by the Lady, I'll slice you open."

Bryn shook his head. "Not today, Niklaus. You're good, but so am I. And you're wounded."

"What do you want?" asked Soki.

Gannon raised his eyebrows and chuckled. "I would have thought that was obvious. To get through the final barrier."

A moment of silence followed his remark.

Then Soki uttered a cant, and hearing her, Aldric spoke one of his own to activate his wards.

But something was wrong. Instead of forming itself to his will and the calculations held firmly in his consciousness, his dawn-tide power lashed back at him, scourging his mind. His stomach churned, and gorge rose to his throat. He spat thick saliva from his mouth and shut his cant down, bottling his dawn-tide power. His sorcery had turned against him. It was … impossible.

Soki was on the ground, head in her hands, mouth open as she screamed soundlessly. She'd drawn far more than him and suffered the worse for it. Aldric stumbled over to her and cradled her head in his lap. He felt a sudden, drowning fear that she might die.

Soki closed her mouth, swallowed, then moaned. She stared at Aldric, eyes wide with dismay. He shared her concern. Nothing he knew could do such a thing. Nowhere in his training had it been mentioned, nor in all the sorcerous tomes he'd read. Perhaps a relic taken from another ruin might have such power … He shook his head. He needed to focus, or they were all dead.

He helped Soki to her feet. Then, taking his khopesh in two hands, his palms damp with apprehension, Aldric raised its crescent blade and stepped between her and Gannon. Without her sorcery, she was helpless. He would defend her even if it cost him his life.

Abruptly, the crackling sorcerous barrier winked out, and Kurio's inert form dropped to the floor with a thud. No one so much as glanced at her.

Niklaus moved to Aldric's side.

Priska edged sideways toward the edge of the platform. Valeria, to Aldric's surprise, stood where she was, staring daggers at Gannon and Bryn.

"That's right," Gannon said menacingly. "Your sorcery has been inhibited. You think I didn't plan for this? Breaching these wards is the culmination of centuries of research and planning. We cannot fail now."

Aldric could hear Soki whispering curse after curse, still hoping they might affect Gannon. She was deathly afraid, he realized. They all were.

"You're Tainted Cabal," said Niklaus, then turned to regard Bryn. "But you, Bryn ... you're just his tool. He'll kill you when he's done with you."

Bryn laughed mockingly. "That's where you're wrong. I know your secret, Niklaus, and I've been promised the same gift. I'll work for the Cabal for a great many years to come. And I'll take your prized sword for good measure."

"Try it," growled Niklaus. He sheathed his short sword and stood there weaponless. "A duel."

"Enough!" shouted Valeria. "This is nonsense. Gannon, you might have disarmed the sorcerers, but my power is still my own. The wrath of the Lady will crack your bones and flay the flesh from them."

She spoke liquid words, flung a hand out, and pointed at Gannon. Cords stood out in the man's neck, and his mouth twisted in a pained grimace. But his knees didn't buckle, and soon the grimace transformed into a smile. Whatever power Valeria had flung at Gannon, he had obviously weathered it.

"You think you know pain?" he snarled at Valeria. "I can endure anything you throw at me, scion of a failed goddess. Years spent in the hells teaches a man many things, a familiarity with pain being one of them."

A profanity escaped Valeria's lips. "Pain is but one of the goddess's dominions. If you—"

Gannon barked a guttural word, and Valeria folded in two and tumbled across the floor as if struck by a charging horse. She came to a rest ten paces away and lay unmoving.

*Holy Menselas.* Aldric hadn't felt any arcane surge from Gannon. If he wasn't a sorcerer, he must be using artifacts for his power.

There was only Aldric and Niklaus standing now between Gannon and Bryn and whatever resided in the metal coffer. This was why Menselas wanted Aldric here, in this moment. And why Niklaus's goddess had sent him too. Together, they were supposed to stop Gannon, but already he had them reeling.

Bryn sheathed his sword to match Niklaus and stepped forward with swaggering bravado. "Your pet priestess can't protect you now, Niklaus. It's blade against blade, and you're already wounded. I'll cut you open and watch your entrails spill to the dirt."

Niklaus glided a step toward him. "Bryn, if you're going to draw, do it now."

"Kill him, Bryn," Gannon said. "You told me you could." His voice carried a note of warning.

*Why all this posturing?* Aldric thought. *Because he's not a sorcerer and can only turn sorcery back on the user. There are limits to what Gannon can do. We only have to find them, and quickly.*

Bryn licked his lips, hand now crossed over his waist, grasping the hilt of his sword. But he seemed to think better of it as he saw Niklaus's right hand remained clear of his short sword's hilt. Bryn moved his hand back.

Niklaus sighed and hooked his right thumb into his belt in a show of nonchalance. Aldric thought his movements were slow and deliberate, as if his wounds pained him.

"He lied to you," said Niklaus. "Poor Bryn. Always seeking to be the best, but falling short."

The two swordsmen were closer than ever, barely three feet apart, hardly room to fight if it came to drawn blades.

Aldric knew he would have to try for Gannon. He edged away from Niklaus and Bryn as surreptitiously as he could, but Gannon wasn't fooled.

"I wouldn't," he warned Aldric. "Or you'll end up like Valeria."

*If he could, wouldn't he have subdued us all by now?* Aldric thought.

*What's stopping him?*

Gannon's eyes flicked to Aldric's khopesh, then back to the mounting tension between Bryn and Niklaus. The epiphany hit Aldric like a hammer. His blade. Star-metal. Gannon's own words: *years spent in the hells* ... Gannon wasn't just a member of the Tainted Cabal; he was a demon or the spawn of one. And star-metal was anathema to demons and perhaps to their sorcery as well.

Niklaus's sword ... it was star-metal too. He should forget about Bryn and aim for Gannon.

Aldric searched for a way to let Niklaus know of his revelation, but the mercenary's focus was purely on Bryn.

"Niklaus!" he hissed.

"Not now," Niklaus said.

And in that instant, Bryn moved to draw. A twitch of his shoulders. His right hand darted as swift as a striking snake.

But Niklaus was faster. As Bryn grasped his hilt, Niklaus drew his short sword with his *left* hand. Before Bryn's blade was half out of its sheath, Niklaus's sword sliced an upward arc, his right hand pushing the back of the blade for strength. Steel sheared through Bryn's side. Blood sprayed, and the swordsman staggered. For an instant, both men stood there, motionless. Niklaus, one foot forward, short sword grasped in his left hand, extended to the side of Bryn's torso. Bryn staggered, a disbelieving look on his face, scarlet flowing down his right side to splash on the ground.

He frowned, his sword falling from limp fingers with a clang. "No," he said.

"Yes," replied Niklaus. "You always did talk too much."

Bryn collapsed to the ground, his blood pooling in the Skanuric script carved into the pavers.

"Niklaus!" shouted Aldric. "Gannon is a demon. Your sword—it's star-metal!"

The mercenary understood straight away, dropping his short

sword and swinging his long sword from his back to his hip.

To Aldric's surprise, Valeria suddenly stood between Niklaus and Gannon. Her robes were dusty and torn, her face and hands smeared with dirt.

"Wait!" she pleaded with Niklaus. "Whatever power is held here, we must be a part of it. You are her Chosen Sword, Niklaus. You hold greater sway with the priestesses than you realize. We can join with Gannon and—"

"You don't even know what he wants!" shouted Niklaus. "And you have no idea what the Lady wants. You see his power, and you lust after it. The Lady sees you, Valeria, just as I do. You have strayed from her path."

"We can join with Gannon," Valeria repeated. "With the Tainted Cabal. It is all clear to me now. This is what our goddess wants. With our powers combined, we will rule the world. Whatever artifacts are hidden here, we can use them well. Kill Aldric and the rest of them."

Niklaus lifted his chin and sneered at Valeria. "You don't even know what's here, and you want to kill everyone?"

"The Lady wants this!" screamed Valeria. "Haven't you realized yet, Niklaus? Gannon wants power, dominion over humanity. The goddess has sent me here to be a part of this. She wants me to use this power. And you will obey me! You are nothing but a tool to her, an anvil that facilitates the real work. I am the hammer. I wield her true power. I shape what the goddess wants."

Niklaus lunged and his sword plunged into Valeria's heart. The tip burst from her back, the blade dripping blood. He grabbed her shoulder and pushed the sword deeper. Valeria coughed. Scarlet dribbled from her mouth like viscous wine. With a jerk, Niklaus yanked his blade free, and the high priestess collapsed to the ground, fingers scrabbling at the cold stone. Her chest heaved as she tried to breathe, and she coughed again, spraying red across the floor.

"That's where you're wrong," Niklaus said, standing over the dying priestess. "I am the hammer. And the anvil. And the blade. And you ... You are a fool."

Valeria's mouth moved as she tried to speak, but no words could get past the blood in her chest and throat. Her eyes closed, and she coughed another stream of crimson.

Aldric sprang at Gannon, swinging his khopesh with all his might.

Gannon reacted with startling speed, leaning to the side to avoid the blow and hammering a fist into Aldric's head. Aldric tumbled to the ground, khopesh jarring from his fingers. Another pummeling strike slammed into his chest and sent him rolling. A sharp pain in his ribs made it hard to breathe, and it took a few moments before he could stagger upright.

Gannon's knee crashed into his head, sending him sprawling. Aldric's vision dimmed, and his ears rang. He tried to move, but searing pain tore at his muscles. He shook his head to clear it, and a surge of nausea almost brought up the contents of his stomach.

Arms and legs trembling, he pushed against the pavers and managed to lever himself to his knees. Gannon stood over him, the tip of his blade inches from his throat.

Aldric looked around for his khopesh and saw it lying close to Valeria's corpse, a dozen paces away. *Too far ...*

"Time to meet your god," Gannon told him.

Behind Gannon, Aldric saw Niklaus rushing toward them. In the dim light, his blade seemed to flicker with an unearthly glow. He was grinning like a madman.

A slight smile flickered on Gannon's lips. He reversed his sword swiftly and jumped backward, thrusting his blade behind him—impaling Niklaus through the chest.

The swordsman gasped, a look of disbelief on his face.

With one swift movement, Gannon jerked his blade free and a

gleam of satisfaction came into his eyes. Aldric watched in horror
as Niklaus fell to his knees. The hole in his chest pumped scarlet
across his shirt and onto the ground. He groped one hand against
his chest, as if hoping to stop his life leaching away. Blood oozed
between his fingers.

With a savage grunt, Gannon raised his blade high and cleaved
into Niklaus's shoulder.

The mercenary cried out in agony and reached up with one
arm, as if imploring his goddess to save him. But it wasn't to be.
Niklaus collapsed to the ground, hugging his sword to his chest,
blood spilling from his wounds.

Aldric couldn't heal himself, but he could use his god's power
on Niklaus. Staggering to his feet, he reached for Menselas's gift.

Immediately, Gannon jerked around to face him, and his fist
slammed into Aldric's head. Aldric reeled on wobbly legs, tripped,
and sprawled across the floor. When he regained his senses
enough to look up, Gannon was standing next to his khopesh. He
kicked the curved blade, and it skidded across the floor, coming to
rest against Valeria's corpse. Gannon stood between the blade and
the three who remained alive: Priska, Soki, and Aldric.

"Your god may have thought you'd be able to stop this," he
told Aldric. "But he is wrong. You are weak, stunted by your
Church and their fears. I knew that when I saw you in Etia's
temple. If it hadn't been for your god's intervention, I'd have
killed both of you then."

Darya was Gannon, realized Aldric. Disguised by sorcery to
appear as a darker version of Soki, a smoldering, sensual portrayal,
manipulating his reaction. She had been beautiful, as Gannon was
handsome.

"*Idmoni*," breathed Aldric. Gannon had manipulated them all
from the beginning.

"Just so," said Gannon. "Niklaus's interference wasn't
foreseen, but it is a sign the gods and goddesses fear what is

coming. And well they should."

Aldric shifted closer to Soki and winced in pain at the movement. A couple of cracked ribs and a severely bruised face, he surmised. He wouldn't be much good if it came to more fighting, but he'd do his best. That was what his god expected from him.

Priska seemed to have folded in on herself, lost to despair. There was a wild look in her eyes, and she'd settled on her knees, staring at Gannon. She thought they were all going to die. She was probably right.

Soki looked exhausted and defeated, but drew herself up straight. "What is it you want from us?" she asked Gannon. "The blood of a sorcerer this time?"

"No. Only Kurio's death was necessary. What I require from you, Sokhelle, is to deal with the sorcery entombed in the coffer. I should warn you: it's quite virulent." He raised his sword and smiled. "Aldric and Priska, come over here."

"Don't," Soki snapped, and reached out to grab Aldric's arm.

"I wasn't planning to," Priska said.

"Come now," said Gannon. "There's no need to make this any harder. It can go smoothly, or slowly and painfully."

"I won't let you kill them," said Soki.

Gannon laughed and took a step forward. "You don't have a choice."

Soki let go of Aldric's arm and backed away a few steps, closer to the edge of the platform. "You need me. If I don't do what you want, your plan fails."

"But you will do what I want."

Soki shook her head and took another backward step. "What would happen if I threw myself over the edge into whatever's below? I mightn't even need to. My sorcery won't work on you, but it'll work on me. One sharp burst, and I could kill myself."

"You wouldn't."

"Try me. What are my options if I don't? You'll get what you want and then kill us all anyway. And what's the point of that? We're of no use to you after. Let us all go free."

Gannon stood motionless and silent. Eventually, he said, "Maybe you're right. And maybe not. Perhaps I should just take my chances."

"Soki …" Aldric warned.

She turned to him and said warmly, though with an edge of weariness, "I'm not going to die here, and neither are you. Gannon gets what he wants, and we go free." She regarded Gannon. "Agreed?"

A nod. "Agreed."

Aldric knew what Soki thought—they could survive to fight Gannon another day, something Gannon himself must suspect. But the man had manipulated them all so far, so he had reason to believe he was untouchable. He must have his claws into Aldric's Church and Niklaus's too. Whether by corruption or simple persuasion was something Aldric would need to find out. If they made it out of the ruin alive.

And would he and Soki be able to stop Gannon once he had what he wanted? He was a member of the Tainted Cabal, and his purpose was the downfall of mankind and the resurgence of demons and their lord, Nysrog. What was Aldric's life weighed against the devastation that could follow?

"No," he said firmly, meeting Gannon's eyes. "We won't do it."

"I will," Soki said.

Aldric flinched as her words hit him like a physical blow. She gave him a brief smile. *Trust me*, she mouthed.

Menselas, Aldric's god, had placed him here. Did he want Aldric to die trying to keep this unknown sorcery confined? Or did he merely want him to witness what occurred? Was Aldric's only role here to open the ruin? He recoiled from the thought.

No, that was not a task his god would assign to him. Evil such as the Tainted Cabal wouldn't be allowed to flourish. Aldric had faith there were unseen currents he could not discern. He didn't understand the gods, maybe he never would, but Menselas worked for the greater good.

History and legends were full of heroes favored by gods and goddesses. But Aldric wasn't a hero. He was a shunned priest and an unexceptional sorcerer. What use was he if he couldn't even save those he cared about? He set his jaw and drew himself up straight despite the pain of his ribs. If Menselas required a last, mortal duty of him, then he would have it.

"I cannot," Aldric said, his words utterly at odds with the confusion in his soul.

Soki's expression turned to disappointment. He cast his eyes down, not daring to meet hers.

"You don't have a choice," said Gannon.

He produced an object from his pocket: a shiny metal cube covered with script. From the shape of the writing, Aldric could tell it was Skanuric. Gannon grinned, placed his metal cube on the ground in front of him, then moved to the side.

He was getting closer—perhaps Aldric could ... No, it was too risky. Though if he came within a few paces, Aldric might have a chance at subduing him.

"Bind the sorcery into this artifact," Gannon told Soki. "Then we're done."

Before Aldric could so much as blink, Gannon lunged at Priska and tangled a hand in her hair. She screamed, and he twisted her scalp, eliciting more cries of pain from her.

Aldric started forward, but Gannon placed the edge of his blade against Priska's neck, daring Aldric to intervene, then dragged the young woman back a few steps. Priska's hands clawed at Gannon's, scoring bloody welts into his skin as her legs kicked and flailed uselessly against the pavers.

Aldric swallowed against a sudden twinge in his chest. "If you hurt her ..."

Gannon grinned ferally. "You'll do what? I'll slit her throat before you can so much as move a finger. Shut your mouth, stupid priest, and do what I tell you."

Soki's hand rested on Aldric's shoulder. "Calm," she whispered to him. And then to Gannon, "I'm ready. What would you have me do?"

"Open the coffer," he said. "Corral the sorcery, and inter it in this artifact. Simple, really."

Soki strode to the orichalcum coffer and with a grunt of exertion heaved the lid off. It fell to the ground with a tumultuous clang. She peered inside. "There's nothing ... ah."

She made a show of fumbling around inside, turning slightly to shield her actions from Gannon. She drew out a bejeweled necklace and slipped it into her pocket, but not before Aldric caught a glimpse. An orichalcum chain with green cat's-eye cabochons—Aldric recognized it from his dreams, and his heart raced. The last time he'd seen the necklace, it was around the neck of Shalmara, Grandmaster of the Evokers. There was a chilling sensation to it, discernible with his sorcerous sight. But his expertise was lacking. He had no idea what it could do, but he did know what it was ...

The Chain of Eyes, a relic from the war against Nysrog.

If Gannon saw it, he was sure to kill them. He wouldn't leave them alive with the knowledge that such a powerful artifact had been discovered and was now in the Tainted Cabal's hands.

"There's a vambrace in here," Soki said loudly, bringing it out.

The armor's metal glinted briefly in the light before becoming as black as pitch. Not a spot of rust marred its surface, which was worked into a pattern of tiny scales. A faint buzz reached Aldric's ears—a weird droning of insects.

"Put it back," he breathed fearfully.

Soki ignored him and, after one last glance inside the coffer, approached Aldric.

"Soki, put it back," Aldric repeated.

"I'll take that," Gannon said. "Toss it over here. Now."

Soki glanced at Aldric, then did as she was told. The black vambrace clattered at Gannon's feet. He gave Priska's hair a savage twist, and she cried out, tears streaming down her cheeks. Gannon forced her to the floor, grinding her face into the pavers and pressing a knee into her back. With her properly subdued, he picked the object up.

"This is an unexpected bonus," he said. "Can you sense its power? You must be able to." He examined the piece of armor, seeming engrossed in its details.

Soki's eyes met Aldric's, and her words were barely a whisper. "If I fail, you must keep the necklace safe. Can you feel it?"

He did sense something ... a sweet, incense-like fog lifting around them.

He recalled the mist deep below the platform and staggered to peer over the side. The membranous substance had changed from a churning, seething fog to placid calm. But the occasional flashes of diamond he'd seen had multiplied and coalesced into large groups, looking like schools of silver fish darting beneath the surface. It was a reservoir of dawn-tide and dusk-tide sorcery— Aldric could feel it. So massive, so extraordinary, that he couldn't comprehend the skill required to manipulate it, let alone imprison it here. And for what purpose?

Was this Gannon's ultimate goal? Did he and the Tainted Cabal plan to use the power to bring Nysrog back?

He cast a glance back at Gannon, who now held the Skanuric-inscribed cube in front of him. His lips moved silently, and with a thin silver rod he made complex movements. It was sorcery of a sort Aldric had never seen before. Gannon's eyes remained fixed on the cube, which he was no doubt preparing somehow for what was to come.

Soki's eyes were filled with pain and regret. Tears ran down her cheeks. She clasped Aldric's head in her hands, pulled him toward her, and kissed him on the lips. He could taste her salty tears mingling with their breath.

She broke their embrace and wiped her eyes. "I'll do my best. If you survive, take the necklace."

"Soki, we have to—"

She placed a finger against his lips. "It's too late. Opening the coffer was a trigger. The sorcery has been unleashed—you must sense it. And it's ... I'm afraid, Aldric. I don't want to die."

"You won't. I'm here for a reason. My god—"

"Your god sent you as an assassin, as did Niklaus's goddess. Only they failed to tell you what they wanted of you. There was ample opportunity to kill Gannon before this, if you'd known of his intention. Now, I have to wrangle a snake." She paused and gave a slight shake of her head. "If I fail, you must take my catalyst and return it to my Covenant, the Sanguine Legion."

Soki and her gaze were like a lodestone to Aldric. He couldn't tear his eyes away, although he knew Gannon was near. He nodded that he understood.

"Promise me," she said fiercely.

"I promise."

But he knew that as soon as Gannon got what he wanted, they would all die.

Out of the corner of his eye, he saw flickers of brilliance crystalize in the dark. Shoals of sparkles rose from the membrane below and floated past the platform, coalescing into a greater mass above them to become one shining accumulation.

"What is it?" Aldric asked.

"Sentient sorceries that could cause another cataclysm. And I have to stop it."

Soki backed away until she pressed against the coffer, as if using it for support. Her dark hair curled about her slender shoulders, and Aldric cursed himself for not being able to help her in her task. He wished he was more skilled with sorcery so he could share her burden, or even take it from her. His weakness angered him to the point of heartbreak. All this time, he had railed against his circumstance, made a badge of his disgrace. All this time he had confused his weakness for strength. His ceding of control to his Church was his undoing. And he hated himself for it.

He wondered now if his god had chosen him for this very task. And he had failed.

Cants flowed from Soki, fluid and flawless. Words of power underwritten by complex calculations. Aldric's tears flowed down his cheeks as he listened to peerless sorcery stream from her blood-red lips. Her dawn-tide and dusk-tide energies answered, and Soki uttered more ancient words. Aldric gasped at their power. Grandmaster cants that he'd studied, but had never thought to see attempted lest they crack the world.

Sizzling lines appeared from thin air, violet and blue. A complex weave of dawn- and dusk-tide emanations.

Aldric did the only thing he could: he reached for his own repositories and sent a thread to Soki, hoping he didn't disrupt her concentration. A request for a consort; a sharing of power. He couldn't add much to Soki's reserves, but if this battle came down to a knife edge, his support might mean the difference between success and failure.

He looked over to Priska, wondering if she might help. Gannon's hand now grasped her dark hair again, and he jerked her head up to expose her neck, resting the razor edge of his blade against it.

"You have to let her help Sokhelle," Aldric said.

Gannon didn't move. His eyes were focused on Soki, but he removed his sword from Priska's throat. She sobbed with relief, wiped her nose on her sleeve, and added her own cants and repositories to Soki's, as Aldric had done.

"She knows what it is," Gannon said suddenly. "Your fearless sorcerer, Sokhelle."

Above their heads, the diamonds whirled and churned, almost too bright to look at. They chased away shadows and cast a rippling radiance around them like sunlight on the ocean. An immense droning filled the air, so intense it set Aldric's jawbone vibrating.

"What is it?" asked Priska, then gasped as Gannon twisted her hair again.

"I may have lied when I said it was sorcery. It is *of* sorcery," he said, and gestured to the metal cube, which he'd placed on the ground. "In here, Sokhelle, if you please—or the sorcery will go free. What would happen then? Tell them."

Soki paused her chanting, anguish on her face. She spoke as if the words were torn from her. "Every sorcerer will die. And without their protection, so will most of humanity. Our civilization would be destroyed. I ... I cannot condone that. I will not be the cause."

Power rose from her like a current, coursing outward and enveloping the shimmering mass. She gasped, and her eyes narrowed in studied concentration. "It's strong. I cannot ... but I must."

"You are witnessing something no one before you has lived to talk about," Gannon told Aldric. "The sorcerers of old named it Revenants. The Cabal terms them the Raveners, because ... well ... that's what they are. Ravenous. They find sorcerers and destroy them. Along with everything around them."

"They?" asked Aldric. "I don't understand." But he recalled one of the dreams the relic had sent him. Sian telling Marthaze of a sorcery the Evokers constructed that would prevent Nysrog from ever rising again. She'd called it 'the Revenants' and said it would save the world.

"After Nysrog was defeated, the sorcerers and priests decided that a certain level of sorcery was inimical to civilization. It turned into a danger. If its adherents became too skilled, too potent, they would tread places best left alone. The evilest and most power-hungry would look toward demons and their power."

Fragments of Aldric's dreams came together. "They wanted to prevent another Nysrog."

"Yes. So they created the Revenants and entombed them in ruins like this one, behind arcane veils that can only be breached by complex sorceries and divine powers. Sorcerers, they surmised, lusted after more power, delving heedlessly into the unknown. They couldn't help themselves."

It slowly dawned on Aldric just what was happening. If every sorcerer died, as Soki had warned, there would be no one to keep people safe from the creatures of the wilderness. Chaos and death would be inevitable. Diseases would desolate the cities, and creatures of the wilderness would be free to rampage and destroy. An entire civilization decimated, all to prevent the return of Nysrog.

"The cataclysms," he said. "The Revenants were responsible?"

How many people had been murdered? Cities destroyed, and civilization plunged into darkness time and time again? And all because some ancient sorcerers had decided that the only way to keep humanity away from power that could destroy them was to deny them any knowledge of such power. It was abhorrent. It was … evil.

He squeezed his hands into fists. What could he do? He'd had a hand in unleashing this monstrosity.

"The Revenants prevent sorcery from progressing and spreading," Gannon said. "That is their only task. Right now, they've only just awoken, so are vulnerable in certain ways. Only now can they be neutralized, and their power will be mine to use."

He cleared his throat loudly. "Sokhelle, hurry, please."

"Be quiet," snapped Soki between cants of intricate sorcery.

Inside her arcane net, the Revenants grew brighter. Bulges appeared, as if testing the constraints holding them. Soki grimaced, rivulets of sweat pouring down her face. Aldric felt his repositories drain as she tapped into his power. Priska gasped; she must have felt the same. All too quickly, Aldric's reserves were drained. Soki was on her own now.

One particularly large bulge pressed outward, stretching the sorcerous net to bursting. Soki cried out and clasped her hands to her forehead. She staggered, and Aldric lunged to support her weight. He held her trembling body against his and marveled at her capacity as she continued uttering cants despite the strain she was under. In his arms, her slender form felt delicate and fragile.

Soki gave him a wan smile before continuing to chant sorceries. Under assault from the Revenants, her arcane mesh expanded further still as they probed for weaknesses. Soki's voice rose, and cants poured from her mouth as she attempted to strengthen her creation, but as soon as one area was reinforced, another came under assault. She couldn't keep this up, Aldric knew. She would make a mistake; or her dawn-tide and dusk-tide reservoirs would drain completely. Even Aldric's paltry sorcerous sense could feel the Revenants' capacity, as tireless as the tides, as complex as life itself.

Soki stumbled over a cant, and a bright sparkle wormed through a fissure. Immediately, she shoved Aldric away from her. The sparkle swooped straight for Soki, catching her in the middle of an unfinished warding cant. Her spine arched, and her skin lit up with an internal radiance. She cried out in agony and fell to the ground.

Aldric scrambled to her, reaching for his god's divine power.

Soki clawed at his arms, fingers digging into his flesh. "Aldric, I've failed. I'm sorry. It has me."

She screamed, a primal sound torn from her throat, ripped from her very soul. Hair-thin slashes opened on her skin, and blood trickled out, infused with minute sparkles. The Revenants were destroying her from the inside.

Aldric opened himself to his god and threw himself into saving Soki. She was their only chance. Only Soki had the talent to confine the Revenants and possibly to stop Gannon. But what really drove him was the possibility of losing her. He couldn't bear the thought. Why should he live and Soki die? It wasn't right.

Menselas's might suffused him, and he directed it at Soki. Her skin had a feverish burn, and every exposed part was streaked with cuts and blood. Weaving the god's power as best he could, he closed her cuts and healed her skin. Then he sent questing surges through her veins, hunting the Revenants. But they were too small. Too many. He cornered groups, only to feel them slip away. He lacked the necessary knowledge. Another side effect of neglecting his healing.

His Church had held him back, and now the world would feel the consequences of their actions. Beginning with the woman he loved.

Aldric screamed in frustration, then threw himself entirely into the struggle, drawing more of Menselas's power than he ever had before. He changed tactics and sent sheets of it pulsing through Soki. So intent was he on saving her, he didn't notice any change until her fingers twisted his ear. He opened his eyes and stared into hers.

"Thank you," she said weakly. "But I fear I'm a lost cause."

"Don't say that. You—"

Her finger on his lips stopped him. "Now's not the time for false hope. You need to keep me alive while I combat the Revenants. They're inside me, Aldric—I can feel them burning, tearing me apart. There's no hope. But if you can give me more time, I think I can contain those still in my net."

"I'm not going to lose you," he said.

Her hand caressed his cheek. "I'm sorry. I wish it could have been different. Now hush, there's no time." Her face twisted in agony, and she sucked in gasping breaths. "You owe me," she croaked through her pain.

Soki tilted her face up toward the Revenants and resumed chanting cants. Weak at first, her voice grew in strength. Far above, caught in the arcane mesh she had created, the Revenants roiled and churned.

Aldric blinked away tears and bent to his own task. There had to be a chance of saving her. His god's power was immense. He drew in as much as he could and set to healing her.

"This is all very touching," he heard Gannon say. "But if you don't finish the job, I'll kill you both. Then your civilization and everyone you love will also die. It's not my favored option, but I'll settle for it."

"Then at least," Soki whispered, "the Tainted Cabal would have to remain in hiding and will be unable to summon Nysrog for fear of the Revenants. Of course."

A soundless shockwave erupted from the Revenants and washed over them all, pushing them off balance. Soki's mesh flared to blinding brilliance. The ruin resonated with a tangible, swelling charge that prickled Aldric's skin. Soki coughed, interrupting her cants for an instant. Blood dribbled from her lips. She wiped it away with the back of her hand and resumed her sorcery. Her effort felt like a spider's web holding back a gale.

A cold pit in his stomach, Aldric continued his attempt to heal her. The damage the Revenants had done was extensive: already, her less vital organs had shut down, and she had internal bleeding in several areas. He wove Menselas's power as best he could, patching in some places, repairing the worst areas. But for every wound healed, another appeared. The damage was immense, and he knew his skill wouldn't suffice.

"Steady," he told her. "I've got you. It's going to be all right."

She returned a slight nod, her eyes wide with fear. Aldric's heart lurched in response. He sensed her distress. Soki was in intense pain, being torn apart from the inside, and still she fought to contain the Revenants.

Power whipped against power. Dawn-tide and dusk-tide sorcery clashed. Time lost all meaning. All that mattered was Soki. Her cants became a distant backdrop as he sought to keep her alive. Energies coursed from her—binding and imprisoning cants to reinforce the vast and intricate matrix she had created. Lights flashed and danced around them.

Her shouts reached a crescendo, and her power crackled and blazed. A tendril emerged from the arcane net she had created, pulled toward Gannon's cube. Its tip touched the metal, then wavered.

Soki's voice was a rasping mess now, but still she continued her chanting. The tendril latched onto the cube.

"Yes," said Gannon, reverence in his voice.

Glittering lights pulsed down the strand, gathering in speed and frequency, more and more power pouring from Soki's sorcerous net into Gannon's metal cube—another prison.

"Only a little more," Gannon said.

Soki stopped chanting and laughed, her lips and chin scarlet with blood. "You want it all? Sorry, not this fragment."

"No!" shouted Gannon.

With a thunderous crack, Soki's net fractured. Scintillating diamonds in the shape of perfect spheres poured through the breach, swirling into a swarm before shooting upward and hammering into the rock of the roof. Their radiance scattered, fading to nothing, the spheres becoming as dark as pitch.

Gannon spat curses in a guttural tongue.

*They can't escape*, Aldric thought. Then swore vehemently as the entire mass seemed to leach into the ceiling, draining away like water through a cracked bath. In moments they were gone.

Soki had allowed a fragment to escape, and now the Tainted Cabal wouldn't be able to summon Nysrog. Gannon's plan was in tatters. But was releasing the Revenants a better outcome? Aldric wasn't so sure.

He threw himself into healing Soki with renewed vigor, drawing strength from reserves he didn't know he had. Weaving frantically, he mended veins and drained pools of blood back into them, repaired slashed organs and skin, all the while chasing the Revenants inside Soki. They were foreign bodies, so he could exert some control over them, but not enough. He managed to corral some, though had to continually concentrate on them or they'd break free.

Soki gave a cry of triumph, and Aldric looked up to see the last of the Revenants disappear into Gannon's cube. A final surge from Soki, and the cube flashed a brilliant blue.

Soki laughed weakly, then went limp in Aldric's arms. She had sealed the cube with her last remaining strength. Only a powerful sorcerer could break it open again, and Gannon wasn't much of a sorcerer.

Gannon's face was a mask of pure fury, but also pale. The strain from the sorcery he'd worked on the cube was showing. He was weak. Was it time for Aldric to strike?

Before he could move, Gannon snarled and sliced open Priska's throat. Crimson gushed out like a wave.

"Save her," Soki whispered. "I did all I could. Now it's up to you. Don't forget the Chain."

Her eyes closed, and she drew in a halting breath. She exhaled once; then her chest was still. Aldric lowered her head gently to the ground.

Taking a deep breath, he lunged and slid across the pavers, hand reaching for his khopesh. His ribs protested and he grimaced. Aldric's fingers grasped his weapon, clamping around its hilt. He rose to his feet, the blade in his hand. Star-metal—anathema to demons.

Gannon snatched up the cube and ran into the darkness behind the coffer.

Aldric let him go and turned his attention to Priska. He stumbled to her side, knees buckling from exhaustion. Tears coursed down his cheeks, hot and salty. He pressed a hand to her throat. Her wide eyes stared at him, imploring. Crimson bubbled from her lips. Her hands grabbed his shirt, clenching tight.

Her face blurred as fresh tears clouded Aldric's vision. Grasping his god's divine power, he sent it into Priska with all his might. Her wound was relatively simple compared to the damage wrought to Soki. He mended the jugular and tendons and fused her skin, then removed his hand, sticky with blood. Priska was safe. For now.

Aldric blinked away his tiredness and stood to confront Gannon. His khopesh felt ten times heavier than usual. He reached for whatever dregs of sorcerous power he had remaining. There wasn't enough for an attack, not that he'd succeed, but he could use it for defense. He didn't hold out much hope, but he had to try. He couldn't let so many die without an attempt at vengeance.

The immense chamber around Aldric shrank, then disappeared as power blazed through him. He tried to withdraw from it, but his mind refused to budge, as if it were nailed in place. He opened his mouth to scream—couldn't. Something had set him in stone. The power scoured through his body like acid. It was an alarm bell, awakening his survival instinct. And it had a familiar flavor …
It was tinged with Menselas.

His god was burning him with holy fire.

Aldric almost let go then, almost surrendered to the purifying heat of the divine. He'd failed, and this was his punishment.

Just as suddenly, the burning stopped. Aldric moaned with

blessed relief as his nerves and flesh soaked up the chill of the ruin. Long moments passed before he gathered himself to wonder what was happening. Something cold and hard and rough pressed against the side of his face. The floor.

A faint chanting came from somewhere, guttural and halting. Gannon.

Aldric moved a finger and immediately regretted it. His muscles and bones felt like they'd been pierced by a hundred needles. He sucked in a deep breath, forced the pain to the back of his mind, placed a palm against the floor, and before he could finish the thought and stop himself, he shoved himself onto his back. He screamed as the pain was multiplied a thousand times. Tears flowed from his eyes. Then he remembered Soki, and more tears followed. Aldric was alone and afraid.

But Gannon had to be stopped.

Menselas knew this, so why had his god prevented him?

A dark need to act woke in Aldric. A craving for retribution and blood. Gannon must be killed.

He turned the thought over in his mind. It was the first time he'd ever considered killing a human being for his own vengeance. It disturbed him, but if anyone deserved to die, surely it was Gannon. What was one life weighed against the deaths of hundreds of thousands?

There was danger in such thinking, he knew. Dread overcame him. He wasn't afraid of dying in the attempt, but feared for the sanctity of his soul.

But he was different, wasn't he? He *understood* the peril. And some deaths were required. Some deaths were ... holy.

Gannon's chanting continued, and Aldric became aware of an unraveling sensation as reality twisted and warped. An unholy stench assailed his nostrils, and he gagged. He blinked away tears and saw Gannon standing in front of the coffer, a fog rising around him. Lines of sorcery scored through the mist, their passing blazing shadowy lines that rapidly dissipated. Demon sorcery, or some kind of innate ability, Aldric thought.

Kurio lay at Gannon's feet, as did Bryn. The swordsman's throat had been ripped out.

*But that's not how he died ...*

Then Aldric saw the hunk of flesh in Gannon's hand, the blood around his mouth. He watched in frozen horror as Gannon brought Bryn's flesh to his lips and savaged off a chunk, swallowing almost immediately.

Aldric felt an immense surge of a dark, arcane energy. The fog surrounding Gannon swirled and churned more densely, and there was a howling sound, like a keening wind in the high mountains. The fog roiled away from Gannon to form a coursing circle beside him that grew darker, blotting out the coffer. There was a brief flash of brilliant light, so intense Aldric closed his eyes, and the roaring sound stopped, as if cut off by a door closing.

When Aldric opened his eyes, the circle had transformed into a picture of a city from an elevated position. He recognized it immediately: Caronath. No, not a picture. The leaves on the trees moved in a silent breeze. Gannon had created a gate.

Tiny dots of black floated above the city, swirling and swooping, like a flock of swallows. They twisted and churned, darting this way and that, forming clumps of dense darkness that split and reformed and split again and again. Aldric squinted, not believing his eyes. It was the Revenants that had escaped; they had already covered the distance from here to Caronath. As the realization formed a pit of ice in his stomach, he saw the spheres form into a mass and dive like a hawk for prey.

A violent silver flash flared in the city. Buildings crumpled, and a speckled dust blasted into the air. With a sick horror, Aldric realized the dust was people. The Revenants were hunting sorcerers and destroying the city. It was their only purpose. Though it was only a fragment of the whole, it still held tremendous power.

Kurio gave a low groan. One hand came up to clutch her head.

"She's alive," marveled Gannon. "Though she shouldn't be." He gathered her into his arms.

Aldric couldn't do anything to help those in Caronath, not from this distance. But he could try to prevent Gannon taking Kurio for the Tainted Cabal to use for whatever unholy purpose. He pushed himself to his knees, retching as nausea overcame him. Surprisingly, he still held his khopesh.

Gannon stepped through the gate, and his clothes rippled in a breeze. The sun bathed him in golden light. Aldric realized it was just past dawn. He lurched to his feet. The tip of his blade scraped along the ground as he staggered toward the arcane gate.

"Gannon!" he roared.

Gannon turned to frown at Aldric. He dropped Kurio into the dirt, and dust puffed up around her. "You are no threat, priest."

Cants flowed from him, accompanied by finger gestures representing the structure and calculations of his demonic sorcery. Slowly, the circle began to shrink toward its center.

"No!" Aldric shouted, stumbling forward. But he knew in his gut he wouldn't reach it in time; it was closing too swiftly.

The contraction accelerated, and in an instant, the gate shrank to a pinprick and disappeared.

Aldric fell to his knees. Gannon was gone. And he'd taken Kurio with him. He clutched at his body as a violent shuddering racked him from toes to crown. A sob escaped his lips as despair overtook him. Never had he felt so betrayed, so shamed.

Never had he doubted his faith, his god. Until now.

"Aldric?" came a feeble voice.

He turned to see Priska rising weakly to her feet. Her hair was a tangled mess, and dust and dirt stained her clothes.

"Where's Sokhelle?" she asked, looking around. A strangled cry escaped her lips as she saw the sorcerer lying lifeless on the pavers. "Is she ...?"

"She's dead," Aldric said. "I couldn't save her."

Priska saw Niklaus and scrambled across the floor to him. Blood was congealed in a sticky mess around his body, but she took no notice as it clung to her clothes, her hands.

"Heal him," she screeched at Aldric.

"I'm afraid there's nothing I can do for Niklaus either," he said.

"What good are you, then?" sobbed Priska.

He took Priska by the elbow and drew her away from Niklaus's corpse. Fresh tears rolled down her cheeks, and her lips trembled. Aldric wanted to heal her tiredness and her minor scratches and bruises—to do something good, to salvage something from this mess. He reached for Menselas's divine power and found ... nothing. His god had abandoned him. For his failure. For his doubts.

Desolation gripped his heart, clenching it tight.

"I'm sorry," he mumbled to Priska. "I can't heal you. I'm sorry."

He couldn't find any more words. Now, in the moment of his greatest need—of the world's greatest need—Menselas had abandoned him.

Aldric rose to his feet. His khopesh lay on the ground, and he almost kicked it over the edge of the platform, but stopped himself. Its curved blade gleamed under Soki's sorcerous illumination. The globe's radiance would soon fade, he knew that, but for now he stood bathed in its light. In *her* light.

Soki hadn't given up. Even when she knew she was dying, she'd kept trying to bind the Revenants despite knowing she was doomed. She'd given up her life so others, like Aldric and Priska, could live; so their civilization wasn't destroyed. And she still carried the Chain of Eyes.

Bending gingerly, Aldric grasped the hilt of his khopesh and sheathed the blade.

Soki's sorcerous globes winked out, leaving them in pitch darkness.

Aldric reached for his own dawn-tide reservoir and spoke a cant, which fizzled into nothing. He was empty. But a gleam in the inky blackness caught his eye. It was tiny at first, a flicker. Then it resolved into a faint glow.

There was no doubting the source. Niklaus's sword.

A gasp escaped Priska.

Someone groaned. Not Aldric. And not the sorcerer.

Niklaus.

The mercenary rolled onto his side, then sat upright. He sucked in a huge breath of air and gasped like a fish out of water.

Aldric was so stunned he couldn't speak.

Niklaus rose to his feet, as though his horrific wounds didn't bother him.

Priska crowed with delight. She rushed over and flung herself at Niklaus's feet, clutching his legs.

"What ...?" managed Aldric.

Niklaus gave a hacking cough, then spat scarlet-streaked phlegm to the side.

"Blood and damnation, Priska," he snarled. "Can you get off me, and find me something to drink?"

# JUDGMENT

TRYING NOT TO RETCH, ZARINA rummaged through the tattered clothes strewn around Mellish's corpse at the base of the cliff. Or what was left of him. Animals, or something worse, had ravaged his flesh; and some of his bones bore teeth marks. A similar fate had befallen his mount. She was only able to confirm the remains were Mellish's from the gear scattered around and the saddle.

When she didn't find what she was looking for, she closed her eyes and sat for a time on the cold hard stone. A sliver of unease pierced her heart. Mellish had carried with him the artifact that controlled the collar around the demon's neck, and an ancient amulet her order had salvaged from a ruin. Both were invaluable to the Order of the Blazing Sun's cause. If they were lost …

The demon Kurio must have taken them. She would be hunted down and destroyed. Her kind had no place in this world. There could be no compromises, no quarter.

Zarina stood and dusted off her hands. She looked across the darkening defile in front of her and decided she'd better scale the cliff quickly; it would only become trickier in the fading light. At the top, she kneeled at the rough edge and surveyed Mellish's resting place one last time. He had been a flawed tool, but valuable in his own way. She had so few to work with.

The forces arrayed against the Order of the Blazing Sun were vast. At times like this she felt she was insignificant against them. And almost everything they did seemed to end in failure. Each setback hardened her heart and mind, but also brought a shard of despair. The Order's successes were few and far between, so diminished were they from their halcyon days many centuries ago. Only a few branches remained—a few dozen individuals against the might of the Tainted Cabal. But they would never give up. The cost of ultimate failure was too great.

As she turned toward her horse, she caught a glimpse of a figure among the stunted trees surrounding the clearing. Zarina stiffened. She wasn't much of a sorcerer, but she prepared a cant anyway, even though it would be useless against a higher-level demon. At the same time, she drew her dagger. In the pale light, the blade shimmered with an unearthly jade luminescence. Another artifact, this one paid for fairly. Its edges could cut stone as easily as flesh.

"Who are you?" she shouted. "Stand forward where I can see you!"

A man moved from the shadows. He was tall and wore a dark cloak over glimmering mail. A hood obscured his face, but she knew what she'd see if it didn't: flawless skin, a flat nose, and eyes that pierced your soul and judged you. A wraithe.

"Another human," the wraithe said softly in Skanuric. "I grow weary of dealing with your petty concerns."

"Did you kill him?"

"I have killed many of your kind."

Zarina gripped her dagger tighter. "The man at the bottom of the cliff. He was a companion of mine."

The wraithe stood unmoving for long moments.

Zarina tried to keep her breathing even. She thought about making a dash for her horse, but it had wandered off in search of fodder and was twenty paces distant. It probably wouldn't make a difference if she was mounted though. The wraithes had far greater arcane powers than most sorcerers.

"I did not kill him," the wraithe eventually said. "What do you know of the events that transpired here?"

*So Kurio must have killed Mellish.* If she could believe this creature.

"We captured a demon. My companion was taking her to—"

"A ruin," the wraithe finished. "You are involved, then."

"My Order fights against the demons and their worshipers. Our cause is righteous. They are invaders, and their lusts are abhorrent."

"As humans are to me." The wraithe turned its head to the left, then back again. "Righteous ... that is an interesting word. Not all demons are malevolent."

Zarina shook her head. "They are all evil."

"You are mistaken, as your kind often is. So, arrogant one, you stand against the Tainted Cabal?"

Zarina knew that if the wraithes were allied with the Cabal, she was likely dead. If they weren't, there was a chance she might escape this encounter.

"Yes," she said, bracing herself. "My Order opposes the Tainted Cabal."

The wraithe stood still and silent again. A breeze stirred the edges of its cloak. Its hood moved, as if it had nodded.

"Then I have information for you."

Zarina let out a breath. *Maybe I'll survive ...*

"The Cabal's plans are coming to fruition. We cannot allow this. They have meddled with a power far beyond them, seeking to use it for their summoning."

Heart pounding in her chest, Zarina could barely speak, so great was her fear. "To summon ... Nysrog?"

The hood moved again. "Resistance was attempted by a sorcerer of great power and two marked by new gods. They failed.

However, the sorcerer managed to release a fragment of the Revenants. It was a bold action. And unexpected."

The Revenants. Zarina knew of them through fragments of ancient histories, although only vague details of what the Revenants were and how they could be released. Mellish had been dispatched to investigate, to bring proof of this puissant sorcery that had saved humanity many times. If the Revenants had been released, there were dark days ahead. But it also meant the Tainted Cabal were hamstrung, which was good news of a sort.

"A fragment?" she repeated. "Then they will be weak. Initially at least."

"Yes."

"You know all this, yet you did not stop them?"

"My pets tried to stop them entering the ruin, but were forced back by demons. So I watched, and I witnessed."

"You failed," Zarina said.

"I did."

"The sorcerer and the others, the god-touched, what happened to them?" *They might prove useful allies.*

"Death and injury, and not only of their bodies."

"Where are they?"

"Gone."

She knew Mellish well enough to scry his location, but she would never be able to find strangers in the wilderness. "What now?" she asked. "Are you going to kill me?"

"No. You are a thread in this pattern. All is not lost. If you do nothing, the Revenants will destroy your civilization. Again. This is not unpleasing to us. If by some means you are able to stop the Revenants, the demon-bloods will be free to summon their infernal lord. Either way, you lose."

*I'll return to Caronath,* Zarina decided, *and get word to the rest of the Order. We'll do our best. It's all we can do. Maybe we'll make a difference.*

To the wraithe, she said, "What do you suggest I do?"

"Hide. Live for as long as you can."

# TO MY READERS,

**Share your opinion.** If you would like to leave a review of any of my books, it would be much appreciated! Reviews help new readers find my work, and also provide valuable feedback for my future writing.

You can return to where you purchased the novel to review it, or simply visit my website and follow the links.

Amazon Author page: http://amazon.com/author/mitchellhogan

Website: http://www.mitchellhogan.com/

There are also websites like Goodreads, where members discuss the books they've read, want to read, or suggest books others might read.

Goodreads: https://www.goodreads.com/book/show/33139241

**New Release Sign Up.** If you enjoy reading my novels as much as I enjoy writing them, please sign up to my mailing list. I promise to notify you only when a new novel is released. No spam emails!

New Release Mailing List: http://eepurl.com/BTefL

**Send me feedback.** I love to hear from readers and try to answer every email. If you would like to point out errors and typos, or provide feedback on my novels, I urge you to send me an email at: mitchhoganauthor@gmail.com

Having readers eager for the next installment of a series, or anticipating a new series, is the best motivation for a writer to create new stories. Thank you for your support, and be sure to check out my other novels!

Made in the USA
San Bernardino, CA
21 November 2017